"Christy, Christy. Wake up, Christy. I need you, Christy."

It was only a whisper—I couldn't tell who called me. But the call was insistent. It would not let me be.

There was silence in the hall outside my room by the time I had slipped into my shoes, and for a moment I was afraid I had lost the whisper. But not for long, surely. I sensed that someone would be waiting for me on ahead.

When I pushed open the door and looked out into the hall, I saw that the lights had been turned out at the far end near the stairs. It didn't matter. I could still make out the figure standing there. As I expected, it was my father. I recognized his plaid sports jacket and I knew he was waiting for me. For just a moment I wondered if I was still dreaming, because in my usual dreams Adam was never dead. I pinched my arm hard and felt pain.

"I'm c̲o̲ ... ̲d floated out int̲ ...

The fig̲ ... d disappeared ... ̲him, of course. ̲ ... ̲ ... my father anywhere. ...

Fawcett Crest Books
by Phyllis A. Whitney:

EVER AFTER
THE QUICKSILVER POOL
THE TREMBLING HILLS
SKYE CAMERON
THE MOONFLOWER
THUNDER HEIGHTS
BLUE FIRE
WINDOW ON THE SQUARE
SEVEN TEARS FOR APOLLO
BLACK AMBER
SEA JADE
COLUMBELLA
SILVERHILL
HUNTER'S GREEN
THE WINTER PEOPLE
LOST ISLAND
LISTEN FOR THE WHISPERER
SNOWFIRE
THE TURQUOISE MASK

ARE THERE FAWCETT PAPERBACKS
YOU WANT BUT CANNOT FIND IN YOUR LOCAL STORES?

You can get any title in print in Fawcett Crest, Fawcett
Premier, or Fawcett Gold Medal editions. Simply send title and
retail price, plus 35¢ to cover mailing and handling costs for each
book wanted, to:

MAIL ORDER DEPARTMENT,
FAWCETT PUBLICATIONS,
P.O. Box 1014
GREENWICH, CONN. 06830

Books are available at discounts in quantity lots for industrial
or sales-promotional use. For details write FAWCETT WORLD
LIBRARY, CIRCULATION MANAGER, FAWCETT BLDG.,
GREENWICH, CONN. 06830

Spindrift

A NOVEL BY

Phyllis A. Whitney

A FAWCETT CREST BOOK

Fawcett Publications, Inc., Greenwich, Connecticut

With my thanks to the Newport Public Library for valuable help in my research and to the Newport County Chamber of Commerce for supplying me with maps and materials.

Also with my apologies to Newport for certain liberties I have taken as a fiction writer. There are, for example, no boathouses along the shore where I have placed mine.

If there is, or has been, any other house named Spindrift, it is not the house of this story. Both Spindrift and Redstones have come wholly out of my imagination, as have all the characters, both dead and alive.

SPINDRIFT

THIS BOOK CONTAINS THE COMPLETE TEXT OF THE ORIGINAL HARDCOVER EDITION.

A Fawcett Crest Book reprinted by arrangement with Doubleday and Company, Inc.

Copyright © 1975 by Phyllis A. Whitney

All rights reserved, including the right to reproduce this book or portions thereof in any form.

All the characters in this book are fictitious, and any resemblance to actual persons living or dead is purely coincidental.

Library of Congress Catalog Card Number: 74-14384

Selection of the Doubleday Bargain Book Club, May 1975

Printed in the United States of America

First printing: March 1976

1   2   3   4   5   6   7   8   9   10

1

While I was in the hospital I kept drifting in and out of the world around me. It was hard to focus on what was real and what imaginary. Joel was real some of the time and I know that at first he came every evening to see me, and sometimes, when he could leave those writers and manuscripts that occupied so much of his life, he came in the daytime as well. Then his mother convinced him that he was upsetting me, and he came less often. It began to seem as though he were a stranger and not at all the husband I had been so much in love with.

Theo came too. Theodora Moreland, Joel's mother, but she always spelled nightmare, whether she merely stood beside my bed as a small, indomitable figure, waiting implacably, or sat across the room staring at me out of those intense green eyes. The look of her elegantly up-swept, expensively perpetuated red hair began to haunt my dreams. Perhaps if I hadn't been my father's daughter I might have died under the balefulness of that watch she kept.

Once I had persuaded a nurse to bring me a mirror, so I knew what she saw—a face too thin since my illness, too delicate to possess the strength to stand up to her. Brown eyes grown too big and cropped brown hair, with the curls damp against my forehead. Her look put me down as weak and without force.

Yet even then I'd had more strength than she guessed. Adam Keene was my father, and he had brought me up to be a fighter, as he was. My mother had died when I was three and I didn't remember her at all, so it was my father who continued to dominate my horizon. Only lately, I hadn't been able to fight.

Perhaps of all my world at that time he was the figure most real to me, most alive—even though now he too was dead. Again and again I could hear his warning voice in my ear: "Stand up to her, Christy. A fight is the only thing she understands. If you give in she'll destroy you. Christy, hon, watch out for yourself and watch out for Peter if you want to keep your son."

My father had never wanted me to marry Joel Moreland. He had worked with the Morelands most of his life —first with the powerful Hal Moreland, who was already a legend in the field of newspaper publishing, and then with his widow, Theo. Joel was the son of their later years, and he was like neither of them. It was inevitable that my father believed him weak and made of poor stuff because the newspaper world was too rough for him. Joel had taken an editorship at Moreland Press, and while the books he published weren't always a monetary success—which had disturbed his hardheaded father— Theo protected him in this at least and saw that he went his own way. Joel's was a dreamer's world—an escape from the brutal reality of the Morelands, and in the beginning I had relished my belief that he was his own man.

I'd had a job with the Moreland Empire too, thanks to my father. Nepotism, perhaps, as much as had been Joel's hiring, but I had worked hard at my column to keep it lively and newsworthy, and everyone said I had a flair. I had begun to be syndicated in a number of areas around the country and I was already receiving bushels of mail by the time Theo fired me. Dad had been furious, though Joel had rather shrugged it off: "Do you mind all that much, Christy? You know Theo likes change, variety. She thinks you've gone a bit stale. And this will give you all the more time with Peter."

In the hospital I would not think of Peter. Even in my fantasy world I could not think of Peter. I dared not until I was stronger or I knew I'd never recover. Theo had him

—and I couldn't leave him in her destructive hands. But first I had to be strong enough to stand against her.

A nervous breakdown, they said, using the kind, old fashioned term. A natural enough result following my father's tragic death, they assured me. After the hospital they put me in a "rest home"—very private and expensive and quiet, where I had sympathetic care and a great deal of covert watching. Dr. Dorfman was all consideration and he listened to me endlessly. When I said, "My father didn't die a suicide. He was murdered," Dr. Dorfman would ask me patiently why I thought this, and I would tell him again and again that I *knew* my father. He had loved life and believed in it. Under no circumstances would he have profaned it by not trying to live it to the hilt, no matter what happened. Dr. Dorfman reminded me gently that the threat of disgrace, the fear of open scandal, the loss of the job he had worked at and loved all his life could drive any man to desperate escape. "Not my father," I said. Dr. Dorfman smiled with compassion and went away, leaving me to stare about my empty sitting room, leaving me to stare at the plaque on the wall that read, "GIFT OF THE MORELAND FOUNDATION." The very hospital I was in had been a gift of the Moreland Empire. There was no escaping it.

I didn't believe in a scandal concerning my father, didn't believe that Adam Keene had been involved with a crime syndicate, or stooped to deal with those miserable little men who brought the accusations against him. While Hal Moreland had been known more than once to color the news to fit his own beliefs and influence the thinking of millions, my father, though he had always responded to the excitement of a good story, had also loved the truth. He thought a good story was the *real* story. In the beginning of what had been a partnership, his had been the imagination, the gifted creation of ideas, Hal Moreland's, the business head and the money. After their first paper, *The Leader,* took hold and jumped its circulation into the millions, rivaling the *World* and *Journal-American,* Hal had assumed command, though my father remained managing editor. The trouble with Adam Keene was that he cared about an honest paper, he cared about doing the job well. Power for itself meant nothing to him. He had his weaknesses, but greed for power was not among them. On the other hand, power meant everything to Hal Moreland, as it did now to his widow, Theodora. Even in her early seventies she had the will and dynamic drive of a much younger woman.

She stood by my bed and I knew she wanted me to die. She had always disliked me because I was Adam Keene's daughter. Once, when they were all young, rumor had it that Adam had been the man Theo wanted to marry. But, already in love with my gentle mother, he had not returned her demanding affection. He had never told me much about this, but I gathered that Theo would never forgive the rejection, even though Hal Moreland was far more suited to her as a husband and they'd had an obviously successful marriage. On the other hand, Hal had been a big man in his way and he had the self-confidence to shrug off Theo's early infatuation with his partner.

With my father gone, I was all that was left to stand between Theo and the grandson she coveted so possessively. She had once lost her son to me, but now she was getting him back, and she intended to keep her grandson, whom she spoiled on every occasion, and whom she encouraged in unruly ways. She claimed that Peter looked like his grandfather Hal, and that he must grow up to be like him. A resemblance to that old pirate was the last thing I wanted. I wouldn't have him damaged like that. So I steeled myself against her—and against Joel, if he was on her side. I wasn't going to die. I had been ill with grief and shock, I had collapsed, but I didn't believe in this sickness of the mind they were insisting upon in lieu of my death. There were times when I knew with all clarity and certainty that it was the drugs they fed me, the tranquilizers and sleeping pills, that clouded my mind and brought this confusion between the real and the unreal.

Somehow I had to escape from this smothering haze and recover what was left of *me*. For two reasons—to wrest Peter from his grandmother's influence and to uncover the truth about my father's death.

During all these months of illness they would not bring Peter to see me. Let him remember me the way I was, they told me. It would frighten him to see me now: *As soon as you are yourself again . . .* But the clear inference was that the Christy I had been—Christy Keene, Christy Moreland—was gone for good.

Oddly enough, it was Joel who saved me, which was not an action typical of him. He was not given to taking hold in a crisis, but this time he did. It had been a particularly bad day for me. I had been ranting furiously about something unreal—completely out of my head, yet at times pleading piteously to be released from a torment that was not entirely imaginary.

"All right," Joel said, "you're coming home." For once he stood up to his mother, to Dr. Dorfman, to the lot of them. Waiting fearfully for my collapse, the nurses ceased the injections, the feeding of pills. My nerves were rocky, it was true, my sleep interrupted by wakeful periods at night, but in a week or so the fantasies left me and my head was clear. Joel took his shaky wife home.

Unfortunately, after all these months of Theo's torment and Joel's support of her, our marriage had gone flat. All feeling for Joel had died in me. I could no longer believe that he had done what he thought was good for me. He was too much his mother's son and I seemed to be seeing him clearly for the first time. I looked at his slender, good-looking face that I had always thought so sensitive, at his gentle mouth and the gray, thoughtful eyes, and I could not remember loving him. Those days nine years ago when I had married him belonged to someone else's life. Another girl. Another world. And love-making was something I could hardly endure. After my first week at home in the New York apartment, he did not come near me again. It was not only I who had changed—there was a difference in Joel. Theo was in control again and I began to wonder if the man I had loved had ever really existed. Perhaps I had only loved a dream.

I could no longer care. For all that I tried, I simply could not respond. The only things that mattered were the truth about my father and the recovery of my son.

By Theo's edict I still had not seen Peter. Once I had been allowed to talk to him on the phone, but the call had interrupted a game he was playing, and he sounded petulant. By this time he was used to being without me, so that nothing at all of the little boy I loved came through. For an hour or two afterward I wavered on the verge of a relapse, but I fought down the all-enveloping sense of futility and I did not call Peter again in his grandmother's brownstone mansion. Desperate and frightened, I faced the unhappy reality. Theo had already made me a stranger to my son and it would take all the ingenuity and guile I could muster to win him back. I didn't even know how to start.

And then Theo Moreland herself opened the way. The letter from her came one morning when Joel had stayed home from the office to work on a batch of manuscripts. There was a strange look on his face when he came out to the kitchen where I was sitting over a late cup of coffee. Almost a look of wariness.

"Theo is reopening Spindrift," he said and tapped the letter with slender fingers. "She wants us to come up there."

The door that opened was at once ajar upon a vista of brimstone and terror. Spindrift was a place I would never return to. It was the scene of my father's death and the beginning of my collapse.

"Don't look like that, Christy," Joel said. "It's not the end of the world to do what she wants," and I knew that he had already given in to his mother as he always did.

I stared without seeing him. "Is she taking Peter with her?"

"Yes," Joel said. "She's planning some sort of party to

open the house again. She wants to take"—he glanced at the hasty scrawl that was so unmistakably Theo's writing —"to take the curse off the place so it can be put into use again. She thinks it will be good for you and Peter to go back and exorcise—that's the word she's used—all that happened there. She suggests that this would be a good time for me to take a vacation. It had to come," he added. "You know Theo would never give up Spindrift for good."

My mouth was dry and I could feel the quivering in the pit of my stomach. My hands had clenched about my coffee cup and I tried deliberately to relax them. Joel put Theo's note on the table beside me and went quietly away. He had always hated to stay with me through any disturbed mood I might experience. I suspect he felt helpless and that pained him. What he didn't have to watch needn't exist. I sat on at the table and thought about Spindrift.

In Rhode Island's famed Newport there is an avenue called Bellevue. It is not a particularly long street—only three miles. It is continued by Ocean Drive running above the sea, and though the entire area is not large, it is an American phenomenon. It was here that the socially elite, the very rich and powerful, built their summer "cottages" in a wild extravaganza of splendor in the years just before and after the turn of the century. The houses were, in fact, *castles,* of a peculiarly mixed breed of architecture. Whatever whim governed the owner was indulged, and if the results were sometimes monstrous in their pretension and display, the grand mansions had the proud self-assurance of their masters—and particularly their mistresses, and were, for that period of magnificence, above reproach.

Theodora Colby (later Moreland) had been born to Boston, but not to Newport. Her father had been an ambassador who lived much abroad and the family had no Newport house. But as a child she had several times visited the "summer cottage" called Spindrift. Those were still

11

the days of huge straw hats and veils, of white flannels, Irish lace collars and croquet on the lawn, and she loved every minute of it. Visiting it later in her teens, she vowed to herself that she would someday live in a house like that. The dream was never forgotten and when she had married Hal Moreland and his fortunes had increased to the point of real wealth, Theo went back to have a look at those cottages of her childhood. Many of the great houses had become white elephants that no one wanted any longer and that taxes could eat up. The Newport Preservation Society was not yet engaged in their rescue work as far as the mansions were concerned. Spindrift was on the market and Theo bought it with Hal's money and his amused consent.

But Theodora Moreland was not in society. She was a businesswoman, involved in her husband's work, and completely independent of what was proper and expected —a born nonconformist. So she put Spindrift to work in rather a grand way. Hal's position and driving ambitions led him to consort with the world's noted and even the deservedly-great. There were times when he entertained royalty and heads of governments, and what could prove a better background for lavish entertainment than Spindrift? Theo paid no attention to "the season." She was as likely as not to throw a Christmas party when the coast of the island was bleak and gray, there was snow at the windows, and the fashionable were in Palm Beach. But the chandeliers of Spindrift would be draped with holly and mistletoe, and never had its ballroom shone with more crystal splendor.

Of course she had the house done over from room to room, using what was there, but also buying the furnishings of other Newport castles outright, acquiring antiques and oriental rugs and marble statuary. Fiona helped her. Fiona Keene was my stepmother, but long before she married my father, Adam Keene, she had been the wife of Theo's elder son, Cabot Moreland. Many years ago Cabot and his sister, Iris, had been lost in a tragic boating accident. Theo had liked Fiona and perhaps she wouldn't have been able to bear her marriage to the widowed Adam Keene if it hadn't been that she simply ignored it. To Theo, Fiona was still Cabot's wife. She had worked in interior decorators' shops and made something of a specialty of the Victorian, the turn-of-the-century, and antiques in general. So hers was the knowledge behind Theo's rather gaudy enterprise.

The house was a great success. Old Newport had raised its eyebrows to see it was used not only to welcome the truly famous, but for office gatherings at high level, for the use of those who might lack either blue blood or wealth, and of course to attract the notorious whenever they were useful to the Morelands. It was mainly for extravaganzas, for sumptuously planned house parties, though sometimes simply used as an escape when Hal and Theo wanted to get away from New York to what they regarded as a simpler, less hectic life. The entourage that went with them often belied this. I had been to Spindrift many times as a child with Adam and Fiona, and later as Joel's wife. Our son, Peter, adored it. All those marble columns and balustrades, all of those spooky old rooms with the vast high ceilings and miles of rich red draperies and swags of gold trim! I had enjoyed it myself, become quite fond of it as an anachronism from the past, until the night of that last New Year's Eve party.

After the shock of Adam's death, Theo herself couldn't bear the place. She closed it up, turned her back on it. Until now, when it was October, and she was making this dramatic gesture of reopening the house that had seen so much bitter grief.

Spindrift to be reopened . . . ! And she wanted me there.

Everything within me shuddered in resistance. I didn't trust her. Why did she want me to come? But still—if I was once more allowed to be with Peter . . . ? I wished that Joel had stayed at the table with me. There was no one else I could talk to. But I had hurt him, and I could hardly blame him for not seeking my company. I had to weigh carefully this matter of stepping once more into the world of Spindrift and facing the remembered terror that waited for me there.

Yet wasn't this what I must attempt? During my convalescence at home I had been unable to do anything about recovering Peter. Theo had blocked my smallest effort. Nor had I learned anything new about my father's death. If both these things could be accomplished by proving that I was well and confronting Spindrift itself, must I not go? Yet somehow I was afraid. Terribly afraid. Though I didn't know exactly what frightened me. Perhaps I was only afraid of failure—of my own weakness since being ill. If that was what I feared I must face it down as Adam would counsel me to do. Courage had been Adam's guiding spirit, and it was courage I must find.

I pushed my coffee cup aside and went into the bedroom I had occupied alone since that first week when Joel had brought me back to the apartment. He had used the convertible couch in his study for sleeping from then on. I couldn't even feel guilty. It was as if a whole facet of my character had gone numb. He had become a stranger to me.

The framed color enlargement of the last snapshot I'd taken of my father stood on my dressing table. I picked it up and studied his strong, life-marked face. Lines ran deep from cheeks to chin and his dark blue eyes seemed to burn with that excitement for life that I remembered so well. The picture was so good, so true that it seemed as though he ought to speak to me, as though his mouth ought to widen in the remembered grin that could be amused and wry, but never contemptuous.

I set the picture down and moved restlessly about the room. I knew I was much better, nearly recovered. Surely I was strong enough now to meet whatever had to be met.

It was only natural to be a little afraid. One was always afraid before going into battle. In a moment I would go to Joel in his study and tell him we would leave for Newport whenever he wished.

But before I could cross the hall the door chimes sounded. I hurried to answer and let Fiona into the apartment, not exactly glad to see her. We had never been close, though I think she had done her best in the beginning to make friends with a rebellious child of twelve who resented sharing her father with anyone, much less a stepmother. I could realize now what a burden I had been, what trouble I must have caused her, and after I had grown up we'd moved nearer to an affectionate relationship. My father's death had changed all that. Fiona had very nearly dropped me. She had visited me in the hospital only once or twice and had been strangely guarded on each occasion. In Theodora's eyes the interlude between Adam Keene and Fiona Moreland had been wiped out as though it had never existed. Fiona was once more her son Cabot's widow, and Theo employed her in all sorts of unofficial capacities.

After a startled greeting, I stood aside to let her pass me into the living room. At thirty-eight she was only ten years older than I—which had partly caused my resentment as a child. She wasn't old enough to respect as a mother. But Fiona's predominant quality had always been a wonderful serenity, against which my angry resentment had battered itself in vain. When my father went on a gambling binge and then drank too much out of a guilty conscience, Fiona stayed calm and self-contained.

As I grew older, I sometimes thought her devotion to my father was almost like that of another older daughter. And once, more recently, I'd had reason to believe that she had strayed into some outside affair. Whether my father knew or not, I could never tell. He continued to turn to her still pool of quiet from his own wild whirlpools, knowing he would meet with no reproaches, no angry emotions. I was the one more likely to be angry, to weep because I idolized my father and I could not bear to see him let himself down.

But today there was a lack of serenity in Fiona. As she strode nervously past me and went to look out at the view of Central Park, there was a disquiet in her every move. Her build was angular in rather a good way—as certain models are angular—and she was wide through the cheekbones, with blue-gray eyes that could often be clearly appraising. She might not criticize, but I sometimes caught her *thinking*. She used to make me uneasy when she came as a visitor because she could bring order even out of an existence like Adam's, and his apartment with her in it had taken on a composure it had never known before, to say nothing of a tidiness foreign to Adam or me. I wasn't quite as heedless to order as I'd been at twelve, but Joel and I liked rooms that were alive rather than carefully ordered, and I could imagine the distaste our comfortable jumble must sometimes have caused Fiona to feel.

She paid no attention now to books and newspapers on the floor, or to the scatter rug that had been tripped over and not straightened. At the window her fixed look was upon a Central Park that I felt sure she didn't even see. There had been tension in her stride across the floor, and her hands held onto each other in a loss of quiet that was disturbing to me, who remembered her calm so well. Had my father's death done this to her? I had been too busy with my own central problems to be observant of others.

"Fiona," I said, "what's the matter?"

She did not look around at me. "You mustn't go to Spindrift. Don't accept Theo's invitation."

"I haven't decided yet whether I'll go or not," I told her. "But why shouldn't I?"

She twisted my father's rings on her left hand. "Theo's plotting against you. Don't give her an opening."

"How can she plot? What can she do?"

"I don't know." She turned around, her light brown pageboy swinging above her shoulders. "But I've got a sort of sixth sense when it comes to Theo Moreland and I think she'll do you in if she can."

"I already know that." I plucked at the sleeves of my blue cashmere. "Anyway, why should you care? You're back in Theo's pocket now, aren't you?"

She didn't answer me right away, but fumbled for a cigarette, fumbled with the silver lighter Adam had given her in contrition after one of his gambling bouts. When smoke curled up she blew it away and flung herself down in Joel's big armchair.

"I know you didn't like me in the beginning, Christy. And I didn't blame you much. You were young, and how could you like someone you thought was taking your father away? I've always understood that. But after you came home from college and married Joel, I thought we'd come to be fairly good friends."

"Adam was alive then," I said.

She winced. "He's gone, but now I still have to live— you shouldn't blame me for that. He didn't leave me anything but debts, as you know. Theo lets me help her as a sort of privileged social secretary. But that doesn't mean I can forget that you're Adam's daughter."

But she had seemed to forget, staying away, coming so seldom to see me—as though she had something on her conscience. Nevertheless, I relented a little and sat on the sofa opposite her, pushing books aside. I didn't want to be hard on her, but I knew I had to be careful.

"We both loved him," I said. "I know that."

Tears came into her eyes, where none sprang to mine. I was beginning to feel very cold and quiet and clearheaded, as one must be when there is danger ahead.

"Yes, I loved him," she admitted. "Perhaps more than you've ever loved a man."

"I loved him too," I said, still quiet in the face of her obvious turmoil.

She seemed to dismiss that as though what I felt didn't matter. "Anyway, I didn't come here to quarrel with you. I came because I'm concerned for you. Don't go to Spindrift, Christy."

My tentative resolve was hardening in the face of her opposition. "Who is Theo taking with her this time?"

"The usual staff. Bruce and Ferris will be there. And I'll stay with her."

I knew Bruce Parry and Ferris Thornton, of course. Both were unmarried. Bruce was Fiona's age and from a distance I had thought him attractive, though a bit formidable. I had never known him well because Joel didn't like him. The job he had done for Hal Moreland could never be pinned down with a title, but he was there when some high-level negotiation was needed. Perhaps he had been a sort of vice president in charge of troubleshooting, accountable only to Hal, and now to Theo. Secretary of State to the Empire. Ferris Thornton was high level too. He was in his sixties and he had been in on the Moreland-Keene partnership from the early days when he was graduated from Harvard Law School and from then on handled all matters of law for Hal and Adam. I'd always liked him and he had come to see me whenever it was possible while I was ill. I had thought of him as my father's friend, though I always remembered that he was Theo's friend first.

"Joel says Theo is taking Peter to Spindrift with her. Is that true?" I asked.

"Of course. She hardly moves without him these days."

"That's what I'm afraid of. That's why I'm going to Spindrift. Peter's been in her hands too long. I'm his mother, after all, Fiona, and I want him back. I will *have* him back."

"She can do more for him than you can at the moment."

"That's not true. You've been brainwashed. He belongs with Joel and me."

Fiona crushed out the half-smoked cigarette in an ash

tray. "Can you possibly be strong enough to stand up to her?"

"I'm strong enough," I said, hoping I spoke the truth.

"You're still terribly young. And she's cold and crafty and strong-willed."

"You don't know me any more," I said. "I'm Adam's daughter, but I'm trying to be my own woman besides."

There was that wince again, at mention of Adam's name—the stab of a reminder that I knew all too well. "All right, Christy. I give up. I can't change your mind, though I think you're being foolish."

"Why? What can she do to me?"

Her look was pitying. "If I were in your shoes I wouldn't want to test her. But do what you will. I've had my try at changing your mind."

"What do you know about what happened that night?"

She didn't need to ask "What night?"

"You know as much as I do. You found him while he was still alive, Christy."

"But you came right after. And they said you'd quarreled with him that night. Why? What happened between you? Was he worried about something?"

Fiona left her chair and walked to the door with her long, rangy gait. I watched her and when her hand was on the knob she turned back and stared at me.

"That only concerns Adam and me. It had nothing to do with his killing himself."

"Do you believe that he was mixed up with a crime syndicate?"

"Of course I don't. Not Adam Keene."

"Have you told Theo that?"

"What good would it do? Theo believes what she wants to believe."

"Then how can you work for her? How can you stand to?"

Strangely, the nervousness seemed to leave her. A mask of her old serenity came down over her face so that the lines of worry were smoothed away and her mouth relaxed. I had seen a pantomime artist do the same thing by moving a hand across his face to erase one expression and leave another.

"You worry too much, Christy," she said. "Let what has happened go. Learn to live with it. I'm learning."

By sheer will power? I wondered. Had that masking been as deliberate as I felt? I jumped up and ran to stand beside her in the small hall area before the door.

"Don't you want to clear Adam's name, Fiona? Don't you want to help me clear it?" The cold and the quiet had left me, and I heard the cry of anguish in my voice.

She gaped at me, the mask of serenity cracking for an instant, then repairing itself. She smiled at me pityingly, kindly.

"Christy darling, leave well enough alone. I think Adam died because he knew too much. It's better not to know too much and I don't intend to. Better for you as well."

"Then you don't believe he killed himself?"

"I didn't say that. I think he was being hounded in some way."

"But not to the point of taking his own life. He never would."

Without answering me, she let herself out the door and pulled it softly shut behind her. I couldn't hear her carpeted steps as she walked away toward the elevator. Leaning my back against the door, I stared at my own reflection in the mirror opposite. Soft cap of curly brown hair, still short from my illness, a too delicately etched face with a pointed chin and eyes that were too large and a very dark brown. I had my mother's fragility, they'd told me, her delicacy and small bones. And I hated all that. I turned my back on it, wanting to be free of my own body and my face. Wanting to be strong and big and able to cope. Wanting to look like a woman who could cope. People put me down too easily because I was small. And yet—Theodora Moreland was small too. Tiny. But there was no lack of force in her, and I wondered if she had ever rebelled against her size. Was her personality a case of overcompensation? I didn't want that either. I felt torn and sore and unsure of myself.

As I wandered back into the living room, Joel came out of his study with a sheaf of manuscript pages in his hands. His hair that was as red as his mother's was rumpled and there was a pencil smudge above his lip. His clothes, as always, were casual and a little untidy, and his gray eyes had that faraway look they could take on when he was deep in work on someone else's story. Lately I'd sometimes had the feeling that he wasn't living in a real world, but could only exist through the words of others. But perhaps that feeling was only more of my tendency to see him without the old veiling of love. Perhaps I wasn't being fair.

"Who was that at the door?" he asked, brought back to earth by the intrusion of voices that had roused him from his work.

"It was Fiona," I said. "She wanted to warn me to stay away from Spindrift."

He looked mildly surprised. "Why should she do that? She knows Mother wants you there."

"Perhaps Fiona sometimes thinks for herself," I said, and hated my own sharpness. Once I had been a more gentle girl.

He didn't miss the inference and I hated the flush that came into his cheeks. A man shouldn't blush like a girl when someone cuts at him.

"We needn't go if you're against it," he said.

"But we are going. You knew I'd agree, didn't you? You knew that nothing would keep me from being with Peter."

He sighed and threw up his hands. "Then I'll go and phone Theo. She asked me to call her to get the day and time when we'd drive up with her."

I found myself being sharp again. "No! We'll fly or go by train. And a day later than Theo."

He stood looking at me helplessly for a moment longer

and I could remember when that helpless look was dear to me. It only irritated me now.

"I'll call and tell her," he said, and went back to his study.

I could hear him on the phone a moment later, the dutiful son reporting that what his mother wished would be accomplished. Once I had thought this sort of thing indicated consideration. Now I judged more harshly and believed it only meant he was under his mother's thumb.

I found myself gritting my teeth as I'd done sometimes in the hospital and I made myself stop immediately. There must be no more of that. If Fiona could slip on a mask of calm so could I.

What was it she had said so angrily? That I'd never loved a man the way she had loved Adam? But what difference did her words make? I knew how full of love I was. For Peter, for my father. And I would go to Spindrift because of them. I would find strength and courage because of them. Nothing else mattered.

2

Spindrift had always seemed to me a whimsical name for a place that was too solid with marble and tile to be anything so wispy and foamlike. A palatially wide expanse of shallow marble steps led up from the driveway, interrupted at intervals with marble urns in which well-nurtured greenery flaunted itself at the visitor. Six stately Corinthian columns crowned with acanthus leaves marched across the top of the steps, supporting the white roof and contrasting with the black of wrought iron that graced five inner balconies at second-floor level. Beneath these were windows rounded by fanlights, and in the center a great double door with grilled ironwork.

The door had been opened in welcome for our coming. The Moreland chauffeur who met us at the airport on Aquidneck Island, to which we'd flown from Providence, was busy with our baggage, while others of Theo's staff of servants rushed out to help and to welcome us. If the old days of Newport were gone and this was October instead of July, one would never know it here.

I watched anxiously for a small boy to come hurtling down those marble steps and fling himself into my arms, but no one but Ferris Thornton came to greet us. He shook hands with Joel and complimented me on how well I was looking. Then we went into the enormous Marble Hall with its vast expanse that was large enough for a ballroom, its ornate ceiling, nymph-painted, its chairs oversized, its tables elaborately carved. A tall vase caught my eye. As a little girl I had stood beside that six-foot blue and green vase from China and woven stories about it. I had ridden on the magic carpets of these Persian rugs and tried to enter the world of the portraits on the walls. Yet now it had little appeal for me. There was beauty, yes, but in a too pretentious sense as Theodora used it.

Ferris came with us toward the stairs while a porter scurried to the rear with a load of luggage. I had always liked Ferris, and I was grateful for his presence. He was more than six feet tall and he had been cadaverously thin as long as I'd known him. His hair seemed more gray at the temples than I remembered, but that only added to the air of dignity that so became him. He belonged to a practically lost generation of polished gentlemen—a category to which neither Hal Moreland nor Adam Keene had ever held any pretensions.

"I'm glad you've come," he told us, a hand beneath my elbow as I mounted the stairs. "Theodora is looking forward to this occasion and it wouldn't be complete without Peter's parents."

He believed what he was saying, I was sure. He had always seen Theo in a far different light than Adam and I had, and he was the only person who called her "Theodora."

Joel said, "I've brought a suitcase full of manuscripts so I can get in some work at least. I'd have thought it might have been better simply to start using Spindrift again without fanfare."

Ferris's smile was austere, but he had never regarded Theo blindly, despite his long admiration for her. "When did your mother ever avoid fanfare? I gather that's the whole idea. The press will be here in full force, and not only from the Moreland *Leader*."

We'd reached the second floor, where the grand, central staircase divided on either hand. I wondered which wing Theo had put us in. Not, I hoped, near that Tower Room on the third floor. To my relief, Ferris was leading the way into the right wing on the second floor. We turned down a cross corridor into the wing that was farthest from Theo's own suite on the upper floor, and I knew she had given us the magnificent corner room—the Gold Room—looking out toward the Atlantic on one hand and off in the direction of exclusive Bailey's Beach on the other. Spindrift occupied a spot with a commanding view and I went at once to fling louvered doors outward upon a marble balcony.

The scene of sloping lawn down to the Cliff Walk, with the drop to the rocks beyond was as it had always been. There was a boathouse down there in a small cove just out of sight. The October sky shone bright blue over its own reflection in the sea. There was no hint of the quick squalls that could blow up and darken the sky, no hint of a cool October wind. And there was no fog. It was out there that a small sailboat had gone aground on rocks off Lands End on a foggy day and had capsized seventeen years ago, when Joel was seventeen. His older brother and sister had drowned and he had been the only one rescued. It had been a tragedy that would have destroyed some parents, but it had only made Theo fiercely strong, focusing her attention on her remaining son, Joel.

Behind me now, Joel spoke in a flat voice. "This won't do. Mother promised us separate rooms. Christy has been ill, and she needs a place for herself."

"You have your own room." Ferris's tone was courteous but faintly disapproving. "Right through that adjoining door."

The flush had come into Joel's fair skin again and a stab of guilt went through me because of what I was doing to him. There had been happier times for us in this house, even though Theo had always made attempts to drive us apart. But there was nothing I could say or do now, and Joel thanked Ferris and went through the unlocked door.

The moment he was gone I faced Ferris. "When will I see Peter?"

He regarded me more kindly. "He's here. I'm sure you'll see him soon. He has been told you were coming."

"How did he react?"

"I don't know much about children," Ferris said evasively. "I should think he was pleased."

But he hadn't said that Peter *was* pleased.

A tap on the door and the arrival of my bags gave him an excuse to escape.

"Theodora will be waiting for you when it's convenient," he said. "She has her old rooms upstairs in the opposite wing."

"I'll come soon," I said.

He went off and I busied myself unlocking my bags, shaking out my clothes and hanging them up in the closet that was the size of a small room. At least Theo didn't bother with the folderol of personal maids, except for herself. As I worked I tried to take in the room that had been assigned to me. I knew it well enough, though I had never been permitted to stay in it before.

The walls were of gold damask, faded to a softer hue than they must have known originally. Most of the damask-covered walls throughout the house were the original, tenderly restored. There was a gold and cream canopy over the painted Italian bed, with a cream satin Empire sofa at its foot. The carpet was a pale buff, deeply piled, and most of the furniture was creamy white with touches of pale gold. It was not a room in which I could toss books around on the floor, or put my feet on the sofa. It made me distinctly uncomfortable.

But all this unpacking and examining of my surroundings was simply a marking of time. Theodora Moreland was waiting for me and her temper never improved when she waited very long. Yet still I postponed, changing to white slacks and a blouse printed with blue cornflowers, brushing my short mop of hair and restoring my lipstick.

When Joel knocked, I was ready. He came in, his quiet look guardedly approving me. Theo liked those around her to dress smartly.

"We'd better go up," he said. "She must be in a good mood or she wouldn't have given you all this splendor. Can you live with it?"

He knew me and I found myself smiling. "I'll manage. I'll move the chairs around and spill powder on the dressing table, rumple the counterpane. I can't live in a museum, but I don't think it necessarily means an amiable intent to put me here."

"Come along then." He moved toward the door and waited for me.

I followed, suddenly hesitant and uncertain. I had forgotten how to love him, but I had not forgotten the old rituals. Whenever we were away from home—in a hotel, or wherever—he had always paused before he opened the door of our room for me and pulled me into his arms. His kiss was somehow a promise that we faced the world together—that I needn't be alone. But I couldn't bear it if he kissed me now.

He didn't, and I couldn't tell if he even remembered as he opened the door and we stepped into the lavishly red-carpeted hall, warm and alive after the cold, classic splendor of my bedroom.

"Be careful with her, Christy," Joel said as we followed the miles of corridor back to the stairs and the left wing on the third floor.

"Careful in what way?"

"Perhaps I mean patient. She's a very loving grandmother, you know. It's going to be hard to share Peter with us again."

"She's a damaging grandmother," I said. "Peter is ours and I don't mean to share him with anyone."

"That's what I mean. You've always worn a chip on your shoulder with her. She *is* his grandmother, so take it easy."

"And you've always been on her side."

"I still am," he said, and the cool note in his voice warned me.

We did not speak again, and I found that as I walked the corridor and climbed the stairs, I was holding off the house. When houses lived long enough, they developed character, just as people did, and I had the curious feeling that this house had turned inimical to me. I had not been in it since the days just after my father's death and I had the feeling now that it did not want me here.

On the third floor corridor a balcony door had been opened upon the mid-October afternoon and I wanted to delay again by running to look outside, raising my face to the gentle breeze. But Joel was moving toward his mother's suite and I had to go with him. He seemed to know where she would receive us and he opened the door of the Green Sitting Room.

She wasn't there and the moment of our meeting was postponed a little longer. Of all her rooms I liked this one best. No austere, socially elite ancestors looked down from the walls as they did in much of the house. Not Theo's ancestors, but those who went with the house and whom she had never removed, adopting them as her own.

The pale green carpet had a woven design of yellow leaves, muted into the background. The sofa and one armchair wore slipcovers of a narrow green and rose stripe and the wallpaper was more broadly striped in gold and green. But this was a lived-in room. Here the marble mantel boasted a row of small framed pictures of Theo's family. I was not among them, but Joel's face and Peter's looked out at me, and there were old snapshots of Cabot and Iris, the two who had drowned. There were also ornaments of glowing jade and carved ivory that I knew were priceless objects from the time when Theo's ambassador father had once lived with his family in Shanghai. She was given, as a consequence, to a devotion for things Chinese. She took her treasures with her when she moved from one house to another, and I suppose they gave her a sense of being at home. A copy of *The Leader* lay waiting on a glass-topped table and Theo's green-rimmed glasses rested upon it.

There was a faint odor of smoke in the air, and I saw that a fire had been lighted on the hearth, though the day hardly required it. The wood had been allowed to burn down to glowing coals and gave off little heat. I dropped into an armchair and Joel went to stand before the fire with his back to me. I wondered what he saw in the coals, what he felt, what he thought. But something in me slammed a door hurriedly upon such thoughts because I wanted to face no self-reproaches of my conscience. I must be wholly occupied with the purposes before me. Joel was Theo's son before he was anything else. I must remember that.

Bruce Parry appeared and as he came to greet me and then went to stand beside Joel, I was aware once more of the contrast between the two men. It was not in Joel's favor. Bruce was only a little older, but he always seemed infinitely more mature. He was dark-browed with heavy, winged eyebrows, a strong, forceful mouth and carved nose. But his dynamic intensity came through most of all in eyes that were almost jet in their lack of color. His appraisal of me seemed sharply alert, and I wondered what he saw.

"She'll be here any minute," he said. "You're looking well, Christy."

"I'm fine," I acknowledged. "Where is Peter?"

There seemed an unexpected flash of sympathy in those dark eyes. "He had some sort of upset yesterday. Perhaps the excitement of coming here. I'm sure she'll take you to him shortly."

I was Peter's mother. I ought to have the right to go to him at once if he had been ill, but I caught the warning glance Joel threw me. It said, "Wait, wait. Be patient."

Without patience I plucked at the crease in my white slacks and would not look at either of them. I wanted neither to be pitied nor to be warned. I would deal with Theodora Moreland in my own way.

As always, she made an entrance, sweeping into the room on a cloud of sandalwood incense because Fiona followed her bearing a brass incense burner in the form of a writhing dragon.

Theo waved her small hands as she advanced, brushing away imaginary wood smoke, jade and diamonds gleaming on her fingers.

"Whoever started the fire forgot to open the draft until after it was lit, the fool!" she cried. "I cannot stand fools. I cannot bear them. Clear out the smell, Fiona."

We all stood silent while Fiona twirled incense aloft until I felt ready to choke on sandalwood. Theo took the center of the room and seemed to be studying every inch of it—except the part occupied by us. She seemed not to notice any presence except Fiona's, busying herself in directing her secretary's spreading of blue incense smoke about the room. I was glad that her immediate focus was not upon me, and I had a chance to study this woman who was once more going to be my adversary—only now more than ever.

She was tiny—perhaps an inch shorter than I was—with a tendency to plumpness kept ruthlessly in check, and she could give an impression of height with the dignity of her bearing. At the moment she was wearing a cheong-sam, one of those Hong Kong sheaths that come with a high collar and a slit to the knees. It was of jade green satin and it flattered a figure that had never been allowed to sag or bulge too recklessly. She wore her red hair in a high-swept pile on her head, lending to the illusion of height, and it was to the credit of her hairdresser that the color had muted with her age and was completely believable. Her skin was still fine-grained and it was well cared for. The only thing about her to betray her age was her hands, with their raised veins and liver spots.

"That's enough—you're smothering me!" she cried to Fiona, who glanced wryly at me behind her back and lowered one eyelid. "Set it down—set it down! Now then, Christy—let me have a look at you."

She seated herself in a straight chair that allowed for no slumping and beckoned to me commandingly. I knew of old the force of any command she issued, and found it impossible to disobey. I left my chair and went to stand before her, where the rosy glow from the coals tinted my white trousers. She considered me for a tormentingly long time and I tried to stare her down—not very successfully.

"You don't look bad," she said at last. "Better than I expected. And your hair is beginning to grow. The sea air at Spindrift will be good for you. Are you eating well?"

I'd had enough. "I want to see Peter," I told her. "I understand he's been sick."

"A small stomach upset. Nothing, nothing. But it's better not to disturb him till he's fully recovered."

"Seeing his mother shouldn't disturb him," I said, and heard Joel make a slight sound behind me—warning me again, I supposed.

She smiled at me—that dazzlingly beautiful smile that always came as a surprise—because she was rather a plain woman. It lifted the lines of her face, brightened those intense green eyes. Joel too used to smile like that.

"My dear. Of course it will be good for Peter to have his mother here with him. I'm glad you were willing to come. I'll take you to him as soon as I feel he's ready. In the meantime, are you comfortable? Do you like your room?"

"It's a bit grand," I said. "But if it's close to Peter's it will be fine."

She did not answer that. "I hope the house won't disturb you, Christy. I hope you'll be well here."

Her green eyes appraised, watching, I was sure, for some chink in the armor I wore against her, and I challenged her words.

"Why shouldn't I be well here? The house had nothing to do with what happened." I had brought it into the open, as had to be done. "Only a person, or persons, was responsible for that."

She shook her red head at me as if in sad reproach. "Christy, my dear! I thought you'd got over that notion before you left the hospital."

"I will never get over it!" I said hotly. "I still want to know what really happened." There—I had thrown down my challenge—let her make of it what she would.

Theo did not pick up the glove. She turned instead to Joel. "You must take care of her. See that she gets lots of rest and is outdoors whenever there's sunshine."

I stared about the room, seeking some support, some sympathy. Fiona had set down the dragon burner that still exuded a thin line of blue aromatic smoke, and she was looking at none of us. She studied the broad-spaced knuckles of her right hand as if they were all that interested her. Joel looked unhappy—with me—but he watched his mother. Only Bruce's eyes were fixed upon me and when I met his gaze I saw again what might have been a flash of sympathy.

There was nothing more for me to say and I knew we hadn't been brought together for idle conversation, so I subsided and said nothing more. The moment I was out of this room I meant to go looking for Peter. But the audience had not yet come to an end.

"I hope you will all help me with ideas for my party," Theo went on. "We want it to be a very gay and imaginative affair. I mean to bring people back to Spindrift the way they used to come in the old days."

"My father hasn't been dead a year," I said, forgetting about subsiding.

"Mourning periods are old-fashioned," Theo said with a slight edge to her voice. "Adam would be the first to say, 'Give a party!' Come—all of you! Give me some ideas. I'd like fancy dress. But something special."

Fiona spoke with the slight drawl she sometimes adopted with Theo, as if she must always drag back a little in the face of the older woman's dynamic surges.

"I've been thinking and I have a possible idea. But I'd like to show it to you—so why not now? Let's go down to the ballroom."

Theo was always ready for action, and she rose lithely from her straight chair—no pushing up on the arms for her—and moved to the door, the slit in her pale jade satin showing a leg that was still shapely.

"Come along then! Let's go look at Fiona's idea. Where is Ferris? I want him in on this. Bruce, do go look for him."

Fiona and Joel had followed Theo to the door, but I still sat where I was, and as he passed me Bruce bent his head for an instant. "Don't fight her openly. There are better ways."

I was surprised, but I left my chair and went with the others into the corridor. Joel was watching me and I felt uneasy. I didn't trust him and I didn't trust Bruce, but strangely I wanted to trust Fiona. Yet they were all under Theo's thumb.

Bruce had hurried off to find Ferris as Theo marched ahead of us down the stairs and through the marble entrance hall to a door at the rear. There Joel sprang to open it for his mother, and the vast reaches of that room I had not seen since the night of my father's death spread out before me. I held back at the door as the others stepped through.

The last time I had seen it, the gold and crystal chandeliers had been ablaze with light, the velvet draperies had glowed a rich and royal crimson and all the gold leaf of the upper walls and ceilings had shone in ornate splendor. There had been dancers out on the polished parquet floor, while viewers in couturier gowns and the men's black gathered on quilted satin benches around the room. There had been warmth and brilliant sound and the chatter of voices. All that was necessary to hide the crack of a shot fired in a distant Tower Room on the third floor.

Theo had reached the center of the great floor. "Well?" she demanded of Fiona.

"Look around." Fiona gestured. "Look at the ancestors. How many Sargents are there?"

"Three, of course," Theo said. "The one of Mrs. Patton-Stuyvesant that I bought with the house, and the two I purchased in Boston and New York."

"How fortunate for us that he painted here in Newport for a time," Fiona said. "And was part of the social life. You could give a John Singer Sargent ball, Theo. The women could come in the styles of Sargent's paintings, and I think they'd love it. That was a day when fashions were becoming."

Theo looked like a small Chinese lady as she went to stand before the Patton-Stuyvesant portrait. "I can't see me with a pink geranium in my hand."

"No," Fiona said. "You'd have to be Madame X."

I had seen the Sargent painting of "Madame X" in the Metropolitan. It was one that had caused something of a furor in its day—damned at the Paris Salon for being eccentric and sex-oriented—though that wasn't the term used then. But Madame Gautreau who had posed for the picture was a celebrated beauty and Sargent had made her exquisite in a sleek-fitting black gown, her reddish-brown hair drawn severely high, graced by a small red flower above the ear and Diana's crescent over her forehead. Her face and bare shoulders were that strange bluish pearl color that had been derided in Paris, but which had been due to the lady's addiction to lavender face powder.

Theo knew the picture too, of course. Now she raised her head and turned her profile haughtily so that we could view her, for an imaginary instant, as that celebrated figure. Without beauty, she could suggest beauty, and the very lift of her chin and its piquant carving bespoke the portrait. I knew she could carry it off, that Fiona's suggestion had been accepted because of Madame X.

"We'll do it, Fiona. Do see where you can find some good Sargent copies and have them framed in time to hang them around the room. We'll have nothing but Sargents here that night—with the real ones in the place of honor, of course."

Bruce and Ferris had joined us, and Theo burst into an animated description of what she meant to do. I had a sense of unreality listening to her. Much of the time

Theodora Moreland lived in a make-believe world. All of Spindrift was part of this make-believe, as would be Fiona's Sargent ball. But my father's death had been real and I must not let any of them lose sight of that.

I watched them all. Ferris appeared mildly amused and tolerant—as he seemed to be of all Theo's whims. Bruce's expression was more enigmatic. I suspected that he must have liked working for Hal on the paper's business better than he did jumping to the tune of Theo's whistling. If he did jump. I had a growing suspicion that she might have a slight rebellion going on beneath the surface here in Bruce Parry, and that he might be chauvinist enough to have a few opinions of his own. If I wanted help with Peter, he might be worth cultivating.

Joel was neither applauding nor deriding. He had seen his mother's enthusiasms before, and he had gone to open one long door that gave onto the rear veranda that overlooked the sea. I went quietly to stand beside him.

"When am I to see Peter?"

He spoke over one shoulder, not looking at me. "There's plenty of time. He won't be spirited away. When he's feeling more chipper he'll be happier to see you."

That hadn't been the case in the past. When Peter was feeling his worst, *I* was the one he had wanted near him, the one he had clung to in illness.

"I won't wait," I said, and turned back to the others.

Bruce Parry was watching me as I came down the long room. Unexpectedly he smiled at me, and his sardonic look lightened.

"You'll have to come to the ball as young Zenia Patton-Stuyvesant," he said.

Startled, I looked up at the portrait of the woman who had once owned this house, who had danced in this very ballroom. Sargent had painted with an elegantly decisive touch, with broad, sure strokes, and it was the quality of his style that was arresting. His subjects told you little of themselves and he was never particularly profound, though in his day he had been considered the best of all portraitists. Yet in the end he had given up portraiture to return to his first love, landscapes, where his reputation had never been distinguished. I respected him for that. But now for the first time I looked at the lady with the geranium as a person. She had posed for his portrait in her midnight-blue gown late in the last century, when she was young and mistress of Spindrift. Her wealthy husband, Arthur Patton-Stuyvesant (railroads, I thought), had built this house for her. Why had Bruce connected her with me? Her look was mysterious and remote—she had been thinking of other things, but you couldn't tell what.

"There was some scandal about her," Bruce said in my ear. "But that came when she was a little older. As you know, her husband died from a dose of poison—whether administered by his own hand or by someone else's was never decided for sure. Suicide was the story accepted by the police, but there were murmurings for years."

I did know about Arthur and I shivered. He had been the first to die in the Tower Room.

Bruce drew me back to the picture of young Zenia. "Don't you see the resemblance?"

I shook my head. "You're making it up. Anyway, I won't be coming to this party. None of this is real, and I—can't bear it."

I moved away from him, left them all to center around Theo's animated discussion of plans, and moved toward the door. There were only about forty-eight rooms in the house—it wasn't as large as some on Bellevue Avenue or Ocean Drive—so I had better start searching them if I meant to locate Peter. Probably his room would not be far from Theo's suite, and I would start there.

There was no one around in the corridors as I went up to the third floor, and the red carpet hid the sound of my steps as I followed it down the wing, stopping at each door to open it carefully and peer within. I knew the woodsy perfume Fiona used. Ferris's room was dark blue and austere, but that was his gold-initialed attaché case

36

on the bed. The next room was Peter's. He lay in a bed far too large for him, his head turned on the pillow, long lashes dark against pale cheeks, sound asleep, and at the sight of him my heart quivered. I stepped quietly through the door and pulled it shut behind me.

The room had undoubtedly been done over just for him. It was all that some decorator might think a boy's room should be. The wallpaper had a fish motif—and Peter used to collect fish in his aquarium at home. The colors were blue and gray, with a few splashes of bright red, and a dash of sunny yellow in the real sunshine coming in from the balcony door. But it was all too orderly. His toys weren't strewn around as though he had been playing with them, and not a book lay open anywhere.

I stood beside his bed with my heart beating thickly in my throat and my yearning feeling of love almost unbearable. I wanted to bend over him, gather him into my arms and rock him as I used to do when something had hurt him and he wanted most of all to be comforted and loved. His skin had that unbelievably smooth, almost transparent look that all children have until they begin to grow up, but there were shadows under his eyes, and his face looked a little wan against the pillow. I knew he needed to rest, to sleep, and I stole softly away. My arms were empty but I would wait a little.

I returned to the central corridor and followed it. One mission had been carried as far as possible for the moment. Now I must give my attention to the next.

This part of the third floor seemed even more hushed than the rest. Probably the house was not yet fully staffed and there were no maids busy with their eternal dusting and mopping. But for me it was a hush like death—though it had not been hushed the night my father died. All the focus of the house seemed to draw me like a magnet toward that one room at the far end of the right wing. The Tower Room, Theo always called it, and it was the room that my father had liked best. When Adam stayed here he insisted upon having it for his own.

Once it had been a favorite retreat for Arthur Patton-Stuyvesant and Adam's wry twist of humor had savored the macabre connection with the former owner. It was here that Zenia Patton-Stuyvesant's husband had presumably taken a draught of poison and gone not too quietly to sleep. The Patton-Stuyvesants and the Townsends, who lived in the next "cottage," had been close friends. It had been Theron Townsend who found the body, and his wife, Maddy, who had stood by Zenia through all that troubled time. Theo Moreland relished Spindrift's history, and it was known to all of us.

It was this room that Zenia was said to haunt—this room and the ballroom, where she was sometimes seen flitting about as she had in her old age, still greeting guests that were only memories in a house where no guest ever came again until Theodora Moreland took it over and brought it once more to splendid, artificial life.

Such stories had been meat to Adam Keene, who also had a taste for the spectacular and dramatic, as any good newspaperman should. What could be more interesting than to consort with ghosts, and if Fiona would not sleep in that room, then he would meet her elsewhere—"clandestinely" was the word he had teased her with. The room had always fascinated me, and even as a child I had always hoped for a glimpse of one of the ghostly owners. A hope that had so far been denied me.

All the doors along the corridor were closed—as they always were when not in use, to keep out dust and the inquisitive. Theo had a thing about closed doors, as though she feared someone behind her back and wanted protection. But every room had been fully furnished, and sometimes Theo had filled nearly all of them at one time when notable world figures gathered at Spindrift.

As I passed one door I opened it and looked in. Red and cream paisley marked slipcovers and spread. No antiques here. The dressing-table mirror waited for its next lady, chastely reflecting the order of the room. I closed the door and went on. The Tower Room was at the end. I had to take a deep breath and brace myself for the return of shock before I opened the door. I put my hand on the knob and steadied myself. Then I turned the brass sphere and pushed a little. Nothing happened. The door was locked and there was no key in the lock. I shook it indignantly to make sure, the feeling rising in me that it was locked only because of me. It would not matter if anyone else went into this room, but Theo didn't want me here. She had ordered it locked.

My hand on the knob began to tremble and a remembered sense of weakness swept through me. There were too many against me here. Too many who would keep me away from my son, and now from my father. I couldn't bear it any longer. Still holding onto that knob that would not help me, I slipped down to the floor, leaning a shoulder against the door. The tears came, wetting my cheeks. I let go of the knob and huddled with both arms clasped around my body—the way I'd sometimes done in the hospital, holding myself because there was no one left to hold me. My temple felt the hardness of the wood as I pressed against it and wept my heart out. For my son, for my father—for all lost love.

3

I did not hear his step as he came down the corridor toward me. I did not know he was there until, through my tears, I saw his brown shoes with the brass side buckles. Then I looked up quickly in resentment because I did not want Bruce Parry or anyone else to find me there, disheveled and crying, with all my guards let down, the weakness I had to conceal so easily displayed.

He didn't ask me what the matter was, as Joel would have done. He simply stood in silence beside me and waited for me to stop my weeping. I felt in my slacks pocket for a handerkerchief, wiped my eyes and blew my nose. Then I pulled myself up, grasping the knob, and faced him.

"The door is locked," I said. "I didn't expect that. It did me in."

"I'll get you the key," he said. "But not now. Give yourself a little time. You have to get used to it all again. I remember, you know. I remember that night very well."

I knew what he meant. He had come with the others when Fiona had gone screaming to call them. They had all come to find me there, holding my father's body in my arms, his blood staining my white dress.

"I want to go in now," I said. "I want to go into that room right now."

He regarded me coldly, somberly. "You're not a petulant child," he told me. "Don't act like one."

His words angered me, strengthened me, which perhaps was what he intended.

"I'm all right," I said. "But I do want to go into this room now. I'm not acting out of weakness. I've had to brace myself to face the room. It has to be faced, and I don't want to postpone it any longer."

He nodded gravely, seeming to understand, and his dark eyes were not unsympathetic. "Yes, I suppose you have to make your peace with this particular place. But it isn't wise to live over what happened there."

I let that go, seeming to submit. I wasn't ready to tell him why I must face this room, what I must try to wring from it. He stood watching me for a moment longer, considering. Then he said, "Wait here," and walked away.

There was a hall window nearby and I went to sit on the window seat and look out toward the ocean. The sunny afternoon was graying and wisps of fog drifted in from the sea, curling about the ragged outthrusting of rock into the water. From this high window I could see the Cliff Walk curling its way above the edge of the rocky drop. The velvet lawns of Spindrift, still green in October, ran down to the walk, with a few plantings of evergreen near the house. Once that winding path had been a contested area. The owners of the castles had wanted it done away with, wanted the citizenry forbidden access to a path which edged their properties. But the town fathers had decreed that the walk should remain open and that anyone at all could use it when he pleased. I had walked along it myself with my father many times, and with Joel and Peter.

But now I was watching the corridor as well as the sea, and I saw Bruce Parry when he came into view. He moved briskly, with purpose, and I knew he had the key. I hoped he would go away and leave me alone with the room and that I wouldn't have trouble with his lingering.

He seemed taller than ever as he came to a halt beside my window seat, and I had to look up a long way to that grave expression that he so often wore—as a guard against the world? I wondered. Perhaps this was what came of working for Theodora Moreland—the development of a constant guard.

"Why do you?" I asked, speaking my thoughts aloud. "Work for her, I mean? Work for Theo?"

He smiled but this time there as no lighting of his face. "I suppose I inherited the job when Hal died."

"I don't see how you can stand it," I said.

For an instant he seemed to withdraw from me, and I felt the unspoken rebuke. Then, unexpectedly, he gave me a reply.

"She needs me," he said.

"I don't think she needs anyone, except to feed her ego. She devours people."

"She won't digest me easily."

I could sense that this man might very well work for Theo without being devoured—as Joel had been devoured. But it was the key he held which interested me now and I reached for it. He did not put it into my hand, but turned to slip it in the lock of the door. When he would have turned the knob, however, I sprang from my window seat and ran to reach across him, cover his own hand on the knob.

"Please!" I said. "Let me open it myself. Let me go in alone."

My plea was too excited, I knew. He would not now think me calm, but he did not try to dissuade me. He offered no admonishments, but simply bowed his dark head courteously and went away from me down the corridor. I watched him out of sight, and then turned back to my own world, forgetting him.

The door opened easily this time and swung upon the unusual architecture of the Tower Room. Part of the room was square, with the tower bulging from the far corner. The bulge was a turret, really, having its being in connection with this room only, and not rising from the ground like a true tower. I closed the door softly behind me and stood in the weighted silence, staring.

Brownish patches stained the beige carpet. No effort had been made to clean them away, or even cover them. In fact, as I saw quickly, no effort had been made to tidy the room or put anything away since that night. Only the bed covers had been taken away.

On the desk in the bay window made by the tower, my father's things still lay scattered—his small pocketknife, a notebook and pen. The closet door stood open and I saw his cowhide suitcase there and the few clothes he had brought with him still hanging from the rod. I had not expected this, and the shock was shattering.

I would have expected his things to be put away, the carpet to be cleaned or removed entirely. I would have thought some erasing of that night would have been attempted. But it was as though the door had been closed in horror upon a dreadful scene and never opened again. It was as though the very air that we had breathed that night had been shut into this space, sealed away, waiting in this deadly hush for someone to return and dispel the memory of what had happened here.

I knew this couldn't be so because the police must have been in and out endlessly, but the air of waiting was here. A waiting that had been solely for me?

Suppressing the quiver at the pit of my stomach, I skirted those disturbing stains on the carpet and walked to the closet where he had hung his clothes. With a hand that I had to steady I touched the sleeve of the plaid sports jacket he had liked best, and it was as though I reached for my father. This fabric had covered his arm, it had been warm with the life in his body. But now it lay inert beneath my fingers. I couldn't find him here.

I looked into the adjoining bathroom, where his oval hair brush lay, his shaving equipment, a bar of soap he had used, a mirror that would never know his face again. Yet for all my inner quivering, I was beyond tears, beyond the weakness of weeping. If I called out his name as I was tempted to do, he wouldn't hear and I would only torture myself.

Instead, I let my emotion spend itself in indignation because none of his things had been put away. This neglect was somehow unseemly. You packed away the possessions of the dead or gave them away. You removed the immediate reminders and let the person you loved go—because that was what you had to do, and there was more dignity for the dead that way. A certain loving respect could be shown in the very act of packing away, and here I would do it myself. I would come back to this room and I would handle the possessions he had owned with tenderness, just as Fiona must have done with his things at home.

But at home in their apartment there had been intrusion. No one had told me for a long while. I had been too ill. But one day Joel had asked me if I had any idea why anyone should break into Adam's apartment shortly after he died and go through everything he owned before there was time to put his things away. I hadn't known, of course, and the knowledge had upset me, so no one talked about it to me again. But the fact remained that someone had searched for something unknown among Adam's possessions. Fiona had no answers. She had been upset too, but she would not talk about it on the few occasions when she came to see me.

I went back to the closet and felt along the high shelf. My fingers met something made of cloth and I took down the folded hat of faded olive-green corduroy that my father liked to wear in the country when it was cool and he wanted to walk outdoors. It flaunted a bright red feather in the band, somewhat the worse for wear, though he refused to give up the hat when it grew shabby.

I was not as controlled as I thought, and touching this familiar possession of my father's broke me up without warning. The hat seemed more a part of him than anything else, and I dropped into a chair, holding that bit of corduroy close to me, as if I held my father, remembering him.

He couldn't have been more wonderful, as far as I was

concerned. Rather ruggedly good-looking and able to dress well at those times when he wasn't working with loosened tie and mussed hair. Courageous—able to stand up to anyone if he had to. Kind, thoughtful to Fiona and me, though not always gentle. Good to those who worked under him, adoring him, for all his blunt ways. Imaginative, brilliant—that went without saying. His was the real mind behind *The Leader*. And if there was any integrity in the Moreland Empire, Adam Keene had furnished it. I had admired and loved him with all my heart. A bit of Oedipus? Perhaps there is a little of that in every loving daughter. If I could have married a man just like him, I'd have done so. Instead, I had married a man almost totally his opposite. But I *had* loved Adam and I'd forgiven him the one weakness he could not help—gambling.

At the windows of the Tower Room the afternoon darkened and fog crept up from the water to smother away the light that had pressed against the panes. As I went to stand at a window I saw Joel down there, walking in the mist. He had always had an oddly melancholy fascination with fog—perhaps because of that day when his brother and sister had died because of it.

I sat down again in the growing gloom, my tears ceasing at last, because one cannot cry forever. Somehow the feeling began to possess me that I was being watched.

When I raised my head and looked about I had to smile faintly. The watcher stood sternly above me in a portrait that had always hung in this room. Even in the dimming light I could see him—a proud gentleman in a frock coat, a broad four-in-hand tie and wing collar. He stood with haughty demeanor between an ornate table and a green upholstered chair, his hand upon a corner of the table. The papers of a busy man lay on the nearby surface, and he must have been hard put to find the time to stand still, posing for a painter. His hair was a graying brown, his mustache gray above a humorless mouth. This, of course, was Arthur Patton-Stuyvesant himself, the original owner of this room, in which he was the first to die. Somehow I could not envy Zenia her choice of husbands.

The eyes of the portrait seemed to look straight at me, and his was a penetrating gaze, a demanding one. It seemed to ask something of me—as all my father's possessions seemed to ask.

"I'll try," I told that formidable presence. "That's why I've come here. I'll try to find out what happened and why it happened. You saw it. I wish you could talk to me."

The corduroy hat lay in my lap as I leaned back in my chair with my eyes closed. I didn't want to see this room as it was in the present. It was time at last to make the journey back to that New Year's Eve ball at Spindrift. Always I had postponed this venture into remembered terror. Everyone around me had said, "Don't think about it." But that was wrong. It was better to bring it into the open and face it once and for all. Answers could only be found if I retraced my steps, watching for some betrayal along the way that would point to guilt. I knew there was guilt. I knew that someone still walked around unaccused although he had killed my father.

It had been one of Theo's gayer parties and guests had come from everywhere, braving the snows of a white Christmas. Not every newcomer who had chosen to give a lavish party in Newport had been easily accepted. In the old days many an aspiring hostess, beautiful, decked in jewels and spending her husband's money freely, had found her party shunned. Just as membership at Bailey's Beach was a coveted and hard-won accolade, so had it been difficult for the newcomer to become a part of old-guard Newport. From the beginning, Theo had never had any trouble. Of course hers was a later, more lenient time, but she and Hal had too many powerful friends, and she made people curious besides. She might act with audacity, but it did not do to be left out of Theo's parties. So what was around of Newport came, whatever the season, along with the outside world, and there had never been a Moreland party at Spindrift that was not a success.

Somehow, that night, I had never heard the music play so sweetly for dancing, never seen Spindrift chandeliers glitter so brightly. I had danced once with my father before he disappeared upstairs because he said he had work to do, and Joel and I had waltzed to an old chestnut of a sentimental tune. Theo was adamant concerning the music played at her parties. There would be no rock, no dancing apart, and she wanted "pretty" tunes of earlier days. For some reason I still remembered that it was "Tennessee Waltz" we danced to. The last time we were happy together, Joel and I.

I wrenched my thoughts away. It was not of Joel I must think now.

I had been down near the front door when Fiona and Adam had arrived early that afternoon, and I'd known at once that something was wrong. Adam's kiss on my cheek was absent and he had a whiteness about the mouth that I didn't like. He went upstairs to his usual Tower Room at once, leaving Fiona to fend for herself. She didn't want to talk to me, any more than Adam had, and I left her alone until after dinner that night. When I was dressed for the ball, I went to her room.

She had been assigned the Red Room on the second floor and I sought her out there. I was allowed in somewhat reluctantly, I felt, and was in time to zip up the back of her green taffeta.

Those were still the days when Fiona had been a serene presence wherever she was, calming my father's troubled waters, balm to his concern, and perhaps going her own secret way in spite of her fondness for him. But that night in the Red Room the edges had begun to crumble a little for the first time.

She bent before the dressing-table mirror, clipping diamonds to her ears—a Christmas gift from Theo. I'd had a pair too, but I wasn't wearing them.

"You look beautiful, Christy," she said into the mirror. "Like a mist maiden. White becomes you. And it doesn't fight this room the way my green does."

"Oh, I don't know," I said. "Red and green always go together at the holiday season."

"Not in this room. I wonder if she put me here because she knows this is the room I detest the most?"

"But it's not a detestable room," I protested. "I've always loved it. The reds aren't strident—they're like dark, rich burgundy."

She turned around on the dressing-table bench. "I've been put here before, and I never sleep a wink. I'm sure someone must have been murdered here in Patton-Stuyvesant's day."

"Why are we talking such nonsense?" I said. "Fiona, what's wrong with Father?"

Something flickered in her eyes and was gone. "He's been working too hard, as usual."

"Is it the gambling again?" I asked.

"Isn't it always?"

There was a new edge to her voice, and I kept silent, waiting for her to go on. After a moment she did. I think for once she felt the need to talk to someone—and I was Adam's daughter.

"It's worse than it used to be. A few years ago he began going into debt. He's always so sure that this time he will win, this time it will be different and he'll make up all his losses. He behaves as though winning depended on him alone—his system. So of course he feels he can win! He flew out to Vegas two days ago and there was some sort of disaster. He won't even talk about it, but I think Theo knows. She's pressing him on all those debts that Hal covered before he died. But I can't talk to him about any of this. We never used to quarrel, Christy, but now we do. And in the beginning I thought I could handle it."

I knew what she meant. Even in my young jealousy I had admired the way she had dealt with my father's very real neurosis. Each month he was allowed so much money to "throw away," to amuse himself with, while Fiona, always practical, took care of the rest. And the system had worked happily for a long while. She hadn't known that he was borrowing until it was out of hand, and the need had finally arisen to tell Hal what was happening. Hal had at once come to the aid of the man he still admired, and for a time Adam had been chastened and had dropped 'back to the old arrangement, while Fiona saved and scrimped to pay Hal back. But the sums were greater than Adam had allowed her to believe and the debts had been left hanging for Theo to pick up when Hal died.

"I don't know what we're going to do," Fiona said. "I have a little jewelry I can sell—these earclips, for instance." She gave an ironic flick of a finger. "And other things Adam has bought for me when he was feeling especially guilty. But it's all a drop in the bucket. I don't know what Theo wants, why she's pressing him. God knows, she doesn't need the money."

Fiona appeared to be talking openly, frankly, but all the while I felt she was holding something back.

"I'll talk to Joel," I said. I knew his mother often made him large gifts, which Joel didn't pay much attention to because, always having had money, it didn't interest him very much.

Fiona moved about the room, the full, long skirt of her taffeta rustling crisply as she stirred. "Perhaps that will help. I don't know. I don't know what to do. Of course if we borrow from Joel and she finds out, Theo will really blow up. She and Adam had a bang-up fight in Adam's office the last time Theo came in. He's been quarreling with everyone. Even Ferris. Ferris's secretary is a good friend, and she told me about it afterwards. I have a feeling that we're boiling toward some sort of dreadful explosion. And I'm helpless to stop it."

I had grown to have an affection for Fiona, and I went to put my arms around her and place my cheek against hers.

"It will work out," I said. "It's got to work out. Theo needs Adam on the paper. That's the big thing he holds over her head. It isn't as if he ever neglected his job. Everybody on the staff knows that *The Leader* is what it is because of Adam."

She seemed to take some comfort from my touch and my words, and for a moment she clung to me in a very un-Fiona-like way.

"Run along to the party," she said. "Thanks for stopping by, Christy."

So I left her for the time being, but when, a couple of hours later, she had not appeared at the ball, and Adam had not returned after that single dance with me, I went back to her room. I didn't go in, however, because I could hear Adam there and the two of them were arguing angrily. It hurt me to hear them, so I ran away and danced with Ferris and Bruce and others who didn't matter—because I only wanted to dance with Joel. After these years of marriage, and with a small boy asleep upstairs, he was at that time all the husband I wanted, and I was happy loving him. But sometimes Joel absented himself too that night—to do some bidding of Theo's, so he wasn't always with me.

The present intruded coldly upon my thoughts and I was aware of the Tower Room around me, with its stains on the carpet and its memories of another man who had died here. I stared up at Arthur Patton-Stuyvesant on the wall and wondered what his marriage had been like. What was the mystery Bruce had spoken of that surrounded Mrs. Patton-Stuyvesant, and why had her husband taken poison?

I shook myself. Past mysteries were nothing I must waste my time upon. It was just that the sudden remembrance of how much I had loved Joel had dropped me back cruelly into this time of so many losses—and there was old Arthur staring at me.

Did "love" mean only that for a time you saw another person as you wished him to be? Then when reality began to intrude, when you saw with clearer eyes that what you had thought was tenderness was only evidence of weakness, spinelessness—then did love evaporate? Or was it possible for it to go down into some deep cold freeze from which it would emerge someday when a thaw set in? I didn't know. I knew only that I could no longer be stirred by my memory of dancing with Joel to an old and sentimental tune.

How much I had lost since that night. My father, love for my husband, my son—how was I to bear it?

Back to that night. Back to the real things about that night—quickly.

My uneasiness about Adam had grown in me. I'd looked for Theo several times and could not always find her. I wondered what she was making of Fiona's absence and Adam's. An invitation to a party given by Theodora Moreland was a command appearance, but neither Fiona nor Adam had obeyed for long that night.

It was ten minutes to midnight when I decided that I couldn't endure not knowing any longer. I told Joel that I was going to look for my father and if I was late for twelve o'clock we'd greet our own New Year's Eve later. He kissed me and let me go. I sped upstairs through a hush that was all the more marked because of the music and sound downstairs. I ran to my father's door and tapped upon the panel. There was no answer and I rapped again, harder.

When I was sure there could be no one in the room I moved restlessly about that end of the corridor. I felt hot from hurrying upstairs and from my anxiety that seemed suddenly urgent and acute. To cool my warm face, I flung open a hall window and leaned out over the snow on the sill. The wind from the ocean was icy cold but it felt good against my face. Across the wide, dark lawn I could hear rough waves breaking over icy rocks below, hear the sound of music from the ballroom.

I had to find my father. I turned back to his room, leaving the window open, and shook the doorknob, calling to him. To my surprise the door opened easily under my hand, though Adam, like Theo, had a curious habit of late of locking doors behind him.

The room was lighted by several lamps and Adam lay on the reddening carpet, the revolver close to his hand. I think I screamed, but no one could have heard me. In a moment I had dropped to my knees beside him, to find him still breathing, his eyelids fluttering, his lips moving as he tried to tell me something. But he couldn't find the words, and he died there in my arms while I cradled him to me and his blood stained the misty white of my dress.

When Fiona came to the open door to find us there, we could hear the strains of "Auld Lang Syne" drifting up from the ballroom—and then the distant sound of whistles, of pans being clanged, of all the uproar that can greet the birth of the New Year. Fiona screamed as I had done, and I remembered staring at her blankly and registering only the fact that one diamond clip was missing from an ear. Then she ran away down the corridor.

In a few moments they were all there—Joel, Ferris, Bruce, Theo and others of her staff. I was raised to my feet, drawn away from Adam. He lay there on the carpet and I became aware for the first time of the terrible immobility of death. It was something that would haunt my dreams for months to come.

I think both Bruce and Ferris looked after me that night. Joel went to pieces with shock. He hated violence and he couldn't bear to see the evidence of it. Once, I remembered, he told me to go and change my dress. But the scarlet stains were my father's blood, and all night long I would not change.

The police tried to question me during this time—though there was little I could tell them. I remembered the talk of suicide—Adam's suicide!—and the way I threw myself upon Theo, pummeling her in denial. It wasn't suicide. It couldn't be! Someone else had fired that shot. But one did not pummel Theodora Moreland with impunity. I was given something in my arm by a needle and when I woke up hours later I was in bed. I think Joel was there beside me, but I couldn't bear the sight of him because he was Theo's son, and I kept sobbing that Theodora had killed my father. Hysteria and hallucination.

Eventually they took me to the hospital. I lived through all those months of being ill, and came out of them a different woman. Now I was here, still with the same conviction driving me. Not that Theodora had killed my father. That was silly, I realized. But that he *had* been killed and that no one but I admitted this or fought to establish it. Now I had to fling down the glove and tell them I meant to find the truth, though there was still the danger that they might send me back again to that white, sterile prison where I could not be my own woman.

Once more I huddled with my arms about me, rocking a little in the big armchair my father had liked. But I stopped that quickly enough. Rocking was something the emotionally disturbed did when they couldn't cope with reality. I was disturbed and emotional, but not in the same way. And I had to cope.

I returned to the closet where my father's few jackets and suits still hung. This time I was methodical. I knew the police must have been methodical before me, but I knew something they didn't know. Sometimes, in a favorite jacket, my father would have a special pocket sewed in. He'd had what amounted to a little boy's love of secrets and concealment, and I remember his saying, "When they search me, they'll never find this." I doubt if anyone ever searched him, though it might have happened in his line of work, since in those early days when he doubled as a reporter he had sometimes turned up where he had no business being.

There was such a pocket in the lining of one gray suit, but I found nothing in it. I searched the other clothes carefully, and the plaid sports jacket last. Something crackled in the lining, as my fingers sought the concealed pocket, and I hurried to draw out a tiny, folded slip of paper.

The writing on it was my father's—a form of hasty printing that he always used. He far preferred the typewriter to the pen, but when he had to write he set the words down in these square, not very neat letters. There were only four words and they meant nothing at all to me: MUTTON FAT AND TYCHE. That was all, and I could have wept with disappointment. But there was no time for that. Bruce might come back looking for me at any moment, and I didn't want him to guess what I was doing.

I went over the few things of my father's that lay on the desk. His wallet was not among them, and I knew it would have been taken away. I searched the drawers, as the police must have done. I even studied blank sheets of the notepaper Theo provided for every guest with the name SPINDRIFT across the top, in order to see if there was an imprint on a lower sheet from what might have been written on an upper. But the sheets were innocent and blank.

Finally, I went into the bathroom and searched through his leather shaving kit, looked along the empty shelves in the cabinet. Nothing anywhere—as of course there wouldn't be. All I had that was secret—and meaningless —were those four words: MUTTON FAT AND TYCHE.

When I heard someone at the door of the room, I ran water in the basin and smoothed my hands over my shock of fluffy brown hair. That would be Bruce, come considerately to see if I was all right. There was no more searching to be done here so I might as well go out and face him.

I went into the bedroom and found Theodora Moreland waiting.

4

Theo stood across the room from me, carefully avoiding those stains on the carpet. She still wore her jade green Chinese sheath, with the slit up the side and the neat, high collar, and she looked fiercely diminutive. If diminutive is the word. I suppose the Rock of Gibraltar might be termed diminutive beside Mount Everest, but the word did not fit that sort of indomitable smallness.

"Of course you would come here," she said. "I knew this room would be the first place you would foolishly head for. How did you get in?"

So Bruce had not betrayed me, and I would not betray him.

"I got the key," I told her.

"From whom?"

I was silent, and she shrugged and moved to the desk where the contents of Adam's pockets lay.

"Why didn't you have these things put away?" I demanded, seizing the attack.

To my surprise she looked a little uncomfortable. I had not thought I could disconcert her. She tucked a strand of red hair into the pile on top of her head.

"I ran away." The bleak note in her voice surprised me. "When the police were through I couldn't bear the place and I shut it up and ran away."

"I thought you never ran away from anything," I said.

She came toward me across the room, still avoiding those dark stains, and stood quite close to me, looking into my face with those penetrating green eyes that she could widen into beauty when she chose. She was so close that I could see the tiny lines raying out from the corners, lightly masked with powder.

"You have grown very hard since your illness, Christy. If Hal had been here with me, everything would have been taken care of. But all that happened shocked me so badly that I couldn't endure Spindrift. Adam's death, your collapse, all the miserable insinuations surrounding his suicide."

"Perhaps if you hadn't pressed him for money, he might not have died." I wanted to hurt her, though I didn't believe my own words.

"Yes. It will be to my everlasting regret to think that I might have driven him to take his life." She waited, regarding me steadily, expecting my immediate response.

I did not give it aloud. I might say to myself, "He would not have died by his own hand, no matter what!" but I would not say it again to her and open myself to those sly looks that meant I was hysterical.

"I'll have everything packed up right away," she said, moving about the room.

"Please let me do it," I said.

"Of course. If that's what you wish. I'm glad to see that you can take this room now without breaking down. That's why I locked it against you. When you decided to come here, I wanted to bring you myself and make sure you would be all right."

Or make sure she observed me writhing? I was glad I had circumvented that. I did not believe in this new attitude of moderation toward me. Something lay behind it, and I wanted to know what it was.

She had paused before the portrait of Arthur Patton-Stuyvesant, looking up at it, smiling a little.

"I remember him when I was small. He was younger than that portrait then—a handsome man with an abundance of self-confidence. They could be arrogant, you know, those men and women who felt themselves born to the blood because of their wealth and position. You've no idea of the exclusiveness of Newport society in those days."

I wanted to say, "Look who's talking about arrogance," but I was silent.

"Of course Zenia led him a merry round," Theo went on. "I understand that he couldn't control her. His best crony, Theron Townsend, lived next door at Redstones, and they were a fine pair of pirates, the two of them. But Zenia and Maddy Townsend outlived them both."

I wasn't particularly interested in this ancient history, but Theo didn't notice.

"Arthur didn't care much for children," she went on, "except as investments which must be encouraged to grow up properly and take hold when he must leave off, so their children turned out rather badly. Zenia had other interests. Did you know that Bruce Parry is Zenia's great-nephew?"

I shook my head. I hadn't known, and it didn't matter. Bruce Parry did not interest me, except as someone who might help me. No one interested me any more, except my son. If there was emptiness I was not ready to face it.

"I think I will go and see if Peter is awake and take him for a walk," I said. "Just a short walk that won't tire him."

She swung away from the portrait at once. "No! He is to rest now. I won't have him disturbed."

The moment had come. There had been times in the past when I had railed against her. But I had never stood up to her and won my own way. I understood her purpose very well. It was not Peter's health which concerned her, but any means at all to keep us apart.

"Theo," I said, "we might as well understand something right now. I am Peter's mother. I am well again, and I mean to *be* his mother. If he feels well enough to take a walk, then I think it will be fine for him to come walking with me. We need to get acquainted again, my son and I."

Theo could turn slightly purple when she was thwarted.

Now there was a faintly bluish tinge to her color that warned me. I turned my back on her and walked through the door, not wanting to face one of her explosions.

"I hope you won't lock this room again," I said. "I'll get to work on it as soon as I can."

I continued to walk away from her down the corridor toward the opposite wing and Peter's room. I fully expected to have the storm brewing behind me break into its own particular fury, but nothing happened. Before I made the turn in the corridor I looked back and saw that she was closing the tall window I had opened. She did not mean to blow me down now. Not yet. She was letting me go. But Theo Moreland never gave in. She only plotted new attacks.

The moment I was out of her sight I hurried, almost running toward Peter's room, as though armies gathered at my back and there might still be pursuit and defeat. No—not defeat. I needn't be defeated by her any more. I was alone. I'd have no help from Joel or anyone else, but I was strong enough now to stand against her. I had proved something to myself in this small encounter. I did not think the war was won, by any means, but I had come out ahead in a skirmish.

Peter was awake when I tapped on the door of his room and went inside. He had dressed himself in jeans and a blue shirt, but his fair hair was rumpled and he sat on the floor listlessly fingering the counters of a game.

I dropped to my knees beside him and put an arm about his shoulders. "Peter darling, I'm so glad to see you."

He edged himself from my touch and there was hostility in the look he gave me. "You're the one who went away," he accused.

"But not on purpose," I told him gently. "You know I was sick, don't you?"

"Grandma Theo said you didn't feel like coming to see me."

"I was in a hospital. Your father must have told you.

58

They wouldn't let me come." I tried to keep the shock of this wicked deception from my voice.

"Grandma Theo said she couldn't take me to see you because you couldn't keep me any more and it would upset me."

I had no answer except to catch him in my arms and hold him to me. "I've missed you terribly, darling. But we're going to be together again now. I'm going to take you home."

He wriggled frantically in my arms and I had to let him go. Released, he stood up and directed a kick at the game he had been playing, so that the counters went flying.

"I like it with Grandma Theo," he said, scowling. "She lets me do things you never let me do. She loves me the most. She told me so."

I rose from my knees and walked to the window to look out toward the ocean, struggling for my own self-control. When I could speak without a quaver in my voice, I turned back to him.

"If you're feeling better we might go for a walk."

"I'm okay," he said gruffly.

"It's a nice day outdoors," I coaxed.

"Where is Dad?" he demanded abruptly.

"I think he's working. He brought some manuscripts along to read."

"Where do you want to walk?"

At least I had won a small advantage. "How about down by the water?" That had always been a favorite place of his.

The faintest look of interest flickered across Peter's face and I went to his closet and looked along the rack. "Which jacket would you like to wear?"

He stood beside me and unerringly picked out the shabbiest, the most frayed.

"Fine," I said, and waited for him to put it on.

We went into the corridor together, silent in our separate worlds. No companionship had been established with him, and I knew that. Theo's destruction was too great for repairs to be made quickly. I was a stranger to him now—someone he was unsure of, someone he distrusted. I wondered if he had seen me when I was so disturbed that what he remembered from the recent past was a little frightening. Now and then he threw me a doubtful look, which might stem from that time, as well as from Theo's lies about me.

We found a back door, meeting no one along the way, and let ourselves out onto the long veranda that ran the width of the house and overlooked the ocean. Steps led down in the direction of a white pergola, guarded by a stone greyhound that had once been a favorite of Peter's. Now he seemed not to see it.

As with most of these oceanside houses, the trees and formal gardens were around at the front, while the lawns that slanted toward the water were left unplanted so that the wind could do no damage, making green expanses to the sea, with only low shrubbery near the house.

As we started across the sloping lawn, I spoke to my son quietly. "You must understand that I have been very sick. That's the only reason why I've been away from you. But I'm well again now and I want to be with you."

He did not answer, but I sensed that his hostility had not abated. I would have to move gently and give him time to believe in me again. His feet dragged a little as he walked, and I put my hand on his forehead, to find it cool. When I asked him how he felt, he said, "Fine," but he seemed listless, interested in nothing. Something more than a brief upset had deadened his eagerness for new experiences, his excitement and wonder over daily living that had been so much a part of him.

I wandered down toward the wall that separated Spindrift property from the Cliff Walk, and he ambled slowly beside me, with no smile on his face.

For some of the way between Lands End and Ochre Point, the Cliff Walk was in disrepair, and in one place there had been deep erosion, so that the path had to be bypassed, and only the hardy came this far. But we at

Spindrift knew how to circumvent the rough, crumbling places of gravel and dirt, and sometimes we still followed the walk. When Peter reached me, he clambered onto the wall and stood sturdily on its top, as I remembered him doing in the past. He didn't seem weak or sick—I was watching for signs.

For a long while he stared down toward the rocks where waves were breaking gently, not flinging spray high as they could do in a gale. The sound was soothing and rhythmic, but when he spoke I knew the voice of the ocean had not quieted him.

"Dad's brother and sister drowned out there." He spoke without emotion, matter-of-factly.

"I know. Did your father tell you about this?"

"No. Dad won't talk about it. I asked him and he got very sick-looking and told me not to bother him with questions. Gran told me. She lost two of her children that day, you know. My Uncle Cabot and Aunt Iris. Now she has hardly anybody and that's why I must stay with her and do what she says."

I slipped down from the stone wall on the other side and held out my hand to my son. "Shall we follow the walk for a way?"

It had been a mistake to hold out my hand, and he ignored it as he hopped down from the wall. We walked side by side, but not really together, picking our way along the broken path.

Now we could look back and see the great houses stretching along the scalloped ocean front, high above the water, all with an enormous spread of ground around them, each vying in magnificence of stone and brick and marble and timber with its neighbors. We had left Spindrift behind and the house we were passing was closed and neglected. Its roofs pointed upward like pricked ears, and its chimneys made dark slashes into the sky. For some reason I had never liked the look of this particular house and I knew it had a slightly unsavory reputation in the town, though I'd never known exactly why. Theron and Maddy Townsend had once lived here—the close friends of the Patton-Stuyvesants.

Even from this distance the house suggested the decay that was surely coming unless something was done to save it. Shutters hung askew, there was a great stone urn over-turned in the side yard, the verandas sagged and bricks were crumbling here and there, though the main structure still seemed in good condition.

Peter gave me a sidelong glance. "That's Redstones. I'm going in there someday. I like places that are old and spooky."

"It would be better not to go alone," I said mildly. "Sometimes floors break through, or ceilings can fall in old places that aren't kept in repair. There needs to be two people at least, so one could go for help."

All his attention was on the abandoned magnificence and he hardly seemed to hear me.

"The Townsends used to live there. John told me about them."

"Who is John?"

"He's Grandma Theo's new gardener, and he's awfully old. She got him because he knows a lot. His father worked at Redstones when John was a little boy. The Townsends were very rich. He said Mr. Townsend was crazy about collecting old armor and weapons, and he built a special room in the basement, where he kept suits of armor standing all around—just as though men were wearing them. He had lances on the walls and crossbows and swords. He even had a dungeon—just like in a cas-tle."

"A dungeon? Whatever for?"

"Well—a sort of vault. That's the spooky part. John said it was dug into the floor of the armor room. Maybe he put people into it to punish them." Again Peter gave me that sidelong glance, as if to see how much I would swallow.

"That sounds like a flight of fantasy," I said.

He paid no attention. "John says it got so servants

didn't want to work for the Townsends any more. They thought the house was haunted. Mr. Townsend was best friends with Mr. Patton-Stuyvesant, who built Spindrift, and John says it was Mr. Patton-Stuyvesant who got Mr. Townsend to board over his dungeon and not use it any more. Then Mrs. Townsend could get people to come and work again. Someday I'm going to explore over there."

"I imagine the place is empty of furnishings now," I said. "Probably all those suits of armor have been sent off to museums by this time. Anyway, I wish you'd take me with you when you go exploring."

His look held no liking in it. "I don't want you. I'd rather go alone."

He had become a little cruel, this darling son of mine, but I tried not to let him see me wince. There was nothing more to be said, and I turned back toward Spindrift, knowing that I had lost this particular effort to regain my son. He came with me indifferently and neither of us spoke until we reached the place where we could climb the low stone wall that edged Spindrift's lawns. Then Peter faced the great white house with a light in his eyes that I hadn't seen before.

"Someday all this will belong to me," he said and I heard the ring of possessive pride in his voice that was an echo of Theo's. "I'm going to be terribly rich when I grow up, and I won't have to work or do anything I don't want to do. Gran says I'm to be her heir—just like in a story. If I stay with her, that is."

His words were like a sick blow in the pit of my stomach. This was something to fight with all my strength, yet I had no idea how to counteract so insidious a poisoning. If I had disliked Theo before I hated her now.

"There are more satisfying things than being rich," I said quietly.

"Grandma Theo says money comes first. Then anything else is possible. That's why Grandpa Adam died— because he didn't have money enough to pay everybody he owed."

I held my breath, held back a wild impulse to shout denials, to denounce Theo. Nothing could be done quickly to cure what had happened to my son, and I had to control my impulse.

Then, without warning, Peter turned suddenly into the appealing little boy I remembered.

"Why do people have to die?" he asked, and there was hurt in his voice.

How do parents answer that question when it comes inevitably? I sought vainly for an acceptable reply and found none—since I didn't know the answer myself.

"Everyone has to die," I said. "Just think how cluttered the earth would be if everyone lived on forever and none of the animals or birds or fish died."

He considered that solemnly. "Aunt Iris and Uncle Cabot died," he said. "And Grandpa Hal and Grandpa Adam."

"And all the people who lived before them," I pointed out. "We all have to take our turn. It's just that we go at different times and in different ways. It will be a long, long time before you die, Peter."

"Even if he didn't have enough money, why would Grandpa Adam want to kill himself?"

I was suddenly angry. I knelt on the rough path and put my hands on Peter's shoulders, looked straight into his eyes, held him when he might have struggled away from me because my sudden move frightened him.

"Grandpa Adam didn't kill himself, Peter. Don't ever believe that. He thought life was wonderful. Even when things went wrong he wanted to fight to make them better, and—"

"But Grandma Theo says—"

"I don't care what she says! It isn't true, and someday I'll prove it. Your grandfather was my father and I knew him better than anyone else. He loved living and I know he wouldn't kill himself."

There was a dawning of horror in his eyes that I hadn't foreseen.

"But then—if he didn't—I mean, then someone else must have—"

Before I could answer that, he twisted from my grasp and ran back along the walk toward Spindrift. I had to let him go. He wanted none of me now. I had shocked him because murder was more dreadful than suicide, and in my anxiety to defend my father I had forgotten the inevitable road his thinking would take.

As I walked slowly back to the house I tried to tell myself that a beginning at least had been made. But there was no conviction in me. Theo's damaging influence had gone much further than I'd dreamed, and how I was to counteract that influence I could not yet see. I only knew it had to be done.

When I let myself in by way of the veranda, and this time passed one or two of Theo's household staff, I had again the feeling that the house had grown inimical toward me. It threatened me. It was an embodiment of Theodora Moreland, threatening me. I had not felt happy or comfortable in it since I'd arrived, and Peter's possessive attitude toward something that belonged to the past and not the present made me detest it all the more.

I remembered that Adam had always disliked Spindrift, and I had thought his attitude too extreme. He had used words like "phony display," and I had argued that there was the true beauty of an era here. You didn't call the Pyramids phony, even though there had been exploitation in their building. But now I was ready to agree with him, though in a more personal way because of what Spindrift might be doing to Peter.

Nevertheless, I knew that it was not the house itself that threatened me. It was the human purpose behind this emanation. Not only because of Theo. It wasn't hard to believe that there was someone within these walls who resented my presence and would like me to go away. Theo would be first on this list, but there might be another. And it was the masked face I must uncover. So far Spindrift was on the side of the guilty, helping to conceal.

During what little I knew of the investigation after Adam was killed, the police had questioned a great many people. If it had not been suicide, almost anyone at the ball or employed in the house could have murdered him. It must have been a great relief to come to the suicide conclusion. No one had listened to me. And I had never thought that some outsider had wandered upstairs and done this. Whatever motive there had been, I was convinced that it lay closer to home. What I had to do was uncover that motive.

When I reached the Gold Room it did not welcome me any more than the rest of the house had, and its stiff splendor held me apart. I was a foreign body introduced into all this gold and cream and crystal. The huge bed did not invite my body, but I went to lie down upon it anyway. I must shut out the room and the house and try to think.

My fingers fumbled in the pocket of my slacks and drew out that folded slip of paper with the words "MUTTON FAT AND TYCHE" written upon it. Why these words in Adam's secret pocket? What could they possibly mean?

Tyche, yes. After all, she was the Greek goddess of fortune—Lady Luck. My father had often worshiped at her shrine. But what had she to tell him—or me—that was so secret? And what had she or anything else to do with mutton fat?

The tap on my door came from Joel's room. I called, "Come in," reluctantly.

He was in his shirtsleeves, and his horn-rimmed glasses were in place, a pencil in his hand.

"I heard you come back," he said. "Did you have a good walk with Peter?"

So he must have looked out his window and seen us go. I had to be evasive.

"It will take a little while to get acquainted again."

"Especially if you must frighten him," Joel said.

Behind the glasses his eyes had a pained look and I knew he was unhappy with me. I waited, questioningly.

"Peter came running to me just now," he went on. "He said you'd told him that someone had killed Adam. He was upset and frightened. He wanted to know who it was. Christy, if you must keep on with these unrealistic notions, you shouldn't trouble Peter with them."

There was no use trying to defend myself. He was right, and while what I had done had seemed natural at the time, I hadn't thought ahead to the consequences.

"I'm sorry," I said. "The last thing I'd want is to upset Peter."

But Joel was upset himself. "If you're going to persist in what is really a delusion, I wonder if you ought to stay. I wonder—"

I sat up on the bed and stared at him angrily. "Of course I mean to stay!"

He made no further attempt to face me down, but turned back to his own door. "Then I think you'd better take another course and not go stirring things up."

I caught at his words with a challenge. "Stirring *what* things up?"

"Theo, of course. She won't have you here if you upset Peter. And if you hold to this particular course, she'll have you sent back to the hospital."

"She can't do that unless you want me to go. Do *you* think I belong in the hospital?"

He met my look sadly. "I don't know. I hope not, Christy. But it remains to be seen, doesn't it—whether you're really well? I'd only like to help you stay here, if that's what you want."

"We've got to talk about Theo," I said. "About what she's doing to Peter. The most appalling things came through from him when we were out walking just now."

He waited, and I went on.

"Peter told me he was going to be Theo's heir. He said this house was going to belong to him and—"

"All of which is probably true," Joel broke in. "Theo believes that anyone who is to inherit a fortune must be prepared for the job while still young."

"I don't want him to inherit a fortune. That sort of money destroys."

"That's why she's beginning while he's young. So he'll grow up knowing how to take care of it. And I'm afraid you can't stop my mother from doing what she wants with her own wealth. I don't think it really matters all that much. She raised me and I haven't suffered particularly because of the Moreland fortune."

"Because you've never cared about money!" I cried. "So you don't think it's worth talking about."

"You're perfectly right about that," he said, and was gone through the door of his room before I could say anything more. I stared up into the gold and cream canopy over my bed, blinking my eyes furiously to keep from crying. There had been enough shedding of tears. I was completely alone in this house, and anything I tried to find out or wanted to do must be done alone and in secret. What Joel didn't understand about Peter was not that he might inherit wealth, but what his growing attitudes toward it were going to be. Theo was heading him directly for disaster. When Hal had been alive and Joel was growing up, it would have been different because of Hal's good sense. But now Theo was on her own with Peter, and Joel wasn't understanding at all.

I lay back on the bed, feeling utterly frustrated and helpless. It must be nearly dinnertime and dinner was the one meal at which Theo demanded absolute punctuality. If you missed what had been served, you missed it, and there was no sending out to the kitchen to bring something back for the tardy guest. Help was scarce and highly valued, and you did not inconvenience the kitchen. Besides, Theo enjoyed her small tyrannies.

I put on a halter dress of peacock blue, with a gold sunburst in the folds of the neckline, and blue slippers to match. It was a Galitzine Theo had given me last year before everything had collapsed, and I knew she would approve my wearing it. Her good graces were hard to come by since I must oppose her on so many points.

When I was ready I knocked on Joel's door and we went downstairs together in silence. Clearly he had not forgiven me for what had happened to Peter or for my outburst of a little while ago. Everything had gone into cross-purposes between Joel and me and we couldn't talk to each other any more. Yet there had been a time . . . no, I didn't want that any more. I could no longer go back to those days. When something came to an end and there was no feeling left—my own thoughts brought me up short. What did I mean by an end? What were the ramifications? There was no time to think this through now, and I put the disturbing thought away from me for the moment.

A fire had been lighted in the French Salon, where several Louis' mixed their furniture, though with Fiona's influence Theo rather leaned to the XVI period, with mahogany and rosewood, and small-patterned silks, all rather classical in style.

Everyone was there and Ferris stood at a small bar that hardly suited the décor, mixing the drinks. Tonight Theo looked regal in a long gown made of Japanese obi cloth, light green, with bright red poppies scattered across it, and Fiona was lovely in pale yellow chiffon. The men wore dinner jackets, *de rigueur* for Newport dining, and tonight there were no guests—just ourselves.

Theo had not forgotten our last meeting, when I had walked out on her to go to Peter, and for a time she carefully ignored me. We went into the formal dining room and Theo took the head of the table, with Joel on her right and Ferris on her left. I sat between Ferris and Bruce, with Fiona and Joel across. Since this was a news-oriented family, the talk at first was about the latest political scandal. I didn't join in but sat quietly at my place, eating very little, but listening and watching. I knew I had to watch them all because someone among these five might know something that I wanted to learn.

Peter, of course, was not at the table. Theo deplored the custom of having children join the adults at dinner-time. This was the one formal meal. Luncheons were always buffet, with everyone coming and going as he pleased. And breakfasts were somewhat on the same order.

Of all the rooms at Spindrift, this was the one I found most oppressive. The carpet was dim green, with a dingy yellow border—very valuable and old, undoubtedly. The fireplace mantel was black marble, the wainscoting dark mahogany, with patterned gold damask above. There was a multitude of lighted candles, set on the long table and on heavy, dark sideboards around the room, but they did little to brighten the atmosphere. Brown velvet draperies flowed from the top of high windows to the floor, adding to the dark oppression. Theo sat in a tall, straight chair at one end of the table, its back rising over her head so that she seemed to occupy a throne royally. The matching chair at the opposite end had been Hal's and no one was ever allowed to sit there.

When the soup plates had been taken away, Theo addressed me directly for the first time, so that other conversation stopped, and the focus was on me.

"You tired Peter out this afternoon, Christy. He wouldn't eat a bite of supper tonight. Besides that, Miss Crawford is very much distressed. She had only stepped out for a moment and during that time you spirited Peter away, without even consulting her."

It was like Theo to make a public accusation, and I could feel myself flushing rebelliously. I had never even thought about a likely governess who had to be consulted. There was no way in which I could answer her without bleating again about motherhood, but I struggled to save my dignity.

"I'll apologize to Miss Crawford," I said. "I'm sorry I disturbed her. I didn't think about a governess when I took him out. Perhaps now I can relieve her of some of her duties."

"She won't thank you for that," Theo said. "You've already made her disapprove of you."

Bruce said quietly, "Perhaps it's Christy's right to disapprove of Miss Crawford."

Theo threw him a look of reproach, but she said nothing, and I felt a little glow of gratitude because someone had come to my side. I looked at Bruce's rock-carved profile beside me and murmured a secret "Thank you."

He turned his head and flashed that smile which could lighten his somber features and I found myself smiling back at him. For a moment we were conspirators, standing against the Empress. He was a little like my father, I thought. Adam had never let Theo blow him down, and he had spoken up when he thought her unjust to others, as no one else ever did.

The meal wound along to its end, and I was glad to escape soon after the crepes and coffee had been served. The others might return to the salon for liqueurs and more conversation, but I'd had enough. I pleaded weariness to Theo and went up to bed.

The Gold Room obviously disapproved of me for coming upstairs at such an early hour, but I turned my back on it and had a good hot bath in a luxurious bathroom which was Theo's innovation, surrounded by marble and mock-gold fittings. When I was replete with jasmine bath salts and hot water, I put on a blue wool robe and stole upstairs to Peter's room.

Miss Crawford sat beside his bed, reading aloud to him. She was a lady of indeterminate age and immaculate nature, as was evidenced by her neat gray dress that was just an edge off a uniform. No wonder there were no toys or books strewn about the room. As I tapped and came in, she put her book down with a faint air of reproach.

Peter looked at me without welcome, ready to endure my presence if that was necessary, but clearly anxious to get back to his story.

I told Miss Crawford that I was sorry I had taken Peter away earlier without letting her know, but I think my apology hardly mollified her.

"What are you reading?" I asked Peter.

"It's a book called *Treasure Island,*" he informed me grudgingly. "It's very exciting."

I wished that I could have been the one to read it to him first. "I know," I said. "I think I must have read it when I was about your age. Have you come to the apple barrel yet?"

He forgave me a little because at least I was not ignorant. "We're way past that. Jim is with Long John Silver on the island now."

"Then I'll go away quickly and let you find out what happens next," I said and bent to kiss him on the cheek. "I just wanted to tell you good night and let you know how much I enjoyed our walk this afternoon."

He barely submitted to my kiss. "Grandma Theo says you're not good for me. She says you excite me too much. And she says it's not true that someone killed Grandpa Adam. She says you get mixed up sometimes. She says everyone knows he killed himself because he was going to be disgraced, and you only believe what you told me because you've been sick. I'm not to listen to you."

I held back my impulse to blurt out hurt, angry words. I had begun to shake inside, but I managed to speak calmly. "At least we'll have to prove to your grandmother that she's wrong about my not being good for you. I'm your mother. And I think it's rather fun to be excited sometimes—the way you were about that house next door."

He looked doubtful and a little confused. I patted his hand lightly, nodded to the immaculate Miss Crawford, who was plainly aghast, and went back to my room.

"I don't like you," I told the array of cream and gold.

"And I suspect you don't approve of me either. Tomorrow I'm going to ask for the Red Room, if it's empty. In the meantime we'll have to bear with each other."

I had brought some paperback mysteries to read during dull hours at Spindrift, and I took out an Agatha Christie and settled myself against the high pillows of the bed. But I really was weary after the long, emotion-packed day, and before long I got up to open the window on a side balcony, turned out the lights, and settled down to sleep, with the distant rush of the sea—one of the things I had always liked about Spindrift—sounding in my ears. You could even smell the sea here—that distinctive scent made up of so many things—seaweed and spume and salt.

I was only briefly aware of Joel when he came in. He did not tap on my door, nor had he come to say good night. That was a formality we'd done away with. I listened as he moved around, but he must have thought me asleep for he went away quickly.

Nothing penetrated the deep slumber I fell into. I heard no sound of an opening door—nothing. No glimmer of consciousness reached into my dreams—if there were dreams—until the touch came on my cheek. It was light as gauze as it brushed my skin, but it was enough to startle me awake. I reached up to brush aside whatever had touched me, and for an instant my hand came in contact with the cold fingers of another hand grazing my face.

I think I must have cried out in alarm, for a voice whispered softly in my ear, "Be quiet. Nothing will hurt you. Be still. But listen to what I say. Go away from this house while there is time. Never come back."

I gasped and was quiet, waiting for whatever might come next out of the blackness in my room. Nothing did. There was a faint whisper of sound as someone moved away from me across the room. There was a stirring of air as a door opened, and for an instant the slit of light from the hall was blocked by a dark figure. Then the door closed and there was only silence.

I came to life and flung myself across the room to open

the door. The long hall with its richness of red carpet lay empty and silent. No door stood open down the endless corridor, and I couldn't guess which blank face the visitor had vanished behind. The house was still and asleep. But my own sleep had been destroyed in that moment of fright when I realized that a hand was touching my face.

I ran about the room, turning on lamps, banishing the darkness. The delayed reaction of my fright was worse than the moment itself when I had still been befogged by sleep. I thought of running into Joel's room to tell him what had happened. But I stopped myself in time. I knew the look of reproach he would give me, knew he would believe nothing had happened, and that I'd been having one of my disturbing dreams that had come so frequently since I had been ill.

Would he be right? Had it been a dream? I had been so deeply asleep that dream and reality might have mingled. The thought made me feel uncertain and as confused as Peter.

At any rate, I was sleepless now. I couldn't go back to bed. Instead, I slipped on my warm robe and slippers and looked in my suitcase for a flashlight. Since I could not sleep, there was something else I could do, and I might as well do it now.

5

When I was ready I turned out the lamps in my room, lest an edging of light show beneath the door and attract Joel's attention. I had earlier thrown back the draperies from a side window, and now moonlight fell through the opening and made patterns of tree branches on my floor. The moonlit scene at Spindrift had always intrigued me and I went to look out the window while my room was dark.

The view opened in the direction of the opposite house, Redstones, which Peter had talked about this afternoon. Its chimneys and pointed roofs stood stark and black in the moonlight, and I had again the sense of pricked ears, as though the house listened for something. But there was a strangeness now—something that should not have been. In a lower room a light was burning—a pale, subtle glow. I stared at it for a time, puzzled and unbelieving. The light did not move, so it must have been set in one place. I could think of no reason why anyone should be about in that house at this hour unless he was a trespasser. Perhaps in the morning I would speak to Theo about it. But now I had a project of my own.

I let myself softly into the hall and closed the door behind me with scarcely a sound. All was quiet down the far corridor. In slippered feet I sped along the red carpet to the turn where the stairs emerged. And as I ran I heard the faintest of sounds behind me—the whisper of another door closing. I whirled about, but the corridor lay as still and empty as ever, and all along the way the doors gave back their empty faces. Yet someone had heard me and looked out, then retreated.

It didn't matter. Even if someone had seen me running down the hallway, he hadn't followed me and probably wouldn't. Whoever it was, it couldn't be Theo because her room was upstairs. I was no longer frightened as I'd been when I first wakened. That hand on my face and the whispered words had been a deliberate attempt to alarm me. Someone wanted me gone from Spindrift. But no one was going to hurt me physically, and I would not be frightened away by such tricks.

A light had been left burning over the staircase, swung high in its cage from the ceiling. I gathered up the blue folds of my robe and ran up the stairs, flashlight in hand. At the top, where the corridor divided into right and left wings, I found I would need a light. The left wing, which housed Theo and Peter and those she wished to have near her, was lighted by a wall sconce. The opposite corridor which led to the Tower Room was dark.

I turned on my flash and made my way softly toward the tower at the end of the corridor. The key was still in place and the door had remained unlocked. I turned the knob and let myself into the room. My flashlight picked out furniture, rested briefly on the stern visage of Arthur Patton-Stuyvesant, and then found a floor lamp I could turn on.

But before I switched on the light, I made my way to the turret window and looked out toward Redstones, realizing for the first time that the Tower Room was directly over the room I occupied downstairs. So the view was nearly the same up here—only higher. That curious lambency still shone in the distant window, across the wide expanse of lawns between the two houses. For a little while I watched that unshrouded window, but no shadow moved across the glass, and I could not see into the room.

Anyway, there was nothing I could do. The emptiness and loneliness of the Tower Room took my main attention, and now that I had come I did not especially want to stay there. I must hurry with what I had come to do.

When I had turned on the lamp, I went to the closet and drew out my father's cowhide suitcase that had been battered in a hundred places around the world. He never allowed anyone to paste on a sticker in his travels, but the scars of baggage handling in all those airports were there. I lifted the case onto the bed and opened it. This was one article I hadn't searched in my earlier visit to this room.

There were a few shirts he hadn't unpacked, some socks and a red and black tie I remembered with a pang. How could a *tie* last longer than the man who had worn it? I felt under and around these things and then gave my attention to the zippered side pockets. But of course the police had been before me, and if there had ever been anything that would interest me, it was gone.

I was about to start packing the case with my father's clothes when the setting of a ring I wore caught on a bit of frayed lining in the lid of the case. As I released it I could feel something flat under my fingers. It took only a moment to slide out the envelope that had been tucked beneath the torn lining.

I carried it over to the lamp and dropped into the armchair nearby. My father's name had been scrawled on the envelope in Theo's black writing. The letter had been opened and I slid the contents out of the slitted end. It was a single page of that same strong script.

Dear Adam:
    If you continue along your proposed course I will see that everything you care about is destroyed. I would not have expected such treachery from Hal's good friend.

                                        Yours,
                                            Theo

Behind me someone tapped on the door, and I whirled about, startled, the letter burning my fingers. Whoever it was must not find me with this sheet of paper in my hands. I folded it quickly into the envelope and tucked it back beneath the torn lining. The tapping came again and I answered in growing alarm.

"Who is it?"

"It's Bruce." His voice came through the door. "Are you all right?"

I felt relieved and at the same time a little resentful.

"You can come in," I said grudgingly, and he entered the room, a tall figure in a navy-blue dressing gown, with tan pajamas showing beneath. He smiled at me ruefully in response to my frown.

"I have the room next to yours downstairs and I heard you moving about, heard you come into the hall. I guessed where you might be going and I was concerned."

"Besides, you've been told to watch me," I said tartly.

There was a brightness in his dark eyes and I surmised that like Theo he was not accustomed to being challenged. His was a position of power in the Moreland Empire.

"I'm not used as a messenger boy," he told me, "and what spying I may have done on occasion was at a different level."

I felt suddenly ashamed of my own suspicion. It was perfectly possible that this man had felt a slight human concern for a disturbed and unhappy woman. Once I had been generous and unsuspicious—but that girl was gone forever.

"I'm sorry," I said. "Everything in this place sets my teeth on edge. Thank you for looking out for me. But I'm really not ill any more and I can manage on my own."

"I'll go away," he said.

I stopped him as he turned toward the door. "No—wait, please. Now that you're here, I'd like to consult you about something."

As I spoke I knew my words were hasty and without plan. Quite suddenly I no longer wanted to be alone in this room, but what could I consult him about? I didn't know him well enough to trust him with my encounter in the dark when that hand had touched my face, and I certainly was not going to tell him about the letter I had found. Yet the loneliness in this room and my terror because of what had happened here were creeping back. I didn't want to be its solitary occupant.

"Then I'll stay, of course," he said.

"I came to pack up my father's things," I told him lamely. "Why don't you sit down for a few minutes? I won't be long, and then perhaps you'll carry his suitcase back to my room for me. I'll tell Fiona I have it in the morning."

He sat down silently, crossing his long legs. He was still waiting, I knew, for me to tell him what I wanted to consult him about. An inspiration came to me.

"Is anyone occupying Redstones?" I asked as I took my father's clothes from the closet and began to fold them into the case.

"Not that I know of. It's been empty for years."

"I looked out my window downstairs a little while ago and saw a light burning in one of the rooms."

That seemed to interest him. He went to the turret window and looked out toward the black roofs and chimneys of the red brick house. I came to stand beside him. Across the lawns the great house stood behind its iron fence like a ghost of itself in the moonlight, more ethereal than solid, but the interior light was gone. Every window showed a blank of darkness.

"I don't see anything," he said. "There's no light there."

Something in his voice made me uncomfortable. It doubted me.

"There must have been someone there to put out the light I saw," I protested. "It was down there in that lower room toward the front of the house."

"Probably the moonlight striking a windowpane," he said. "You'll see that effect sometimes."

I didn't think it had been the moon, and the effect wasn't there now, though the moon was climbing the sky. I felt suddenly faint and shivery—one of those spells that used to come over me in the hospital and which I hadn't suffered for a long time. The very faintness frightened me—I couldn't go back to those days! As I moved from the window, I stumbled, and at once his arm came about me, supporting me, helping me to a chair. He looked anxious and a little distraught himself, as though rescuing fainting maidens wasn't in his line.

"Would you like a drink of water?" he asked.

I took myself in hand and sat up straight. "No—I'm all right. It's just foolishness. So much seems to have happened today. And—and this room—"

"Hadn't you better stay away from it until you are stronger?"

His very words strengthened my resolve. "No! If I'm going to be like this, I'll come here every day until I get over it. I won't be faint. I won't be sick. I won't be sent back to that place!"

He was bending over me with a certain anxiety in his eyes and he touched me lightly on the cheek with one finger. "I don't think you'll be sent back. I think you're strong enough—if you'll just give yourself time. Be a little lenient with yourself."

His finger seemed to burn my cheek, bringing my senses tingling to life as they had not been for a very long time. I turned my head from his touch and was aware of his slight amusement. I suspected that this was a man quite accustomed to conquests when it came to women, and I didn't mean to be one of them. The portrait on the wall gave me a quick topic of conversation, under which I could hide my moment of discomfiture.

"Theo says you're related to the Patton-Stuyvesants. Did you know Arthur?"

He grimaced slightly, looking up at the picture. "The relationship is a dubious distinction. Zenia was my great-aunt on my mother's side, and we used to visit her sometimes when I was small. But Arthur was gone long before I was born, and I only remember Zenia as a very old and somewhat eccentric lady. She fascinated me."

I was glad Bruce had picked up the gambit. "In what way?"

"She was always promising to tell me secrets and I used to have a pleasantly creepy feeling about her. I suspect that she took on more than one lover in the early days, and that she probably drove poor Arthur up the wall. Have you ever seen her sitting room?"

I shook my head.

"I'll show it to you sometime. Theo remembers her in the great days and she had the whim of leaving Zenia's room untouched."

I'd recovered myself by this time and I stood up. "I'll get back to my packing now," I said, feeling my knees wobble only a little and commanding them silently to be steady.

Bruce helped me, not troubling me with idle talk, simply bringing Adam's things from the closet, from the desk, from the bathroom, and as I put them away I felt an unexpected warmth of gratitude just for his calm presence and his silence. He did not intrude on my sorrow for my father or on the feelings of recognition that stabbed through me as I handled Adam's worn possessions. I welcomed such pangs. Not to feel them would be to forget, and I owed it to Adam Keene not to let his death—or the possible cause of it—ever be forgotten.

"Do you know if my father's wrist watch was found here that day?" I asked Bruce.

"I think Theo has it."

"Why? It would mean nothing to her. A Japanese friend gave it to him when he was in Yokohama one time, and he was quite fond of it."

"If you'd like to have it, I'll try and get it for you," he said.

Bruce puzzled me. Why was he helping me? Why had he obtained the key for me, and why was he now offering to recover my father's watch?

I spoke the word aloud bluntly. "Why?" I asked.

For a moment he stared at me and then, unexpectedly, he laughed. "Don't you know?" he said.

"I don't know anything. I don't see why you should put yourself out for me. Unless this is something Theo has told you to do."

This time I'd angered him. His face darkened and he stared at me so coldly that I could hardly believe I had seen warmth in his eyes earlier.

"I admired Adam," he said. "I'm not altogether sure I admire his daughter. If you're ready with that case, I'll carry it back to your room."

He had put me down thoroughly and I felt disconcerted and annoyed with him and with myself.

"Thank you," I said coolly, and slammed down the lid of the case. Then I drew my robe more closely about me and walked past him to the door. He followed me down the corridor, not walking beside me, but staying in my wake, like a bellhop showing me to my room, I thought scornfully.

But he was no bellhop, and when we'd gone downstairs and reached my door, he set the suitcase down with a bit of a thump, told me a grave "Good night," and vanished through the next door. I wrestled the big case into my own room, still feeling at odds with myself. It had been a long time since I had met a man who had left me feeling so unsettled and unsure. I was accustomed to Joel's absolute predictability, and I didn't know what to make of a man whose actions I couldn't fathom, whose thoughts were a mystery. There was no way to tell whether he was friend or foe.

Carrying the suitcase into my room had made a noise as I bumped it on the door, and before I'd had time to get back in bed, Joel was tapping on the panel between our rooms.

"Is anything wrong?" he called.

"No—nothing. I've just been sleepless."

He opened the door and a sliver of light from his room fell into mine. "You've been up, haven't you?"

"It's all right. I'm just going back to bed."

"Where were you? I called to you a little while ago and there was no answer." Here it was again—the watching—and I couldn't help but be suspicious.

I hadn't wanted to tell him where I'd been, but now I had to. "I went to the Tower Room. Since I couldn't sleep, I packed my father's things."

This seemed to disturb him and he came into the room and turned on a lamp. I didn't want him asking questions, probing my emotional state, and I got into bed with my robe still on.

"I'm all right," I repeated. "Don't fuss over me."

He stood beside my bed, more persistent than sympathetic. "What awakened you, Christy?"

Abruptly I decided to fling the truth at him and see what he made of it.

"Someone came into my room. Whoever it was touched my face and told me to be quiet, told me to go away from Spindrift."

His incredulity was evident. "Oh, come now—not this again, Christy! You've been free of such imaginings for weeks."

"I can go even further," I told him, my voice hard. "When I looked out toward Redstones there was a light over there in a lower window. A light in an empty house, Joel."

At once he went to push the draperies aside, and I spoke quickly. "You won't see it now. It's gone."

Nevertheless, he stepped out on the balcony, looking out toward Redstones.

"There *was* a light," I said and felt the tightening of my muscles against his disbelief.

When he had closed the draperies he came back to my bed. "Can I get you something to help you sleep, Christy?"

"I don't want anything. Except for someone to believe me!"

Obviously, he couldn't give me belief and his eyes were evasive. Resentfully, I tried a new attack.

"Joel, do you know that your mother was threatening Adam about something?"

"What do you mean?"

"She was accusing him of some sort of treachery."

"You'd better tell me what you're talking about."

But I had no intention of showing him the note or explaining any further. I had just wanted to see what sort of reaction I might get from him.

"Never mind," I said. "Unless you can tell me something about it, I'll try to go to sleep now."

He waited a moment longer and I could sense his increasing disbelief in everything I said. With a shrug he gave up, turned out the lamp and went away. The strip of light from his door narrowed, disappeared, and my own room was enveloped again in darkness. I sat up and took off my robe. Then I slipped out of bed and ran to the window for a last look out toward Redstones. The house slept in the moonlight. All was quiet and there were no lights anywhere. I went back to bed and this time I fell soundly asleep out of sheer weariness.

It was late when I awakened in the morning. Sunlight was bright outside, but except for that one balcony window, my room was dim with drawn draperies. I lay quietly for a little while, trying to orient myself.

I thought of Peter first, and of how I must work out some time with him every day. Then I thought of those four things I dared tell no one else about. The touch on my face—which I had better dismiss as a dream. It seemed too incomprehensible that anyone would come into my room and *touch* me. Someone might come seeking for some reason—though I couldn't guess what—but such a search would certainly be secret, with an attempt not to rouse me. Of course if the intent had been merely to frighten me, it had briefly succeeded.

Next there was the light I had seen in a lower window of Redstones. Again, mystery, but this time none of my affair. Since Bruce had not seen it later, I had no proof that this was not another hallucination, and it was better not to mention it further—though I'd already told Bruce and Joel. I was curious about Redstones, but the house was of interest to me only as it interested Peter.

The third and most ominous thing was the note from Theo to my father. What that meant was important and I needed to find out why she had written it. Though how I could go about investigating, I hadn't the faintest idea. And there was still that strange "mutton fat" notation of Adam's.

As soon as I was up and dressed I removed Theo's note from the lining in my father's suitcase and hid it with the "mutton fat" slip in my handkerchief box. Then I went downstairs to breakfast.

I far preferred the smaller room where breakfast and lunch were served to the formal dining room. It was a room of rose and cream. The walls were paneled and had been painted a warm ivory, while the oriental carpet was a faded rose, and so were the tapestries of a screen that hid the serving door and decorated the comfortable chairs around the informal round table. The mantelpiece was white marble with touches of gold, and a firescreen with an embroidered Tudor rose design stood before the empty fireplace. Over the mantel a portrait of the young Zenia—not a Sargent—looked down upon the room and there seemed to be mischief in her eyes and a sense of gaiety that had been lost in the Sargent painting.

Apparently everyone else had eaten, though hot dishes still awaited me on the buffet. I sat in comfortable solitude and had scrambled eggs and bacon, toast and hot coffee. No one disturbed me, or showed the slightest interest in what I would do with my day. Not until I was nearly finished did Ferris Thornton come into the room.

"Ah, Christy," he said. "I'll join you with a cup of coffee."

He was the only one in this house whose presence I could welcome at the moment, and I was glad to see him. True, he had been vocally critical of Adam's gambling, but I had always believed that his criticism grew out of fondness for my father, so I had willingly forgiven him.

He poured a cup from the plugged-in percolator and brought it to the table, black. In the light of bright morning flooding the windows, he looked thinner than ever and the bones of his face marked its structure with narrow cheeks and long chin. As he had aged, his eyes had sunk a little in their sockets, but they were still an alert hazel and I had always had the feeling that Ferris Thornton missed very little of what was going on. There might be things I could learn from him, but I would have to step cautiously because his devotion to Theodora was well known.

"What was it like in the beginning?" I asked. "I mean when you and Father and Hal came together to start a paper?"

"We all went to Harvard at the same time," he said, "though I was in Law School and it was pure chance that threw me in with the other two. I was dating Theodora and she introduced me to them. I expect I was a bit of a Boston snob in those days. Hal was from what I regarded as the wilds of Chicago and Adam from the streets of New York, so I considered myself privileged. But those two had a vitality and creative energy that quickly took any wind out of my sails. I knew from the beginning that they would go places and that if I had my wits about me I could get them to take me along."

"It seems that you succeeded. Were you and Theodora in love in those days?"

He seemed to regard me as a little girl asking questions and forgave my impertinence.

"Theodora was in love with Adam. And he was in love with Hester, your mother. It was a good thing for all of us probably that Hal had the exuberant confidence to sweep Theodora off her feet. I don't think she ever regretted it."

"Did you?"

Ferris Thornton seldom smiled and there was no great warmth when he did, yet now there was just a hint of wry humor in the parting of those thin lips.

"I expect I was relieved. Theodora was enough of a tumult in my life from afar. It might have been too painful to be any closer."

I liked him for his admission. Yet he had never married and all his life had been devoted to the law affairs of the Moreland Empire.

"I think Theo listens to you," I said. "More so than to anyone else."

"Perhaps because she knows I'm asking nothing of her. She knows she can trust me."

I left my role of the wide-eyed questioner. "You gave your loyalty to Hal too, and to Adam. You liked my father. So now will you help his daughter?"

A veil of lawyer's caution seemed to come over his face. I reached out a hand and touched his arm lightly across the table. For a good many years he had been "Uncle Ferris" to me, bringing me dolls and games and candy.

"I want my son back," I said. "I don't think Theo's good for him. Not as I would be."

"Are you so sure you are good for him?" Ferris asked.

"What do you mean? We used to have a wonderful relationship, Peter and I. We loved each other and we could laugh and play together. He was mine."

"No child can be owned," said Ferris judiciously, the long-term bachelor giving parental advice.

"Of course not. But I was encouraging Peter to find his own way. Theo spoils him. She gives him anything he asks for without question, and he's learning how to be clever and use her. Everything is being made too easy for him, so that he's losing interest and getting bored. Even worse, she's making him think of money as the most important thing in the world."

"The man who has it must learn to use it wisely."

Ferris could be hopelessly stuffy.

"Oh, Ferris, I've heard all that! But there are such things as values. What Peter is developing is greed and the idea that he doesn't need to work for anything. It isn't a matter of taking him away from Theo, but of counting me into the picture where I belong. The way it is now, Miss Crawford stands on guard. There are rules to shut me out. I broke them by taking Peter for a walk yesterday, and now everyone's angry with me."

He unbent with a nod of sympathy. "I can see it must be hard for you. But what can I do?"

"Talk to her. Persuade her that I'm well again and perfectly fit to be a good mother. Even that I have a few rights along that line."

"And are you well again? Completely?"

I stared at him. "Of course I am!"

"At breakfast this morning Bruce said you claimed to have seen a light in a window at Redstones last night. Theodora said you were imagining things again."

I could not thank Bruce for telling, though it might have been a casual remark.

"I did see a light. It wasn't moonlight and it wasn't hallucination. There was someone in that place last night."

He was not persuaded by my vehemence and there was a new coolness in his look. "Theodora thinks it very unlikely. She is concerned about you, Christy."

I knew the course Theo's concern could take, and I answered indignantly. "I wasn't imagining it! Why is it so impossible? Perhaps some kids have camped in there. Or it could be someone who likes exploring empty houses. Or a thief looking for treasure."

He considered all this quietly for a moment. Then he made a suggestion. "What do you say we go and find out?"

"You mean just go over there now and walk in?"

"I have a key. It would be quite official. There's some interest in turning the house into a school, and I've been keeping something of an eye on the place for the present owner. I don't want to pass up investigating any signs that someone has been in there. If it's true, it should be looked into."

"Then let's go," I said. "I'll change my shoes and get Peter."

"Why Peter?"

"Because he wants to explore that old place, and this would be a much safer opportunity than if he should get the idea to go in alone."

"I'll wait for you at the side door," Ferris said.

I ran upstairs eagerly, happy to take some sort of action. There was the possibility that whoever had been inside Redstones last night had left some sort of evidence behind which Ferris Thornton would be sure to recognize. And besides, this would be a way to spend some time with my son.

I put on navy-blue slacks, my red turtleneck sweater, and a pair of loafers, good for clambering around on uncertain territory. Then I went to the top floor to look for Peter.

Miss Crawford was on guard again, while Peter sat listlessly on a window seat staring out toward the sea. "Some people have swimming pools," he was remarking as I reached the door. "Why doesn't Gran have a swimming pool? She can buy anything she wants."

"October is the wrong month for swimming." Miss Crawford evaded the issue and she looked up at me from her knitting with no welcome in her rather pale eyes.

"I've got a better idea," I said. "Uncle Ferris has offered to take me through Redstones. How would you like to go along?"

Once Peter would have sprung up in delight, but now I could see that the habit of sulky resistance had become too ingrained.

"I'd rather go alone," he said indifferently, waiting to be coaxed.

"All right," I agreed. "I'm going anyway," and I turned toward the door.

Peter slid from the window seat. "I guess I could go along if you want me to."

"But we have a math lesson to do," Miss Crawford objected. "You know that if you're permitted to stay home from school for a while, you have to have lessons."

"Isn't it possible to do math this afternoon?" I said. "Or even later this morning? I don't think we'll be gone too long."

"Gran will let me go," Peter said with smug confidence and I found myself torn between my own wishes and the right that was obviously on Miss Crawford's side.

"When will Peter be free?" I asked.

The governess gestured toward an open notebook on the desk. "We believe in a full schedule. His time will be completely occupied all day."

I suspected that she had been told to confront me with obstruction, but before I could say anything more, Peter took matters into his own willful hands.

"Oh, no it won't!" he cried, and hurled himself past me out the door to run down the hall toward the Green Sitting Room, where Theo was dealing with her morning's work of dictating letters to Fiona. I followed him to the doorway reluctantly. Nothing was simple any more, and I was finding myself in the thankless role of a disruptive force. What was worse, Joel was there beside his mother's desk to witness what I had wrought.

Theo, as always, looked smart and I guessed that her gray suede dress was a Halston. She welcomed Peter with an outstretched arm and kissed his cheek lovingly. Then she took off her green-rimmed glasses and stared at Miss Crawford and me, crowding her doorway. Peter, however, gave her no time to ask questions.

"Mother and Uncle Ferris are going to explore Redstones this morning and I want to go along. Crawfie says I can't. Tell her to let me go!"

I glanced at Fiona and saw that she was watching intently, her pencil poised over her notebook. I couldn't look at Joel.

Theo's beak of a nose pointed in my direction and her straight lips did not smile. "Why should you explore Redstones?"

"Last night I saw a light there," I said. "It's possible some trespassers have broken in. Ferris wants to take a look and I'd like to see the house. Since Peter has been dying to go through the old place, I thought this was a good opportunity for him to go along. But I didn't realize I was interrupting lessons. I really think we'd better postpone—"

"I want to go, Gran!" Peter broke in, and returned her kiss fulsomely on the cheek.

I hated to see my son coaxing his way around his grandmother so disgustingly. But the matter was already out of my hands.

"You shall go, darling," Theo said. "And what's more I'll come along myself. It's all right, Crawfie. Peter's bright enough to catch up on whatever work you planned for him this morning."

Miss Crawford knew who was boss and she retreated with a straight back that was more disapproving of me for causing all this than of anyone else. What had looked like a pleasant morning's adventure was now to be taken over by Theodora Moreland.

"We can finish this matter later, Joel," she said, and rose from her chair, always surprisingly small when she was on her feet. "And, Fiona, you can work on your notes, dear. I'll pick up that letter later."

Fiona raised her eyebrows at me and I could only give her a helpless shrug. One did not stem the tidal force of Theo Moreland once it had been released to some purpose.

Joel came with us when we went out of the room and downstairs, to find a somewhat surprised Ferris Thornton waiting for us. He had hardly expected this to turn into an expedition, but he greeted Theo and Joel, nodded to Peter and led the way out through a side door.

6

The chimneys of Redstones stood up from among ancient beech trees whose leaves were turning bright in the October sunshine. Red bricks that dated back to the last century had softened to a muted rose color with the passing years, so that the house no longer lived up to its name. The evidences of neglect were everywhere. Walks that were overgrown, flower beds lush with weeds, the great stone urn tumbled in deep grass, all bespoke owners no longer interested. An iron fence guarded the house and we could see all this through its spears as we walked around to the front entrance.

Here the great wrought-iron gate confronted us, its intricate pattern thrown in detailed shadow on the sunny gravel driveway beyond.

"This was an extravagantly expensive gate in its day," Ferris said, and touched his fingers regretfully to rusty scrollwork. "But such a gate has to be sanded and painted every year to keep its perfection."

"Look at the cobwebs," Peter cried.

Between all the involved scrollwork and loops of the iron pattern, spiders had wrought their own intricacies, the strands shining in fragile beauty in the sunlight, still twinkling with a few beads of dew.

"Don't break them, Uncle Ferris," Peter pleaded.

This was Peter as I remembered him, with a quick and sensitive eye for beauty. Once I would have exchanged a look of pleasure with Joel over our son's response, but now Joel walked beside his mother and there was a gulf between us.

"Nonsense," Theo proclaimed. "Spider webs are only

spider webs, and we have to get in." She reached out a careless hand and shook the gate, but it did not open. The webs trembled and broke in places, scattering crystal drops.

Peter promptly lost his temper as I had never seen him do before. He flew at Theo with a force that nearly pushed her off her feet, and she tried to hold him away, laughing. Even Joel seemed startled and he collared Peter firmly and pulled him back while the boy shouted angrily.

Theo made no effort to suppress her amusement. "I'm sorry, darling. But there will be new spider webs by tomorrow morning. There are always more spider webs."

I looked at Joel, shocked because I had never seen Peter throw a tantrum before. Theo had been insensitive to the beauty and fragility of a spider web, but Peter should never have made a physical attack upon his grandmother. Yet I was no longer in control and in no position to reprimand him as a mother should. Joel met my eyes briefly and I knew that whatever either of us might say would be countermanded by Theodora Moreland. Nevertheless, Joel set his son down hard on his feet, and Peter subsided sullenly.

Ignoring the entire outburst, Ferris took out a ring of keys and fitted one into the old-fashioned lock. The great double gate creaked open as he pushed it, sagging on its hinges. Weeds sprouted on the once clean gravel drive as we moved toward the house. Peter ran ahead, still rebellious, turning his back on all adults. Joel helped his mother along the uneven walk, and she leaned on his arm possessively.

I still felt shaken by the scene we had just witnessed. Peter had always been a sunny little boy, agreeable and reasonable most of the time. He could be as cross as any other child now and then, but he had always recovered quickly, and he had never put on a display like this. One more count had to be made against Joel for allowing this to happen, for allowing this new Peter to develop.

We were approaching the house, and I looked up at the

high roofs, feeling depressed and frustrated. It had been built with a domed rotunda at its front, and four marble pillars circling the bulge. A flight of wide, shallow steps led up to the front door, cracked in places and overgrown with clumps of weeds which had worked their way between the bricks. The tenacious tendrils of vines clung to the pillars, seeking for cracks in the marble. Over the front door the fanlight had long since been smashed and the space boarded over against the weather. Above was a wide balcony at the second-floor level, with tall french doors leading into the house. Again there had been glass damage.

Once more Peter's eyes were quicker than ours, but now there was something faintly malicious in his tone. "Look at the faces, Gran! Look at the wicked faces! Maybe they don't like us."

By some whimsy the columns that supported the inner balcony were decorated on each side by a gargoyle face carved in marble and looking down at the visitor with evil grins that offered anything but welcome. I could see why some people might once have been afraid of this house. On either side of the marble protrusion of the rotunda, red bricks spread away in two long wings. Architecturally, the house was anything but all of one piece, yet it had aged and weathered like an elderly dowager who made her own fashions and looked grand in whatever she pleased to wear. Grand and forbidding.

Again Ferris produced a key. The double front doors opened easily, with scarcely a creak, seeming to indicate recent use. Peter stepped ahead of us into a circular front hall crowned by the huge dome, and stood looking up the wooden staircase that rose broadly on our left and then swung across the rotunda as it mounted to the floor above.

It was a dark entryway. Perhaps daylight had once been intended to flow in through the dome overhead, but boarding had taken the place of glass, and there were no windows. Ferris left the double doors open to let in a little light and I stood in the shadowy dusk looking about me with a curious sense of uneasiness.

I was glad for Theo's matter-of-fact tones breaking the silence. Theo would never be impressed by a haunted house.

"We have a much finer entrance hall at Spindrift," she said with satisfaction.

"You must remember how it used to look," Ferris reminded her. "There were Chinese rugs and tapestried chairs. And all that paneling around the walls and up the stairs was polished till it gleamed."

It was dull and dark now. Joel went to stand at the foot of the stairs and look up at the great tapestry, a medieval hunting scene that hung above the stairs, threadbare and faded. The hall was empty of furniture and there were scratches on the fine wood of the floor. At the back there still remained a partial suit of armor, without legs, that had been fastened to the wall, and it was this which caught Peter's interest. In spite of his wish to be sullen, he was coming to life with excitement over exploring this empty house. I would have been pleased, except that it seemed a tense and nervous excitement—too overwrought.

He flew back to the armor and reached up to raise the visor. Nothing looked out at him and he seemed disappointed.

"It used to be polished every week," Ferris said. "Maddy Townsend ran a strict house and since her husband was enthusiastic about collecting armor, every bit of it had to be kept gleaming. There used to be several full suits up here and they could shine like mirrors."

"There was armor downstairs too!" Peter cried. "John told me. A whole room of armor. Can we go down and look?"

"It's still there, but that room is kept closed until something can be done about the Townsend armor collection."

"There was a dungeon too," Peter ran on.

"That's a fable, I'm sure," Theo told him. "Poor

Maddy. She had to put up with a lot when it came to her husband's tastes."

"It was a vault, really," Ferris said. "Theron had a phobia about being robbed, and he built safes into that underground room. Since there's interest in the house, we've been down there, and I've had a look at the place."

"Then it wasn't a dungeon for locking people up?" Peter asked, sounding disappointed.

"Hardly. Though it was the sort of place rumors grew up about. Not that Theron ever cared, from what I've heard. But I imagine his wife did."

"Anyway, Maddy outlived him," Theo said.

"What happened to her?" I asked.

"She was left a widow, like Zenia, and in her later years she was too arthritic to come downstairs." Theo spoke as though she too had belonged to those great days of Newport, when she had really been only a visiting child. "She's gone now. One day at eighty-four she tried to come downstairs to look over her house and she had a bad fall. That was the end of her."

"A better end than Zenia Patton-Stuyvesant's," Joel said.

I had developed a mild interest in Zenia, since Bruce had said I resembled her.

"What happened to Zenia?" I asked.

"In the end—madness," Joel said. "She used to go wailing around the halls at night when she was a very old woman. But they let her live out her years at Spindrift."

"I didn't know you knew that much about Zenia," I said.

His mother answered me. "Moreland Press is thinking of publishing a book about Zenia and Spindrift, so Joel has informed himself."

Once I would have known about such plans. Now he never talked them over with me, and perhaps that was mostly my fault. But it wasn't anything I could seem to help. So much was slipping out of my hands because of Theo's machinations.

Ferris decided to take charge of our idle sightseeing. "We're here for a purpose, aren't we, Christy? Suppose we take the downstairs rooms one at a time and look for any evidence of an intruder. Can you tell us which room you saw the light in?"

Somehow I was aware of Joel in the background, watching and listening intently. As if he waited to see me trapped and proved unbalanced, I thought.

"I saw the light from my room," I said. "So it was at the side of the house. On the first floor and toward the front."

"Then it was probably the room beyond this door," Ferris said.

He opened a door beneath the high swing of the staircase and stood aside to let us through. Peter ran ahead into dim and echoing emptiness and I stepped after him into the long, bare expanse that must once have been a handsome drawing room. The ceiling had been painted with scenes from mythology and the walls were interrupted by columns of veined yellow marble. But there was nothing else left that could be removed.

Even the chandeliers had been taken away and there were scars in the ceiling where they had hung. The plaster molding of the upper walls was elaborate, and though a little dingy, still intact. Two great marble fireplaces graced each side of the room, veined in black and brown, their broad mantelpieces empty. Above one of them a huge mirror, now cracked, had been built into the wall, framed ornately in gilt. On either side, tall windows ran the length of the room, most of them shuttered, though some of the shutters were broken and hung askew, letting in a filtering of daylight. Peter began galloping noisily around the big room, pretending he was a pony.

Theo ignored the uproar. "As you can see, there's nothing here to place a light on," she pointed out.

I thought about that. "It didn't have to be on a table by a window to show light. It could have been put on the floor, or even on one of those mantelpieces. I didn't see the source of the light itself."

"If it was on the floor or a mantel in this room," Ferris said, "then you'd have seen a glow behind more than one of those broken shutters."

That seemed to be true, and I looked helplessly around the long drawing room, seeking for some clue. There was dust everywhere. Wreaths of dust and cobwebs hung from the mantels and rimmed the plasterwork of walls and ceiling. Curls of it drifted across the floor and our footsteps had disturbed the floor coating in places. But there were also marks where we had not walked, and I pointed them out to Ferris.

He shook his head. "I'm afraid that doesn't mean anything. There have been people in looking at the house. We aren't the first to disturb the dust in the last few months."

Theo was watching me with an air of satisfaction, and I knew why she had come along. "You see? There was really nothing here, Christy. It's as we all thought—you were dreaming again."

I hadn't been dreaming and I had seen a light, but there appeared to be nothing here to substantiate what I'd told them.

Joel said, "Where does this door go?"

He had wandered to the front wall of the room and I saw for the first time that a small doorway led to what might be another room at the very front of the house. I ran past Joel to open the door upon a small anteroom off the drawing room and main hallway. Here there was more daylight, as the shutters were gone.

"This is the place!" I cried. "If the light was here and the door closed, I would have seen it at this window only."

They followed me into the small space that was as bare as the drawing room, except for a round table with a broken leg, propped against one wall. Peter lost interest in being noisy, and came with us, adopting our search as a game.

"Somebody could have put a lantern on that table," he said, "and then my mother would have seen the light at the window."

I went to stand beside the table and Theo and Ferris joined me there. Its surface should have been dusty, and if a lamp or a lantern had been set upon it, there should have been an imprint. But except for one diagonal across a corner where a pale fuzz still coated the surface, there was no dust. Someone had wiped the table clean.

"You see!" I pointed. "Peter's right. Someone was here."

"As Ferris has told you, a good many people have been through this house recently," Theo said. "Because the table is free of dust doesn't prove that someone was here with a light last night. The committees who have been looking over the place certainly wouldn't come here at night."

"And they wouldn't be likely to do any dusting either," I said.

"Why not?" Theo was bent on disproving my claim. "They could be women with handbags and folders of papers. If they wanted to lay something down, they wouldn't want all that dust to soil their possessions."

I moved around the room, as convinced as ever, but unable to convince the others. Ferris had said nothing, but he was regarding the small table thoughtfully, perhaps more inclined to believe me now.

Peter was already tired of a room which offered no further excitement. "Let's look at the rest of the house. Let's go upstairs, Gran. I wish I had been here last night. I wish I'd been here when it was dark and spooky. Did you really see a light, Mother?"

"You don't wish anything of the kind," Theo said. "You'd be frightened to pieces here. This is no place for a child, and you are never to come here alone."

I didn't think it was a place for him either, but it was hardly wise to order this new Peter so flatly not to come.

"I really did see a light," I told him. "And I think it's a good idea to look at the rest of the house."

"Why?" Theo challenged. "We've discovered what we came for—that there is no evidence of anyone being here last night. So let's go home."

"Oh, no, Gran!" Peter was vehement. "We came over to see the whole house. My mother promised me I could."

"Your mother?" Theo challenged, bristling.

He grinned at her and I glimpsed once more that hint of a malice that had always been foreign to him. "Sure," he said. "Mother says I'm going to be with her now."

The words were spoken as a return to her challenge, and I saw that he was quite shrewd enough to play each of us against the other.

"I agree with your grandmother that you should never come here alone," I said firmly.

Peter might have continued the argument unpleasantly, but at that moment something thumped to the floor overhead and we all stood still, staring at one another. It seemed to me that Joel looked the most startled of all, and before any of us moved, he had started toward the entryway.

"There's someone in the house right now," I said, and ran after him through the main hall to follow him beneath the frayed tapestry of a hunting scene, up the shadowy stairs.

Peter raced after me as I went up, and I had to take his arm and hold him back at the top.

"Wait," I said. "Let your father go first. We don't know what has happened. These old houses can be rotten. Something might have fallen apart up here."

"I doubt that," Ferris said behind me on the stairs. "These houses were magnificently built and this one is perfectly sound. I've been all through it. But something could have fallen over of its own weight—if there was anything to fall."

I was already moving ahead of them on the second-floor corridor, still holding onto Peter, and Ferris and Theo came up behind us. Again it was dark and the stale air was oppressive. This floor was cut by cross corridors, and there were closed doors stretching blankly on either hand. A number of them must lead to rooms above the drawing room. Peter wriggled away from me and ran to the nearest door, thrusting it open. There was nothing inside. The room was bare of carpets or furniture and here the dust had not been disturbed for a long time. I didn't know where Joel had gone.

We began to take each room in turn along the corridor that led to the front of the house. We heard no further sound, but if anyone had been up here, he must have heard us downstairs, and he could have made off quietly down some rear flight. Then Joel called to us from the front of the house.

Peter and I ran to the front bedroom where Joel waited, and I knew this must be the room in which we'd heard the noise.

"Here you are," Joel said as Ferris and Theo joined us.

I saw what he meant. A stepladder stood in the center of the room opposite a side window. On it rested a cracked saucer with a candle stuck into spilled wax, its wick blackened from burning.

"There's the light I must have seen!" I cried. "I was right, but I saw it downstairs."

The others came into the room and stared at the candle, while I looked at Theo and Ferris. I think Theo was merely disappointed to have my claim of a light proved correct. But it was Ferris's expression that held my attention. For some reason the presence of the candle surprised him inordinately. I had only a fleeting realization that he was startled, and then his usual guarded look was in place. Since we had come here searching for a possible source of light, why should it so astonish him to find it?

But he was already accepting the fact and speaking calmly. "I think you may very well be right, Christy," he said. "I suppose the candle could have been used downstairs easily enough."

Theo flung out an accusing hand. "But who would be using a candle here?"

"What is equally important," Ferris said, "is who made the sound we heard just now. I think I'll have a quick look around. Do you want to come with me, Joel?"

When they'd gone, Peter went to a door off the room and opened it upon a generous closet.

"Look, Gran," he called. "There's a flight bag on the floor."

I reached the closet ahead of Theo and saw the blue and red canvas bag lying on its side.

"I think this is our intruder," I said. "It could have teetered off that shelf up there just now, and we heard it fall."

But even as I spoke, I felt a new misgiving. I carried the bag over to the window, turning my back on Peter and Theo. It took only a moment to zip it open, look inside at a flashlight, a small Thermos that I recognized and more candles. Then I zipped it shut and carried the bag back to the closet, shoving it more securely onto the shelf.

"It's just a discarded old bag," I said. "There's nothing in it."

Theo didn't question me. She had no interest in the bag. And I had held it too high for Peter to see into. When I closed the closet door and turned away, Theo was picking up candle and saucer. She sniffed at the wick dubiously.

"This may have been here for ages," she said. "There's nothing to tell us it was lighted downstairs last night."

"Except that I saw a light," I reminded her quietly.

Ferris and Joel rejoined us in time to hear. "If anyone was around, he's gone by now," Ferris said. "And I must admit the candle was not on that ladder the last time I was in this room."

"I don't think there was anyone here just now," I repeated, but I was watching Joel. "Peter found a canvas flight bag on the closet floor. It must have fallen off the shelf and made the sound we heard. Anyway, that's of no importance. It's this saucer and candle that matter."

Joel said quickly, "I agree. We've found Christy's light, Mother." But I was aware that he was watching me, and I wasn't sure why I kept silent.

"Anyway, this is all quite meaningless." Theo dismissed our opinions. "Peter, if you've explored enough, let's leave this place to its own nightmares. Empty houses make me uncomfortable."

Peter looked ready to pout again, disappointed with his adventure. Undoubtedly there had been too many people along, and he hadn't been able to follow his own bent in the house. I thought he might ask to go up to the third floor or down to the armor room, but he did not, and I wanted no more exploring either. I had recognized the flight bag and the things in it and I had a strange reluctance to let the others know that they belonged to Joel.

"Are there other keys to the house?" Theo asked Ferris as we went downstairs.

Ferris shook his head. "Just those in the hands of the real estate dealer, and he has furnished them only to legitimate visitors. But I don't suppose it would be difficult to get over the fence and break in, if anyone wanted to. I'll take a look around outside before we leave."

Theo sat down on the stairs to wait for him, and Peter busied himself examining the forlorn suit of armor that was the only occupant of the bare entryway. Joel went to look at it with him, and I watched them uneasily. What was the future to hold for these two who loved each other? A future that might lie in my hands. This was a choice I didn't want to make and I put it away from me as I stepped through the front door and out between vine-covered marble columns. There were other questions in my mind.

Why would Joel have gone over to Redstones last night? Why would he have brought along that flight bag with its odd contents? Had he really been there in that upstairs room, and had he moved about the house carrying a lighted candle, so that I had seen its glow when he was downstairs? And would I confront him with these things when we were alone? I didn't know the answer to any of this. I only knew that a growing uneasiness possessed me. If he suspected that I had looked into that bag, he had said nothing.

Ferris returned to report that basement windows could be easily opened if someone wanted to get in, though there was no particular evidence of intrusion.

We all walked back to Spindrift across the intersection of lawns where russet leaves were drifting down from the few sheltered trees. When we reached the house Peter was dispatched to his lessons and Ferris and Joel went their separate ways. I waited for no invitation to follow Theo upstairs to her sitting room.

Fiona was working busily on invitations for Theo's Sargent ball, and she looked up curiously when we came in.

"We found a single candle over there," Theo admitted reluctantly. "I think it might have been there for a long time. It meant nothing. What is it, Christy?"

"Peter has changed," I said. "I've never seen him throw a temper tantrum before."

She shrugged my words aside. "All healthy children have tempers. That didn't mean anything. Peter is devoted to me."

I knew it would be hopeless to discuss Peter with her. The only real solution was to get him away from her influence, and I couldn't do that yet.

She glanced at me again. "Is there something you want?"

It was an effort at dismissal, but I stood my ground. "I just wanted to tell Fiona that I've packed up Father's things, and I have them in his suitcase in my room. There's a pen I'd like to keep, and I'd like to give his penknife to Peter."

I sensed worry in Fiona, but I couldn't place its source.

"Of course," she said. "Keep anything you want. I could never bear to go back to that room."

"There's one thing I'd especially like, if I could have it," I went on. "Do you know what has become of his wrist watch?"

"I have it," Theo said readily. "It's the one thing I picked up as having some value the last time I was in the Tower Room. I'd forgotten about it. Of course it belongs to either you or Fiona."

"Let Christy have it, if she wants it," Fiona said. "I have other things I've kept of his."

"Come, we'll get it," Theo said to me, and led the way through a door into the long, narrow room she called her Jade Gallery.

When Theo's ambassador father had lived in Hong Kong he had become fascinated by the entire subject of jade, and he had begun a fine collection, which Theo had later inherited. She herself had grown very knowledgeable on the subject and she had prepared a room at Spindrift where she could show off her collection whenever she was here. Ferris had always been disturbed about the insurance angles in moving valuable pieces of her collection around with her, but Theo liked to take her familiar world into whatever house she happened to be occupying, so she did as she pleased.

The room was really a hallway connecting one section of this wing with another. The ceiling was vaulted and Theo had had it painted with oriental scenes to fit the purpose for which she meant to use it. A pine tree protruded from the vertical rocks of a cliff, and a heron waded in the stylized ripples of a stream below. Down the length of the gallery ran a row of delicate vitrines, with their tall, spindly legs, their glass sides and shelves shining in the lights she turned on. Theo herself had arranged her collection of jade and carved ivory in these cases. No one else was allowed to touch these pieces, except by Theo's express wish.

While she went to a small locked desk at the far end of

the gallery, I paused before one of the vitrines and looked at a lovely horse of gray-green jade in the center of a glass shelf. It was curled into a resting position, its legs bent beneath its body, graceful head turned back on its flank. Its ears were pricked forward alertly and its mane had been carved in flowing strands over the smooth neck of mottled green jade.

Theo came to stand beside me, Adam's wrist watch in her hand. She noted the direction of my attention.

"It's amazing the lifelike qualities they could capture—those ancient jade carvers. That piece is very old. It probably belongs to the Han dynasty. The carver tries to see a picture in the round in his stone, and the idea is to abrade away as little of the jade as possible to bring the creature or thing that hides in the stone to life. Look at the delicacy of that little blue water buffalo on the shelf above. That translucent blue is very rare, and the shape of the stone must have suggested the result."

Theo's voice was warm with feeling, and I wondered if she ever showed as much warmth toward human beings.

She opened the case and drew out a piece about six inches high—a pitcher made of yellow jade.

"Of course part of the charm of jade is to touch it with one's fingers. Do you see what I mean, Christy?"

She gave me the small pitcher and closed my fingers about it, so that I could feel the smoothness of the stone as it warmed in my hands.

"Tranquillity, purity, wisdom," she said. "Those are the qualities the Chinese claim for jade. I have a small pebble of apple green that I keep in my desk to play with when I'm disturbed. Like the worry beads of the Middle East. It's quieting to hold it in your hands."

She took back the pitcher and replaced it on its shelf, closed the cabinet and moved on to the next, where small carvings of ivory were displayed.

"Here is something I found one time in Kyoto. Adam was fond of it."

She reached among the pieces in the second cabinet

and drew out a delicately carved ivory figure of a Japanese lady—a tiny geisha about two inches high. One tiny hand held up the folds of her kimono at the front, while against the other rested a fan. The small face was exquisite, the hair above piled in intricate traditional arrangement.

I took her into my hands admiringly.

"Turn her over," Theo said.

Upside down, the lower folds of the kimono were carved in ripples, and among them were revealed the bottoms of two small feet, in properly pigeon-toed position, wearing the two-toed Japanese sock.

"She's lovely," I said and gave her back to Theo.

Theo sighed as she replaced her on the glass shelf among other carvings. "She had a twin sister whom Adam liked even better. The second lady held her fan more coquettishly, and she was barely smiling. For some reason Adam said she was a lucky piece. He nicknamed her Tyche—Lady Luck."

My attention was suddenly arrested. Tyche! That had been one of the words on that slip of paper I had found in the pocket in Adam's plaid jacket.

"Could I see the second lady?" I asked.

Theo shook her head regretfully. "She disappeared some time ago from my New York house. I've always wondered if Adam took her. Once he wanted to borrow her from me for some special occasion when he thought she might bring him good fortune. But I didn't trust him. He might have sold her for money he could gamble with."

I answered her sharply. "My father would never have done that!"

"Yet she disappeared," Theo said blandly. "Of course Adam would only have called it borrowing. But I never saw her again."

The inference made me angry and I held out my hand for my father's watch. "Thank you for letting me have this," I said, though I felt she'd no right to it in the first place. I wondered what she would say if I asked her what she had meant by Adam's "treachery" in that note she had written him. But I wasn't willing to bring that into the open yet.

She noted my suppressed anger with amusement and perhaps a little pleasure. I had often thought that Theodora Moreland enjoyed upsetting people, making them furious. The anger of others gave her power over them. I took the watch from her and went down the gallery toward her sitting room. She let me go, to stay behind and further savor her jade collection.

Fiona glanced up from her address file as I came in. "You look ruffled. What did she do to you?"

"It's something she said about Father. She accused him of taking some little piece of carved ivory that she said he used to call 'Tyche.' Do you know anything about it?"

"Oh, that. Yes. He brought it home for fun one time—mainly to annoy Theo. He said she was too careless about her collection and he wanted to teach her a lesson. But he meant to give it back to her, of course."

"You didn't find it among his things?"

"No, of course not. Adam wouldn't have kept it."

And where was Tyche now? I wondered, and did the name he had set down have anything to do with the little ivory figure that was missing?

"At least," I said, "I wasn't dreaming when I told them I'd seen a light in the window of that old house last night."

There was uneasiness in Fiona's eyes. "Who could have left that candle there? Apparently your light was real enough."

"Yes. And I'm beginning to think something else was real, though part of the time I've tried to convince myself that it might be a dream. Fiona, last night someone came into my room while I was sleeping."

Uneasiness gave way to barely concealed alarm. Something was disturbing Fiona deeply. But she managed to answer me with a question.

"What do you mean—someone came into your room?"

"Just what I said. I woke up because whoever it was touched my face ever so lightly. And a voice told me that I must go away."

I had never seen Fiona so distraught. She stared at me wide-eyed and when she tried to speak her lips trembled. "Oh, Christy—that's what you must do. Go away. Just go away!"

I had slipped the metal bracelet of my father's watch over my fingers and the cool links had warmed in my clasp, as if I held his hand. I bent above Fiona.

"What do you know? Tell me, Fiona!"

She turned away from me, reaching for her cigarette case, opening it. Her hand steadied as she lighted a cigarette.

"Stop it, Christy. I don't know anything in the sense you mean. But I'm sure you can do no good by staying here, and you may do a great deal of harm."

"To whom?"

"Yourself. Perhaps to others."

"You mean I'm to give up my son, leave him behind, run away from Theo?"

She had recovered herself, though her old serenity was still lacking. "If you stay here and prove you aren't stable —as you're already doing—how will it serve you? There's trouble, Christy. I don't know exactly what it is, but I think if you stay here you're likely to get hurt."

I wondered if I had heard a veiled threat behind her words.

"I'm not going to run away just because someone is trying to frighten me," I told her.

I would have said more, but Theo came back into the room at that moment and looked at me with displeasure, as though she had expected me to be gone. She ignored me after the first glance and spoke to Fiona.

"I've thought of a woman in Providence who used to be good at whipping up costumes. We'll get her down here to make our dresses for the ball. What are you going to wear, Fiona?"

"I haven't decided. Perhaps Sargent's Ellen Terry."

"Lady Macbeth? Lovely! You'll look the part, dear. We'll make you a copy of the royal crown of Duncan to carry around with you."

Fiona gave her a rather curious look and bent her head over her address file again. Theo turned reluctantly to me.

"Bruce seems to have settled the matter for you. That blue dress in the Patton-Stuyvesant portrait? We'll see what we can do. If you're here that long."

"I'll be here," I said, "if Joel and Peter stay. But I don't feel like partying these days."

"Nonsense. If you're still here you'll come to my ball, of course. I can't have you sulking in a room upstairs. Everyone would wonder where you were. Fiona, look up Mrs. Polter's number and get her on the phone for me. We'll need to get the dresses started."

Neither paid any attention to me as I walked out of the room. Adam's wrist watch was still warm in my hand as I went down the corridor. I was sorry it was too large for me to wear, but holding it gave me a sense of his presence, of his encouragement. He would never want me to run away. He would want me to stay, to face up to them all—to know the truth. And he would want me to rescue Peter from Theo's appalling influence.

When I reached Peter's door I tapped on it and looked in. My son was working earnestly on a math problem, a scowl of concentration ruffling his forehead. I had been away from him for so many months and the old yearning to touch him rose in me. I loved him so intensely, yet I must never smother him with my affection. He needed more than love from me now—he needed a wisdom I wasn't sure I possessed.

Miss Crawford was regarding me with her usual lack of welcome.

"May I see Peter's schedule, please?" I asked her.

She handed me a clipboard with time entries made neatly down its length. I examined the afternoon listing.

"I see he has an hour off for play around three o'clock.

I'd like to see my son then, if it can be arranged. Perhaps we can plan something together."

Peter looked around at me. Breaking his fixed schedule probably appealed to him, though he gave no sign of eagerness. Since I was his mother, Miss Crawford could do nothing but agree, however much she might have preferred not to. I wished that I could make friends with her, but it was Theo who still set the rules, and I was not in favor with Theo.

"I'll see you then," I told Peter. "I have something for you. Perhaps we can go down to Thames Street and have tea at one of the wharfs."

He gave me an unexpectedly winsome smile and I was foolishly pleased to have won that much from him. I must be careful lest I find myself bribing him to return my affection.

I went downstairs to my room and put Adam's watch away in my jewel case. Next I considered Joel's closed door for a moment. I didn't know whether he was in there or not, or whether I was ready to confront him, and I decided to let the matter of those things of his I had found over at Redstones go for now. I must talk to him about Peter too, but I didn't feel ready for that. However, there was an immediate plan I could put into motion.

I reached Theo's housekeeper on the telephone and asked her if the Red Room down the hall was empty, and when she said it was, I requested that I be moved into it.

There was a surprised pause at the other end of the line. "I'll have to check with Mrs. Moreland," she said. "I'll call you back as soon as I've reached her."

The telephone extension was in the hall just outside my room, and I left the door open while I waited for her call. Then I took my clothes from the closet to lay them across the gold counterpane, and packed the things on my dressing table into my suitcase. I was nearly ready by the time the telephone rang.

This time it was Theo herself. "Why do you want to move, Christy? I've given you our very best guest room."

"That's the trouble," I told her. "Its altogether too splendid for me. I like the Red Room better, if you'll let me have it."

If she could have thought of any good reason to refuse, I think she might have, because that was Theo's temperament. But there was no reason and she gave her reluctant permission and said she'd let the housekeeper know.

A few minutes later I was told I might move in, and was offered the help of a maid. An offer I refused. Once more I considered Joel's closed door. I supposed I should let him know I would no longer share an adjoining room. But I still didn't want to face him. A sense of indecision and foreboding held me back. I tossed a load of dresses and pants suits over one arm, and went across the hallway. Bruce opened his door as I reached the Red Room, and at once he came out to help me.

7

"Moving?" Bruce asked as he took dresses from my arm.

"Yes. I couldn't stand all that gold. Besides, that room doesn't like me."

He opened the door of the Red Room and let me go in ahead of him. "And this room does?"

"At least it doesn't reject me," I said, and looked about with satisfaction.

I had always thought it a beautiful room. The red glowed warmly without being strident and there were buffs and a good deal of beige to complement it. The soft carpet had a red oblong center surrounded by a beige border, and the narrow red and buff stripes of the wall-paper were broken at intervals by the folds of beige-colored hangings. The bed was Tudor, with its high carved backboard that echoed the dark wood of the mantelpiece. Two red roses bloomed in a vase of milk glass on the bed table, indicating that someone had hurried to welcome me to the room, and the easy chair wore a muted pattern of green vines and tiny red flowers on a cream background.

I must have given a little sigh of pleasure as Bruce laid my clothes across the bed, because he smiled that rare, rather shining smile of his.

"It's possible that rooms and houses too have auras, as well as people," he said. "For you this could be a friendly aura."

"But not for Fiona. She hates this room," I told him. "She says it keeps her awake. But I know I'll sleep better here."

"Perhaps her human aura doesn't match the room's," Bruce said.

It surprised me that he could be whimsical. "Do you think mine does?"

"I haven't that gift—to see auras. I can only sense them. But I think you'll be comfortable here."

I went to a window and drew aside the draperies. The room had its own small balcony, and I opened the french doors and stepped outside. Like the Gold Room this one looked out toward Redstones, but it was a side, not a corner, room and did not face directly on the ocean. However, from my little balcony I could see the Atlantic rolling in to break over the rocks below the winding Cliff Walk. And I could hear the crash and soughing of the waves. Redstones stood quiet in the morning sunlight, its windows shadowed and empty. Bruce Parry came out to stand behind me.

"I did see a light last night," I told him.

"So you all trooped over there this morning? What did you find?"

"There was a candle in a room upstairs. But there's no telling when it was used, as Theo has been emphasizing."

"Good," Bruce said.

I glanced at him questioningly. He stood very close to me on the small balcony and I was aware of him, as I had not been aware of a man for a long while. For the first time I wondered a little about *him*. Why had he never married? What would it be like to have those nearly jet black eyes kindle when he looked at a woman?

My own thoughts startled me, frightened me a little. I wanted to come back to life. But not in this way, not for this man. Infinitesimally I moved away from him on the balcony.

"Why did you say 'Good'?" I asked.

"It's just that I'm glad there was a light. Though I wonder who was there. What could he be doing? It sounds a bit nefarious. At least Theo can't make anything now of your seeing a light over there. Not if someone is burning candles."

"Why should she want to make anything of it?"

"You'll have to ask her. But I think she probably does. It needn't matter. Just stand up to her, Christy."

"You sound like my father."

"Then I'm complimented. He's the only one of us who really went his own way against the Morelands."

I looked up into Bruce's lean face, searching—for what I didn't know. "I think you've gone your own way."

"Not as much as I could. I've compromised a bit since Hal's death."

"Why?"

"You like to ask blunt questions, don't you? The way Adam did. I suppose because—in a strange way—I'm sorry for Theodora Moreland."

"Sorry for her!"

"Is it so surprising? I think she's the loneliest woman I've ever known. She talks to me sometimes. And I listen. It's the least I can do."

"I suppose I have a blind side when it comes to Theo, since anyone can see the way she's damaging Peter. I want to get away from here and take him with me."

"Don't be too ruthless," he said. "Take him back gently. She has feelings too."

"Sometimes I wonder." Unwillingly I heard the harsh note in my voice.

He turned back to the room behind us and I sensed that I might have been rejected, condemned. Unexpectedly, I didn't want that. Perhaps Bruce Parry was the closest I could come to having a friend in this house, and I didn't want him to condemn me. Yet I could entertain no kindly thoughts toward Theodora Moreland. Bruce had never known her as the victim she had made me.

"Anyway," I said as we returned to the room, "my son is coming out with me this afternoon. We're going to have tea in town."

He nodded coolly, and moved toward the door. "If there's nothing else to help you with—"

I didn't want him to go away. All my feelings were

contrary. I wanted him to like me, to continue to be kind to me. I needed something to hold onto.

"You said you'd show me Zenia's sitting room some-time," I said. "Could you do it now?"

He seemed to relent, to unbend a little. "Why not? The room is in the other wing, right on this floor."

I left my things on the bed and followed him through the door and down the hall to the opposite wing.

"Theo found the room exactly like this when she moved in," Bruce said as he reached the door ahead of me, "and she was delighted to keep it this way in Zenia's memory."

The door was not locked and it opened easily. No one had ever told me about this room before, and I walked into a rather small, crowded area with the feeling that I was stepping into the past. This was late Victorian at its last ebb, with touches of the Edwardian and turn-of-the-century American. A red velvet Hepplewhite sofa with a brocaded seat nudged a deeply buttoned red velvet chair that might have come out of the Crystal Palace. A tapestry footstool was set close to the chair and a small rosewood table held sewing things. The carpet was undoubtedly Aubusson, while the lamp on a round table was a Tiffany and belonged to this century.

What could be seen of the walls was a periwinkle blue, but the color was almost completely hidden behind the pictures, plates, framed needlework and other oddities that covered them. Some of the paintings and prints were good, others were mawkish and luridly colored, like calendar art. Zenia's taste had been catholic, to say the least.

I moved about, intrigued and delighted with this personal museum. Because of her portrait as an appealing young woman and because of the tragedy of her last years, Zenia was coming to life for me, and I wanted to know her better. I paused before a small rosewood desk with a drop leaf on which rested a silver inkwell and a silver pen holder, noting that Madam's morning book lay open on the desk, as though she had just put it down. The faded directions to housekeeper or butler could still be made out in a rather deliberate script.

"I wonder if she still comes and sits in this room sometimes?" I said. "It must have been so totally hers—her private haven."

Bruce nodded. "I can't see old Patton-Stuyvesant spending much time among all these frills."

Above the white marble of the mantelpiece a mirror with an ornate gilt frame reflected the room. I looked into the glass at the man behind me and caught his eyes upon me with a certain solicitude I hadn't expected. Perhaps Bruce Parry was sorry for me too—and I didn't want that. I turned away from the glass and faced him, bringing back the present.

"Ferris is going to keep an eye on things over at Redstones from now on," I told him, "but at least I've been vindicated as far as the light goes."

"Ferris?" There was a questioning note in Bruce's voice that alerted me. I waited.

"Never forget that Ferris Thornton is Theo's man," he went on.

"Not always," I said. "Not any more than you are. I've heard him counsel her when what he said wasn't welcome at all. But he's been my friend too, since I was a little girl. I trust him."

There was a closed look about Bruce's face, as though shutters had come down over his thoughts. It was a look that made me uneasy and I caught him up quickly.

"Do you know something in particular about Ferris that I don't?"

He regarded me steadily for a moment and then shrugged. "No, nothing."

"All right," I said. "Don't tell me if you don't want to. My father thought the world of him."

"Did he?"

The quiet phrase was disturbing in its challenge. I remembered what Fiona had said about Adam quarreling with Ferris a day or two before he died. But then, Adam seemed to have been quarreling with everyone those last few days. Something had driven him, but I had no idea what it was.

"I believe I'll go over to Redstones and have a look around for myself some night," Bruce said, and I knew he had closed the topic as far as Ferris was concerned.

He was studying me again, directly this time, not just in the glass, and I couldn't tell what he was thinking. It was a tantalizing look, not pitying now, but rather curious, as though there was something about me he couldn't make out.

Uncomfortably, without knowing why, I turned back toward the mirror and began to examine the small ornaments on the mantel. That was when I saw it—the tiny object that did not seem to belong in Zenia Patton-Stuyvesant's room. Here again was a tiny Japanese lady carved in ivory, and surely sister to the one Theo had shown me. Her fan was raised coquettishly beneath her chin, and the hint of a smile curved her lips. She stood upon a long, narrow box with a lump of jade for a handle, but it was not the box which interested me. For all the assorted knickknacks, I did not think this little geisha figure had ever belonged to Mrs. Patton-Stuyvesant.

Bruce had turned away from me and was roaming the room, stopping beside Zenia's desk, opening its drawers. With a quick movement that he did not notice, I cupped the carving in my hand and slipped it into the pocket of my slacks. If this was the same figure that had disappeared from Theo's New York house, then it was the one Adam had called Tyche, or Lady Luck. I didn't know how she had come to this room, or what she could possibly tell me, but I had to keep her with me for now. Perhaps later I would return her to Theodora Moreland.

"Sit down over there in the button chair," Bruce said from across the room.

There was such a peremptory note in his voice that I looked at him, startled.

"Why do you want me to?"

"Don't argue and ask questions," he said. "You can be as obstinate as your father. Just sit down. I want to try something."

He had found a pad of paper in Zenia's desk, but he had rejected her silver pen for a ballpoint from his own pocket. When I went in puzzlement to sit in the chair he had indicated, he began to draw swiftly on the pad.

"Are you an artist?" I asked.

He smiled at the word. "Perhaps I might have been, if I hadn't gone in other directions. Sometimes the urge to catch something on paper still comes to me. Sit still— don't wriggle."

No one had ever wanted to draw me before and I felt faintly flattered, but while he worked my mind turned to other things and I touched the small ivory figure in my pocket. How had Tyche come to this room? Had my father placed her here? And if Theo had missed her, why hadn't she been discovered here? Or could Theo herself have put her on the mantel?

Bruce paused in his swift sketching to regard his work with dissatisfaction. But when he started to crumple the paper from the pad, I jumped up and held out my hand.

"No fair! The model has a right to see what the artist drew."

He handed it to me reluctantly and I examined the sketch in surprise. I didn't know why he should be dissatisfied, because in its hurried way it was very good. Except that he had made me look too young, with my hair tousled and my eyes wide, gazing off into distance. This was a young girl with a soft mouth that somehow held an entreaty.

"I'm not like that," I said regretfully. "Not any more."

"I think you are," he contradicted. "But I haven't done you justice. Not nearly. Do you see the chin line? I've made it soft, and yours isn't." He reached out and drew a finger impersonally along the line of my jaw and my skin tingled at his touch. "Your chin belies your mouth. You've got a bit of Adam's chin."

I don't know why his words reached me so unexpectedly and poignantly, but suddenly there were tears in my eyes. Tears that spilled over and ran down my cheeks. Why should it be, I thought ruefully, that this man was always around on the occasions when I burst into tears. I had never been a weeper before, but lately my emotions were all too close to the surface.

He put a hand gently on my arm. "Well, now," he said, "go ahead and cry if you want to. But I didn't mean to upset you."

His words undid me further. "It's just that—that everything came back and hit me so suddenly. It does sometimes. And then for a few minutes I can't bear it that Adam is gone Where is he? What has become of him? Why can't he speak to me?" I was wailing now, without control.

"I know," he said. "I know. I've felt like that."

I didn't know what he meant or whom he had lost, but there was understanding in him and he wasn't just pitying me—he was feeling *with* me.

I fumbled in my pocket and when I drew out my handkerchief the ivory geisha flew out with it and fell to the carpet a little way off. Bruce heard the thud and went to pick it up. He didn't return the carving to me, but stood examining it. Then he whistled softly.

"Lady Luck!" he said. "Christy, where did you find this?"

I waved my hand. "Over there on the mantel. I knew it didn't belong here. Theo showed me its twin sister this morning."

"I'll return it to her," he said. "She'll be glad to have it back."

That wasn't what I wanted, but there was nothing else

to be done—since I didn't want to explain. And there was nothing the small figure could tell me anyway. At least I had recovered myself.

"Why did you call it Lady Luck?" I asked.

"Because that's what Adam nicknamed it. Or Tyche. I don't know what a geisha would have thought of being given those names, but perhaps she'd have been tolerant toward such whimsy, as any geisha was supposed to be tolerant of the whims of men. Like Fiona."

"Is Fiona tolerant?"

"She used to be. At least of Adam's gambling."

"I'm not sure now," I said. "For one thing I think she's afraid of something."

Bruce made nothing of that and the shutters were down again as he looked at the carving in his hand. If he knew anything of Fiona's fears, he was not going to tell me.

"Fiona says Adam carried that little figure home from Theo's house one time," I went on. "He had a theory that it brought him luck. But he would have given it back. So how did it come to be here at Spindrift in Zenia's room?"

"That's something of a mystery, isn't it? I'm afraid I couldn't guess the answer."

"May I keep your drawing?" I said.

He smiled at me and my wayward heart turned over a little. "Of course, if you want it. I wish I could do something better."

I walked to the door and out into the corridor because I didn't want to be alone with Bruce Parry another moment. Something was happening to me that mustn't happen. I was Joel's wife. Peter was our son. I mustn't feel this attraction to another man.

He was too perceptive and I think he was aware of my lack of ease as I moved back toward the Red Room, and I sensed a faint amusement in him that stiffened my spine.

"Thank you for showing me Zenia's room," I said a bit curtly. "Now I'll go and get settled in my new place."

I hurried away and he didn't follow me down the hall.

When I glanced back at my own door, I saw him heading upstairs—probably to return to Theodora Moreland.

I was thankful that this was another room to which Theo had attached a bath, and before I hung up my clothes I washed the tear streaks from my face, more than a little angry with myself, more than a little impatient. I wasn't a young girl, to be bowled over by unexpected sympathy and consideration. I was alone in the problems that faced me, and I had to remain alone. Besides, Bruce Parry's very kindness might be the tactic he used with foolish women, and I didn't mean to be betrayed by it. I wouldn't be again.

Yet I couldn't help carrying Bruce's sketch to the window where I might examine it more carefully. He had portrayed me sympathetically, and with some strange perception he had drawn the girl I used to be. She wasn't so far away in time. Only months ago she had existed—until that New Year's Eve when music in Spindrift's ballroom had hidden the sound of a shot fired in the Tower Room. She had died too that night, the girl Bruce had drawn. Of course he had known me then, and he could have drawn this from memory, perhaps not wanting to sketch what he really saw in me now.

I put the sketch away in a drawer, regretting something I had lost, and went to tap on Fiona's door. Probably she was still upstairs with Theo and I wouldn't find her here. But her voice bade me enter and I went into the room.

She still wore the yellow sweater and gray skirt I had seen her in earlier in the day, but she had kicked off her shoes and stood in her stocking feet by a long window that looked out toward the ocean. There was a glass of faintly colored liquid in one hand, and by her blurred look as she turned from the window, I suspected it was not the first today. I wanted to protest that Adam would have hated her drinking alone, and in the morning, but I held back for the moment.

I told her about my excursion to Zenia's room with Bruce and of finding the carved ivory figure.

"I'm glad it's turned up," she said. "Theo's been making nasty cracks about Adam's taking it."

The face she turned toward me with its wide cheekbones seemed thinner and more drawn than I remembered. Her light brown page boy hair had lost some of its luster and her eyes had that blurred look as she faced me. With a start, I realized that I hadn't really been noticing Fiona lately.

"But why was it there?" I pressed her. "Could Adam have put it in that room? If Theo missed it, why hasn't it been noticed there?"

She took a long swallow of her drink and shrugged. "Who knows? Perhaps no one ever looked, since it disappeared from the other house. Theo hardly ever goes to that room, and the servants here are all new and wouldn't know about it. Anyway, what does it matter, so long as it's been found?"

"A lot of things matter that no one is paying attention to," I said. "For instance, what's troubling you, Fiona?"

She drained the rest of the liquor in her glass and her eyes did not meet mine.

I had to speak out. "Adam wouldn't like this."

"Adam, Adam!" She waved the empty glass at me. "Adam's gone. He's left me to fend for myself. I never thought he would. I thought he'd always be here to take care of me, Christy. He was so strong, so dependable."

No, I thought—not always dependable. Not with his gambling.

There were tears of self-pity in her eyes, liquor induced, no doubt, since I never remembered Fiona as self-pitying.

"It's time you told me what you quarreled about the night my father died," I said. "I came to your door earlier in the evening and I heard you, so there's no use denying it. Unfortunately, I went away without staying to listen. But now I want to know what was wrong. *Is* wrong."

"Why? What good will it do to dig up old pain, old problems?"

"It may help me find out why my father died. That's the reason I'm here—to find out the truth. And I think the truth begins with you."

"All right," she said, capitulating unexpectedly. "I'll tell you. We had a fight over something Adam wrote in that log he kept."

I knew what she meant by his log. For as long as I could remember my father had kept a sort of running listing of happenings in what he called a "log." There were stacks of these long, narrow notebooks that he had kept over the years, all written in his own sort of printed shorthand that he adopted when he wasn't using a typewriter. He would scribble about plans, or comment on happenings or people he had met during the day. The notes were useful to him when he wanted to refer back to any happening. He used to sit at his desk in the apartment every night and write them up before he went to bed. There had always been an unspoken law that the current pages of his log were private, and I would never have thought of opening one of those books.

"How did you happen to see what was in it?" I asked.

"I looked. Oh, I knew about the sacred rule, but I had to find out what he was up to."

"And did you?"

"You'll never know because I'm not going to tell you."

"What happened to that last log?"

"I don't know. It disappeared and never turned up among his things."

"Was that what someone ransacked your apartment to find after his death?"

"If it was, they never found it, because I'd looked first. So I could destroy it."

"Do you think he destroyed it?"

"Never. I think he brought it here with him when he came to Spindrift that last time. If it's anywhere it must be around here. There were too many important matters set down in it for him to destroy those pages."

"What sort of matters?"

"I'm not going to tell you," she repeated, looking suddenly stricken. "It's dangerous enough that I read some of what was in that notebook. I wish I hadn't. Oh, God, I wish I hadn't!"

She moved toward the bed with her usual angular yet graceful gait and flung herself across the spread. The empty glass dropped from her fingers and rolled under the night table.

"There—I've told you the cause of our quarrel. Now just go away and leave me alone. If you had any sense at all you'd get away from this place while you still can." She drew an arm across her face, hiding the look in her eyes.

"Because there's a killer around? Is that what you mean? Because I might be in danger too if I don't keep still like a good girl?"

She turned over on her stomach and began to cry into the pillow—long, wracking sobs such as I had never heard from her before.

"I don't know what to do," she moaned. "I don't know what to do!"

I hated to press her further when she was obviously suffering, yet this was not the time to be merciful—not when I might be close to something I needed so badly to know.

"It would help if you would tell me the truth, Fiona. Don't shut me out."

She only went on crying and I knew there was a hopeless impasse between us.

"Can you tell me which one of them you're afraid of?" I asked. "Which one of them has you so terrified?"

The sobbing ceased and her shoulders were still. The voice that reached me was choked and barely distinct. "Oh, Christy, most of all I'm afraid of *me*. Where have I gone? I'm not like me any more. I'm not like the woman Adam married."

She had struck a note that made us sisters. I too had lost the self I used to be, and I reached out to touch her shoulder in sympathy.

"I'm sorry, Fiona. I feel that way too lately. What has happened to change you?"

She answered with unexpected perception, considering the fog that was upon her. "The same thing has happened to change me that has happened to change you. Adam's death. Everything I was stops there. And I can't ever go back. It's all done. Destroyed. Finished."

"Destroyed, but not finished," I said. "Go on—please tell me what you know."

There was a long silence from the woman on the bed. Then she seemed to make an effort to rouse herself, to recover a semblance of what she had once been. She sat up and drew her knees to her chin, looking at me directly with those blue-gray eyes, and with nothing blurred about her gaze. She spoke as calmly as though she were still the old Fiona, always serene and unmoved by others' passions.

"It's time for you to stop being so stupid, Christy. If you weren't Adam's daughter I wouldn't listen to you. But you are, and I owe him that at least—to try to save his daughter. You don't need to be as reckless as he was. You don't need to ask for your own death."

"So he *was* murdered! And you've known it all along!"

Her look told me that she did not really like me. That all her efforts to be a mother to me in the past had been false and contrived—something she had attempted to please Adam. The breach between us, which had closed momentarily with our mutual grief, widened. I tried to strike through her guard.

"Had you stopped loving him by the time he died? Is that why you've let everything go? Is that why you've never spoken up, as I've spoken up? Because you didn't care any more? Because his death didn't mean to you what it meant to me?"

If I expected my tirade to sting, I was disappointed.

She regarded me calmly, without liking, but without anger.

"You've always thought you were the only one who could love Adam as he deserved to be loved," she said. "Why you ever married Joel, I'll never know, when it's only the image of Adam you can love. But Adam is dead. He killed himself. Because he couldn't face the exposure of what he'd been doing. Be satisfied with that and get back to your own life. You owe that to Peter, at least."

If she was speaking truths, I didn't want to hear them now. She didn't understand, couldn't understand. Adam would never rest—nor would I—until his death was— was what? Avenged? Or at least until the truth of it was exposed.

But I could be surface-calm too and turn away from her hurtful words. I moved about the room, noting its Fiona-neatness, stopping before my father's cowhide suitcase set beside the closet door, where I had not noticed it before.

"I see you've brought Adam's things here," I said.

"I asked a maid to bring them from your room. You said I could have them."

"Of course. They belong to you. I have his watch. There's nothing else I want."

We were both oddly calm, as though hot words had never been spoken between us, as though a sort of truce had been declared. Fiona was going to keep her secrets, however terrible, and I was not going to give up my purpose in coming to Spindrift. But we were through for now with railing at each other. Or so I thought.

I paused beside the hall door. "Tell me about Bruce Parry. I've known him for years, of course, but I've never known much about him. Was he ever married?"

"Yes, he was—when he was quite young. His wife was killed in a plane crash years ago. And he never married again. But that's not for want of women being interested in him. Or he in them. Why do you want to know?"

"When he showed me Zenia's room he seemed sympathetic. He said he understood loss. He must have been thinking about his wife. Did you know her?"

Fiona shook her head. "No. She was an invalid much of the time. He was always taking her to new doctors to try to help her. Things must have been hard for him then. Perhaps it was a mercy when she died."

The pang of loss struck through me once more, and I had to deny her words. "It's never a mercy when anyone dies. It's a loss and a tragedy and an insult. Do you think it was a mercy when Adam died? Because you were tired of marriage?"

Her calm had been broken, and the truce was over. The serene Fiona picked up a book from the nightstand and threw it at me.

"Get out! I don't care what happens to you. And the sooner the better!"

The book missed my head, but her sudden passion startled me. My words had uncovered something unexpected. I realized that I knew very little about Fiona Keene. I had lived in the same house with her for years, but my selfish young gaze had always been turned inward —or toward my father. I didn't know what she was really like and I certainly didn't know what turmoil was stirring in her now. I went out of the room and closed the door softly behind me. It did not give me a good feeling to know how much I had upset her. Yet what else was I to do?

It was nearly lunchtime and Ferris Thornton was going down the hallway to his room.

"Hello," he said. "You look thoroughly ruffled. Have you been solving any more mysteries?"

"One or two," I told him, not lingering to talk. I didn't want any lunch. I was too upset myself. Some of the things Fiona had said had begun to burn in my mind, and I wanted to be alone until I could shake them off.

"Have lunch with me," Ferris said. "I want to talk to you. About Theodora. If we're early no one else will be there. So hurry and get ready and I'll meet you downstairs."

He went on to his own room and left me standing there, helpless to refuse his suggestion. I went into my room and once more bathed my hot face with cold water. When I came out of the bathroom I found Joel sitting in one of the flowered chairs.

"I hope you don't mind my coming in," he said with stiff formality. "I just found out that you'd moved."

"I'm sorry," I said. "I should have told you. It was just that I couldn't stand that room any longer. It made me nervous. I like this one better. It's a warm room, and it likes me."

There had been a time when Joel would have understood such a reaction. Now he said nothing, and his very silence set us apart.

"I suppose Theo is disappointed to find my vagaries real for once?" I asked.

"You're too hard on her," Joel said. "You always have been."

And he had always been deceived by her. In his presence she dissembled.

"With good reason," I told him. "She hated our marriage. She couldn't forgive me for being Adam's daughter when there was a time when she wanted Adam herself."

"All that is buried in the past."

"Where the present has its roots. Fiona tells me that the last log Adam kept is missing. And that she read something in it that frightened her before he died."

Joel was listening intently now and, I thought, a little warily. "So?"

"So I'm going to find that log if it still exists—as it probably does. Fiona thinks Adam hid it somewhere—perhaps in this very house. I don't believe anyone has found it yet and that's why this atmosphere of uneasiness and distrust exists."

Joel left his chair to roam around the room, tossing words at me over his shoulder.

"Oh, Christy, let it alone! We know Adam was involved in something unsavory. It has all been exposed. The log would tell the same story and that would make everything worse for you. And for Fiona."

"No! It would tell the truth. The truth that is frightening Fiona and making her a coward. Adam wasn't a coward and I won't be."

Joel had reached the balcony window in his turn about the room and he stood before the french doors staring out toward Redstones.

"Those were your things I saw over there this morning, weren't they?" I said abruptly. "Your flight bag, with articles in it that belong to you."

He did not move from the window. "I thought you might have guessed. But you didn't say anything to the others."

"No. I don't know why, but I didn't."

"Don't tell them," he said.

"Why not? What are you up to over there?"

He turned about slowly and his smile had a wry twist. "Perhaps after you'd told me what you'd seen, I just wanted to plant the evidence of a light over there. So no one would think you were imagining things again. It's too bad I didn't put the candle in the right room."

I stared at him in surprise. "You'd protect me like that? When you believe I was imagining that I saw a light?"

"I don't know whether you saw one or not. But I hate all these clashes with my mother, Christy. I know what you've been going through, but I hope it will stop."

"But why the flight bag with a flashlight and extra candles—as though you meant to return?"

"Perhaps I do. Perhaps I'd like to find out whether there really is something going on over there. If I go over some night and stay for a few hours, perhaps I can find out. In any case, all this isn't why I came to talk to you. Christy, do you know what Mother believes about us?"

I didn't want to know, and I shook my head.

He spoke quietly, with his usual restraint. "She thinks there is no point in our continuing a sham marriage."

Something inside me began to tremble, and unexpected tears burned behind my eyes. Tears for the loss of a love that could never be recovered? I couldn't go back, but I could still remember. I blinked my eyes, trying to steel myself against memory. I knew very well what Theo meant by this. I knew she wanted Peter.

"What do you think?" I asked Joel.

He hesitated and his eyes did not meet mine. "I won't oppose you if you want to go, Christy."

No, he wouldn't oppose me. He wouldn't fight for me! It was unreasonable for me to condemn him for this. If he had fought for me I would fight him back. Yet I couldn't help measuring him beside Adam. In a similar situation Adam would never have behaved like this. Nor, I thought, would Bruce Parry. If Bruce wanted a woman, if he felt she was worth it, he would fight for her against all odds. I didn't know how I knew that, but I did. However, there was Peter to consider, and I could not yet risk being free. Not until I could prove myself strong and worthy as a mother. Too much of the time lately I had been close to an emotional brink and I would not let Theo push me over.

"For the time being, I'm satisfied the way things are," I said. "There are things we both need to think out. For one thing, we've got to talk about Peter. He's turning into a child I don't know, and you've stood by and let it happen. Theo's influence on him is vicious—poisonous."

I could sense the stiffening in him. "Those are strong words, Christy, and I can't accept them. All children go through phases. Peter will pull out of this."

"Not without help," I said. "And we need to work together. The sooner we take him away from Theo, the better."

"We can't do that until you're well, Christy. The last thing Peter needs is an emotional mother tearing at him."

The injustice of his words, considering the care I had taken with Peter, stung me to the quick. This, of course, was something Theo had convinced him of.

"I've been trying very hard not to upset Peter," I said.

He gave me a long, thoughtful look and walked quietly out of the room.

I was not without guilt. I sensed that I had hurt him. Even though he would not raise a finger to stop me if I wanted to go, I knew his hurt went deep. Yet I could do nothing to prevent this. I couldn't deal with everything at once.

The palms of my hands felt damp as I went downstairs. No one believed I was well again, and sometimes in this state of helpless frustration, I doubted it myself.

8

Lunch, like breakfast, was served on the buffet in the smaller dining room, with its Tudor roses and ivory-paneled walls. Ferris was already there when I came in and he got me a plate and served me from the hot casserole of lamb and peas. We were alone in the room and we sat together at the round table. Joel had not followed me downstairs.

"You wanted to talk to me about something?" I asked him, buttering a hot roll. I had to try to eat. To keep up my strength.

"Yes. We'd like your help in influencing Joel—Theodora and I."

Nothing could have surprised me more. I was about to say that if I'd ever had any influence with Joel, I'd lost it—but with Theo seeking the breakup of our marriage, that wasn't wise.

"You'll have to tell me how you want him influenced first," I said.

"I've been talking to him," Ferris went on, "and for the first time he seems receptive to Theo's wishes concerning the books he's been publishing at Moreland Press."

In the past I had been proud of Joel's publications. They might not make a great deal of money, and you wouldn't find them on the best-seller lists, but they usually received excellent reviews and they were distinguished publications. The other editors at Moreland Press did not, in my opinion, do nearly as well.

"What about his books?" I asked.

Ferris had the grace to look faintly uncomfortable. "Theodora feels he is getting nowhere on the course he's following. Of course she doesn't read what he publishes, but she thinks it's a waste of time and a loss to the company to get praise and poor earnings. Oh, he needn't compromise when it comes to quality, but she feels that he could give a little more attention to a wider market."

There had been a day when Theo had placed herself on the other side of this argument and against Hal, humoring Joel in whatever he wanted to do. But now that Theo had the managing of income in her hands, she might very well see matters in a different light. Once I would have been angry about this, but for months now the only emotion I was capable of feeling was tied up with Peter and Adam. I didn't really care any more.

"Why should you need my help? Why doesn't Theo just tell him what she wants?"

Ferris smiled. "She's a little afraid of him."

"Afraid? Of *Joel?*"

"Only when it comes to his work. He has never let anyone interfere with him there."

I supposed that was true and it added to my contrary sense of resentment. Joel would let me go without a word, he would bow to whatever Theo chose to do with Peter, but let anyone raise a finger toward one of his authors, and he would turn into a pillar of ice. He simply froze his opponents out and went his own way. Once I had admired him for this. Now it seemed a narrow and unimportant course in which to play the untouchable knight-errant.

"He'd be unlikely to listen to me," I said, "even if I wanted to argue Theo's premise. Which I don't. Joel is doing a top job in the books he edits and publishes. Adam always said so."

"And you would never go against anything Adam ever said—is that it?"

The cut of unexpected sarcasm startled me. Ferris had never been unkind to me before.

"I've read Joel's books," I said. "I know how good they are."

"For a special audience, yes. But I think Theo is right when she feels that he could reach many more readers if he would compromise a little."

"He won't compromise," I said flatly. My feelings were contrary indeed. I was a little proud of Joel's obstinacy, even while I resented it.

"Then you won't try to influence him?"

"It would be useless." I changed the subject abruptly. "There is something I've been wanting to ask you, Ferris. Fiona says you had a quarrel with Adam a few days before he died. Will you tell me what it was about?"

Only a slight hesitation before he spoke hinted that I had caught him off guard. Then he answered me quietly.

"I wouldn't call it a quarrel. A disagreement, rather."

"What was the—disagreement about?"

"A private matter, Christy, my dear. Nothing that would help anything that faces you now. Your father was planning a course of action which I couldn't approve. I had to argue against it."

"A course of action that threatened someone—so that he had to be stopped?" Was this the answer to that note of Theo's I'd found, accusing Adam of "treachery"?

Ferris's look warned me. "I wouldn't go around saying things like that, Christy."

I felt that someone I had always loved and trusted had turned suddenly against me. This was not the Uncle Ferris of my childhood. But before I could say anything more, his tone softened and he spoke to me more gently, so that I wondered if there had really been a warning in his words.

"I've been discussing with Theodora your request to have a freer hand with Peter, and she agrees that this should be made possible. Your plan for an excursion into town this afternoon has been approved."

I was still upset. "I'm not seeking her approval or disapproval. I simply mean to take my place as Peter's mother. We would go to town this afternoon whether she approves or not."

"I'm not sure you would," he said evenly.

I started to make an indignant response, but just then Joel and Fiona came into the room. They greeted us and went to the buffet to fill their plates.

Fiona did not look at me, but she seemed to have recovered a semblance of calm, probably because of another drink or two, and she seemed very pleased about something.

"What do you think?" she said to Ferris. "Joel is going to take on Jon Pemberton as one of his authors! Moreland Press has coaxed Pemberton away from his present publisher, where he's been dissatisfied, and Joel will be his new editor."

I nearly spilled the coffee I'd been drinking. Jon Pemberton was nothing if not a big seller and his books were enormously popular. Which in itself didn't damn them. But he wasn't Joel's type of author and I couldn't see this at all.

I must have been staring at him in astonishment because he gave me a grim look and nodded to Ferris. "I'm doing this as a favor to Theo. I've met Pemberton and I like him. Perhaps we'll do each other some good."

I couldn't withhold my indignation. "But he's cheap!" I cried. "His books are often trash."

"Often, but not always," Joel said quietly. "Perhaps we can do a good one together."

"It's not like you!" I was almost pleading now. "You've never compromised your standards. You're letting Theo change you!"

Ice was beginning to close in and his look told me this was none of my business and I had no right to be heard.

Fiona broke in quickly, with an effort to soothe. "I think this is a good idea all around. It's what Theo wants, and Pemberton is pleased about it."

"He's not known for being agreeably modest," I said. "Joel is likely to have as much influence on him as—as any one of us has on Theodora."

"Someone is having an influence on Theodora," Bruce

said from the doorway, and we all looked around as he came into the room. "Do any of you know what's upsetting her?"

No one answered and there was an odd quiet at the table, with no one looking at anyone else. Except for me. I looked at each one of them in turn and none of their faces told me anything.

"What's up?" Joel asked.

Bruce helped himself at the buffet and brought his plate to the table. "I wish I knew. She has suddenly developed the idea that someone is out to do her physical injury."

Ferris looked relieved. "This isn't anything new. She's often had recurring nightmares that set her off along this line. Probably anyone in a powerful position is apt to think himself threatened at times. Hal had this idea more than once. She'll get over it."

Bruce looked at him with no particular liking. "I don't think we'd better shrug it off too lightly. I couldn't get much out of her, but perhaps you can, Fiona."

Fiona shook her head. "Not me. Not today. I've just been banished from the presence."

"I think we'd better leave her alone," Joel said. "Someone to argue with always sends her further in any disturbing direction. Ferris is right. She'll get over it."

I think Bruce did not agree with them, but he said nothing more, and gave himself to eating his lunch with a good appetite. I watched him covertly, wondering about him. And about myself. He had given me a single swift look as he came into the room—a look in which there was a question I couldn't answer. I had fled from him rather precipitately earlier and there was no explanation I could give him that would not amuse him further. I did manage a direct question of my own, however, to Bruce.

"How did Theo feel about getting her ivory lady back?"

"She was pleased, of course," he said, "but she was still pretty hard on Adam for taking it in the first place."

The others wanted to know what we were talking about, and Bruce told them about my finding the ivory figure in Zenia's sitting room. How it came to be there puzzled them all, and while they were talking my thoughts turned to my own speculations.

What was disturbing Theodora Moreland? Why should she suddenly develop this notion that someone was making a threat against her? This was a matter I wanted to know more about, and as soon as I'd finished my lunch, I left the table and hurried upstairs. Theo's sitting room was empty, but a door stood ajar to an adjoining room and I went into it to find that Mrs. Polter, the dressmaker, had already been set up there with a sewing machine and all the accouterments of her trade. As I came in, she stood at a table—a small woman with bright blue eyes and a cheerful smile. She was cutting material from a pattern and her hands moved with accustomed skill.

When I introduced myself, she reached without delay for a tape measure and advanced upon me with authority.

"I've been anxious to see you, Mrs. Moreland. Mrs. Keene has shown me the painting you're going to portray at the ball and I think the gown will be perfect for you. Will you let me take your measurements now?"

"I'm really looking for Mrs. Theodora Moreland," I told her. "Do you know where she is?"

"She was here just a few moments ago. She wasn't feeling well and she said she might lie down for a while. Come now, raise your arms—let me get these figures down."

I gave in to her persistence. This might be the wrong moment to seek out Theo, and a little postponement wouldn't matter.

Mrs. Polter chattered brightly while she measured and wrote down entries in her notebook. Apparently she had never visited Spindrift before and she was entranced by all she had seen. Theo had sent Fiona to take her down to the ballroom, so she could better visualize the background for the costumes she was to create. Fiona had supplied her with color reproductions of the gowns she and Theo would wear, and she was particularly taken by Sargent's portrait of Ellen Terry as Lady Macbeth. She had the enthusiasm of an artist herself and I knew her dresses would be perfection, but I couldn't really care.

When she was through with me I went down the hall to Theo's room and tapped on the door. Probably she would snap at me and send me away, but I had to make the attempt to see her while she was in this disturbed state and might be willing to talk to me. No one answered, and I rapped again. She wouldn't be pleased with me for waking her, but as I raised my hand to knock again, I heard a faint sound from the other side of the door—as though someone had moaned. I tried the door. For once Theo hadn't locked it, and I went in quickly.

At first glance the room seemed empty and I was aware of a green carpet and pale green walls, of a gold coverlet rumpled on the bed, and of gold-topped bottles and jars on the glass of the dressing-table top. Then the moan came again and I ran around the end of the bed in alarm.

Theodora Moreland lay on her back on the green carpet beyond the bed, her legs sprawled beneath the hem of her citron-yellow robe, and blood seeping from a wound on her forehead. I dropped to my knees beside her and she opened her eyes and looked at me dazedly.

"I'll get someone," I told her. "Don't move, Theo. Lie very still."

A phone call to the dining room got no answer. Luncheon was over and the diners had gone their various ways. I called the housekeeper, told her to find anyone at all and send them here to Mrs. Moreland's room—and then to call a doctor.

With linen handkerchiefs from a drawer I stanched the wound on Theo's forehead, murmuring to her that someone was coming, that it would be all right. She endured that for only a moment and then pushed my hand aside and sat up.

"Don't make such a fuss. It's nothing. I was dizzy. I slipped and fell. I struck my head on the bedpost."

She tried to get up, but she was weaker than she thought, and she accepted my arm reluctantly as I helped her up from the floor and over to the bed. The broken skin on her forehead had stopped bleeding, and the bruised flesh was already swelling and showing angry color.

Fiona was the first to rush into the room, with Joel following. Theo pushed Fiona away and scowled at Joel. "I was dizzy. I fainted. Don't make such a fuss."

Joel stood quietly beside her bed, while Fiona rushed into the bathroom for cold cloths to place on the bruise.

"You're not usually given to fainting," Joel said. "Suppose you tell me what happened."

Their two red heads were close together as he bent over her, but she pouted at him, her green eyes flashing resentment that anyone should catch her in a moment of weakness.

"I'll faint if I please. I was worried, upset. I wanted to get away by myself."

"With your door unlocked?" I said. "You always lock your door."

The green malice enveloped me as well. "Get someone sensible in here!" she cried faintly. "You three are no good to me at all. Get Ferris."

"When did you come back to your room?" Joel asked.

She lacked the strength for the moment to fight us all and gave up with a rebellious sigh. "I left Mrs. Polter at one-fifteen. I know because I looked at my watch."

I glanced at mine and saw that scarcely fifteen minutes had passed. Whatever had happened had occurred while I was talking to Mrs. Polter.

"Did you see who struck you?" Joel asked.

She answered grumpily. "I didn't see anything or anyone. I was just walking around the end of the bed when I became dizzy and went down. When I opened my eyes

140

there was no one there, but Christy was rapping on the door."

I wondered if she was telling the truth—it was hard to know. If someone had been in the room with her, there must have been a lapse of consciousness in which he had gotten away.

"I've sent for a doctor," I told Joel.

He nodded and moved aside while Fiona pressed cool cloths on Theo's bruised forehead. I bent toward her and whispered a question.

"Is it because of Adam this happened, Theo? Is it because you know something about how Adam died?"

Fiona cried out indignantly and Joel pushed me away from the bed.

"Leave her alone," he said. "Don't torment her now."

"*You* were asking her questions," I protested, but he paid no further attention to me, taking the cold cloth from Fiona's hand.

Fiona turned to a chair and sat down abruptly as though her knees had given way.

"I'll stay here with her," she told Joel. "She shouldn't have a roomful of people hovering about."

"I'll stay myself," he said. "You and Christy go along. I want to talk to my mother."

Fiona got up as though still uncertain of her legs and moved toward the door. When she spoke there was a note of hysteria in her voice.

"I think someone did strike her down. Someone who waited for her here in her room."

"Who?" Joel said. "Did you see anyone, Christy?"

I shook my head and Fiona went on. "Your mother asks for trouble. She asks for trouble constantly. Now it's caught up with her."

"Go away," Joel said, with more heat in his voice than was usual.

I put a hand on Fiona's arm. It wasn't like her to criticize Theo, especially in her presence.

"Come along," I said. "You need to lie down yourself." It was hard to tell whether her unsteady movements were due to shock or to the drinks she had had that day.

Theo stopped us as we reached the door. "You'll be the next," she said.

We both turned back in surprise, and Fiona said, "Oh, God!"

"Not you," Theo told her. "Christy. You'll be next, Christy. If you stay here at Spindrift, you can't escape."

I started back toward the bed, but Joel shook his head at me. As always he was protecting his mother and the look on his face stopped me. He didn't believe what Theo was saying, and he only wanted me to go away. Fiona plucked at my arm and I went with her into the hall.

"I feel a little faint," she said.

I helped her to her room and when she had flopped down on the bed and flung an arm over her eyes, I pulled off her shoes and drew the coverlet over her. But I couldn't afford to be merciful. I bent over her and spoke softly.

"What do you really know, Fiona? Who do you think tried to kill Theo?"

She rolled away from me on the bed. "No one tried to kill her. If someone had, she'd be dead. It was only a warning. But after the warnings can come the real thing."

"A warning of what?" I could imagine Theo being behind any trouble that might develop, but I wouldn't expect her to be a target.

"Perhaps she's found Adam's log," Fiona said, her voice muffled beneath the arm that shielded her face from my view.

"I don't think she'd need to read anything Adam may have written," I said. "If there's something to know, she's known all along. Just as you have."

The arm came away from her face and she stared at me, stricken. "But I don't know anything, Christy. How can you believe that I do?"

There was no use talking to her. I couldn't help feeling

sorry for her in this pitiable state. "Go to sleep if you can," I said more gently. "Get some rest."

As I went downstairs I heard voices coming from the direction of a room at the rear of the house that had once been used as an office by Hal Moreland. Without hesitation, I walked to the open door and saw that Ferris and Bruce were sitting at a long refectory table with papers strewn between them. This was clearly a business conference and they were so engrossed that they did not see me there in the doorway as I looked about the room.

It was a brown room, without character. Only a picture over the mantel gave it interest—a portrait of Arthur and Zenia Patton-Stuyvesant, perhaps painted around the time of their marriage. Zenia's young face looked eager for life, and grimness had not yet touched Arthur. They had been beautiful people in their day—what had happened to them?

Ferris saw me first and rose to his feet without welcome.

"Someone struck Theo down in her bedroom," I said, choosing the more dramatic explanation. "She has a bruise and a cut on her forehead."

Both men stared at me in disbelief, and if either had been upstairs in Theo's room he betrayed nothing. Bruce came toward me.

"Who would do such a thing? How is she?"

"Not badly hurt. And who did it is something we'd all like to know. Part of the time she claims she was simply dizzy and fainted. Joel is with her now. Fiona has gone to pieces. I've put her to bed."

"I'll go up to Theodora right away," Ferris said. "This is a terrible thing. I didn't believe in her suspicion that someone was going to attack her. I should have taken better care."

He hurried out of the room and I faced Bruce, still probing. "That leaves you," I said. "Sometimes I don't think you like her very well."

He stared at me for a quiet moment, his dark-browed

face more somber than ever, his deep-set eyes regarding me with a certain intensity.

"I am still in her employ," he said, and I knew that meant he would make no criticism against her, whatever he might feel.

I sat down at the table, though he remained standing. "Anyway," I said, "it wouldn't be like you to make a petty attack. If you had reason and wanted to kill someone, you would."

A faint, rather grim smile touched his straight mouth. "You are probably right. And now that we have that out of the way, suppose you tell me exactly what happened."

It was easy to talk to him, and I stopped trying to hold back my own reactions of alarm and fear.

"She said I would be next," I told him when I had described my going to Theo's room, finding her there on the floor, summoning the others. "She'd already denied being struck, so why would she say a thing like that?"

"You'll have to ask her when she's feeling better," Bruce said. "Though I suppose she's unlikely to tell you. I wouldn't take her words too seriously. You already know that she'd like to frighten you away from Spindrift so that Peter will stay in her hands."

"Yes, I know that. But is there another plot against me?" I said.

"Do you think she would tell me? You've already drawn your own conclusions, haven't you? You've already been victim to her tricks."

"And you think this is another one?"

"I didn't say that. I haven't seen her. I don't know anything about it. But what if she really did fall against that bedpost? It wouldn't be beyond her to make the most of a dramatic situation. She's done that plenty of times before, God knows."

"It's possible," I agreed. "Anyway, I've had enough of it all for a while. This afternoon I'm going to take Peter into town for tea at one of the wharfs. He's been behaving badly, and I'd like to get him into a different atmosphere for a while."

He dropped into the chair across the table and began to shuffle the papers together in a pile. Some of the somberness had fallen away and when he spoke again it was with a certain hesitance that surprised me.

"I envy you," he said. "I envy you your son and the chance to run away from the Morelands. Once a long time ago I hoped—" He broke off and flipped the stack of papers down on the table.

"Fiona told me about your marriage," I said gently. "I'm sorry."

He was silent for a moment. "It seems very long ago. Sometimes I can hardly remember her face." There was a sadness in his tone that I had never heard before. "That seems a betrayal, doesn't it? But it happens. With time. And I won't ever really forget her."

I had the unexpected impulse to comfort him—and that was ridiculous. I had never known a man as strong in his own right as Bruce, except perhaps Adam—and I knew how quickly he would reject sympathy from a stranger like me. Yet I wanted to offer him something. When I spoke I made my words light, almost playful.

"Why don't you run away with us too? Peter likes you and he'd welcome your company."

He smiled and reached across the table to touch my hand. "You're kind, Christy. That's a quality that's hard to find in a woman these days."

Kind? I wondered. Perhaps to a few people. Not to everyone. Not lately. It wasn't a word I could accept deservingly and I shook my head.

"In any case," he went on, "I wouldn't think of intruding when you want this time alone with your son."

"I'm not sure I'm ready to be alone with Peter," I admitted. "We're still a little wary of each other because Theo has come between us. It would help me to have you there. You'll know what to say to a little boy."

"You put it well," he said, and there was warmth in his

rare smile. "I'll come. And thank you. Shall I take you in my car?"

"That will be fine," I said and stood up. "Let's meet at the front door at three o'clock."

So it was arranged and I left him and went upstairs to my Red Room. I pulled an armchair over to where October sunshine fell through the opened draperies, brightening the red of the carpet, and curled myself into it, basking in warmth and light. For a little while the sense of darkness had slipped away and I felt curiously content. Yet I dared not analyze why. I had no desire to seek disturbing answers in this quiet moment of suspension.

It was possible now for my thoughts to follow other roads almost impersonally and without suffering distress. I didn't feel afraid now. I could live through whatever tricks Theo might play upon me because they would be no real threat. After all, she wasn't going to harm me physically. And there was no reason why anyone else would try.

I began to think of Joel, and suddenly, unnervingly, the thing happened that Bruce had said could occur long after someone had died. I had seen him only a little while ago, yet I couldn't see his face clearly. For a few moments I couldn't see it in my mind's eye. It was as though all my past life with him had never been, and I had moved on into a separate world in which he had no part. Lately he had looked at me without liking; he had supported his mother against me and refused to recognize the harm that was being done to Peter. Whatever we might have owed each other in the past had been evened out, and perhaps we would both be better off free. But there was still Peter. As long as I was strong and well balanced and in good health, my son could not be taken away from me. All the more reason why I mustn't let Theo's plotting unsettle me. I respected Bruce for not speaking against her while he still worked for the Morelands but I knew that he'd wanted to reassure me, stiffen my spine against whatever Theo might try to do to me. All this I could cope with.

Surely I *was* strong again and in full possession of my senses. What had frightened me was only Theo's vindictive scheming, and I must never again let this disturb me. She was a tyrannical and rather foolish old woman, but not dangerous if I stood up to her. Foolish because she thought the world must revolve about her wishes and that whatever she wanted must be brought to happen. Well, she was not going to have her way. I would stay at Spindrift. She should not be allowed to confuse and weaken me again. I would stay and fight for Peter.

I drew in a long breath of relief and let it slowly blow away. Already I was feeling stronger.

And yet—Adam was dead.

Without warning, my paper house of courage collapsed into thin air. Adam was dead, and he had not killed himself. Somewhere there existed his own writings which would tell me the truth about what had happened. I was not safe. Not if I was about to discover the truth. Evil did exist. It wore a masked face and I was still threatened.

I glanced at the watch on my wrist and saw that it was a long time until three o'clock. I mustn't waste whatever hours I had. I'd said I would search, but I was doing nothing, and there was one obvious place where I could begin.

I went to my door and looked into the empty hallway.

9

No one crossed my path on the way to Zenia's sitting room. Her door opened to my touch and I closed it softly behind me, to find the darkness hushed and empty. I fumbled for the light switch near the door and the Tiffany lamp on a Victorian table that dripped red plush balls came on, sweeping the shadows up the walls. I went quickly to a window and drew back the heavy velvet draperies so that sunlight touched the room. From the walls Zenia's strange collection of pictures and plates looked down at me. I was beginning to feel rather close to the woman who had once used this room as a haven. But now it was not upon her possessions that I must concentrate.

If it had been my father who had set the ivory carving upon that mantel, perhaps he had meant it as a marker for something else he had placed there. I looked at the spot where the small figure had stood and saw again that it had rested upon a wooden box with a curious fanged creature upon its lid, carved of some whitish stone used as a handle—probably jade. Was this another of Theo's treasures?

I raised the lid of the box by the carving and looked inside. There were long, thin slabs of stone piled in the box—jade again? I picked up the top slab and saw that it was inscribed with Chinese characters in gold. So were the slabs which lay underneath. They meant nothing to me. I replaced the lid and moved uncertainly about the room. I had no hint of what I might be looking for. "Tyche" had been one word my father had written on that slip of paper and Tyche, identified and found, was still meaningless to me. The other words "mutton fat" left me as hopelessly in the dark.

I spent some time moving idly about the room, admiring a cabinet of inlaid satinwood where vases of cut glass and Meissen and Crown Derby were displayed, picking up a tarnished silver pomander from Zenia's desk, moving on to discover an arched doorway in a corner of the room which had been hung with a bead curtain.

The rustling clatter the beads made as I parted the strands was startling in the silence of this quiet room. In a place as huge as Spindrift with its long corridors and high ceilings, it was possible to be thoroughly isolated, even though many people were under its roof.

I stepped through the bead curtain into what seemed to be a small dressing room. There was a wardrobe—empty —a dressing table of light ash wood, with a mirror in the shape of a shield, now faintly crazed as I saw when I bent to peer at myself in the glass. Here sunlight did not penetrate and I was only a shadowy figure among other shadows. This small room in turn gave off another room that was probably a bedroom, but the door was locked and I could explore no further.

As I moved back toward the curtain to return to Zenia's sitting room, I heard the soft sound of a door opening beyond. Opening and closing. Someone had come into the sitting room. I parted strands of beads for a thin aperture through which I could look. Fiona stood with her back against the door, her gaze roaming the room. If she was surprised to find a lamp burning in the room, she gave no sign. She had put on a garnet-colored caftan that swept to her slippered feet. It seemed to me that there was almost a sleepwalking quality about her, her eyes a little glazed and staring as she viewed the room. Her light brown hair, usually sleek with brushing, hung rumpled, framing her white face.

She must have come to look for what I had come to look for, I thought—Adam's log—and I watched as she left the protection of the door behind her and moved slowly about the room. Her gaze flitted from one object to another without recognition, but for a few moments she did not touch anything. Her search seemed as fruitless as mine.

Then she appeared to make up her mind and walked directly to Zenia's desk. I had thought of the desk earlier, but had postponed searching it because I wanted to know the over-all pattern of the room first. Now it was too late. Fiona would look through it before me.

Strangely, however, she did no searching. She simply opened a bottom drawer of the desk and bent over it. From among the folds of the caftan she drew some object I could not see, and thrust it into the drawer, pulled the contents of papers over it and shut the drawer quickly. With no further look about the room, she moved with her rangy stride toward the door and disappeared into the hallway. I think she had never been conscious, one way or another, of the lamp burning on a table.

In a moment I was through the bead curtain to bend over that lower drawer. Beneath the notebooks and papers within lay a lumpy object, revealed in its cold black lines as I thrust the covering away. What Fiona had hidden in the drawer was an automatic pistol. She had not come here to find anything—she had come for the purpose of concealment.

Even though I didn't understand her action, the physical presence of the gun did not surprise me. The Morelands had always been gun-oriented. Hal had been a hunter when he was young, and he had a prized collection of guns—both rifles and handguns. In fact, he had made a hobby of collecting handguns of the old West. Theo didn't like her guns to be "alive," but I knew she kept an old derringer, borrowed from Hal's collection, in a desk drawer. My father had owned a gun—the one that had killed him—and so did Ferris. Bruce scoffed at living with such fearfulness, and Joel would have nothing to do with firearms.

This pistol, however, was not from Hal's collection. It was what Theo would have called "live," modern, and I wondered why Fiona had hidden it. I did not investigate to see whether it was loaded, but restored the covering of papers and closed the drawer. Then, as all those crowded pictures on the walls watched me, I went through the other drawers of the desk. But if Adam had chosen to hide his log in this room, he had not picked so obvious a place. Methodically I examined everything. I opened cabinets, looked in boxes, and even under the cushions of chairs and sofa. And I found nothing at all except a tortoiseshell comb that might once have belonged to Zenia herself. If the log was here it was so disguised that I did not recognize its identity.

When I was ready to leave, I opened the door cautiously to make sure the hall was empty before I went out. As I passed the foot of the stairs to the third floor I met Joel coming down.

I tried to speak as though a void had not opened between us. "How is your mother? Did the doctor get here?"

Joel nodded. "He says the bruise is superficial. She's already up and she won't have anyone fussing over her."

"Do you think someone struck her down?"

"It seems unlikely." Joel's look was suddenly guarded. "I understand you're taking Peter into town this afternoon."

"Yes. It's time we had an outing together."

"I hope you won't try to prejudice him against his grandmother."

I could only stare at Joel helplessly. "I'd love to do just that but it's not going to happen so quickly. Anyway, Bruce is coming with us, and he'll probably look out for Theo."

I wondered almost impersonally if Joel would offer to come with us himself, but he only nodded and moved away from me down the hall.

I hurried after him. "Is it really true you're going to publish a book by Jon Pemberton?"

He didn't break his stride. "Theo and Ferris both think it's a wise move."

"But you've always stood up to them before! You've always refused to have any interference with what you chose to publish."

"Then perhaps it's time I changed," he said, and walked away from me toward the door of his room.

I let him go and went to my own room. There I opened the balcony door and stepped out where I could see the Atlantic rolling in, listen to the sound of it and smell the familiar tang of salt on the breeze.

What I wanted was to give myself up to the pleasant anticipation of my outing with Peter and Bruce, but my earlier sense of contentment was gone. Too many unsettling things tugged at my consciousness. There were too many unanswered questions, too many disturbing new emotions moving me. There was a restless questing in me, yet I didn't know what I searched for, what I wanted. While there was no longer any close relationship between Joel and me, I could be upset by the change in his approach to his work. And I was disturbed about Fiona and why she should steal into Zenia's sitting room to hide an automatic in that desk drawer. My double purpose in coming to Spindrift remain unchanged—I wanted to recover Peter and I wanted to know the cause of my father's death, but now all sorts of perplexing strands of happenings had begun to weave themselves in and out among these purposes, so that nothing was clear cut any more and new emotions had begun to motivate me. Fear of something unknown was a part of all this, and so was the odd new excitement that gave my life a savor it had not had in a long time. An excitement that had to do with Bruce Parry and was in itself frightening. This was only attraction, I knew, and nothing more. But I couldn't afford to be attracted, didn't want to be. Besides, Bruce himself was a complete enigma.

I returned to my room and managed somehow to fill the time with small tasks of preparation. I got out of my slacks and sweater and put on my brown gabardine suit. Then I brushed my hair which I'd been letting grow since I came out of the hospital, though it was still short.

When I went upstairs I found Peter ready for me, neatly dressed in gray slacks and a green sweater, his brown hair brushed and his hands clean. Miss Crawford had done her best, but Peter was clearly anxious to escape her, and while he didn't greet me warmly, at least his earlier sullenness had lifted.

We went downstairs to find Bruce waiting at the wheel of his Aston Martin and as we hurried down the wide flight of front steps he came around to open the car door for me.

Driving along Bellevue Avenue with its big trees, its iron fences and sometimes shabby mansions, Bruce pointed out to Peter some of the special houses—Chateau-sur-Mer, The Elms, Kingscote and the old Newport Casino.

We continued on to little Touro Park, with the famous Stone Mill in its center. The squat, round tower, open to the sky, its doorways arched, was once supposed to be a relic from the days of the Norsemen, and local legend claimed it had inspired Longfellow to write his "Skeleton in Armor."

As we left the ridge of the Historic Hill we could see the graceful white steeple of old Trinity thrusting up from among gambrel and gable roofs that dated back to the 1700s. Bruce drove down narrow streets, turning odd corners so that we could pass more of the old houses before we went down to Thames Street, with its wharfs stretching into the harbor. No Newporter called it "Tems"—the "h" and the "a" were pronounced. Bruce was up on his Newport history and even Peter seemed fascinated by the small tour he gave us.

Some of my misgivings and concerns had begun to slip away, and when Bruce parked his car and we walked in the direction of Bowen's Wharf and neighboring Bannister's Wharf, I sensed that something of the old spirit of adventure had seized Peter. It was clear that he liked Bruce and I listened to Peter's questions and Bruce's answers with a pleasure that I had not felt for a very long while.

We spent some time on the wharfs, looking over the windjammer *Bill of Rights* and the brig *The Black Pearl,* before we went to our restaurant and found a table beside an upstairs window, where we could look out at the harbor and Narraganset Bay beyond. Sunlight sparkled on the water, and dozens of small boats were out on this beautiful day. The sound of the buoys had no menace with such clarity of weather, and gulls soared and darted, graceful to watch, but raucous to hear.

The restaurant was nearly empty at this hour, and we had all the privacy we wished. While we ate ice cream and Bruce and I drank hot tea, Bruce talked about Spindrift as he had known it as a boy when his great-aunt Zenia was an old lady, but not yet in that unhappy last phase.

"She was still beautiful," he said. "She had been a wealthy widow for a long time, but she never wanted to marry again. Instead, there were always beaux dancing attendance on her, and more than one man who loved her clear into her eighties. Even though there was always something a little strange and sad about her."

"Like Grandma Theo," Peter said.

I looked at him in surprise. "Strange and sad—Theo?"

Bruce laughed. "He doesn't mean that. Who do you think is in love with your grandmother Theo?"

"Uncle Ferris, of course. Grandma says he always has been."

"At least he seems to have served the Morelands well," Bruce said, and I heard a dry note in his voice. "In Zenia's case it was a little different. Of course I suppose there were fortune hunters who wanted to marry her because she was rich. But she really did have a certain glamour, as well. I've heard some wild stories about her, and I've seen a good many pictures of her in her youth, even though I never saw her as a young woman. She was never tempery, as Theo can be, but I think she must have been equally self-centered and autocratic. She had the complete belief of her Newport contemporaries that she and they were the favored of the earth and I expect she was more of a snob than Theo has ever been."

"Have you seen the portrait of her painted by Sargent —the one that hangs in the ballroom?" I asked Peter. "I'm going to be dressed like that picture for the ball. Though I'm afraid I can't carry off any real impersonation of Zenia."

"I'm not so sure," Bruce said. "You have a touch of Zenia in you. Determination and a willingness to defy anyone who opposes you to get your own way. She was like that too."

I looked at him in surprise and then busied myself with my teacup to hide my confusion. These were hardly attractive traits that he'd mentioned, but they were admittedly mine and he must have watched me observantly to be aware of them.

"I have some of those traits of Zenia's too," he went on. "Perhaps we're two of a kind, Christy. And both of us subversives when it comes to Theo's plans."

"What are you talking about?" Peter demanded.

We both laughed and I relaxed a little. Peter let our adult laughter pass and went on to talk about the coming ball.

"Grandma Theo says I can stay on the orchestra balcony for a while, if I like. So I can watch the party. She's going to put the band right down on the floor because the room is so big. She says there will be lots to see, with all those ladies dressed up in beautiful costumes. She's already been talking to some of them on the telephone—talking about what they're going to wear. And she's asked Jon Pemberton to come. He's going to be Dad's new author, and he's very famous."

I could find nothing to say to that, but Peter paid no attention to my silence, running on excitedly with further items he had picked up about the ball. I was glad to see him once more a lively and interested little boy.

"I think Fiona will have the most beautiful dress of all. She showed me a colored picture of it in a book. It will be a shiny blue, like metal, and she'll have long green sleeves and a golden girdle. Sometimes Fiona sleepwalks like Lady Macbeth, doesn't she? Oh, I don't mean really. She just gets a staring look in her eyes, like she's thinking of something else, and she walks past and doesn't see me. This afternoon she was going down the hallway from Grandma Theo's rooms, and I said, 'Hello, Grandma Fiona'—because that makes her mad—but she never looked at me at all."

It was hard to remember that Fiona was Peter's step-grandmother. She had never liked to be called a grandmother, so he always used her first name alone. But he had touched on the thing I too had noted about Fiona when she came into Zenia's room—that blankness of vision, as though she were driven by some inner purpose, or inner fear, that allowed her no attention for side matters.

I let Peter's remarks pass and asked Bruce to tell us more about Zenia Patton-Stuyvesant. If I was to wear a dress like hers and echo the pose of her portrait, then I wanted to know more about her.

Peter grew quickly bored, and when I noticed a boat coming in to the wharf, I suggested that he go to the end of the room, where he could watch it better. He jumped up gladly and ran to the far window.

Bruce was willing enough to talk about the Patton-Stuyvesants. They had apparently been close friends with the Townsends of Redstones. Theron Townsend was in railroads too, and they were friendly rivals. It was Zenia who was most interesting to me, however. Rumor had it that while her husband, Arthur, was alive she had had a secret lover—the one love of her life—and there had been an occasion when she'd hidden him in one of the empty rooms at Spindrift and Arthur had found him there. No one knew exactly what happened, but the young man disappeared from the Newport scene and for a time Zenia was tragically subdued.

I wondered aloud whether that was why Arthur had taken poison.

"No, I don't think so," Bruce said. "That poisoning came much later, and no one was ever sure whether it was suicide, or whether someone else could have administered the dose. He had a good many enemies and there were always business acquaintances as well as friends coming in and out of Spindrift."

"I've never found the man in the portrait that hangs in the Tower Room especially sympathetic," I said.

"I imagine he had his problems. And now Spindrift has a new problem."

"What's that?" I asked, quickly alert.

"You," Bruce said. "You seem to have turned the house upside down with this talk about a log of Adam's."

"I only told Joel," I said.

"Who told his mother, who told the rest of us. So your plan to search the house isn't much of a secret. But it's certainly upsetting the beehive."

"That's fine," I said.

Bruce dropped his voice to a lower tone. "Christy, be careful. That log of Adam's could concern a lot of people. Some of them outside of Morelands. I wish Theo hadn't talked so openly about your looking for the log. We can't tell who may have outside connections that go back to a dangerous time."

"What do you mean?" I pressed him. "What dangerous time? What do you know about that log?"

"I didn't even know it existed until today. Fiona has kept still about it. But I can imagine some of the things Adam might have written in it."

"Then tell me what they were."

His look darkened. "No, Christy. You're getting in over your head. Don't stir up the sleeping beasts."

"Beasts who went to sleep when Adam died? Because they knew they were safe, once he was out of the way?"

Bruce stared out over the harbor and I knew that whatever he might suspect, he was not going to tell me.

Peter returned to the table, full of chatter about the docking of the boat, but while I was glad to see him come to life, my pleasure in this outing had vanished. Some dark knowledge underlay Bruce's words, and he wasn't going to reveal it to me.

I wondered what he would make of Fiona's hiding a pistol in Zenia's desk. Was it a gun that belonged to her? Or was it one that belonged to someone else and that she feared might be used? Had she been hiding it so it wouldn't be taken from her, hiding it for a quick recovery if she should want to use it? My thoughts whirled into a morass of speculation from which it was difficult to extract them. Yet out of some lingering loyalty to the woman who was my stepmother, I could not tell Bruce.

However, there was still something I wanted to do before we returned to Spindrift. I opened my handbag and took out my father's penknife.

"Do you recognize this?" I asked Peter and set it down on the table before him.

He did not touch the knife, but stared at it as though it frightened him. "It's Grandpa's knife."

"Yes. Would you like to have it?"

He looked at me and his eyes filled with tears that he brushed away angrily. "You're trying to make me cry!"

"There's nothing wrong with crying, Peter. I miss him too, and sometimes I cry."

Quietly Bruce got up from the table and walked to another window, leaving us alone for a little while, as we needed to be.

"But Grandma Theo says I mustn't cry over him," Peter went on. "She—she says he was a w-worthless person and did a lot of wrong things and I'm not to cry about him!"

There was no one but Bruce in the restaurant to see, and I left my place at the table and went to kneel beside Peter's chair. For once he did not draw away when I put my arms about him.

"You're not to believe such things of your grandfather. He was a wonderful man and we must never forget that, or let anything make us believe any different. It's all right to cry for him, darling. You can cry right now, if you like."

My son clung to me for the first time in nearly a year. He leaned his head against my shoulder and when I bent my own head I felt his wet cheek against mine. Down by the window Bruce glanced around at us, his look warmly sympathetic.

When all the held-back tears had been shed, Peter pushed me gently away, and Bruce came back to the table to offer a big linen handkerchief. Peter took it and wiped his eyes, and swallowed with a last, gulping sob. I went back to my own place and he reached out to pick up the penknife.

"Is it all right to keep this, Mother? I mean, Grandma Theo won't like it."

"Grandpa Adam would want you to have it," I said, chalking up one more mark against Theo. I looked at Bruce, still shaken by the emotion that had swept me when I'd held my son in my arms again. "I think we'd better go now, please."

He nodded and signaled for the check. When he had paid it, we walked back to where Bruce had parked his car. Somehow there was a greater closeness between the three of us than had existed before. The afternoon had been unexpectedly satisfying, and it had brought Peter closer to me. One of my purposes, at least, was beginning to show some results.

We drove back to Spindrift by a somewhat different route and Bruce talked to Peter, in the seat between us, about what an interesting place Newport was. Some people, when they heard the name "Newport," he said, thought only of the wealthy who had lived here and made themselves high society, or they thought of the current popular music festivals, or the yacht races for the America's Cup. But Newport had been settled in the early 1600s and until the Revolution it had prospered and been a center of commerce. When the British had occupied the town they had confiscated and destroyed, so that much of Newport's historical past had been wiped out. Fortunately, many of the old houses had been left standing, and eventually the city had returned to a position of influence and prosperity. Today there were more colonial houses in Newport than in any other city in the country, so there was a great and varied heritage to be preserved.

In the telling, Bruce made the story come to life so that Peter's eyes shone and when Bruce told him he would take him sometime to look at more of those old houses, Peter jumped at the suggestion.

By the time we reached Spindrift, something of my earlier pleasure in our excursion had returned and I could thank Bruce warmly for making the trip so interesting for Peter—and for me. But if I had managed to draw a little closer to Peter by this time, I knew Bruce had wanted to discourage me from my present course and did not approve of my determination to follow it—as did no one else.

He must have had some perception of what I was feeling because when he came around to open the car door and Peter had jumped out past us to run up the steps, forgetting to thank anyone, Bruce held my hand for a moment.

"I'd like to see you safe, Christy," he said. "It's better not to stir up those beasts."

In an instant everything was spoiled and I snatched my hand away. "Who is it you're trying to protect?"

The sardonic look was back in his eyes. "Perhaps if I knew, I wouldn't protect them."

"You're not sure?"

"Sometimes I'm not sure of anything," he said, and he went around the car to the driver's side.

I didn't wait for him to drive off, but ran up the steps in Peter's wake. Something we had been moving toward had been blocked, and in a way I was relieved. This afternoon I had felt increasingly attracted to Bruce, and while I was glad of his help with Peter, I didn't want that. I didn't dare want it. Now I was all the more sure there was something to discover about Adam's death, and all the more sure that I was going to discover it before very long. Nothing else mattered.

Peter had disappeared and Fiona was waiting for me at the first-floor landing of the stairs. She no longer appeared to be sleepwalking, but her face, so much thinner than when my father had been alive, had a harried look about it.

"Theo wants to see you," she told me.

"So you're back in her good graces. What's up now?"

"I don't think it's anything special. She just wants to hear about your taking Peter to town."

I went up to the third floor with her and found Theo waiting for me in her sitting room, upright in a rose-striped chair. She still wore her citron-yellow robe, and the bruise on her forehead had been covered by a patch of bandage. If it had not been for that evidence, she would have looked none the worse for her fall.

"How are you feeling?" I asked as she waved me toward a chair.

Fiona followed me into the room and went back to her addressing of invitations, while Theo's green eyes studied me as though something profound was to be learned through that penetrating gaze.

"I'm feeling like anyone who has an enemy," she said.

So she was now going to admit to an attack upon herself. But she went on quickly.

"That's not what I want to talk about. How was your tea with Peter and Bruce?"

How quickly she knew about everything that happened!

"We had a very pleasant time," I said, trying to sound as neutral as possible.

"Peter enjoyed himself?"

"I'm sure he did."

"You didn't upset him then?"

"Why should I upset him?"

"Come, Christy dear, we know you've been ill and that there have been times when you've upset him very much."

"I'm not ill any longer."

"I'm delighted to hear that you are so sure about that —in spite of your seeing lights after dark, where there couldn't be any lights, and roaming the corridors on strange errands in the middle of the night."

I had to resist her goading. She wanted to upset me, and I made myself answer quietly.

"There *was* a light over at Redstones. We all saw the evidence of that candle. And when I have a sleepless night I often get up and walk about."

Fiona's pen moved rapidly on the envelope she was addressing. I had the feeling that she was forcing herself not to stare at me, not to listen.

"I've just talked to Miss Crawford," Theo said. "She tells me Peter was terribly excited when he came in. I don't think I like that."

"Small boys need healthy excitement once in a while. If they don't find it in their everyday lives, they can get into mischief. Though I can't say anything very exciting happened. One thing I did was to give him my father's penknife. Adam would want him to have it."

She stiffened in her chair and I knew she detested the way I was standing up to her. She couldn't know that she was having her old effect on me, and that I'd begun to tremble in the pit of my stomach.

"What did he do when you gave him the knife?" she demanded.

162

"He cried. We both cried."

"Hah!" It was a sound of triumph. "That sort of emotionalism isn't good for him."

"I don't agree," I said. "It's very good to let your feelings go now and then. Peter has needed a good cry. He felt better for it afterwards."

"Boys shouldn't be encouraged to cry." It was her typical pronouncement, and I began to get a little excited myself.

"That's nonsense! Tears can be healthy. Little boys cry as well as little girls. And so do men."

"Have you ever seen Joel cry?" she asked me.

"I suppose you taught him not to. And perhaps that's one of the things that's the matter. He can't ever let go and suffer openly. But when feelings have to be suppressed like that there can be a real explosion when they finally break out."

"You are a psychiatrist, I presume?"

"As much as you are." I knew I was being as snide as Theo, but I couldn't stop myself.

Fiona's pen had ceased to move. I glanced at her and saw that she was regarding me with something like horror. Because if there was a Moreland Empire, Theo was the empress, and one did not argue with the ruler of the realm.

But since I had gone this far, I might as well go all the way, and I continued. "When I have finished what I've come to Spindrift for, you might as well know that I mean to take Peter away. I'm grateful to you for helping Joel and me by looking after him while I was ill. But now I'm well again I'm ready to be his mother properly."

The purplish look came into Theo's face and I tried to soften my tone.

"I know Peter loves you very much as his grandmother, and we'll want him to see you often. There needn't be any change in his relationship with you. It's just that Joel and I want to have our own say about raising him."

" 'We'?" Theo echoed my pronoun. "Is it really to be

we? Joel tells me your marriage hasn't gone well since you came back from the hospital."

"That's between Joel and me," I said flatly. "It's for us to work out."

Theo put her hand to her head as though she had grown weary of our whole discussion. When she was unexpectedly silent, and Fiona's pen began to move again, I found I couldn't sit still any longer. The tremor in the pit of my stomach was quickening, and I left my chair abruptly to walk to a corner shelf where the carved figure of the little Japanese lady had been placed. I stared at her for a moment, as though I might gain from her my self-possession and the courage to stand up to Theodora Moreland.

A sound behind me made me turn, and I felt a slight shock to discover both Theo and Fiona standing very close behind me.

"Are you all right?" Theo said.

"What do you mean? Of course I'm all right."

She and Fiona looked at each other.

"You didn't answer when I spoke to you," Theo said, "and you started to sway. You must have gone completely blank for a moment or two."

"Blank? Of course I didn't go blank. I was just looking at your little Japanese lady."

Theo nodded at Fiona. "It was one of her lapses. She used to have them at the hospital. I'd hoped she'd recovered from them."

"There wasn't any lapse!" I cried. "I've been perfectly conscious every minute."

Theo regarded me sadly. "I know. That's what you always say. But Fiona saw this too. Didn't you, Fiona?"

"Yes, of course," Fiona said, but her eyes didn't meet mine.

I felt shaken enough to return to my chair. Theo told Fiona to get me some water, and then nodded to someone in the doorway. As I sipped, Ferris Thornton came into the room.

"Theodora, you look flushed and upset," he said and went to bend over her in concern.

She pushed him away and sat down at her desk. "I'm not the one who is upset. It's Christina we're concerned about. She's just had one of those forgetful spells she used to have at the hospital. If these are to return, Peter mustn't be trusted to her."

I made a sound of protest and spilled water from my glass. It was hard to speak because I was so shaken and disconcerted. I couldn't tell for sure whether there had been some lapse of consciousness, or if this was simply one of Theo's tricks, in which she was aided and abetted by Fiona.

Ferris gave me his searching lawyer's look that revealed very little, but he made no comment.

Theo went on tartly. "If you've recovered, Christina, you can tell me what you meant by saying you had come to Spindrift for a purpose."

I'd always hated to be called "Christina," which of course was why she was doing it. I tried to answer her quietly, tried to keep myself from trembling.

"I think everyone knows what I want. I told Joel and he seems to have publicized it. If my father left his last log anywhere in this house, I'd like to find it. Or if someone else has found it, I want to see what he wrote in those pages."

Ferris coughed gently. "I doubt that there is any such log to be discovered at this late date. Or if there should be, I hope it will be destroyed unread at once."

"Why?" I said. "Why are you all so afraid of what my father might have recorded in the last days of his life?"

Fiona had given up her pretense of working and she was staring at me as if hypnotized. Theo flung up her hand in a gesture of impatience, but Ferris spoke to me in that dry, even tone that was typically his.

"Your father was involved in some pretty nefarious dealings before he died. Some of these came out in the papers, but not all. He was ready to do anything to get money for his gambling. Theodora could not go on supporting this, as Hal had done. Adam was at the end of his resources, and he knew it. So he turned to some blackguardly schemes that were about to blow up in his face. If he kept any record of what he was mixing into—which I doubt—it would be kinder to you to have that record destroyed without reading it."

I managed to speak into the waiting silence, knowing they were all watching me. "I don't believe one word you're saying! I never did believe those stories that someone invented for the police and the newspapers. All those lies about Adam having dealings with the underworld."

He regarded me almost sadly. "Have I ever lied to you, Christy?"

I tried to see him in his old, loved role of the Uncle Ferris who had been good to a lonely little girl without a mother, but the picture had blurred. He belonged to the Morelands and I could no longer trust him. If he chose to lie to me he would.

I stood up and moved toward the door. "If that's all you want of me now, Theo—"

"You may go," she said shortly. "But we'll talk about some of these plans of yours again. Perhaps you'd better go and lie down now, give yourself time to recover from what has just happened to you. All this emotionalism isn't good for your state of health."

Ferris said, "I'd like to speak with you alone for a moment, Theodora."

She flicked her fingers in dismissal at Fiona, who followed me out the door. Just as Fiona closed it, we heard Ferris's voice from inside the room. He spoke softly and not all the words were distinct, but I heard two of them—"gun" and "missing." Then the door had shut and we were walking along the corridor together. If I had heard, Fiona had too, but she gave no sign as she moved along at my side, and I knew she was lost in her thoughts and sleepwalking again. She still wore the dark red caftan I'd seen her in earlier, and she moved beside me, drifting as though without direction.

When I put a hand on her arm, she started as though she had forgotten I was near, and gave me a quick, startled look, then hurried away from me down the hall.

I knew it would do me no good to follow her and I paused beside a long window overlooking the lawn which sloped toward the ocean. A single, lonely figure stood down there beside the stone wall on the edge of the Spindrift property. It was Joel, looking out over the ocean he hated.

Memory quickened in me, suddenly as real as the present. I could recall a time when Joel and I had followed the Cliff Walk clear to the Forty Steps. It had been a windy day with the spray flying high as it broke over the rocky shore of the island. We'd walked hand in hand and we had been very close that day, and terribly in love. There had been an earlier scene with Joel's mother, and for once he had walked out on her and brought me with him. I could still remember his words.

"Don't fight her, Christy. She only gets stronger. Yield. Bend with the gale. And then go your own way."

That was what he had always done. But it hadn't been my way—or Adam's. And was it I who had been wrong? Was it true that I had always put Adam's ways first? Until, after his cruel death, there was only Adam who seemed real in that numb, hospital world where I had lost myself. What if I could wake up and find myself loving Joel as I used to? Had I really tried? Hadn't I just shrunk within myself and shut him out until his own pride would no longer allow him to reach out to me?

If only everything could go back to the way it used to be, perhaps I would be safe again. Safe from the new emotions that stirred in me when it came to Bruce, and that I wanted none of. Safe to cope with the changes in Peter which Theo had wrought. If Joel and I could go home together and take Peter with us, perhaps our old relationship could be re-established. I hadn't tried hard enough since I had left the hospital. There had been no reasoning in me, no real thought of Joel. Yet when I'd married him I had loved him enough to put him first.

Joel hadn't changed alone, of his own accord. It was I who was making him change, and the time had come for me to recover myself and do something about what was happening. Theo wanted our marriage to end, and I must defeat her purpose, if it wasn't already too late. I had made too many accusations against Theo for Joel to accept them when he truly loved his mother. I had made angry attacks against everyone, including Joel, and now I must get myself in hand and try to heal the wounds I had made in my anguished slashing. Never mind if Theo wanted to play tricks, to shake my very sanity. If Joel and I could once more find each other, there would be nothing she could do. And this was what *I* wanted—only to go back and be the gentler, more contented girl I had once been. If some wilder, stronger emotion stirred in me when I thought of Bruce, I would thrust it down, stifle it. I only wanted to be Joel's wife.

I hurried downstairs and went out on the long veranda that overlooked the water.

10

For a moment I stood on the veranda watching the lone figure down by the wall, strengthening my resolve and my courage. What I had to do would not be easy. Then as I watched, I saw him climb the wall and knew I had better hurry if I was to catch him.

Outdoors, though the sun was dipping down the sky, the day was still bright and warm with Indian summer. The breeze from the sea had not yet turned chilly as it would when the shadows fell. As I ran across the lawn, Joel disappeared and I knew he must be climbing down the rocks beyond the Cliff Walk.

As I went over the low wall I saw in surprise where he must be going. A boatshed was built out into the little sandy cove below the rocks, with a path carved down to it, and Joel, who would have nothing to do with boats since his sister and brother had died, was following the path to the shed.

Spindrift kept a speedboat down there that Hal had liked to use, and when I reached the boatshed behind Joel, I saw that it had not yet been put away for the winter. The boat bore Spindrift's name and it floated between two docking platforms inside the shed.

Joel still did not know I was back of him when he stepped down into the cockpit and slipped behind the wheel. He had already untied the boat from the dock and he was clearly going to take it out. I moved quickly, stepping down into the seat beside him.

"Do you mind if I come with you?" I said.

He showed no astonishment at finding me there, but seemed indifferent, and I hid my own alarm. Joel had been afraid of the water ever since the accident, and I didn't know why he was taking the boat out. But I asked no questions and he offered no explanations. For a moment we sat there in silence and there was no sound in the boatshed except for the gurgling of water in the slip and the rush of the ocean over the rocks outside. By this time the sun was slanting behind us into the west and the shadows were dark under the shed roof, with only the opening to the sea a square of sunlight ahead. It was cold here in the shade and I wished for a jacket. Joel wore only a sweater with a rolled neck, but he didn't look cold.

Now that I was here I didn't know what to do. This hardly seemed the moment for the sort of talk I wanted. The man beside me seemed impossibly remote. The Joel I had been thinking of, wanting to return to, was another man—far removed from this quiet stranger.

"Is anything wrong?" I asked, making at least a beginning. The words echoed in the hollow shed and I was sorry that I'd spoken.

He did not answer but reached for the switch, and suddenly the motor roared into life. I braced myself against whatever was to come as we headed out of the cove. It was a calm enough day, with only a slight breeze, and the sea was blue green and smooth, stretching ahead to the far line of the horizon. We moved straight out across the water as though the coast of Europe were our destination. The *Spindrift* shivered with power and pointed its bow like an aimed arrow toward the invisible distance. Water curled away from either side in two great waves and the wake behind us widened, frothing and swirling. Gulls screamed as we left the shore. The roar of the motor prevented any talk, and I watched a gleam of sunlight strike off the brass cleats on the bow, washing the varnish to a golden brown. It was as if by fixing all my attention on that gleam of brass, I could still the rising of fear that had started up in me.

At last I had to speak. "Are we going to France?" I shouted over the roar.

If he heard me he paid no attention. His thick red hair shone in the sun, hardly ruffled, with the glass shield breaking the wind. His profile was as fine and clear cut as I remembered it—and it was still, as a cameo is still, without emotion, without life, carved.

This time when I spoke I reached out and touched his arm. "Let's follow the coast," I shouted.

He heard me and cut the roar so that we idled into a mere bobbing on the water. No one else seemed to be cruising this coastline and except for a ship in the distance we had the open ocean to ourselves.

Joel turned so that he could look back toward the shore. "They died on those rocks in there near Lands End. Because it was a foggy day. Because I wanted to go out in the fog."

Why had his mind turned back to old tragedy? I wondered. Why must he torture himself? Yet now he seemed to want to talk.

"Tell me what happened," I said.

He had never spoken about it to me before. What I knew I'd heard from other people. But now he began to tell me.

"Cabot lost his direction that day because of the fog. Our sailboat crashed into those rocks and capsized. Cabot tried to swim for shore, while Iris and I clung to the boat, but the seas turned high and he never made it. Iris was frail. I can still remember how beautiful she was. How beautiful she looked that day with her hair plastered back from her forehead so that her face was all pure beauty. I can still remember her frightened eyes. God knows, I tried to help her to hold on. And did for a long time. The fog was thinning as the wind rose, and the waves were beating against us, breaking over us, so that we didn't dare to try to make our way around the boat where we might be thrown against those daggers of rock. When she went under I still held onto her for a while, but my own strength was gone. I couldn't hold her above water in that

171

rough sea. When the Coast Guard came she was dead. I'd just had my seventeenth birthday."

I wanted to touch him, console him, but his face was like rock and I did not dare. I didn't know what had caused him to come out here now to face old terrors, old grief, and I could not ask. All the things I had wanted to talk to him about were swirling through my mind, but I could say nothing. I was too late. He had gone into some distant place that I could not reach and I didn't know him any more. Yet I had to try. In some way I had to try.

"I'm sorry," I said softly. "I'm sorry for everything, Joel. About what happened to you in the past, and what is happening to us now. When the time is right I'd like to talk to you. There must be a way back. For us, I mean."

For the first time he turned his head and looked at me and there was a gray void in his eyes, as though he didn't know who I was. It frightened me.

"Because of Peter we have to try, Joel. We have to try!" These were the reasonable words I had meant to speak. But they sounded like a cry of desperation.

He reached for the starter switch and the roar of the motor engulfed us once more. We headed at high speed back for the shore, and I found myself wondering what strange land of the mind we had visited. Joel had met some private test of his own, but I didn't know why, or what result he had found. I only knew that he had gone away from me completely and that no recovery seemed possible between us. I had intruded on some vision of his own, and now I had lost whatever chances I might have had. I'd never felt so alone in my life as when the boat shot arrow-straight back to shore and we sat there side by side.

Now the coast of Aquidneck stretched before us, with the great houses strung along the cliffs above the water, one after another, enormous as they crouched there brooding over a past that was long gone. The surf broke upon the rocks at their feet, and among them Spindrift stood out proudly, still alive, its white grace rising from lawns that retained their summer green, from among trees on the far side that were the color of October.

As we neared the shed Joel cut the speed and we idled neatly into the slip. If he had not handled a boat since he was seventeen, he could still do it skillfully. He got out on the dock, secured the line and then held out his hand to me impersonally. I made one last attempt when I was out on the dock.

"Joel, when can we talk?"

"I know everything you can say," he told me. "There's nothing left to talk about."

He went out of the shed and back up the rocks, and I followed more slowly, feeling bewildered and lost. I had done this. I had brought this about. Or had I? How well did I know my husband? Had there been a change in him long before I went into the hospital? I didn't know. I could no longer remember clearly what it had been like before my father died and I felt even more shaken than when Theo and Fiona had come to stand behind me in Theo's sitting room. I had told myself before that I was alone, but now for the first time I realized it fully. When I had told myself before, I hadn't truly believed it. Fatuously, I had always thought Joel would be there to return to when I really needed him, that it was I who had changed, not Joel. Now I believed that wasn't true. Theodora Moreland had won.

I wanted only to regain the quiet of my room and lie on the bed and rest—as she had advised me to. Yet when I reached my room and opened it, I realized that I was not yet going to rest. I put out a hand to steady myself on the side of the door as I stood staring at the strange scene before me, feeling as though I'd at last been pushed too far and was going a little mad. I had not been in my room since I had dressed to go out with Peter and Bruce, but someone else had been here.

Someone had taken my smaller possessions one by one and made a parade of them in a curving line across the red and beige carpet. Shoes and handbag, perfume bottles, lipsticks, coin purse, brush and comb, and other small articles had been lined up one after another to make a path across the room. Nothing seemed to have been damaged. The disturbance of my things lacked destructive malice, yet there was something enormously troubling about it. Troubling, perhaps, because I could not understand the intent. This was a childish thing to do. Childish?

I stepped back into the hall, closed the door, and ran down the corridor and up the stairs to Peter's room. When I knocked and went in, I found him curled on the window seat reading, while Miss Crawford knitted one of her endless anonymous garments in blue-gray wool. They both looked around as I came in.

"Hi," Peter greeted me cheerfully, and there seemed no malice in him.

"Peter," I said, "have you been down in my room since we got back from our trip?"

He shook his head. "No. I came right up here and Miss Crawford said I wasn't to go out again."

I didn't tell him what was wrong. "I just wanted to thank you for going out with me this afternoon. It was a lovely time."

"I liked it too," he admitted, and gave me the warm smile that I had not had from him for a very long while.

I went to where he sat and put an arm around him, held him close for an instant, and he did not struggle against me. Theo had not changed him irrevocably.

"I'll come back this evening and kiss you good night," I said.

He said, "That's fine," and returned to his reading. But I did not come back after all, that evening.

I left Peter with Miss Crawford and went down the hall to Theo's rooms. Fiona was not there, but Theo sat at her desk looking over bills and writing checks. She frowned at me absently as I came in.

"I think it's time," I said, "that someone tells me what is going on here at Spindrift."

She took off her green-rimmed glasses and looked at me. "Just what do you mean by that?"

"There are too many tricks being played on me. Are they by your order?"

She made an impatient gesture. "Christina, I am busy. You'll have to explain what you mean."

I told her what I had just found in my room, and she regarded me with maddening skepticism.

"Oh, come now! Why would anyone play such a silly prank?"

"That's what I'd like to know. I've checked with Peter and he wasn't the one."

"Are you sure you aren't imagining things again?"

"I'm not imagining anything. Come and see for yourself if you don't believe me."

She stood up reluctantly, a small, erect figure in her robe of citron-yellow. "Very well. I'll come."

At my side she moved more slowly than usual and I was aware of the patch of bandage on her forehead.

"Have you come to any conclusion about who struck you?" I asked her.

"Struck me? But no one struck me." She had done an about-face again. "I told you I'd become faint and then fallen. You're confused, Christina dear."

I could feel my hands tightening into fists until the nails bit into my palms, but I didn't answer her. The sight in my room would have to prove my point this time. Though as we neared the door I had the sudden anxiety that I would find all once more in order—and then how would I explain anything to Theo?

But when I opened the door the parade of small articles still marched across the floor and I waved my hand at them in triumph. Theo came into the room and stood looking down at the wavering line of objects at her feet. Then she leaned over and picked up a lipstick, examining it before holding it out to me.

"Is this yours, Christina?"

"Of course it's mine. All these things are mine. But when I came to my room just now I found that someone had taken them from where they belong and made this line across the rug."

Theo sighed. "Oh, dear. I truly don't know what to say to you, dear."

"You don't need to say anything. You just need to find out who did this and why."

"I'm afraid that's obvious, isn't it?"

"What do you mean—obvious?"

She took a quick turn about the room, the yellow of her gown shining against the red heart of the rug. Then she came back to me and put both hands soothingly on my shoulders.

"Christina, my dear, don't you see? You've just forgotten—the way you used to forget in the hospital. The way you forgot a little while ago in my sitting room. No one else has been in here. No one has touched these things but you."

I stepped back from her, staring. "You mean you believe *I* did this?"

"I know it's hard to face, dear, but that is what I think. And it will be best for you if you do face it and don't expect too much of yourself too soon."

I began to lose any last control of my poise. "Of course I didn't do it! I'm perfectly well. Someone came in here who wants to upset me and make me believe what isn't true. So that I'll not try to take Peter away from you. So that you can say I'm unbalanced and not fit to be a mother. That's it, isn't it? That's behind everything that has happened to me since I've come here."

"Oh, Christy, Christy," she said, at least dropping the Christina. "I don't know how you can make such accusations. You hurt me very much, dear."

Once more she reached out to touch me and I pushed her hand away.

"Stop pretending to be sympathetic. I know how you feel toward me. I know what you want."

With that same sad air she gestured toward the dressing table. "Look, Christy. Look in the mirror."

I didn't want to look. I was suddenly afraid of what I might see, but her tone compelled me. I stepped toward the dressing table and bent to look in the mirror. My brown gabardine was creased and stained. My hair had blown in the breeze from the ocean and it looked wild and unkempt. My eyes were staring glassily and my lips had begun to tremble. I turned away from the reflection of a woman I remembered from those first dreadful days in the hospital when I had been beside myself and helpless to fight the authority which surrounded me. But even that woman, for all her weakness and fright, had not been out of her mind. Theodora Moreland was not going to do this to me.

"I'll leave you now," she said. "Do lie down and rest, Christy. I'll send you something warm to drink. You've had an upsetting day. Don't try to come down to dinner. Everything will seem better after a night's sleep."

This was the way they used to soothe me in the hospital, when all I wanted was to find someone who would believe with me that my father had been murdered and help me to find his murderer. But there was nothing more I could say to her. If she had engineered all this, then I was wasting my breath.

When she had gone I knelt and scooped up my possessions a bit wildly, to toss them onto a chair. I would put them away later, but in the meantime I could not bear to see that straggling line across the floor, pointing at something that was untrue and that I must not for one moment believe. Ignoring the chill that crept over me, I flung myself across the bed and lay there inertly.

There had been no "lapse" from consciousness during that scene in Theo's sitting room. Nor had I been the one to strew those articles across the carpet. Not for a moment would I believe that these things were possible.

I don't know how long I lay there. Light faded from the room and I made no motion to turn on a lamp. If it was dinnertime, it didn't matter. I was freezing cold and I couldn't rouse myself to get up and pull the covers over me. It was as if any movement at all would plunge me into some terrible reality that I dared not face, that I must fight against with all my will and sanity.

When the knock came on the door I tried to ignore it, hoping whoever it was would go away and leave me alone. But it came again and Joel's voice called to me. There was nothing to do but tell him to come in.

He opened the door and crossed the room to set something on a table. I could just make him out in the light from the hall. Then he switched on a lamp and I saw that he had brought me a dinner tray. When the room was lighted, he came over to the bed and looked down at me impersonally, put out a hand to touch my forehead. He no longer looked like a man carved from rock, but he was still a stranger.

"Mother has told me what happened, Christy," he said. "Upstairs in her sitting room, and here in your room. I've brought you something to eat and something hot to drink. You're freezing cold. Don't you want to get out of your clothes and under the covers?"

"Nothing happened!" I cried. "Nothing happened! Just go away and leave me alone!"

He didn't go away. Instead, he rolled me over to one side of the bed and pulled the spread from under me, pulled down the blanket and sheet. Then, as impersonally as before, he pulled off my shoes and rolled me back into the center of the bed. My teeth were chattering by that time and I couldn't stop them.

"Hot soup first," he said, and plumped up a pillow behind me, lifted me up in the bed and piled covers around me. He held the spoon to my lips and I took the soup, grateful for its nourishing warmth, even though I wouldn't thank him. He believed what his mother had told him to believe. He belonged to the enemy camp. My sense of being totally alone increased. This was a man I couldn't reach, didn't want to reach.

When I had finished the soup as he fed it to me, a little strength returned and I reached for the bowl of hot milk toast and fed myself. An invalid's diet. There was even a cup of hot chocolate, a little too bitter for my taste, but it too warmed me. Joel sat down in a chair and watched me eat. As the chill left me, I was surprised to find myself hungry and a little less weak and shaken. At least I could speak now and when I finished I pushed away the tray.

"Thank you, Joel," I said politely. "What did your mother tell you about me?"

His eyes were as evasive as Fiona's. "I'm afraid you've had a slight relapse. There's been too much excitement for you here. Too much unrestrained emotion."

"That's the kind of emotion you've never understood, isn't it?" I said. "The sort that's unrestrained."

"I've tried to. But it's not for me. Perhaps I'm beginning to see a good many things that weren't clear before. My mother has been a lot sharper than I have. I don't like to be made a fool of, Christy."

"I don't know what you're talking about."

"This new interest of yours in Bruce Parry. Somehow I wouldn't have believed that of you, Christy. But my mother has seen what was happening."

I could only stare at him in helpless outrage. What could I say, what could I do? There was the merest whisper of truth in his words, but I had recognized the danger of casual attraction and I had already turned away from it.

"I suppose there's no way to make you believe that Theo is lying again?" I said.

His face darkened and he left his chair to pick up my tray. "Get into your night things and go to sleep. You'll feel better in the morning."

Hollow words. I wouldn't feel better in the morning, and he knew it very well. Nothing in Theodora's book of refined torment had been changed. It was getting worse with these new lies to Joel, and tomorrow it would continue. Until I cracked under it. That was what they all wanted. That was what they waited for. Theo, Joel, Fiona, Ferris. Bruce? But I would not think of Bruce. I hadn't seen him since our trip to town this afternoon and I must put him from my thoughts for good. I didn't mean to prove Theo right.

I watched Joel as he went out of the room. Ministering to me was not an unfamiliar role. On occasions when I had been ill with a cold or something else innocuous, he had brought trays to my bed, sat with me soothingly, comfortingly. And he had kissed me good night tenderly when he went away. This sort of thing he could cope with. But not anything more serious. There was no tenderness in him now, no liking for me, and I was glad when he went away. When the door was closed and he had gone, I left my bed, meaning to get into my night things. But the chill and weakness seized me again, and I removed my stained suit, pulled on slacks and my red turtleneck. Then I turned off the lamp, opened a window in the direction of dark Redstones and crept back into bed in slacks and sweater, shivering again under the covers.

But not for long. I began to feel languid and sleepy rather quickly, and I wondered if Theo had put anything into that hot chocolate. It didn't matter. If she had given me a sleeping potion I would gladly go to sleep and thank her for it. I couldn't bear consciousness any longer—with all its pain and confusion.

I closed my eyes and drowsed and dreamed. The dreams were vividly colored and dramatic, and at first they did not seem to be wholly unpleasant. Once I thought a loving Peter had come to sit beside my bed and read to me from his favorite storybook. Once it was Joel who came and for a little, little moment I thought I loved him again. Then he turned horribly into something that lay immobile on the floor of the Tower Room and I could feel warm blood on my hands, on my clothes, so I began to scream.

But the screaming must have been silent, because no

one came and the vision faded and left me awake and drenched in perspiration. Now I became aware that the windows were rattling and that a storm had blown up outside. The voice of the ocean had become a roar. I had always liked the sounds of rain and rushing wind. I knew that waves could be crashing high upon the rocks below the Cliff Walk, and it would be rather fun to go down there and watch them. My changing mood encompassed the storm and matched it, rising to meet its intensity. I wouldn't mind being outside in the rain, my clothes plastered against my body, my hair streaming moisture. There was inner elation in contemplation of such a vision. If only I didn't feel so physically languid, I would go out there and meet the wild elements.

But I was too drowsy. I fell asleep again, and dreamed, and wakened once more to the sounds of storm. In the waking moments I couldn't remember all I dreamed. Once I was being held in comforting arms, I was being told that nothing would ever be allowed to hurt me again. I had been alone and deserted, and I opened my eyes to see Bruce's face. But he was not as I knew him. There was a greater gentleness there, and I knew that I meant to him what he was beginning to mean to me. The rejection I felt when I was wide awake was gone, and I only wanted to hold to this all-enveloping comfort, but the dream would not stay and a kaleidoscope of colors took its place, weaving the darkness of my room into a bright pattern, delighting me with glorious hues. Outside I heard thunder, and lightning flashed at my open window, matching the brilliance of my inner visions. It was through this pulsing of color and sound that I heard the voice calling me.

"Christy, Christy. Wake up, Christy. I need you, Christy."

It was only a whisper—I couldn't tell who called me. But the call was insistent. It would not let me be. I cast off the bedclothes and discovered with surprise that I was warm and fully clothed in slacks and sweater. When I got out of bed my legs weaved a little and there were flashes of pulsing color as I made my way across the room. The whisper was retreating now. It was not so close. I would follow it, of course. Nothing seemed more logical. With some small semblance of care, I put on my loafers so as not to go roaming about Spindrift in my stocking feet. It was reassuring to be able to reason so well.

There was silence in the hall outside my room by the time I had slipped into my shoes, and for a moment I was afraid I had lost the whisper. But not for long, surely. I sensed that someone would be waiting for me on ahead. I felt quite calm and happy, and I seemed to float a little as I walked.

When I pushed open the door and looked out into the hall, I saw that the lights had been turned out at the far end near the stairs. It didn't matter. I could still make out the figure standing there. As I expected, it was my father. I recognized his plaid sports jacket and I knew he was waiting for me. For just a moment I wondered if I was still dreaming, because in my usual dreams Adam was never dead. I pinched my arm hard and felt pain.

"I'm coming, Adam," I said softly, and floated out into the hallway.

The figure near the stairs beckoned and disappeared downward. I would follow him, of course. I would follow my father anywhere.

11

As I had known he would, Adam waited for me on ahead. When I reached the stairway I could see him near its foot. There was only a dim light burning on the main floor, and the figure in the plaid jacket moved away from the stairs as I came down.

I was pleased with my floating motion. I hardly needed to touch the broad banister—just a tap with my fingertips now and then as I ran lightly down. Ahead of me he drifted through the dimly lighted Marble Hall and I was aware again of the storm flashing at tall windows, the thunder booming and reverberating, rain slashing against the glass. But I had no time for storms. I ran across Persian rugs and expanses of cold marble to the far doors that opened on the ballroom, and through which the figure of my father had disappeared.

He had left the double doors open behind him, and I stepped through into darkness. Here there was no light at all and the windows were made of black glass. I stood near the door, waiting for the next flash of lightning to show me where Adam had gone. But when it came it flashed brilliantly upon nothing. The great area of floor was empty, for an instant shining and polished in the explosion of light, with rows of sedate satin benches marching around the walls. But with nothing living to be seen. Then darkness swept down again and I knew I had lost him.

I called softly in the black room. "Adam, where are you? Adam, don't go away from me. Wait for me, Adam."

But there was nothing—only the violence of the storm

outside. I was waking up a little and my visions, my confident sense of floating to a sure rendezvous were fading, and in their place came a paralyzing fear. What was I doing down here in this great, dark room with the storm crashing all around? No longer was I tempted to go out and meet its fury. Someone waited for me in this emptiness that now seemed terror haunted, and I knew it was not my father. My father was dead.

The turbulence outside was subsiding a little as the storm swept on. Lightning flickered less often now and thunder rumbled intermittently in the distance, leaving in between its drums a strange, listening quiet throughout the room. A listening I knew was meant for me. A listening that had a sense of watchfulness about it that frightened me. But I listened too.

Was that a creak far across the ballroom? Had a foot moved upon some ancient board that groaned beneath its weight?

Shelter. I must find shelter—a hiding place. Without being fully aware of it, I had moved away from the door and now it was only a faint oblong of dim light far behind me. If I ran toward it I would be intercepted. I no longer felt that the spirit which had led me here was benign. There was menace around me—something that threatened my sanity.

Moving as softly as I could I went toward the nearest window and slipped behind the long crimson draperies that hung there. I remembered the crimson, though now their color was black. No one could have seen where I'd gone. There had been no flashing light for many seconds now. Only sound could have betrayed me. The heavy brocade was warm and smothering about me and I was beginning to perspire again, even though I could feel a cold draft from the window behind me, and its pane chilled my damp skin when I touched it.

I could see nothing of the ballroom, but I continued to listen, and at the same time I looked out the window toward Redstones. Black trees thrashed out there in the wind and the other house was a crouching monster in the cloud-strewn night. No light illumined any window.

My brain seemed thick and fuzzy, and there was no longer the wonderful clarity I had felt when I'd floated down the stairs following that vision of my father. I was wider awake now, but I couldn't think properly and the devastating terror of my earlier dreams was still upon me. Only now it was real. There was danger waiting for me in this room.

Somewhere a door opened and closed sharply, without effort to conceal, but I had lost my sense of direction in the dark, and I didn't know where it was. Then footsteps started boldly down the ballroom and I knew utter terror. Whoever it was knew my hiding place and was coming directly toward me. I froze as the steps paused beside me, and a hand came through the draperies and touched me. Touched my face as I had been touched in my own bed once in the middle of the night. But this hand grasped at me, caught me roughly by the shoulder. I struggled wildly as the heavy draperies were thrust aside and a flashlight beam blinded me. I tried to cry out, to scream for help, but my throat had closed. The hands that grasped me shook me hard and a voice I knew spoke to me.

"Christy, Christy! Stop fighting me. Open your eyes. I'm not going to hurt you. What on earth are you doing here?"

I obeyed and ceased my struggling as I looked up into Bruce's face. Then I sagged limply into his arms and he held me gently.

"You frightened me terribly!" I gasped.

"I'm sorry. I thought I'd caught our nighttime intruder. Tell me why you're here."

My words must have been nearly incoherent, but I poured them out with my cheek against the wetness of his raincoat that told me he had just come in from outside. I explained breathlessly about following my father downstairs, about losing him here in the ballroom, and about the menace that hid in the darkness until Bruce had come.

When the outpourings were done, he released me gently.

"Stay right here while I turn on the lights," he said and walked away from me to a wall switch.

The chandeliers blazed, so that the great ballroom glittered with light and I could see Bruce standing by the switch in his wet raincoat with the flashlight in his hand. There was no one else there. Whoever it was had escaped. As Bruce came toward me his eyes were troubled and questioning.

"I'm all right now," I said in answer to that question. "I think Theo put something in the drink she sent me before I went to sleep. It was like some of those drugs they gave me in the hospital—I had wild dreams and things happened that seemed real when they weren't. But, Bruce, I saw my father. I'm not hallucinating now and I know what was real and what wasn't. I saw him."

"Yes, Christy." His tone was still gentle. "You thought you saw him. Look. Look here."

He walked to a near corner of the room and picked up something that had been dropped behind another concealing drapery, with only the edge of it showing. But Bruce had seen. He drew out my father's plaid jacket and held it up.

"This is what you saw, Christy, but someone else was wearing it."

"To lure me," I said. "To make me think I was mad."

I took the jacket from him and clasped it to me, as though I held my father. The terrible shivering was upon me again.

"If you hadn't found me—" I faltered. "If you hadn't—"

"Hush," he said and drew me into comforting arms again, as though I belonged there. It was like the dream I'd had of him, when I'd known I wasn't alone any more.

"I knew there was someone behind that drapery the moment I moved my flashlight around the room," he said. "The bulge gave your presence away. I'm sorry I frightened you."

I couldn't stop my trembling, even in his arms, and he began to propel me across the room.

"Come along, Christy. We'll get some hot coffee. I need some myself by this time."

I went with him without question as he turned out the lights and led the way to the small rose and cream dining room, sat me gently in a chair and busied himself with the coffeepot on the buffet. When the brew was percolating, he came back and drew a chair up to sit close to me, took my two hands in his and held them in comforting warmth.

"You're all right now. You can stop shivering. No one is going to hurt you."

"They want me to go mad. They want to frighten me so badly that I'll believe I'm ill again and go back to the hospital. Then Theo can have Peter to raise and there will be no threat to whoever it was who killed my father."

He said nothing. He neither agreed nor disagreed. He simply held my hands and let me draw strength from his strong clasp. When the bubbling stopped he went to pour us each a cup of black coffee. I sipped mine gratefully and felt my shivering lessen. But there was a great weariness in me, a helplessness because I lacked the strength to struggle any longer against Theo's ingenious methods of torment.

"She'll stop at nothing to get rid of me," I said between gulps of hot coffee. "And I'm not strong enough to go on fighting her forever. Fighting them all. Perhaps it's time to give up and go away."

"Don't go away," he said. "Stop fighting them, but don't go away. You're winning Peter back. Isn't that what matters?"

I finished the coffee and set my cup on the table. "I don't know what matters any more. I'm frightened and confused. Who is doing this to me?"

"We're always more confused and discouraged when it's nighttime. And you know who is behind it."

"Yes—Theo. But who is her surrogate? Right now I feel beaten by a dreadful night and by all those accusations Theo made. Though of course you don't know about them."

"I know. She talked of nothing else at dinner."

"What did Joel say? Did he believe her too? Because if he did, between them they'll have the power to send me back to that place."

There was pity in Bruce's eyes. "I don't know. But look, Christy, you're not alone here. For whatever it's worth, I'm with you. I spoke up pretty sharply at dinner. They all glowered at me because that isn't what Theo wants."

His words brought me a certain reassurance. I had been so terribly alone and now, somehow, I wasn't. I didn't think he or anyone else could really stand up to Theo's machinations, but it was something for him to offer. A thought came into my mind that I hadn't considered till now. A question.

"Why were you out in the storm at this hour? Were you over at Redstones?"

"Yes," he said. "I've been there, waiting, for some hours. If anyone came, if anyone lighted a candle, I wanted to know who it was."

"And did you find anyone?"

"No. Nothing stirred in the whole house except mice and the usual creakings in an old place."

"It's lucky for me that you were coming across just when you were. Thank you for rescuing me. I think I'll go back to bed now." I sounded stiff to my own ears, but I had been so recently in his arms, letting myself go, and I had no knowledge that he really wanted me there. He had offered me protection and comfort. As anyone would, but I was still alone as I came to my senses.

I picked up my father's jacket, but before I could leave, Bruce stopped me and there was a sudden lighting in his eyes.

"No, Christy. Don't go yet. Do you realize that the night is nearly over? It's already dawn and in a few minutes the sun will be coming up. The storm has blown away, and you mustn't miss sunrise over Lands End. Are you warm now? Can you stay up a little longer?"

I slipped my arms into the sleeves of my father's jacket and pulled its comforting bulk around me.

"I'll be fine," I said. "I'd love to see the sun come up."

I took the hand he held out to me and he led the way to a side door. We went out into a dripping wet world and I saw that the sky had lightened in the east.

The grass was wet as we ran across it and so were the stones of the wall beside the Cliff Walk as Bruce helped me over. We went to stand where the rocks began, with the white froth of waves breaking beneath. The ocean was still angry after the storm and it boiled and chopped against the rocky barrier, sending its spray nearly high enough to reach us. There were still clouds low on the horizon to catch the tints and the sky was turning a glorious azalea color, with a fury of black clouds still scudding by overhead.

Bruce put his arm about me and I stood close to him, asking nothing more than this moment as the sun came up, turning the sky rosy gold over the water, gliding a path straight to our feet. I looked up at Bruce and saw the brightness of the sun in his eyes. He bent his head and kissed me and I gave myself to the caress. This was what I needed, what I had not dared to face or accept in myself.

"Christy," he said, "Christy," and put his face against my hair.

I clung to him until he held me gently away.

"We'll go back now," he said. "I haven't wanted this to happen. I thought I was resisting it. It wasn't in my plan to love you."

"Plan?" I echoed.

He started toward the house and I went with him, that single word echoing in my mind. He did not answer until we were over the wall and crossing the wet grass, with the

189

brightening world at our backs. When he spoke there was a harsh note in his voice that troubled me.

"Exactly," he said. "Plan. Theodora Moreland's plan to break up your marriage. I was to be the instrument."

I looked up at him with swimming eyes. So this was why Theo had said those things to Joel. She had meant this all along. She had even involved Bruce, and now I was truly frightened. I didn't want this comforting moment to slip away and be lost forever in the acting out of a lie.

But Bruce was speaking again. "I told her I wouldn't go along and she got a bit threatening—which I don't like. It's possible to work for other news chains. After I met you and saw the way you've become since you left the hospital, I was all the more anxious not to see you hurt in any way. I don't want to hurt you now."

So perhaps he had not acted a lie. Perhaps he had kissed me because he wanted to. He was like my father, I thought. He would stand up to Theo. He would do only what he chose to do.

"I'm not hurt," I said. "I'm happy. For this little moment I'm happy."

"I don't know what the answers are," Bruce said. "I don't know what to do about you. Perhaps I'd better tell Theo where to get off. I'd better cut and run—go back to New York."

"I can't bear it if you go away," I said. "Not until I can leave. You're my only friend here, and I can't leave yet. You have to understand that. I was only speaking out of fear a little while ago when I said I must go away."

"I do understand. But I don't think it's sensible if you have to go on as you've started. There's too much working against you here. Some of it's silly, and some of it could be dangerous. It depends on how aroused Theo gets, how much of a threat she considers you."

This past night had been dangerous, I thought. The threat had been real. I looked at Bruce as we neared the house and I wanted to be in his arms again. But it was bright daylight outside and all the windows of Spindrift seemed to be watching us. It was better not to bait the house.

"A little while ago I was nearly ready to give up," I said. "Nearly beaten. But you were right—that was partly night vapors and the fright I'd had. Besides, I haven't shaken off all the fumes of that drug, whatever it was. But I've got back my courage. I'll stay now and see this through."

"On one hand, I'm sorry," he said as we went through the door. "But on the other, I'll always salute courage. A brave woman is my kind of woman."

We did not touch each other again, even though no one stirred in the downstairs rooms. I think we were both a little afraid of what might happen if we gave in to the longing for one more embrace. All the problems were still there between us. Joel and I were ready to part, but whether I could leave him I didn't know. Because of Peter. Always because of Peter. Too many battles still lay ahead of me. I would need my vaunted courage.

Bruce let me go upstairs alone, so that we wouldn't be seen coming in together, but I didn't go straight to my room. Early as it was, there was something I had to know. I went to tap on Fiona's door.

"It's Christy," I said softly. "I want to see you, Fiona."

I heard her bed creak, heard her moan as she tried to rouse herself. Then she called to me weakly to come in.

I went into the room still wearing my father's jacket and she stared at me with something like horror in her eyes. I stood beside her bed relentlessly.

"Did you come to my room wearing this last night? Did you run ahead of me down the stairs, knowing I'd be dizzy with whatever drug it was Theo gave me with my supper? Did you know I'd follow you?"

She seemed too startled by my presence to speak. I bent over her, took her shoulder in my hand and shook her.

"Wake up, Fiona. Wake up and tell me the truth. Was it you down in the ballroom?"

She pushed my hand away and sat up in bed. "I don't know what you're talking about. I took a sleeping pill myself and I'd still be asleep if you hadn't wakened me."

"How did this get out of your possession?" I said, slipping out of Adam's jacket and holding it up before her.

"I don't know. I had it packed away in Adam's suitcase in my closet."

"And you didn't put it on and go to my room? You didn't try to fool me into thinking Adam was calling me?"

"Of course not, Christy. I—I've done some things, but not that."

"Then who do you think did?"

"I don't know. I don't know at all."

"You didn't hear them plotting, working out this scheme to terrify me?"

She squirmed under the covers and tried to slide down beneath them. "I don't know anything about it, Christy."

I thought she did. But there would be no way to get the truth out of her, and I gave up, throwing the jacket over my arm.

"I'm going to keep this," I said. "Maybe it means more to me than it does to you."

As I walked to the door she was silent and I didn't look back at her. When I reached my room I hung up Adam's jacket among my clothes. It would be good to have it there to comfort me. Then I stood for a moment looking down at the disturbed blankets and sheets I had tossed aside last night. I could remember all too well my sense of conviction as I'd followed that lure to the stairway. I had really believed I was following my father. But that had been the drug they'd given me. I wasn't confused any longer. I hadn't fallen into the trap of believing in my own madness—which was undoubtedly what Theo wanted. Joel had brought me that tray. He had handed me the cup of bitter chocolate. Had he known what his mother was doing? Could it have been he who had worn that jacket? But no—the Joel I'd known would never have done a thing like that. And he had seemed scornful about my possible interest in Bruce. Hurt, perhaps?

Weariness enveloped me suddenly—and a terrible sense of hopelessness that I had been able to shake off for a little while when I was with Bruce. This time I undressed properly and put on my nightgown. Then I got into bed knowing that all I wanted for the moment was to sleep.

I tried to put away all terrifying remembrance, and think only of Bruce—of his arms about me and his kiss on my mouth. But the belief I'd felt so strongly while he held me was already fading. Now, in the loneliness of my bed, I could no longer be sure of what I felt for him. To love so quickly—that was too easy. It might not be real for either of us. Love was something that grew with intimacy and knowledge. And it was something that declined. I turned my face against my pillow and cried myself to sleep.

I must have slept for several hours and then only a knocking on my door awakened me. Drowsily I called, "Come in."

To my surprise, it was Miss Crawford and she was looking thoroughly flustered and not at all her self-possessed self.

"Is Peter with you, Mrs. Moreland?" she asked.

I sat up at once. "No, of course not. I won't take him again without letting you know. What's happened?"

"He's slipped away from me." She was practically wringing her hands. "I left him for only a few moments and he was deep in a book, so I never thought he'd go out. But he's vanished completely."

"Is he with his grandmother?"

"No. I went to her rooms and he's not there. I—I didn't tell her I couldn't find him. I wanted to check with you first. His outdoor things are gone, so I thought you might have taken him out."

I was already reaching for my clothes. "Don't worry. I

think I know where he may have gone. I'll get dressed and go look for him. You needn't say anything to anyone till I get back."

She gave me a look of gratitude and scurried away. Poor thing. She probably knew her fate at Theo's hands if Peter's grandmother found out that he had slipped from her care.

I splashed water on my face and once more got into slacks and a sweater. Then I left my room and hurried down the hall. A maid asked if I wanted breakfast brought upstairs and I told her, "No," but I saw no one else.

A bright sun overhead had dried the grass, though some of the trees still glistened with rain from last night. I ran across the lawns to Redstones and went around to the front gate. It was locked, but the scrolls and grillwork of wrought iron gave me hand- and footholds and I climbed over it as Peter could have done. I ran up the drive to the front steps and from the balcony columns the two gargoyle faces grinned at me evilly. The front door too was locked and I walked around the yard past the tumbled urn until I found a basement window I could get through. It had been left ajar, so perhaps Peter had been there ahead of me.

It was not difficult to squeeze my body through the opening, though I snagged my sweater. Uncertainly I felt for some foothold, but there seemed to be none, and I let myself drop to the floor. My legs went out from under me as I landed and I sprawled on the gritty cement, but I was not hurt and I jumped up at once and began to look around.

The basement was a dank, musty place, crowded with furnace, washtubs, old refrigerators, water tanks and other bulky objects discarded from the floors above. Very little light seeped through the few dirty panes of high windows, and the place seemed oppressive in its silence. I didn't think Peter was down here. Where the back stairs were, I didn't know, but I disliked the idea of wandering through the darkness of an expanse of basement that ran beneath this entire monster of a house.

Before I moved away from the window, however, I tried calling Peter's name, just to make sure. My shouting sounded eerie in this dim, echoing place, and there was no answer, and I didn't really expect one.

Within a few steps from the window I was lost amid the clutter of generations. Cobwebs streaked clammy strands across my face and once there was a skittering at my feet that made me step back hurriedly. I wasn't going to take fright over a mouse, but there might be rats in a place like this. I must find the stairs quickly.

As I stumbled about, the heavy dusk of the huge area began to seem like a palpable threat, impeding and smothering me. The stale, unaired smell made it hard to draw a deep breath, and now and then I stood very still, listening. For the first time I wondered if Miss Crawford's plea for help had been genuine. What if this were another trap? What a good idea to coax me over to Redstones where no one would hear me even if I screamed, and where I would be at the mercy of anyone who might be hunting me.

But I shook off the thought determinedly. Crawford had been upset and concerned. I doubted if she was that good an actress to convince me otherwise. And besides, no one could know that this was the place I would come to first to look for my son if he had run off on his own.

I found the stairs by banging into the side of them in a dark corner and bumping my knees. The door at the top was closed, but I ran up to it and found it unlocked. Once through the door, I was in a narrow hallway off the kitchen at the back of the house. I followed it to the main dining room, hurried through the smaller morning room and a library with nearly empty shelves, then into a wider hall. This crossed to the big drawing room where we'd been the other day. Now I knew my way and I began to call again for Peter.

My voice rang startlingly loud in the emptiness and

echoes threw it back to me as though in mockery. I found my way to the front entry hall that Theo had put down as being inferior to Spindrift's. The partial suit of armor that had intrigued Peter still stood guard, and the threadbare hunt scene of the tapestry looked down from the high stairwell with its bounding hounds and fleeting deer.

There was no answer to my calls, but at least it was not as dark up here in the main part of the house. While windows were mostly shuttered and doors closed, sunlight had a way of trickling through any crack, and shadowy though it was, I could at least see my way.

I didn't call again until I'd mounted the first flight of stairs to the second floor. Then I set the echoes ringing once more with my son's name. There was no answer at all. Of course he might be hiding. He could know very well that I was looking for him and mischievously keep his presence secret. I was still convinced that he was here somewhere at Redstones. If he had run away from supervision, this was the most likely place for him to come.

But bedroom after bedroom stood empty. When I reached the small room where we had found the candle, I looked in the closet and saw the flight bag had not been disturbed. I opened it and took out the flashlight. There might well be some need for it in my search.

On up the flight of stairs to the third floor I went. I had never been up here before beneath the eaves of the house. Redstones was not as large a place as Spindrift, but it was still a castle compared with modern houses, and there was room after room to look into. Most were bedrooms on this floor, smaller rooms, which had undoubtedly belonged to the servants in those great days of entertaining which Newport had once known, when an army of live-in help was the pattern. But there was nothing here of any interest, and no small boy sprang out in a delighted attempt to frighten me. My calls brought no answer and while I disliked the clamor they aroused in the emptiness, the stillness when I was silent was even worse. At least I needn't fear a trap. If there had been one it would have been sprung before this.

I went back to the head of the third-floor stairs and stood listening. It was darker here in the hall than in the rooms, where daylight shone between shutter slats, and I turned my flashlight upon the steps. They dropped away from my feet more steeply than the stairs to the lower floor, carpetless and scuffed. I must go down them carefully. It wouldn't do to fall and break something in this lonely spot. No one might come to my help for days. The fear of falling prompted a frightening thought.

What if that was what had happened to Peter? What if he had fallen somewhere and hurt himself? What if he were lying helpless in some corner that I had missed in my searching? But surely he had a good pair of lungs and he would have managed to answer my shouting if he needed help. He would have answered if he could.

There was a clamminess of sudden dread that made my palms damp. Peter might not have come here at all, in spite of his interest in the house. He might have gone down to the rocks along the ocean, or even to the boat-house. Motors of any sort had a fascination for him and in my mind's eye I could see him heading out to sea, joyfully daring in a boat he could not handle. If I hadn't been wakened so suddenly from sleep, I might have thought things through a little better. I shouldn't have come rushing over here alone. I should have gone to Joel and Bruce so that we could each search in a different place. Peter wasn't here and I had wasted time making the wrong try.

I ran down the steep steps with less caution than I'd planned, and I didn't pause at the second floor, but went on again, down to the main hall. There I had the feeling that I was being peered at from between the hinges of that tarnished visor on the suit of armor. But the armor was legless and empty.

Armor! What was it I had heard? Had it been Peter

197

who had told me that Theron Townsend of Redstones had collected suits of armor and weapons, and had a room for them in the house? He and Ferris had talked about this. If Peter came here alone, that was the room he would want to see. But I had found no such room in my searching. Wait—whoever had mentioned this had spoken of the basement—of a special room built into the basement. Of course.

I ran back through the rooms of the main floor till I found the basement stairs, glad now of the flashlight whose beam could light my way into those dark regions. There was a skittering again across the broken cement floor, but it did not stop me, and I only brushed cobwebs aside impatiently as I turned the flashlight from side to side.

The door was at the back of the long expanse and it was closed. Its knob balked at my first effort to turn it, but I tried again and the door swung open upon blackness. There were no windows here, so that the sense of airlessness was greater than ever, and the smell of dust was stifling. The floor was of damp, cold stone, like the floor of an ancient castle.

I choked and coughed as I swung the beam of my flash in a wide circle that caught the gleam of metal from all those armored figures which stood about the room rusting now, with the passing years. Everything was here, from helmets and visors to breastplates, skirts of chain mail, loin guards, kneepieces, greaves for the shins and sollerets that covered the feet. I knew something about armor because Peter and I had spent some time reading about the knights of the Middle Ages and we had visited museums to look at armor more than once. If Peter was anywhere in this house, it should be here.

I called to him again and kept the beam of my light moving inch by inch around the room, but no small boy answered me. Only those leering visors stared, an occasional gauntleted hand was raised toward me, and I could almost hear the clatter of hollow laughter from all these empty men. Above the mounted suits of armor the walls had been used to display weapons of various sorts—spears and swords and axes, along with the shields that had been raised against them. When I turned the flash beam upward I saw that the ceiling was vaulted, carrying out the medieval character of the room. Where no weapons had been hung there were tapestries, mildewed now, and the worse for neglect.

Peter would love this place, but he was not here.

I turned off my flashlight to save the batteries and stood still in the center of the long room, listening. If my son were hiding he would surely make some sound in the darkness. But there was not even the skitter of mice in here to break the silence. Yet there was something—not a sound, but something my eyes began to make out as they grew accustomed to the black room about me. It was a faint glow that seemed to come from a far corner.

I turned on my flash and followed its beam, but with the light on there was nothing to be seen—nothing but a patch of blackness on the stone floor. I walked toward it, puzzled, and when I switched off the light again that faint yellow glow seemed to come from the black square.

In moments I had hurried to the corner, my flashlight beam revealing what appeared to be an opening in the floor where a sliding wooden hatch cover had been drawn back. It was from this opening that the faint glow emerged. I remembered that Ferris had spoken of an underground vault in the room of armor—and this must be it. My light was too weak to penetrate the depths, but it showed me a ladder that dropped out of sight, showed me a broken wooden rung. The break in the wood looked raw and recent. My heart began to thud.

Kneeling above the opening, I tried vainly to see into the room below where a pinpoint of light burned, giving off the glow I had seen. Once more I called for Peter. There was no immediate answer, but something down here moaned faintly.

"Peter!" I called again. "Peter, can you hear me?"

199

The faint mumbling and moaning came again and I began to talk softly, coaxingly.

"Peter darling, everything is going to be all right. I'm going to get you out of there as soon as I can. Peter, can you tell me if anything hurts?"

The faint tremor of his voice reached me. "My head hurts. And my leg."

I examined the ladder with my flash, but I didn't dare trust my weight to a rung lest I too be dropped into the pit of this underground vault. This time when I turned off the flash I realized what made the glow that had caught my eye. Peter had brought his own flashlight with him and it had remained on when he dropped it in his fall. It was still glowing down there, but it might not last too long and he would soon be left in darkness.

"I'm going for help," I told him. "We'll have you out of there as quickly as we can. Do you hear me, Peter?"

"I can hear you, Mother," he said weakly.

I used my flashlight to get back through the rows of armor and through the bulk-obstructed basement to the window that had let me in. I had to find a packing crate to place beneath it so I could clamber out. Then I was up and through, out into the sunlight again, to climb the gate and run toward Spindrift and the help I must get for my son.

12

Before I had gone far across the grounds, I came upon Peter's friend John, the head gardener. I didn't want him to try to get Peter out alone, and I told him quickly what had happened, sent him to find Joel, or anyone at all who could come at once to Peter's rescue.

"Tell him to bring ropes," I said. "I'm going back and stay with my son. So hurry, do!"

The old man went off at a good pace and I ran back to Redstones. I had become adept at climbing gates, tumbling through windows, and I hardly noticed my barked shins and bleeding knuckles. My anxiety was growing, and so was my self-blame by the time I reached the armor room and ran to kneel at the opening in the floor.

"Somebody will be coming soon," I called to Peter. "I've sent John for help. Are you all right?"

He answered me with a muffled sound of pain, and I knew I had to get down to him. This time it wouldn't matter if I was dropped into that space beside him. I thrust my flashlight into the band of my slacks to free my hands, and then knelt at the top of the ladder to feel gingerly backwards with one foot for a rung that would bear my weight. The third rung seemed to hold and I began my descent, step by step, testing first and holding tightly to the sides of the ladder as I went down.

The next-to-the-last rung broke, but I dropped only a few inches, landing safely on the stone floor of the room. My flash beam picked out Peter where he lay, curled up in pain, and when I knelt beside him and raised his head, I could feel the lump at the back.

"I think my leg cracked," he told me. "It hurt a lot when I fell, and it still hurts now."

The light beam showed me his twisted leg and although his pain seemed my pain, I tried to reassure him. "Someone will come soon. We'll get you to a doctor quickly. Just lie very still, darling."

"I've never had a broken leg before," he said with a certain pride, and I laughed softly with tears in the sound.

"I could hear you calling me when you went through the basement," he went on. "But I couldn't make you hear me. I tried, but my voice wasn't strong, and after a while I didn't try any more. Mother, before the others come, will you do something, please? Maybe it will scare you, but I have to know."

"Whatever you want, Peter."

"You've got a flashlight. Go look at the suit of armor down at the end wall of this place. Don't be afraid—just look at it."

His request seemed an odd one, but I turned my light on the rest of that small room and walked about it. Now I could see the steel safes built into the walls, which were the reason for the room's being, their knobs and dials gleaming as light swept over them. The rusting suit of armor that stood in a corner against the wall seemed out of place, and I wondered why it had been brought down here. As my light beam flashed over it, however, I could see nothing unusual.

"I'm looking at it," I called to Peter, "but I don't know what I'm supposed to see."

"Don't be scared," he repeated. "But just open that visor and look inside."

His warnings alerted me to some unexpected horror, and I was reluctant to raise the grinning metal shield.

"Please," Peter said. "Mother, I have to be sure."

I held the flash in one hand and fumbled with the other for a way to part the sections of the visor. The closed edges opened with a clatter upon what would have been the face of the wearer. But what looked out at me was a naked skull—hollow-eyed and lipless, the strong teeth grinning more fearfully than the visor had grinned. I let the visor fall and went back to Peter.

"How did you know? What did you mean—you had to be sure?"

He roused himself to answer me. "The first time I came down today it was because I found the hatch open and I was curious. The ladder was okay and I didn't fall. So I was poking around down here with my flash and when I saw the armor I opened the visor. I guess what I saw scared me a lot, and I climbed back up the ladder and was going to run home to Spindrift. But before I climbed out the basement window I began to wonder if I'd really seen what I thought I saw. Because if I had maybe the thing that looked out at me was real, and not just a joke of Mr. Townsend's. If it was real I would have to tell somebody. I didn't want to really, because then Grandma Theo wouldn't want me to come here any more. Not alone, anyway."

For a moment he was silent and his mouth tightened in the light from my flash that I'd set on the floor beside us. His hand reached out to touch me and I held it in my own cold one. Perhaps we comforted each other.

"It was awfully scary coming down the second time," he went on. "I guess I wasn't as careful as I was at first, and that rung cracked and I fell from near the top. My head hurt and my leg was twisted, and I was awfully afraid nobody would find me here. It got worse when I heard you calling upstairs and I couldn't make you hear me. And all the time that awful thing was over there. If it really was what I thought. So I wanted you to check and see. Do you think it's real, Mother?"

"I'm afraid so," I said. This hardly bore thinking about. If there was a skull behind the visor, then there was likely to be what was left of the whole man concealed in that suit of armor. Concealed because murder had been committed?

"After a while, I guess it won't be so scary," Peter said.

"When I'm away from here and I get used to it, maybe it will seem exciting—like an adventure. But I'm glad you came. I didn't want to be here alone with—that. I couldn't even reach my flashlight because it hurt so much to move, and I knew the beam would burn out after a while, so I'd be in darkness. Then after enough time went by, I'd be just like that—thing in there."

"Hush, darling," I said, squeezing his hand. "I did come, and soon there'll be others and we'll get you out of here." But the possibilities of his imagining chilled me.

"We'll have to tell, won't we?" he said.

"Yes, of course. But that's not the most important thing now."

In the distance I could hear voices. I had told John where to find us, and I called out as loudly as I could. There were answering shouts, and before long footsteps were sounding overhead. I heard Joel's voice calling me, but inevitably Theo had come too, and I could hear her crying out in alarm, with Ferris trying to quiet her.

"Down here!" I shouted again. "We're down here in the vault. There's an opening in the corner. But watch the ladder—it's got a broken rung."

They had brought lanterns, which lighted a greater area than our torches, and when Joel held his above the opening, the small room of the vault glowed, showing up its horrid interior. All three were peering down at us through the opening, and I warned them quickly that Peter had a broken leg and a bumped head, so they would have to take care about getting him up. Theo exclaimed in distress and Ferris spoke beyond Joel.

"There's an old hammock around here somewhere. I'll see if I can find it. It will make a good sling for getting him up."

He went bumping about the basement and Joel called down to his son. "Hang on, Peter, and we'll have you up in no time."

I could see Theo's face in the lantern light and the shadows thrown upward made her look old as a witch and as menacing. That she was angry was clear, and of course it was with me.

"What were you and Peter doing in this dangerous place? Why did you bring him here where he could be hurt?"

Peter answered before I could speak, weak but indignant. "Mother didn't come with me. And it wasn't Miss Crawford's fault. I didn't ask anybody. I just waited till I had a chance to sneak away, and then I came by myself."

"Then how do you come to be here, Christy?" Joel asked, his tone colder than his mother's and without the passion of her anger.

I tried to explain. "When Miss Crawford couldn't find him, she came to see if he was with me. I thought I knew where he might have gone because I've heard him talk about wanting to explore Redstones."

"Then you should have come directly to me," Theo said severely. "If you had used your head that's what you would have done, instead of coming over here alone and letting no one know."

In this case she was right and I had to agree. "I know that now," I said meekly. "But I did find him and I did get help."

They both looked down at me with disapproval and I was glad when Ferris came back with the woven hammock in his hands.

The two men climbed carefully down and Peter was folded gently into the hammock. Between them they carried him up through the opening. He groaned once or twice, but he was trying to be brave and cause as little extra trouble as possible. Theo began to croon over him and I knew his care had been taken out of my hands.

"Can you get up the ladder, Christy?" Joel called down to me, still cold and remote.

"Yes, of course," I told him. "I'll come right up."

The lanterns moved away from the opening in the floor, so that once more I had only my flashlight. I picked it up and started up the ladder. But it had taken enough strain on its rotting rungs, and the first one I stepped on broke beneath my weight. The ones above felt rickety too and I was doubtful about trusting them. In the basement above everyone was moving away, and I could see myself left behind and helpless to get out.

"Somebody help me!" I called. "The ladder's breaking up."

Joel must have given the burden of Peter over to Ferris, for he came back with a lantern. "I've got a rope here," he said when he saw the problem. "If the ladder won't hold, I can pull you up."

"Can you come down first?" I said. "There's something here you need to see."

He looked down at me impatiently. "I'd like to get back to Peter. This is no time to be whimsical, Christy. Whatever's down there can wait."

"Yes," I said. "I'm sure it can. It's a dead man and he's probably waited quite a while already."

I heard his gasp of disbelief and knew he thought I was having aberrations again. But he busied himself fastening the rope to some well-anchored object in the room above, and then came gingerly down the ladder, holding onto the rope. The rest of the rungs held.

"Now show me what you're talking about," he said.

Reaction was beginning to set in and my teeth had started to chatter. I couldn't bear to go over and open that visor again. I handed him my flashlight.

"Look inside that suit of armor over in the corner, Joel."

It took him only a moment to walk to the corner and open the visor. He came back to me at once. "I don't know what's there, but we'll have to report this. Now let's get back to Peter."

With Joel behind me and the security of the rope to hold onto, I managed the ladder safely and crawled out on top. The others were gone from the basement and we hurried upstairs to leave through the front door Ferris had left open. The wrought-iron gate was open too and when we'd gone through it and walked around the house in the direction of Spindrift, we saw Ferris ahead of us carrying Peter, and Theo a tiny figure in sweater and green slacks beside his tall one, fairly running to keep up with his long stride. We caught up with them as they went into the house and Ferris carried Peter, hammock and all, to one of the brocaded sofas in the Marble Hall.

"Rest there for now," he said, putting him down gently. "I'm going to phone the doctor. Then we'll get you upstairs."

Peter looked white with strain and his eyes were closed, his lips firmly shut against the sound he might have made. I pushed past Theo and knelt beside him.

"It's all right to cry if it hurts," I said. "You have a right to feel frightened and upset. But it's over now."

He turned his head against my arm, wanting my comfort, and my sense of self-blame increased. If I'd been able to be a better mother none of this would have happened.

Theo stood beside me, her fury growing. "It's your fault that he was down there," she accused. "You've been encouraging his interest in Redstones, so of course he'd have to run away and go over there."

I was silent. She couldn't blame me more than I blamed myself.

Joel put an arm about his mother. "Don't get any more distressed over this. Peter will be all right now. There's no use blaming and accusing."

"You don't mean to tell me you think Christina is a proper mother to Peter, or that she has behaved like one?" she cried.

"I'm afraid she hasn't," Joel said and his look condemned my actions. "You could have at least let us know, Christy. You haven't been acting with good judgment lately."

There was nothing to say. They were all against me,

and this time with justification. Ferris came back from the phone, and Joel picked Peter up and turned toward the stairs.

Theo spoke to me sharply. "Don't come with us. We don't need you and you'd only weaken Peter with your emotionalism."

I started to answer her heatedly, but she turned her back on me and followed Joel up the stairs. I heard Peter's faint cry, "Mother, come with me!" as they bore him away. But when I would have run after them, Ferris held my arm.

"Let them go, Christy. Peter really doesn't need you now. His father is there. And you can't go on upsetting everyone like this."

He turned from me too, as the others had, and I stayed behind, helpless and useless, trembling with frustration. I wanted to cry out against them all, but I knew no one would listen, and in a moment I might go thoroughly to pieces in weak anger. I didn't want that and I ran to the nearest door and let myself out of the house. There was release in running down toward the ocean and I was out of breath by the time I reached the wall and went over it.

I climbed onto the rocks above the water and sat where the spray would touch me as it broke, where I could feel a part of that green energy that rolled in so fiercely from the ocean deeps. Somehow I could take strength from the elements, and feel myself growing calmer in the face of forces so much greater and so much more eternal than myself. I tried not to think of what had occurred, or what was happening back at the house. Eventually, of course, I would go to Peter. They couldn't keep me from him. But not now. Last night and now this! Nevertheless, I somehow managed to let go, to let anger and fear and the terrible sense of helplessness drain out of me as I listened to the rushing of the waves.

I don't know how long I sat there with the sun warm on my hair and the wind from the sea cold against my face. Once I put my head against my drawn-up knees and dozed for a moment or two because I'd had very little sleep last night. Then I awakened and thought of Bruce. He had held me and kissed me down here at sunrise, a long time ago. And he had said that he hadn't meant to love me. How much did that mean? For now I wanted only to have his arms about me comfortingly. I wanted a friend who would stand beside me against those who would take my son away and put me back in the hospital. Yet if I went to the comfort of his arms I would give Theo the power to move against me and take Peter away.

It seemed natural, and almost expected, when I heard a step on the rocks behind me and turned my head to see Bruce standing there. He was like the man of last night's dream, with a gentleness and affection in him, a consideration that no one had given me for a very long time. Not since my father had died. Yet Theo had in a sense hired this man to break up my marriage, and he had not altogether refused to do her bidding. What was I to believe?

He sat down on the rocks, making no move to touch me. "I thought you might like to know that the doctor has come and he has set Peter's leg. It's a simple fracture, though he'll be in a cast for a while. His spirits are good. He's beginning to look on the whole thing as an exciting adventure."

"Thank you for coming to tell me," I said. "Is everyone still angry with me?"

He looked for a moment as though he did not want to answer that. Then he shrugged. "You might as well know that Theo is busy whipping up criticism and prejudice against you. It's to be expected."

"And Joel goes along with it?"

He didn't answer that, but looked off toward the waves that rolled endlessly in upon the shore of the island. Perhaps he was wondering why I had ever married Joel, though he would never ask me that question. I answered it, unasked.

"Joel was in love with me in the beginning," I said, and sounded unintentionally defensive.

"That isn't hard to believe."

"I was having a difficult time at home. Fiona and I didn't always get along, and my father was gambling heavily and making us both miserable."

"I remember," Bruce said. "I don't mean I remember that particular time, but I knew about his compulsion to gamble. I'm not a gambler in the same way, but I think I can understand what Adam felt. There's a fascination about insecurity and danger. Life can seem very flat when there is nothing to be risked."

I glanced up at him. "You *are* a little like him."

"But Joel never was?" he said.

"Not at all. And I knew that. But at the time it seemed wonderfully safe to find a man who didn't want to take risks. I was angry and disgusted with Adam. I had quarreled with him. Running off with Joel was a way of flinging all my hurt and resentment in my father's face. So that's what I did. Though it wasn't as coldblooded as all that. I loved Joel. I think I loved him."

"I don't think you'd found out what love is," Bruce said. "Perhaps you will someday."

Was I finding out now? I wondered. And did I dare to find out?

"Adam used to say that all life was a gamble," I went on. "Marriage, the work one went into, how one invested money. Even painting a picture or writing a book was a gamble. This was always his defense—that he was no different from anyone else—only more honest about his gambling."

"The catch is that his sort of gambler produces nothing," Bruce said. "That's the difference."

"But he produced too!" I cried. "He was good at his job. The gambling wasn't his whole life as it is with some men. He could even let it alone for months at a stretch when something important was brewing on the paper."

"That's right," Bruce agreed. "He couldn't be beaten at his job."

We were silent for a while after that, and then, slowly

at first, and more quickly as the words began to pour out, I told him the whole story of what had just happened over at Redstones. And I asked for no mercy over my own misjudgment. I told him about finding Peter and getting help, about going down to join him in the vault. And of opening that visor at Peter's bidding and seeing the horror that was inside.

"I know," Bruce said. "They were talking about that too. Theo has phoned the police."

"Have you any idea who it could be?" I asked. "Has anyone been reported missing around here?"

Bruce smiled at me a bit grimly. "Not lately that I know of. But I might have a theory. Whoever put that body down there must have known about the armor—and about the underground vault. I suppose it depends on how old those bones prove to be. Eventually, this may answer a few questions."

"What questions?"

The grim smile was still there. "When a man dies—or it may be a woman—and the body is hidden, there must be questions somewhere on the part of someone."

I supposed they would be answered eventually, as Bruce said, but it was all long in the past and my attention returned to my own unhappy moment.

Bruce took my hand in his and I felt his strong fingers around my own. "Don't let anyone make you believe you're not the right mother for Peter, Christy. You've been under more pressure than most women ever have to face, and you're standing up to it with courage. Don't lose confidence in yourself. Don't let them break you down."

I warmed to his sympathy. It had been so long since anyone had believed in me.

"One thing at a time," he said, and let my hand go. He was not relinquishing me. He was only making a postponement of what might lie between us, and I was grateful that he would not press me. I suspected that he was not a patient man, but I wasn't ready yet for an enormous decision. A decision that would not only separate Joel and me, but which would take Peter away from the father who loved him. I felt a little sick when I thought about that. Yet it might come to this. If I had to make a choice, I would never leave Peter in Theo's destructive hands.

"You'd better go back to the house," he said. "You've had your respite and the war is still ahead of you."

I braced myself. "Yes. I'm ready for it now. Thank you."

His look told me the things that could not be said. I wanted to hear them—but later. I dared not listen now. Being with him had helped strengthen me. I could face Theo, face Joel, and whoever else tried to stand between me and my son. He let me go and I returned to Spindrift alone.

13

When I reached the house I realized for the first time that I had had no breakfast, nothing but a cup of coffee at dawn. It was long past the breakfast hour and nothing was left on the buffet in the small dining room, but I found someone to get me orange juice and toast and coffee. Since there were confrontations ahead of me, I needed my strength.

When I had eaten I went upstairs still buoyed by Bruce's words and his belief in me, still warmed by the knowledge that I was coming to life again, that it was possible to feel an emotion. Just what that emotion was, I was not yet ready to face.

First I would go to Peter's room, and then to talk with Theo.

Peter's door was ajar and as I stepped to the opening I could see him asleep in his bed. Miss Crawford was not in her usual chair and for a moment I thought he was alone. Then I pushed the door wider and discovered Joel sitting by the bed with his back to me. He too was asleep, his head against a wing of his chair. The chill and disapproval I had last seen had been washed away, and he looked young and unguarded, the way I remembered him in the beginning when I had first known him. I still carried the memory of love, even though I had lost the ability to love Joel as I once had. A sense of my presence must have penetrated his sleep for he opened his eyes and saw me there. At once the chill was back, and he was again his mother's son.

"Don't waken him, Christy," he whispered. "You've done enough damage for today."

I turned and walked out the door, fighting the familiar sense of helplessness. I couldn't afford to be helpless, and I wouldn't let Joel and his mother do this to me. I must hold to the courage Bruce had given me. Determinedly I turned down the hall toward Theo's sitting room.

Here the door was open and I heard voices inside. A uniformed officer stood near Theo's desk, and a man in plain clothes who was obviously a detective sat in the chair opposite her. Theo, rather pert in green trousers that matched the room, looked around at me.

"Come in, Christina. Don't stand there staring. Lieutenant Jimson will want to talk to you."

When I had been introduced as Peter's mother and Joel's wife, I took my place on the sofa across the room. Fiona was nowhere in sight and I wondered if she had begun her drinking early this morning.

The officer in uniform was young and blond, with blue eyes not wholly schooled to concealing his curiosity as his glance moved from Theo to me and on about the room. Lieutenant Jimson had a square, rather rugged face, with a nose that bore the indentation of a long-ago break, and his look gave nothing away.

"I understand you made the discovery of the—uh—body," he said to me.

"My son found what was there and showed it to me," I corrected.

"Suppose you tell me what happened from the beginning."

Once more I explained about going to search for Peter, and of his account of looking through the visor in that suit of armor in the vault.

"Is anyone missing?" Theo asked the detective, who only shook his head.

"We'll have to check that out, Mrs. Moreland. But maybe she"—he nodded at me—"can come with us now and show us the place."

"Of course," Theo said. "Go along, Christina. And then come back and report to me."

The last thing I wanted was to return to Redstones. I was being moved about like a puppet again, but what the police wanted would have to come first, so I went outdoors with the two men and led the way across the lawn. Ferris had left everything unlocked. They merely needed a guide and they didn't make me go down into the vault. Both of them had brought flashlights and they let themselves down holding onto the rope Joel had left hanging beside the ladder.

I found a rickety kitchen chair in the basement and sat down to wait for those two to complete their grim investigation. When they came up both men wore carefully blank expressions.

"Get on the phone," Jimson told the young officer, and when he had gone off to Spindrift, the lieutenant looked at me. "You sure you don't know anything helpful about this?"

"I don't know a thing," I said. "How could I? I've never heard of anyone around here being missing. But then, I haven't been here for quite a while, and I've never stayed very long in the past anyway."

He was eying me dispassionately and I wondered what Theo might have said about me.

"You've been having a few troubles of your own lately, haven't you?" he said.

I could feel myself stiffening in resistance. My troubles had nothing to do with this.

"My father died," I said. "If that's what you mean. And I was in the hospital for a time."

"I remember about your father."

"I don't think so," I said evenly.

He stared at me, and for a moment I thought he was going to ask questions. Then he seemed to reconsider and his shrug let the matter drop, as if my father's death were unimportant.

"I was ill, but I've recovered," I told him. "I know my father didn't commit suicide and I think his death should have been investigated more carefully."

"It was investigated," he said. "I was on the case. There was no reason to suspect anything else but suicide."

"Oh, I know," I said, nettled by his calm assurance. "I know about the gun in his hand and all the rest. But I still think there is more to it than that. Adam Keene wasn't the sort of man to kill himself."

"I wanted to talk to you at the time," he said, "but you weren't entirely coherent. They had to take you to the hospital. Your father's wife, Mrs. Fiona Keene, was the one to answer most of our questions, and she hadn't any quarrel with the findings."

"Well, I do." I tried to keep my voice calm, reasonable. "But no one has ever listened to me. No one has ever let me talk. From the beginning I was drugged so that I couldn't make sense—even to myself."

He seemed suddenly more alert than before. "What do you have to talk about?"

"Nothing—yet. That's the trouble. But something is being hidden. Someone is lying. I've been sure of that from the first."

"There were reasons for suicide. Your father was in debt and involved with something pretty bad."

"I don't believe it!" I was losing all vestiges of calm. "Theodora Moreland was in a position to make things look any way she chose."

The alertness died away in the face of my excitement. "You're a loyal daughter," he said. "That's to be expected. But you've been pretty sick and upset and maybe you haven't been able to see things as clearly as you might."

"Oh, I don't expect you to believe me! But someday you will. Someday I'll find the truth. Can I come to you then?"

"Come ahead," he said. "I'll listen."

He had given me nothing. He didn't believe in anything I had said, and yet I had a strange feeling of reassurance. As if for the first time there was someone who would listen to me without arguing if I could come up with any facts.

The young officer had made his contacts and was back in short order. "They're on their way," he said to his superior. I knew what that meant. Picture-taking and all the rest—an examination of what had been found in that suit of armor.

"How old do you think those bones are?" I asked Jimson.

"We'll have to have tests made to tell," he said. "I'm not guessing. You can go now, Mrs. Moreland, if you want to. If you've told us everything that might help."

"I've told you what I can," I said.

I knew my way to the basement stairs by this time. I went up them into the silence of the house and followed the halls toward the main entry. Ferris Thornton was waiting for me there.

"How did it go?" he asked me.

I shrugged. "What could I tell them? I just led them to that room."

"It's all very strange," he said. "A skeleton in armor— shades of Longfellow! Theodora is upset about it."

"She seemed to be taking it in her stride all right."

He ignored that. "I've come to bring you back to her."

"That's where I was going. She told me to report, and I want to see her anyway."

"She was afraid you might not come back right away. You've been a bit headlong lately, Christy."

I went past him out the front door. What did they expect of me under the circumstances?

He came with me when I crossed the intervening ground between the two houses and I was glad to have him with me. I wanted him to hear what I had to say to Theodora Moreland.

She was waiting for us in her sitting room, and now Fiona was there too, pale, but apparently quite sober, working at her own desk.

"Tell me what happened," Theo said the moment I entered the room.

I took my place on the sofa opposite her, and Ferris went to stand beside the window.

"There's nothing much to tell," I said. "Lieutenant Jimson asked me if I knew anything about what we found down there and I told him that of course I didn't. He has sent for the usual people to examine what is there. He didn't need me to stay."

"I don't like this at all," Theo grumbled. "There will be unpleasant publicity in some of the papers. I'll want Bruce to get on the phone to New York and play down the story as far as we're concerned. Perhaps I'll send him in."

"Why are you so uneasy?" I asked. "Redstones has been closed for a long time and this probably has nothing to do with you."

"Those bones may have been there when Redstones was still occupied, for all we know," Ferris said. "The story is going to be pretty remote from us. I don't think that's any recent murder over there. I wonder if it's a man or a woman."

Theo had moved the ivory carving of Adam's "Lady Luck" to her desk, and she picked it up to turn it about in her fingers, as though she played with worry beads. After a moment of silence she looked up at me, her green eyes spiteful.

"All right, Christy, you may go. I don't suppose there's any use in talking to you further about the damage you've been doing to Peter. We'll just have to see that you have no further opportunity to harm him."

I kept my temper with difficulty. "I came here to talk with you. I don't think you know what happened to me last night. Or perhaps you do?"

She looked up sharply from the ivory figure in her hands, and Ferris turned from the window to listen. Fiona

218

was very still at her desk. She, at least, knew what was coming.

"What do you mean, Christina?" Theo asked.

"You had some sort of drug put in the hot chocolate that Joel brought me last night. It must have been what they gave me in the hospital that used to send me out of my head and bring on strange dreams."

"I don't know what you're talking about," she snapped.

"I think you do. Anyway, sometime in the night my name was called at my door. I felt a compulsion to see who it was and I got up and looked into the hall. Down at the far end there was someone wearing my father's plaid sports jacket. Because the drug was making my brain fuzzy I thought it was Adam and I followed him downstairs and into the ballroom."

"The ballroom!"

"Yes." I looked around at Ferris, but he had his back to me and he did not turn. "Whoever it was disappeared there and it was very dark except for flashes of lightning. But someone was there. Someone who meant me harm. That's why I'd been lured into that place."

"Lured? Oh, Christina, I don't know what you took before you went to sleep—*if* you took anything, but obviously something was befuddling your brain."

"I wasn't that befuddled. I was aware of what was happening to me. By that time, of course, I knew it wasn't my father, and I was terribly afraid."

Theo held me with her steady green stare. "I rather think you are making all this up, Christina. This is the way you used to talk in the hospital. You often thought things were happening that hadn't occurred at all."

It was all I could do not to jump up and rush over to confront her there at her desk, but I managed to sit quietly. That much control I managed to achieve.

"These things did happen," I said. "Bruce knows. He came across from Redstones just in time, and he frightened whoever it was away. He found Adam's jacket, and I brought it upstairs with me. I took it to Fiona's room. So she knows too."

Fiona expelled a soft breath and Theo glanced at her sharply.

"How did that jacket get away from you, Fiona?"

She shook her head helplessly. "I haven't any idea. I put it in a suitcase in my closet, as I told Christy."

Theo turned back to me. "I rather think you are playing games with us, Christina. Or else you've become completely unbalanced."

"You can ask Bruce. He was there. He rescued me."

"I shall ask him. But what he may say proves nothing. You're quite interested in Bruce, aren't you?"

"I know what you tried to do," I said. "I know how you planned to use him. He told me. It's not going to work. I mean to stay with Peter."

Theo sighed as though she dealt with a recalcitrant child, and glanced at Ferris. "You used to have some influence with Christina. Talk to her, will you?"

Ferris had said nothing till now, but he turned from the window and came to sit on the sofa beside me. His tone was kind, his manner gentle, but I thought he looked decidedly wary. He would believe what Theo wanted him to believe, and he half expected me to fly apart.

"Christy, my dear, this is rather a wild story, and you can't blame us for questioning it. Are you sure it wasn't you who carried that jacket of your father's down to the ballroom, where Bruce picked it up?"

I'd begun to shake again inside and it was all I could do to hold onto myself. "It was either you or Joel," I said. "It wasn't I. But I wonder which one of you was trying to fool me, trying to coax me down there? Maybe it was even Fiona, or you, Theo?"

Ferris put an arm about me and I jerked away, not wanting him to sense my trembling. "Don't try to soothe me. I know something is happening. I know you want to drive me away, keep me quiet. I think you'd drive me out of my mind if you could. But I'm going to stay right here where my son is and I'm not going to let you injure me."

Deliberately, Theo set the ivory carving down on her desk and picked up a piece of yellow-green jade to hold it up for Ferris to see.

"I don't think I've shown you this." She spoke as though nothing I had said mattered and it was perfectly natural to change the subject. "It's something I found in New York a few months ago—down in Chinatown."

Ferris took the piece from her and examined it. "Another *lung-ma?* Very interesting."

"Give it to Christina to hold," Theo said.

I was trembling and angry, but I took the curiously carved piece of jade from him. It seemed to be some sort of mythical animal with a dragon's body and a horse's legs. Stylized waves were breaking around its feet in the carving, and it looked vaguely familiar.

"It's a dragon-horse," Theo told me. "A lung-ma. You can see that it is rising from the waves of the Yellow River and it carries the Books of Knowledge at its side. Let your fingers explore it, Christina. Jade has a calming effect upon the nerves."

I wanted nothing more than the courage to throw the bit of jade right in Theo's face, but of course I didn't. I let my fingers smooth the rounded back of the creature and explore the carving. Jade, I knew, was as hard as a diamond, but where a diamond flashed fire, jade was translucent. It caught and reflected the light with a glowing quality that was unlike that of any other precious stone. In my fingers it felt cold, hard, smooth and strangely pleasant to touch. I let myself concentrate on it because I wanted to be calm.

"I used to have another lung-ma," Theo went on, speaking to Ferris. "The one you remember. It formed the handle on the cover of the box that held my jade book. It was one of my most valuable pieces, but at some time or other it must have been stolen back in New York."

"I've often warned you about carrying pieces of your collection around with you when you travel," Ferris said. "The insurance problem is enormous when anything is lost."

Theo flicked her fingers at him, and the ring of green jade and pearls on her hand glowed in the lamplight from her desk.

"You know I mean to enjoy these things. If I have to lock them up or leave them behind, they do me no good. And I haven't lost much over the years. The ivory carving has come back to me. So only the lung-ma is missing. It was a particularly good example of mutton fat jade."

My fingers froze on the small creature in my hands. The term she had used was ringing through my mind. *Mutton fat.* "MUTTON FAT AND TYCHE," my father had written on that slip of paper I'd found in his secret pocket. Tyche had proved to be the ivory lady. Mutton fat was apparently a type of jade.

"What's the matter, Christina?" Theo was staring at me. "You look positively transfixed. Is my jade having such an effect upon you?"

"Perhaps," I said lightly. I stood up and gave the lung-ma back to her. There was no point in remaining here any longer and submitting myself to her insinuating attacks. I had better things to do.

"If I were you," Theo said as I moved toward the door, "I'd go and lie down for a while. You've obviously had a bad night, whether real or imagined."

I went through the door without answering and fled down the hallway and down the stairs to the second floor. Just one place was my goal at the moment and I hurried down the wing that led to Zenia's sitting room. I had found Tyche there, and I remembered now that she had been resting upon a box with a jade handle. If Adam had put these things in Zenia's room, he had set them together on the mantel—and made that record on a slip of paper. Temporary hiding, perhaps, but with the intention that they should be found if he did not have a chance to produce them? The maid who dusted this room would be new, and she would see nothing amiss. Theodora, I gathered, had not been here since her return to Spindrift.

No one had closed the window draperies since I had last opened them, and daylight flooded in so that I needed no additional light. On the mantel sat the long box with a white jade dragon-horse on the lid. But it could wait a moment. Before I looked into it I wanted to check one other thing. I opened the drawer where I'd seen Fiona hide Ferris's automatic pistol. The gun was gone. I searched beneath the papers in the desk, but it was not there. No matter. There was nothing I could do about that now.

The wooden box was heavy in my hands as I picked it up and carried it to a table. I had to thrust aside a basket of shells and several small china birds to make room.

Mutton fat was an unlikely and not particularly attractive name for jade that seemed to glow with a white light. I took the little dragon creature in my fingers and lifted. The lid of the long wooden box came free easily, as it had done before, and I saw again the green slabs inscribed with gold characters. A "jade book" Theo had called it. I lifted the top slab out and there was another underneath, and another under that, until the box was nearly empty. Eventually there was only one slab of jade left. But where I had stopped before when I'd thought that the box contained only these slabs, this time I took out the last one and saw that long sheets of paper had been folded double and placed in the bottom of the box.

The hand-printed scrawl sent a pang through me because it was as familiar as a loved face. My father had written these lines, and these undoubtedly, were pages from the missing log. The dates were right—this was the time just before he had died. I sat down in Zenia's rocker and began to read, completely absorbed, oblivious to everything around me. The scrawled phrases were clipped, hurried, a sort of shorthand to record his thoughts.

The Martin Bradley affair. An old scandal in his past. The "woman in blue" the papers called her. They said at first that she was selling him out. Then they said worse. That he was involved in handing over the documents in the case. Bradley is a ruined man. The same with Malcolm Courtney. A photograph of him in the notorious Amber Club. "Gay" isn't all that acceptable in politics as yet. He tried to fight, but Hal Moreland was too strong. A brilliant career finished.

I stopped reading, remembering. My father had admired both men. He had known them both, and had been concerned with the crash of their careers and with the suffering they had experienced, the damage to their families. But they had both dropped from the public eye several years ago. Why had my father been interested enough in them to make this record in his log and then hide it away? Hal Moreland, it was true, had helped to break these stories and expose both men. But what had that to do with my father's death, or with anything in the present?

The next line stood alone and the words leaped at me:

That wasn't Courtney in the faked picture.

The movement in the room behind me was so swift, so quietly secret that I heard only a faint rustle before the smothering folds came over my face. My chair rocked wildly as I fought up from it, to struggle against the deadly pressure across my mouth, my nose, covering my face and stopping my breath. I could feel the strands being knotted at the back of my neck and I clawed at them, gasping for breath. Hands seized me and flung me across the room so that I fell against Zenia's desk, striking my temple as I dropped to the floor.

I must have been stunned for a moment. Then my hands were tearing at the soft material across my face, snatching it away so that deep breaths of air could flow into my lungs. I got shakily to my feet, looking about the room. There was no one there and I ran to the table where the slabs of the jade book lay. The pages from my father's log were gone. I had led someone to them and he had taken advantage of my absorbed reading to whip this silk stuff across my face so that I would be prevented from stopping him, so that I couldn't see him.

I looked at the silken material for the first time and saw that it was one of the bright batik scarves which Theo had brought back from a trip she'd made to Thailand with Hal. The soft blue and gold strands had been torn by my ripping, but I remembered the scarf. It was one Theo had given to Fiona after that trip.

My head was thumping and I felt the small swelling at the hairline gingerly. I wasn't seriously hurt, but I had lost what I'd come here for.

I tried to remember any sound I had heard just before the attack. Had there been a slight rustle—like the movement of beads in that curtain? Someone could have stood there watching me through the beads, just as I had watched Fiona.

The jade book was of no further use to me, but I put the slabs back in the box and covered them with the lung-ma lid. Then I went out in the hallway, carrying the box in one hand and the torn scarf in the other. I was going upstairs to see what Theo made of this.

But before I reached her room Joel came out of Peter's and looked at me in surprise.

"What's the matter, Christy? You look white as paper."

I dangled the scarf at him. "Someone just tried to smother me with this. Because I'd found the pages of my father's log and I was reading them."

"Christy, what are you talking about? Is this more of your—"

I interrupted impatiently. "Whoever it was threw me across the room and I struck my head as I fell. You can see the lump, and I assure you I didn't put it there myself."

225

He examined the bruise on my head with a light touch that nevertheless made me wince. "I don't like this, Christy. How much did you read?"

"A little. Enough to get an inkling of what may have been going on."

Joel looked alarmed. "There's been enough of this. I'm going to take you back to New York and—"

"You're going to do nothing of the kind," I told him sharply. "I've had a hint of what my father was about, and I'm not going to run away. Whoever used this scarf is the person who shot Adam. I'm sure of it, and I'm going to find out who it was."

Joel was hardly one to be masterful or argue me down, and he said nothing more as I walked past him along the hallway, carrying scarf and box. Theo must be told about this. She could not go on blaming everything that happened on my imagination.

But when I reached the Green Sitting Room only Fiona sat at her desk, and she looked around at me guardedly as I came in. I placed the jade book on the glass-topped table and stood for a moment twisting the scarf about one wrist.

Fiona began to make nervous conversation. "I've just been addressing an invitation to Jon Pemberton for Theo's party. She's decided to invite him."

I couldn't help flinching at mention of that particular name. I still hated to think of Joel lowering his standards to work with Jon Pemberton. But other matters were more important now. I held up the scarf to Fiona.

"I think this is yours, isn't it? Have you worn it recently?"

"Why, yes—I suppose I have. But I couldn't find it the last time I wanted it, and I couldn't remember where I might have left it."

"Perhaps you left it in Zenia's sitting room," I said. "It was used just now in an effort to smother me. Because I had found the pages of Adam's log and started to read them."

Fiona gasped and put a hand to her mouth. I couldn't tell whether her surprise was real or counterfeit.

"What was it about Martin Bradley and Malcolm Courtney that Adam wanted to uncover?" I asked her.

"I—I don't know what you're talking about."

"There was a published picture of Courtney, supposedly taken at the Amber Club. Adam said it was a faked picture."

Fiona crossed her arms over her body as though she protected herself from a blow. Once she tried to speak, but the words would not come. She looked so dreadful that I went to the cabinet where Theo kept a few bottles and glasses, poured some brandy and took it to her. She drank a long swallow and seemed to steady herself.

"Fiona, why did you hide Ferris Thornton's automatic pistol?" I asked.

She had recovered enough to look carefully blank. Or perhaps she was beyond being startled by anything more.

"I don't know what you're talking about."

"Of course you do. You carried it to Zenia's sitting room and you hid it under some papers in her desk. I was there in the dressing room. I saw you through the bead curtain."

For a moment she hesitated, and her eyes avoided mine. Then life seemed to come into them and she reached out her hand and clasped me by the wrist.

"Then you'd better forget what you saw, Christy. Forget all about it and stay out of trouble."

"There is trouble, isn't there?" I said. "I *have* stirred up the sleeping beasts, as Bruce says."

She choked and took another swallow of the brandy. I had been standing beside her desk and now I drew over a chair and sat near her. I had upset her again and I needed to let her recover.

"Yesterday Joel took me out in the *Spindrift*," I said. "For the first time he talked about the day when his brother and sister were drowned."

Fiona looked surprised. "Joel on the water?"

"Yes. I think he was testing himself in some way. Fiona, what was Cabot like?"

My effort to distract her had succeeded and she was quieter now as she began to talk about the past.

"He was the oldest of Theo's children—twenty-six. I was only twenty when I married him. I suppose he was a lot like Hal, and Theo loved that. I guess I did too. I wanted someone strong, someone I could trust and lean on. I wanted someone to take care of me, and I thought he would for the rest of my life."

I listened to her in pity. Twice she had chosen such a man, and each one had failed her by dying.

"Is that why you married Adam—to be taken care of?"

She hesitated. "Partly, I suppose. I don't think I really loved him in the beginning. I was only twenty-two and I was trying to make the pain of Cabot's loss go away. I was trying to find a way to live. Adam taught me how to be calm, how to accept. He brought me to life again. I know you disliked and resented me in the beginning, Christy, but I did try with you. I honestly tried."

"I know you did," I said gently. "And eventually we got along pretty well. Perhaps right now you and I are closer to each other than to anyone else at Spindrift. So why can't you talk to me? As you'd have talked to Adam. I'm Adam's daughter, and you're his wife."

She heard me but she went off at a tangent. "You were right about something you said recently, Christy. You said I had stopped loving Adam. That was true. How could I love him when he was destroying everything that we had built up together? He didn't care about anything except that one driving aim of his. Gambling!"

"Is that why you looked outside your marriage for the sort of love you wanted?"

To my surprise, she made no denial. "What else could I do? He was hardly a husband to me any longer. But what I did was a mistake too. It didn't go anywhere. And

228

in the end, Adam didn't care about you or me or anything else."

I managed to speak evenly. "That's not true. My father and I were close up to the very day he died."

"Were you? When you knew nothing at all about what he was doing, what he was involved in? And I don't mean just gambling."

"You're not going to expect me to believe that underworld story Theo and Ferris cooked up?"

"No. I'm sure that wasn't true. But I couldn't fight Theo, any more than you could."

"Then what was he involved in?"

Her anxiety returned. "Don't tell anyone what you've told me, Christy. Don't say you've read any of that log. What happened to Adam mustn't happen to you."

I pounced upon her admission. *"What* happened to Adam? What do you know?"

She moved so quickly I had no chance to stop her. She flew up from her chair and ran past me out of the room. There was terror in her face, and I think she was partly afraid of me, afraid of the pressure I might put upon her. I let her go and dropped into Theo's chair. My fingers played idly with the mutton fat lung-ma on the lid of the box, but it told me nothing and it carried no soothing quality for me now. I had been so close to the answer to all that had happened. If ony I had been able to finish reading those pages, the truth might have come clear. But they had been snatched away by someone who had been watching me, knowing that I searched, that I followed some clue, fearful lest I might find what I looked for. Or perhaps hopeful that I might lead the way to the goal?

For the first time reaction swept through me. This assault upon me had been real. I might have been near death if I hadn't fought so hard. I spilled a little of Theo's brandy as I poured some into a glass for myself. I was drinking it when Theo came into the room.

"What's all this?" she cried, coming to stand before me, a small indomitable figure. "I met Fiona in the hall just now, and she's half out of her wits."

I gestured toward the box I had set on a table. "There is your mutton fat dragon-horse."

Momentarily distracted, she pounced upon the jade book with delight. "How wonderful! Where did you find it?"

"Where my father must have put it," I said bluntly. "In Zenia's sitting room, where he put the carved Japanese figure. They were both on the mantel there."

"But why? Why would he—?"

"The box was a hiding place for pages from his log. He must have wanted to put them in a place where no one was likely to look quickly, yet where they would be found eventually if anything happened to him."

Her eyes widened, matching the green jade she wore on her finger. "What are you plotting now, Christina?"

I reached up to touch the swelling on my forehead. "This," I said. "The same thing that happened to you has happened to me. I was reading the pages of the log when someone tried to smother me with this scarf." I held it up while she stared. "Then he threw me across the room and I fell and struck my head."

For once she made no attack on my emotional state or my veracity.

"Why aren't you trying to find out who is behind all this?" I pressed her. "Or do you already know? Are you protecting Adam's murderer, Theo? Is that what you've been doing all along?"

This time I had touched her on the quick. Without warning, her hand flew out and slapped me hard across the cheek. I set the brandy glass carefully down on her desk. Then I got up and walked out of the room. My cheek was stinging from the blow, but I walked quite steadily downstairs to my room and went to stand before the bathroom mirror. I was white as Joel had said, except for the red streak across one cheek and the red swelling at my temple.

But at least I knew one thing. I had come very close to the truth with Theodora Moreland. She knew more than she pretended. If she had really been struck down, she must have a good suspicion of who had done it, yet she was keeping still. Because she was protecting someone she didn't want to expose, or because she was afraid?

I left the mirror and stood looking about my room. Everything was in order. No line of my possessions marched across the floor, but I stood there uneasily, once more twisting Fiona's torn scarf in my hands. For the moment I would keep it as "evidence" and hide it away. I looked for my canvas tote bag that had an inner zippered pocket, but it was not in my closet, and I wondered if it had been left in the Gold Room when I moved.

I needed to be doing something. I didn't dare sit down and think, lest the waiting reaction of fright should engulf me, and I went across the hall to the big corner room where Theo had first put me. Sure enough, the tote bag had been left behind in a closet there. I took it out and opened it, put the scarf away in the inner pocket. I was about to carry the bag back to my room, when there was a scraping sound overhead, as though someone had dragged a chair across a bare floor in the room above.

Doubtfully, I looked up at the ceiling, and as I waited someone walked across the floor. That was the Tower Room up there. The carpet on the floor should have muffled such sounds. But someone was up there now—and suddenly I wanted to know who it was. I would be careful now. I would take no risks, but I would find out who was in that room.

I carried the tote bag across to my room, left it on the bed, and hurried down the corridor to the stairs. I ran up them and turned down the wing that led to the room where my father had died.

14

In the hallway I looked about for a hiding place from which I could watch for anyone who came out of the Tower Room. There were long blue draperies on either side of the nearest window that might serve. But first I paused before the door, listening. From inside came the sound of voices—low, almost secretive, so that I could not recognize the speakers. Once I heard a soft sob, as though someone wept. Fiona?

But why had she come to this room? I had to know. And if there were two people there, it would not be dangerous.

The knob turned quietly under my hand and I thrust the door open and stood looking into the room. The carpet with its stains had finally been removed. An armchair had been drawn beside the tall window of the turret, and in it sat Fiona, her face tear-stained and drawn. Joel was walking about the room, pausing sometimes to speak to her, then walking again.

I stepped into the room, closing the door behind me, and they both looked around. I asked no questions, I said nothing at all, but went to the desk where my father used to work when he stayed at Spindrift, and sat down in the straight chair. From the wall the portrait of Arthur Patton-Stuyvesant looked down upon us with stern rebuke. Irrelevantly, I wondered once more how Zenia had ever managed to put up with him.

Joel seemed clearly discomfited, but Fiona was too far gone in misery to care who saw her, or who came and went in this room.

"Perhaps you can deal me in on this conference," I

said. Fiona looked so unhappy that I could only pity her, and when no one spoke I turned to Joel. "What have you done to upset her?"

"It seems to me that it's you who have upset her," he said. "I found her running down the corridor to this room and I followed her into it to see if I could offer any comfort."

I looked into the bleak gray of his eyes and knew that he was a stranger to me. I didn't understand his motives any more.

"I just want to know what it is that Fiona is trying to run away from. I want to know what she knows."

Joel spoke to my own rising emotion. "It could be, Christy, that you've become blind to everything but the one purpose that drives you. It might be better for everyone if you could accept your father's death the way it was, and stop rushing roughshod over everyone else's feelings."

In a way, he was right, and yet how could I stop? No one else would face the truth—perhaps because each one of them had so much to hide. But I had been pushing too hard, and I didn't want to hurt Fiona any more—though perhaps I'd have to in the end.

"It's possible that Fiona came to this room because she misses Adam, just as you do, Christy," he went on.

"Is that so?" I asked Fiona. "Are you here because you miss him so much?"

She looked at me as though I had cornered her in some desperate way and she was casting about for escape.

"What *are* you up to?" I said.

Joel had turned back to the restless pacing that seemed uncharacteristic, but now he came to stand before me.

"I wonder if Mother is right, Christy? I wonder if you've really recovered from what was wrong with you in the hospital."

I shrank back from him because there was a threat in his words—the one threat that could frighten me.

He must have seen the look in my eyes, because he

reached tentatively for my hand and his manner softened. "Christy, I only want to do what is best for you."

Now I was on guard. I remembered how gently, how considerately he had once before sent me away to what was hardly more than a prison. I snatched my hand back from his touch.

"I would never have believed that *you* would shield a murderer!" I cried.

His face darkened and he turned to Fiona. "Let's get out of here. I want to talk to my mother."

But before they could leave, there was a knock on the door. For a moment no one answered. Then Joel went to open it. Bruce stood looking into the room and his gaze turned first to me in my shocked state, then to the weeping Fiona, and finally to Joel. But he asked no questions.

"Theo wants you, Fiona," he said. "Do you think you can pull yourself together? Or shall I tell her you aren't feeling well?"

Fiona gave her eyes a last desperate wipe and stood up. Oddly enough, she looked relieved—as though she had been provided with some unexpected reprieve.

She and Joel went out of the room together, leaving the door open. I didn't move from my chair because I was trembling with reaction, and Bruce stood watching me.

"What have you been doing, Christy?" he asked ruefully. "Ferris is with Theo now, trying to quiet her. She's full of wild accusations, and you don't seem to be in very well with Fiona and Joel either. What have you done to throw Spindrift into such an uproar?"

I was nearing the end of my strength. "Don't," I said. "Please don't. Not you too. I've been having a bad time. And now Joel—just now—"

Bruce came directly to me and knelt to put his arms around me. I clung to him and he soothed and quieted me until I was able to speak more calmly and tell him what had happened to me in Zenia's sitting room. He listened quietly, questioning me once or twice, and when I was through he went to sit in the chair Fiona had left by the window and become deeply thoughtful.

"What shall I do?" I said after a few minutes had passed, and I heard the wail of helplessness in my own voice.

"I suspect that it's over now," he said. "You've led the hunter to his quarry and there should be no further need to track you or use any violent means to stop you."

"I read some of the log," I said weakly.

"Obviously you didn't read enough to give you any answers. If you had, you'd already be storming the ramparts." His tone was still faintly rueful, yet he respected my purpose—as no one else had.

I went on, trying to make him understand and believe. "Adam meant to expose something that Hal Moreland had been doing. I never told you, but when I was going through Adam's things I found a note from Theo that accused him of treachery. Perhaps Hal had been falsifying news to destroy those he opposed. If Adam found this out he'd never have rested until the truth was known. He would have suffered deeply over the things that were done to those two men, Courtney and Bradley. He'd want the truth published."

Bruce nodded. "Yes, I'm sure he would have wanted that. But I don't think, even under such circumstances, that Theo would have taken such extreme action against him."

"I don't know," I said helplessly. "I think she'd want to guard the reputation of the Moreland papers at all costs. And such an exposure might bring court action even now."

Bruce was silent. He knew he couldn't dissuade me and I was grateful to him for not trying. It was possible that I had even begun to persuade him.

"Help me, Bruce," I said.

He looked into my eyes and I seemed to gain courage from his courage. "For whatever it's worth, I'll try to help

235

you, Christy. Have you any first steps you want me to take?"

"If I knew of a single first step, I'd take it. Help me by thinking, by figuring it out, by helping me to know what to do. That's where Adam would have started, and you have Adam's sort of brain. It's possible that those two men, and others besides, were injured through false stories concocted by Hal Moreland. Bruce, did you know about any of this?"

He shook his head. "Sometimes I distrusted Hal's methods, but I didn't think he'd go this far."

"But you believe that this should be mended now, don't you? Adam started something, and perhaps he died for it. I have to know the answers."

"We need more to go on," Bruce said. "I'll have to think where to begin."

The relief of having someone on my side, someone to help me, was enormous.

"I just don't want to beat my head against the barrier by myself any longer," I told him.

My fingers went absently to the bruise on my forehead and he came out of his chair and pulled me into his arms. This was where I wanted to be, and I clung to him again, the cold that was so often a part of me these days thawed by his closeness, melted by the touch of his lips on mine. After a moment he held me from him and looked down into my face from his tall height.

"There's a danger in all this, Christy. I wonder if you've really faced it."

"It seems to me I've been facing danger ever since I came to Spindrift."

"I don't mean physical danger. I think that's over for the moment. But there's the danger of what you may find, what you may expose about someone who is close to you."

Close to me? Was it Joel he meant? But that was ridiculous. Wasn't it? And even if Joel had taken some part in the plotting, I would still not protect him. He could never again mean to me what he had before.

"No one is close to me any more. Whoever it is, the truth has to be told. What was done to Adam is more important than protection for anyone else."

"All right," he said. "If that's the way you feel, I'll try to help you. Not here. Theo wants me to keep the sensational side of the discovery of what was found at Redstones out of our papers. I've already been on the phone to the managing editor. But she wants me to go to New York and supervise what's being done myself. There are a few things I can look into there. I can reread those old stories about Malcolm Courtney and Martin Bradley. Perhaps there's something to be learned from them."

I knew I could trust Bruce to do a careful and thoughtful investigation.

"What has become of those two men?" I asked him.

"Courtney's still around, though he's out of politics. But Bradley killed himself."

"Another death," I said. "It's Hal who is guilty in all this, but he's beyond punishment. Just the same, Theo is left and I think she'd do anything within her power to save Hal's reputation and the paper's."

"To the extent of your father's death?"

"I don't know. I don't know what Theodora Moreland might be capable of."

"All right," he said. "Let the chips fall where they may. I'll drive back to New York after lunch. So I had better go and get ready."

He started for the door and I ran after him. "Bruce, be careful. If you get into this there may be danger for you too."

He smiled and pulled me to him again. "You'll have to be doing some thinking too, Christy. About the future."

I knew what he meant. I'd known all along that Bruce

Parry would not stand still and wait forever. The choices that I feared still lay ahead of me, and I would have to face them sooner or later.

"I'll think," I promised him, and he kissed me again, gently, and went out of the room.

When he had disappeared down the hall, I went to close the door. This room was as good a place as any to start my thinking. Here, where Adam had died. I no longer felt uneasy about being alone, no longer felt myself in danger. Bruce's words had reassured me about that. The recovery of the log pages by whoever had sought them had put a stop to that fear. Theo might still try to torment me, but even this I could now meet with equanimity. I wouldn't let her drug me again, and I would prove to her that I couldn't be driven into another breakdown by anything she might do. Not even Joel could hurt me now—not with Bruce beside me.

The other part of the threat against me had been more serious—an effort to stop me if I knew anything dangerous, or to keep me from finding out something that would be dangerous to an unknown hunter. This was the part that was over now unless the hunter still feared that I had read too far into Adam's pages. Perhaps I could dispel this by letting everyone know just what I had read. I had begun to do that already. What little I'd had time to discover had pointed no finger of guilt at anyone.

But there was still more that faced me. There was the whole problem of Bruce. Now I felt that if he wanted me to, I would go to him. I owed Joel nothing any more. Yet how could I turn to Bruce unless I could take Peter with me? That was what Theo would fight. Even if Joel never lifted a finger to keep me, Theo would see that he kept Peter. When Bruce held me I wanted only to be with him. Yet when I was out of his arms I was tortured by the problem, not only of keeping Peter but of the hurt I would deal my son by taking him away from his father.

The whole thing was too big for me, but at least I had an ally now. I would put all this aside until Bruce came back to Spindrift and told me whatever he had been able to discover.

I stood up, bracing myself to return to the household. I must now try to make myself an agreeable part of it, try to shrug off Theo's cuts and Fiona's weeping, try to face Joel as though nothing had happened. But first, I would find Peter and see how he was faring since his ordeal at Redstones. He would probably be awake now, and perhaps I could have lunch with him in his room.

But as I walked toward the door the Tower Room seemed to pull in around me in some strange way. It was as though it were saying to me, "You must remember what happened here. *That* is what you must think about while you are in this room." Arthur's portrait looked sternly down at me from the wall and I wondered what terrible sight that unwavering gaze had witnessed here last New Year's Eve.

When I had gone into the hospital my thoughts had been confused and I had been unable to understand what had happened. I had been instinctively sure, knowing my father, that he had not killed himself. Yet the gun had been his. No one had come to this room bringing the weapon with him from outside. Nevertheless, nothing I knew about my father could make me believe that he had turned that gun upon himself. If he had carried it, it must have been for protection, because he knew that someone might try to stop him from what he meant to do.

Suppose that person had come here. Suppose it was my father who had turned the gun on him to stop him. Suppose there had been a struggle, so that while my father held the pistol it was twisted against him and the trigger was pulled. It could have been intentional—it could have been an accident. But it had never happened because my father had intended it. Whoever had forced the pressing of that trigger had had time to get out of the room and out of my sight before I came in to find my father dying. Such a struggle could have been equally possible for either a woman or a man.

There seemed to be a new clarity in my thinking, as though for the first time I had stopped floundering in a morass of grief and denial, and had begun to look at my father's death with an objective appraisal that I had never managed before. For the first time I had begun to accept its reality, and this was another step toward the healing of grief.

First, in the beginning, I had been numb and disbelieving. Everything had seemed unreal—not to be accepted. Then, as grief gradually enveloped me, I had tried desperately to recover him through memory, through old pictures and the news stories he had written. Perhaps, under normal circumstances, I would have evolved from that morass to the place where I could accept his death as real, and true healing would have set in. Then I might have comforted myself with happier memories, without trying to force him to be alive again. But I'd had no chance, because into the deepest period of my grieving had been thrust the lies about Adam, about his death, and when I had fought them in a hysteria that was part grief, part helpless frustration, Theo had seen her chance and I had been sent to the hospital.

It was as though a wound which was open and raw and ready to fester had been frozen into that state. What they had done to me in the hospital with the help of drugs had drawn a deceptive skin of supposed healing over pain that throbbed beneath the surface. The wounds of my father's death and of the withdrawal of my son from my care were never allowed to heal properly. The cure of the second wound was clear as I drew closer to Peter. Healing was effective there. But I had convinced myself that the first wound could only be healed when the truth was known and justice was done. I had become numb and insensitive to all else. Only now, because of my new feeling toward Bruce, had some of these things been shaken into a truer perspective. Adam was dead and I must stop hurling myself blindly into danger because of an unreal belief that exposure of the truth would somehow bring him back to me. I still wanted the truth to be known. I owed him that. But I wanted it less wildly and recklessly. My father was dead and nothing would ever bring him back. Acceptance of this fact had at last put me upon that long road to healing after loss from which I had been detoured and held back from the true goal.

I could at last look about me more calmly in this room, and try to find what it had to tell me. If only that person who had struggled with my father had left some evidence of his presence behind. But the police had found nothing and there had seemed to be no reason to believe that Adam had been attacked. If I could only discover something—something real which I could take to Lieutenant Jimson, whose ear I believed I might now have, however skeptical he might be—then perhaps we would be on the way to the truth.

But there was nothing. Nothing at all. Even the rug upon which two people might have fought, and which had borne the stains of my father's blood, had been taken away. The closet was empty of my father's clothes, and the desk of the few things he had left upon it. The bed had long ago been stripped of sheets and blankets. There was nothing here the police had not examined and re-examined. And mute furnishings could not talk, any more than could a watchful portrait on the wall.

I made one more cursory search of the room, to no avail. I even got down on my hands and knees and looked under the desk, patted the floor beneath it to the very molding—without result. If the carpet had been removed, undoubtedly a maid had been sent here to vacuum and dust as well, so even if the police had missed something, it would be gone by now. It was only my own sensitivity to this room that made me feel it might have something to tell me.

I was still on my knees, searching idly, when my fingers touched some tiny object wedged in a crack against the molding that the vacuum had missed. I drew it out to find in my hand a single diamond earring clip. I knew whom it

241

belonged to. I remembered seeing Fiona with both clips on her ears when I had talked to her the evening of the ball. And I remembered her later, wearing only one clip.

Whether it meant anything, I couldn't tell. She had been in this room later, along with the rest of us. She could have lost it at any time. But I would keep it and when it seemed opportune I would confront her with it. She might be startled into telling me something.

I went out of the room in search of Peter, eager to have lunch with him, if that was possible. But when I reached his room he only looked at me with new resentment.

"It's your fault this happened to me," he said, gesturing toward the cast on his leg. "Grandma Theo says it's all your fault."

So now I must begin all over to find a loving relationship with my son. But I would do this. I had to do it, and there was more courage in me now.

I talked to him as gently as I could about the need to place first blame where it belonged. *I* could blame me, but he must first examine his own actions and see if any blame was to be found in him before he looked outward. Whether my words had any effect on his thinking I couldn't tell. He remained sulky and withdrawn, and I didn't stay for lunch with him after all.

15

In the days that followed, there seemed to be a change in the climate at Spindrift. Perhaps some of this was due to a change in me. I was no longer entirely alone, and I was no longer the center of a whirlpool, so perhaps they all reacted to this in varying degrees, however warily. When Joel and I met again he was studiously polite and I treated him with equal courtesy. We were not even friends any more, and it didn't seem to matter. Only now and then would some reminder of the life we had shared arise to stab me with old memory. But I hardened myself and refused to be vulnerable. What was over was over.

Perhaps during this time I even matured a little when it came to my attitude toward Adam. I loved my father no less, but I tried to think of him more objectively. I could see now that I hadn't always been fair to Joel in the comparisons I had made between him and Adam. In this new and developing relationship with Bruce I must beware of doing the same thing. I must remember that Bruce was his own man. I must stop being too much Adam's daughter. I still owed my father the truth, but I did not owe him my life.

During this time there was a little unpleasant publicity in the papers concerning the grisly find at Redstones, and perhaps there were more sightseers than usual following the Cliff Walk for this time of the year. But their interest was an outside thing, and we were only aware of it from a distance.

Theo had now been fully caught up in her plans for the Sargent ball and had little time for considering anything else. I was giving no immediate trouble, and perhaps she had postponed dealing with me until after the party. Fiona seemed to have relaxed to some extent and she appeared calmer as she ran errands for Theo, wrote letters, consulted with Mrs. Polter, the dressmaker, and went with her to Providence to purchase materials. I sensed that she was avoiding me, but I didn't mind. I was not afraid of Fiona, or of anything she might do. That single diamond earclip hid its fire in my jewel case and I waited for my right moment.

Even Ferris seemed to unbend toward me and regard me with a less critical eye. One morning he stopped me outside of Peter's room and spoke to me in the old way, almost fondly.

"I'm glad to see you more like your old self, Christy. It's as though you've crossed some area of white water and come out into a calmer pool. And I'm glad you've decided to stop tormenting Theodora."

For an instant the old indignation rose in me, but I thrust it back. "I thought it was Theodora who was tormenting me," I said. "Though for the moment she seems to have forgotten me."

We smiled at each other in almost friendly fashion and after that he was more approachable, more like the man I remembered from my childhood. Once he even took Peter and me for the Ten Mile Drive out along the ocean, looking at the old "cottages" and talking about the days when they had been the center of life for Newport. Peter was in a "walking cast," using crutches quite agilely, and rather impressed with the drama of his situation.

We eventually had had a good talk about his escapade at Redstones, and for the time being Theo was too busy to work against me with my son. Peter was not always agreeable, and I often came upon disturbing traces of Theo's influence, which I had to work subtly to counteract. But at least he accepted me as a mother again, and we had some good times together. I put out of my mind the unhappy questions of the future. I would have to face them—but not now.

Only with Joel was I unable to show this new and calmer self. I was on edge and wary whenever he was present, and I think he felt just as wary with me, for all our attitude of cool courtesy. Once he too made a trip to New York and I gathered it was for a consultation with Jon Pemberton. He talked to his mother about it when he returned, as I heard from Ferris, and he brought another stack of manuscripts back with him from the office. But he avoided the subject when I was around and I wondered if knowing how I felt gave him any sense of guilt in having lowered his standards. Once he had shared so many details of his work with me. But that was long behind us. He turned entirely to Theo now, and there was the coldness of antagonism between us. I no longer knew the thoughts which moved behind those remote gray eyes.

Mrs. Polter had finished my dress for the ball and was working hard on Theo's "Madame X." She had finished the Lady Macbeth costume for Fiona first of all, but Fiona had refused to model it for anyone but Theo, who was enormously pleased with Mrs. Polter's work.

Bruce stayed away no more than three days, and of course when he returned he became a central part of this halcyon time for me. What he had found in his study of back issues of *The Leader* appeared to corroborate what I had suspected from reading those few paragraphs of Adam's log. But it did not advance matters in any way. In a strange sense, I was almost relieved. I had developed a certain resistance to trouble—as though I could hold it off for a little while, if I let everything alone.

I was thriving, not only mentally, but physically in this new atmosphere which pervaded Spindrift, and I felt a reluctance to disturb it with disquieting news. There would be time enough later. Let me rest for a while and recover from all that had happened to me. I didn't want to start a new trend of upsetting events. Not yet. And so I ate and slept well, and gained a little weight, which Bruce said became me. I put off coming to grips with the situation between Joel and me. I ceased to prod for answers concerning my father, and I grew well, grew almost happy. Bruce was near and there were moments when his eyes sent warm messages, or his hands might touch me lightly in passing and I knew what lay ahead between us. Yet I was not ready to take any steps toward bringing it about. I clung to my calm and postponed.

Of course all of this was deceptive. It was only the lull, the quiet eye of the storm, and the real hurricane still whirled on its course just out of sight.

Only one thing of interest occurred during this period. Lieutenant Jimson came to see Theodora Moreland. Fiona had developed a cold and was staying in her room, so Theo had asked if I would type some letters for her.

She was in an amiable mood and when she chose she could be agreeable and charming. While she worked at papers piled on her desk, I sat in Fiona's place and tried to recover my rusty skill at the typewriter. Someone phoned from downstairs to say that the lieutenant was here, and Theo asked that he be sent up to her right away.

Since she did not dismiss me from the room, I stayed where I was and Jimson nodded to me when he came in. Theo waved him into the chair near her desk.

"You've some news for me?" she asked.

"In a sense. Laboratory tests indicate that the bones which were found over there at the next house are fairly old. They probably date back forty years or more."

Theo seemed relieved. "I'm glad it isn't someone from the present. That might mean more nastiness, investigations and all that sort of thing. But bones that are more than forty years old needn't concern us. Have you any sort of theory?"

Jimson considered her question soberly. "I don't like to deal in theories. And no identification seems possible at this late date. He was put into that armor without a scrap of clothing to identify him. And there doesn't seem to have been any missing persons recorded from Redstones or Spindrift in the past years."

"You said 'he.' Does that mean you can tell definitely?"

"Yes. The bone structure is that of a man. And the chances are he died a violent death or his body wouldn't have been hidden like that."

Theo looked interested. "Can you tell how he died?"

"His neck was broken. Could have been a fall, of course. But then why hide the body?" Jimson stood up. "I had to be out this way and I thought I'd stop in and tell you."

Theo thanked him and he said good-bye, gave me another nod and an unexpectedly inquiring look before he went out of the room. I wasted no time pondering the mystery of unknown bones, but finished the letters Theo wanted me to do and gave them to her.

"Thank you, Christy," she said, still agreeable. "You are looking much better these days. There's a sort of bloom about you. As if you were going to have a baby. Or as if you were a woman in love."

I didn't rise to the bait. "If you're through with me, I think I'll go look in on Fiona," I said.

She didn't try to hold me. "You do that, Christy."

It was all too amiable. Too pleasant. I didn't trust her, but I was thankful to accept this lull in hostilities while it lasted.

I found Fiona propped up in bed with the sniffles, a red nose, and a box of tissues beside her. She was reading a mystery novel open against her hunched knees.

"I won't ask how you feel," I said. "But is there anything I can do? Can I get you anything?"

"Thanks, Christy. There's nothing. I just have to live and weather this."

I told her about Jimson's visit and what information he had given Theo. "It seems strange to think of some man whose name we don't even know dying from a broken neck and being hidden at Redstones in that weird way. There are all sorts of violent possibilities in that story."

"There are violent possibilities everywhere," Fiona said huskily.

I didn't want to follow the morbid course of her words.

In the past few weeks I had begun to insulate myself from horror. I didn't know whether this was true healing, or just an escape from events that could no longer be borne.

"I don't know what's happened to Theo," I said. "She couldn't be more pleasant and agreeable. Do you suppose she's thinking up some new torment?"

"She doesn't confide in me," Fiona told me. "Not any more. I suppose I've disappointed her too many times."

I sat down in a chair beside the bed. "Was it you, Fiona, who came to my room and touched my face that first night?"

She closed her eyes and turned her head away. "Don't start that again, Christy. You've been so much better. You even look a lot better, so don't go giving Theo any new handles to hold onto."

"All right," I said, "if you don't want to talk. But I wish I knew why Theo seems so pleased these days."

"It's pretty obvious, isn't it? You wouldn't look the way you do if you hadn't done exactly what she wanted and fallen in love with Bruce Parry."

"Since I'm not sure of that myself, I don't see how it can be so obvious."

"You'd better be careful. Theo's only biding her time. When you bring things into the open and tell Joel and Theo what you mean to do, she'll whip out all her weapons. She'll let you leave Joel—she wants that. But she'll never let you take Peter away."

"There aren't any weapons she can use. I'm well now. In fact, I'm getting better every day. I don't think she could upset me any more, no matter what tricks she might play."

"You ought to know her better than that. She and Hal were both destructive. They destroyed anyone they didn't like."

"Just as they destroyed Courtney and Bradley?"

Fiona pulled herself up in bed and stared at me. "I thought you were through with all that. I thought you were going to let Adam rest in peace."

"I'm not through," I told her quietly. "Bruce went to New York to find out more about those two men. It's all waiting to be opened up again."

"Christy, no—no! If you go on you'll be in deeper trouble than you've ever been."

Her face had changed and she looked a little wild. I thought of the earring in my jewel case, but I wasn't ready to confront her with that yet.

"If there's nothing I can get you I'll run along," I said.

She let me go and when I looked around from the door she was lying with her eyes closed and her book had fallen to the floor.

The days moved along with a pleasant quiet toward the night of Theo's ball. Quiet, that is, as far as untoward circumstances went. The bustle of pressure as time approached for the ball was enormous. Now and then Theo made use of me to run errands or to spell Fiona on writing letters, but mostly I was apart from what was going on. No threats were made toward me, no tricks were played, and if anyone found my presence undesirable the fact didn't emerge. Fiona recovered from her cold and no one else was stricken.

On the day before the ball the house was full of strange faces. Extra help had been brought in, made up, as was the custom, from moonlighting Newporters who were willing to help out at parties.

Guests who were arriving from New York and from other places appeared and Theo was enjoying herself to the full as hostess for Spindrift. She didn't need me now, and time hung heavily on my hands.

That afternoon I found myself wandering idly around the first floor. It was a gray, rainy day, with the ocean sending in long rollers under the slanting rain, and the beeches dripping a steady patter on the leaf-strewn grass. I had run out of paperbacks, so I thought I might have a look at the formal library downstairs and see if I could find something to read.

The massive mahogany door opened on a vast, empty

room, and I was glad to have the place to myself. I had always thought it an attractive room, much too seldom used. The carpets were a soft yellow gold and ran practically wall to wall. The walls themselves echoed the same dull gold, and the draperies that shrouded ceiling-high windows were of golden-brown velvet. Against their panes the rain beat incessantly, blurring the vistas of lawn and garden beyond. Over the white marble mantel with its green veining hung a great mirror, framed in gilt, that rose to a peak of clustered wreaths at the apex. Flanking a square-faced English clock, silver candelabra set with white candles graced each end of the mantel.

On either side of the fireplace two modern sofas, slip-covered in oyster white, faced each other invitingly, with a round coffee table between them set with a bowl of golden chrysanthemums. At one end of the room stood an oval Chippendale table with chairs ranged about it and magazines strewn across its polished surface. Other parts of the room contained small furniture clusters, conducive to conversation or even to solitary reading, and all around the walls were ranged tall, built-in mahogany cabinets well stocked with rows of books.

As I walked into the room, I saw that a thick book with a modern jacket rested on the coffee table and I picked it up. The name JON PEMBERTON stared at me in black type, larger than that of the title *Ganymede*. I flipped the book open and glanced at the blurb on the front jacket flap. There was reference to the youth who had been cup-bearer to the gods, but I gathered that Pemberton's hero bore that name in a later, but still swashbuckling time. This was one of his roistering historical novels, I supposed, and I turned the book over to look at the photograph on the back.

The author's face was clean-shaven, with a thatch of light, unruly hair above, and a pair of wide-set eyes that had an almost hypnotic effect. The man must be in his fifties, at least, to have written his long string of popular novels, but he looked younger and I suspected great energy there. Perhaps I would read his book, I thought. Even though I did not like it, it might give me some clue as to why Joel was taking him on. I returned it to the coffee table for now, and wandered on around the room.

Hal had been a great reader, so the shelves were lined with novels and nonfiction of distinction from past and present. The feature of the room that most interested me, however, was the balcony.

The high ceiling had allowed generously for construction of a gallery that began halfway up the wall and could be reached by a curving wrought-iron stairway. Most of the old-fashioned books were kept up there, and there were chairs and a small writing desk, where one could have complete seclusion.

I climbed the stairs and moved idly along the shelves, pulling out a book here and there. There were volumes of poems by Longfellow, Whittier, the Brownings, Byron, Scott and others. I looked in the flyleaf of *Childe Harold* and found an ornate bookplate with the Patton-Stuyvesant name. Perhaps most of these books dated back to their day.

From the room below a sound reached me and I looked over the iron rail to see one of the men who worked about the house come in with a basket of logs. He knelt by the hearth and went to work lighting a fire. Perhaps in preparation for guests who were visiting for the ball. I paid no attention but went back to exploring the shelves. When the fire had caught hold he went away, and I stood for a moment enjoying the way leaping flames lent a reddish glow to the carpet and sent shadows dancing up the walls. Perhaps I'd go down in a little while and read Jon Pemberton's book beside the fire. Its warmth would be all the more pleasant with gray rain at the windows.

But for the moment I returned to my study of the shelves. The titles moved on to a later, less literary time and I found books by George Barr McCutcheon, Gene Stratton Porter, Harold Bell Wright and others, now almost forgotten. I was blowing dust from the top of an old edition of John Fox, Jr.'s *The Trail of the Lonesome Pine* when the door of the library opened again and I looked down to see Fiona come purposefully into the room. She wore still another caftan of a pumpkin color, deeper and more orange than the carpet and walls, and she moved gracefully to the fire to warm her hands.

I debated whether to call out to her, or pretend I hadn't seen her come in. Probably she was only checking over the room and would go away shortly, so I made no effort to attract her attention and she did not look up to see me.

When the fire had warmed her, she busied herself lighting the eight candles on the mantel and then seated herself on one of the oyster-white sofas, turning sideways to me, as she drew a handkerchief from the inner folds of her robe. Traces of her cold, I thought, but that wasn't it. She dabbed at her eyes and began, rather deliberately, it seemed to me, to cry. I was fascinated now and I had no intention of attracting her notice. This entire scene looked like a calculated staging and I wanted to know for whom the performance was intended. Anything Fiona did interested me, and under the circumstances which existed at Spindrift I had no compunction about spying. I was, however, too easily exposed to anyone in the room below who happened to look up. I sat down on the floor behind the balcony rail, trusting that I was thus lost in its shadow, and waited for whatever was about to happen.

Fiona had not indulged her tears for more than a moment or two when the door opened again. The end of my balcony blocked it from sight and I couldn't see at first who had entered. Fiona saw. She looked up, gulped tearfully, dabbed at her eyes and began to cry fresh tears.

Ferris Thornton walked across the room and stood beside the fire looking down at her. Now I understood. Ferris had always been susceptible to feminine tears. He was a sort of gallant throwback to the last century, when women were weak and tearful—or supposed to be—and men were strong and all prevailing. It was really rather strange that he had been devoted to Theodora for so long when she possessed none of these weaker traits.

"My dear," he said to Fiona, "you mustn't cry your heart out like this. How can I help you?"

"I can't bear what is happening!" Fiona wailed. "I can't go along with it for another day. Christy is going to be hurt, and Christy is Adam's daughter."

"I appreciate your loyalty to Adam," Ferris said, dropping to the sofa beside her and patting her gently on the shoulder. "But Adam hasn't been your real concern for a long time. Nor has Christy."

Fiona wept the harder at that and I pondered the fact that any woman could have so complete a personality change as my stepmother had shown since my father's death.

Ferris might be touched by feminine tears, but he was also made uncomfortable by them, and there was a slight impatience in the way he continued to pat and soothe.

"Suppose you tell me exactly what you plan to do," he said to her.

"I can't talk to Theo at all. She won't listen to me. I thought you might. I can't go on like this, Ferris. The truth has to come out."

"Who will believe anything you say at this late date? And what is the truth anyway? Are you so sure that you know as much as you think you do?"

She looked up at him with an air of fright that I could discern even from my balcony.

"Oh, I don't know everything! You needn't be afraid of my talking out of turn, if only you and Theo will let Christy off."

"I don't believe you're really thinking of Christy," Ferris went on. "What you want to protect is yourself and your own hopes for the future."

"I haven't any hopes! Not any more. Everything is over for me. But I can still stop what is happening."

Ferris spoke gently, yet there was an ominous quality in his tone. "No, my dear, you cannot."

"There's still Joel!" she cried. "I can go to Joel!"

Ferris considered her thoughtfully for a moment, as though what she had said surprised him. "Joel won't lift a finger. He has his own neck to consider. Have you forgotten that? Haven't you seen how vulnerable he is? He must protect himself. Because he's part of the Moreland Empire."

"He's changed too. Since that night. Everything changed the night Adam died."

"What you must remember"—Ferris's voice dropped so that I barely heard his words—"what you must remember is that you know nothing about what happened in the Tower Room that night. Isn't that true, Fiona?"

"But I can guess."

"Silently," he said. "Not out loud. You might be guessing wrong."

She bent her head and the soft brown pageboy swept her cheeks. "For now I'll be silent," she said. "But only for now. Ferris, be kind to me."

The appeal seemed to touch him once more and he bent and kissed her lightly on the cheek. "I want very much to be kind to you. You are Cabot's widow and important to Theodora. And what is important to Theodora is important to me. We're moving into a busy time now, and these things have to be kept in abeyance. Afterwards, plans must be made for Christy. We will expect you to help us then."

He stood up, looking down at her for a moment, and when she covered her face with her hands and did not answer, he went quietly out of the room. She waited for a moment after he had gone and then wiped her eyes carefully with what must have been a very damp handkerchief. I watched between the rods of the iron railing as she stood up and went to the mantel to blow out the candles. All had obviously been staged for an appeal to Ferris, who was usually sensitive to attractive surroundings. And whatever her purpose, it had all been in vain.

When the candles had been snuffed and blue smoke

drifted upward from the wicks, Fiona spoke into the silence of the room.

"You can come down now, Christy."

Caught and half-embarrassed, I stood up and looked down at her over the railing. "How long have you known I was here?"

"I saw you in the mirror," Fiona said. "Ferris was already in the room, and it was too late to do anything about you. Come down here, Christy."

She was my stepmother, commanding me as she had sometimes done long ago, and there was nothing tearful about her. I went to the stairs and descended them to the main room, feeling a little cold, so that I wanted to stand by the fire, where its warmth could touch me.

"What was that all about?" I asked.

She looked at me with that calm assurance I had not seen her wear for a long time. Suprisingly, she had again turned into the woman Adam had married—calm, unruffled, self-controlled. And clearly she did not mean to answer my question. It was I who felt awkward and disturbed.

"How can you change like that?" I cried. "How can you weep at one moment and then be perfectly calm the next?"

She smiled ruefully. "Because I'm a chameleon. I always have been. I am what the moment requires."

"Not always," I denied. "You've been a very frightened woman several times lately, and I don't think that has been faked."

"I'm still frightened," she said, "but I'm tired of letting go and wallowing."

"What did you hope to accomplish with Ferris?"

"Respite," Fiona said without hesitation. "A break for you."

"That's an about-face," I told her. "You haven't been offering me much in the way of respite before this. Besides, how could you hope to win Ferris away from any plans Theo might want him to carry out? We all know that famous story of his lost love, and how he has devoted himself to her ever after."

"He doesn't love Theo," Fiona said. "He detests her."

I was startled. "That's hard to believe."

"It's true. He's caught, as all the rest of us are caught in Theo's webs. The Moreland webs. He's part of the Empire too—and has been for all his life. You're not free of them yet, and neither am I, nor anyone else in this house."

"Bruce is free. I don't think he's ever been fully caught."

"All the worse for him. If you care about him, Christy, you'd better make him see how dangerous his position is if he defies Theo."

"Dangerous? That's a strong word."

"Is it? Adam defied her."

"Is that why he died?"

Fiona took a quick turn about the room, her yellow caftan seeming to float with her long strides. "Do you think I'd answer that—even if I could?"

"So we're back where we were—with you denying any knowledge of anything. Isn't it time you stopped playing that game, Fiona, and gave me something to go on?"

Her assumed calm was cracking a little around the edges. "That's the last thing I'd do. Because you don't know how to buckle under, any more than Adam did. I'm the worm in all this—but I'm going right on being a worm for as long as I can. It's safer that way."

"But someone tried to injure Theo. Someone must be standing up to her."

She gave me a long, thoughtful look. "*If* she was injured by anything but a fall. We don't really know that."

"I suppose you're right. Besides, if she really was injured by someone, why would she ignore it? Why would she claim nothing happened and make no effort to expose or punish whoever it was?"

"How do you know that she hasn't?"

I threw up my hands in exasperation. "Let's not talk

about it any more, Fiona. We go around in circles and run into our own arguments coming and going."

"There's only one argument I've ever been interested in," Fiona said. "The one that would persuade you to leave this house and stay as far away from Theo as possible. The less you know, the safer you are."

"Then I'm very safe, because I don't really know anything."

"That would be lovely, if true. But you already know more than you think you do and you've read some of what was written in those pages of Adam's."

"Yes. There was some sort of plot to discredit and destroy those two men, wasn't there—Courtney and Bradley?"

"And how many others who displeased Hal Moreland?"

"My father would have exposed the whole thing."

"I thought you said you didn't know anything."

"I don't know as much as you do, and you appear to be safe enough."

"I'm Cabot's wife, in Theo's eyes, and therefore sacred and untouchable."

"I don't think you believe that either. Fiona, I found something the other day in the Tower Room. A single diamond earclip. You were wearing them both when I saw you earlier that New Year's Eve. But later, after we found Adam, you wore only one."

She stared at me and one hand flew to her left ear and touched the pearl she wore—as though she expected the lobe to be bare.

"You were there earlier that night, weren't you, Fiona?"

Already she was recovering herself. "Why shouldn't I be? Adam was my husband."

"But you saw something, didn't you? You know who came into that room after you left."

She threw me a look that was a little wild and stalked out of the room. But she had denied nothing.

I dropped onto a sofa by the fire and sat watching the flames. I no longer wanted to read. I only wanted to ponder the things I had seen and heard—some of them old and few of them startling, except for Fiona's claim that Ferris Thornton had no love for Theodora Moreland. That was something to think about, though I couldn't see what good it would do me.

Bruce found me there. I looked up with sudden pleasure to see him in the doorway. Perhaps the attractive setting wasn't going to be wasted after all.

He closed the door after him and crossed the room to stand before me.

"I was looking for you. Fiona said you were in here. She's upset about something again. Has anything happened?"

"In a way," I said. "Sit down and I'll tell you."

He sat beside me on the sofa, not touching me, but close, so that I could note the way his dark hair grew back from his forehead and the way his fierce eyebrows drew together as I talked. I told him all that had happened, all that I'd heard, and he listened to the end without questioning me.

"It doesn't matter," he said. "None of it matters because after this idiotic ball is over, you are going to be away from Spindrift."

I opened my mouth to speak, but he put out his hand and turned my head toward him, kissed me almost angrily, silencing my words of protest.

"Now listen," he said, "and don't imitate your stubborn father. When I went to New York a few days ago it wasn't only to look up old news stories that will do us no good at this late date or to run errands for Theo. It was for another purpose. I went apartment hunting."

I stared at him, knowing what was coming.

"I found a small, pleasantly furnished apartment in a good neighborhood that I can lease in your name," he told me. "As soon as this ball is over I'm going to drive you to New York and see you safely into that apartment. Be sure your things are packed so that I can take them to the car. When you're gone, I'm going to tackle Joel and Theo. I know you haven't been willing to do this so far, so I'll do it for you. I think I can wring an arrangement out of them. I don't think they'll stand up to me."

I thought of Fiona's words. "Because you know too much? Because Theo might be afraid to cross you?"

He flashed his bright smile, but it was not one of amusement. "You'll have to leave that to me."

I moved myself away from his protective arm, his nearness, and went to sit on the opposite sofa where I could think more clearly than when I was close to him.

"No," I said. "Stay where you are, please, Bruce. I can't go along with any of this. If it was done your way I'd have to give up Peter. I won't do that, and I must try it my own way. I can't just walk out on Joel and go into hiding without talking to him first. He deserves better than that of me."

He challenged me. "Can you do anything else?"

"I don't know," I said. "But I'm going to try. I won't put you in a position of risk. That's where you'll be if you use any threats against Theo."

"So you'll put yourself in just that position by staying here?"

"Part of this is still my problem alone," I said. "Because of Adam. I still can't run away from that."

His eyes were warm on my face and some of the fierce determination, the smothered anger went out of him. It had never been against me—that anger—but now he quenched it altogether.

"I suppose I love you because you are the way you are, Christy. I suppose I admire stubborn determination and unswerving courage."

"Courage?" I said. "I have very little of that."

"Those who have it don't always recognize it, Christy. Just the same, I'm going to hang onto the idea of that apartment."

"I won't go away now," I said.

"All right. I'll bow to that for the present. And tomorrow night we'll dance at the ball."

I felt a tiny thrill run through me—as if I were a young girl going to her first dance and in love for the first time. No man had ever affected me the way Bruce did, so perhaps this was the first time.

He left me sitting there beside the dying fire and I made no effort to replenish it. A new determination was rising in me. There was no need to wait about talking to Joel. Even when I told him what I planned, I needn't leave Spindrift right away, unless Theo chose to banish me. I could still stay and pursue my questions about Adam. After all, Joel and I were not living together. All that had been over before we ever came here. So I would go to him now and tell him what I meant to do. I needn't say anything about Bruce yet, but only tell him that I wanted my freedom. It was foolish of me to feel timorous about taking this step. I didn't think Joel would oppose me in any way. And there was no reason to try to take Peter away from me, since I was well again. He would go to Theo with this news, of course, but what did that matter? It was Joel I must talk to first.

I picked up Jon Pemberton's book from the table and walked resolutely out of the room in search of Joel. A passing maid told me she had seen Mr. Moreland going into the ballroom, and I crossed the Marble Hall and opened one of the tall double doors at the end. Rain beat against the windows of the room, as it had done the last time I was here on that dreadful night when I'd thought I was following Adam. But now there was gray daylight at the windows, instead of black glass.

Joel was not there, but the portrait of Zenia Patton-Stuyvesant had been hung in the place of honor, along with the other true Sargents which Theo had acquired, and standing before it, studying the picture was a man I had never seen before.

Not finding Joel, I was about to go back through the door, when the man before the portrait turned and looked at me. He was a big man with a thick crest of blond hair, intensely blue eyes, and a full blond beard. He looked vaguely familiar, but I didn't know why. Certainly I had never met him before.

Since I had been observed, I spoke to him. "I'm Christy Moreland. You're one of Theo's guests?"

His bright blue eyes seemed to spark with unexpected interest. "So you're Christy? I've heard about you. I understand you're going to wear a dress like that tomorrow night?" He nodded at Zenia's portrait. "I'm glad John Singer Sargent is part of the story. He deserves more attention than we give him these days—especially as the recorder of a society long gone."

I didn't know why he was so interested in the portrait, or Sargent, or me, or why he had been told what I would wear tomorrow night. Apparently my bewilderment cut through his enthusiasm.

"Oh—sorry! I might have introduced myself. I'm Jon Pemberton. I see you've got hold of one of my books."

I turned the book I carried over and looked questioningly at the photograph.

Jon Pemberton laughed. "That's an old picture. I've grown this shrubbery since."

He came toward me with his hand outstretched and enveloped mine in his bear paw of a grasp. He was rather overpowering, and I felt more than a little confused.

When he released my hand he stepped back and studied me as a painter might study his subject. "I'm anxious to see you in that costume. You'll help to bring her alive for me."

"Bring her alive?" I echoed, completely lost.

"Yes. Zenia, I mean. Your husband is going to be my editor. But of course you know that."

I nodded. "Yes, I know." I couldn't say that I was glad.

"And you don't approve." His grin was boyish. "Can't say I blame you. And ordinarily I'd run from Joel's sort of editor. I'm an entertainer, not a literary type. But I respect my job, and for this book he's exactly right."

"May I ask why?" I inquired thinly.

He waved his hand at the portrait. "Because of her. Zenia Patton-Stuyvesant. Because hers is the story I'm going to write. Joel knows her history and he has entrée to this house. His mother knew her when she was young. Bruce Parry is related to her. So Joel and I understand each other. We should get along well. So long as he doesn't interfere too much—and I don't think he will."

I could only gape in astonishment at all this lusty exuberance and the information he was giving me. For the first time I could see the reason behind Joel's acceptance of Jon Pemberton as one of his authors, and I could almost forgive him. But why hadn't he told me the reason?

"Have you seen Joel just now?" I asked. "I believe he was down here?"

"He brought me to the ballroom to commune with the portrait and the room. But I think he's gone back to finish some work with his mother."

"Thank you," I said. "I'll go find him."

"Right. I'll see you at the ball. I'll probably get carried away and fall in love with Zenia as she must have been. I always fall in love with my heroines."

He was quite absurd and outrageous, but somehow I had begun to like him. "I'll look forward to seeing you again," I said, and went off in search of Joel.

When I reached the Green Sitting Room I found them together—Joel at Fiona's desk, and Theo marching resolutely about the room, electric in a long gown of scarlet watered-silk taffeta, apparently dictating a list of plans for the coming days.

They both looked around as I paused in the doorway and I braced myself against whatever was to happen.

"Joe, may I speak with you?" I said.

"Come in, come in," Theo ordered. "And don't take too much of his time. He's helping me, instead of Fiona, who seems to be of very little use to me when I need her."

"I'd like to speak with you alone, Joel," I said.

Theo stared at me. Perhaps she saw determination in my face, because she shrugged. "Very well. I have plenty to do in the rest of the house. You can talk to him here, if you like."

She swept past me with a swish of taffeta and I went to sit in a striped green chair near Fiona's desk. Joel set aside the list he was working on and waited, not helping me at all.

I made the plunge almost breathlessly. "Nothing has worked out for us lately. I don't think we'll ever come together again, Joel. I'd like a divorce."

He regarded me quietly, his eyes gray ice, remote, as though I had been a stranger making some request in which he was scarcely involved. As always, he was on guard lest he reveal his own feelings.

"Are you planning to marry Bruce?" he asked after a long moment.

"Bruce is something for the future," I said. "I don't know what I'll do then. But I can't go on as we've been."

"You're right," he agreed slowly. "You came out of the hospital a different woman. There's no point to our going on."

Even though he'd hesitated, the capitulation was swifter than I'd expected. I felt both relieved and empty. No matter how thoroughly a marriage has crashed, it isn't an easy thing to end it.

"I'm sorry, Joel," I said.

"You needn't be. I suppose it was inevitable from the beginning."

"Inevitable?"

"You've only loved one man in your life, Christy. Your father. You married me when you were angry with him, rebelling."

He had touched me on the quick. "I did love you, Joel. I loved you a great deal. But we've both changed. I don't know what happened to me after Adam died. It seems as though I've been numb ever since."

"Because you lost Adam," he said. "And you can't love anyone else. No matter what he did, you're tied to him forever."

"That's not true," I protested. "And what do you mean about what he *did?*"

"Since you found his log I've been talking to Mother, Christy. I've been able to get a few things out of her. A beginning. Adam knew what Hal was doing, all right. He wasn't blind. He saw men being destroyed and he didn't always try to stop it. Because he knew if he did, he was finished with the Morelands. So he went along and kept still."

"No!" I cried. "That isn't true!"

"I didn't expect you to believe me. But I felt you should know the truth, whether you're able to face it or not. When do you plan to leave?"

I tried to recover the cool and purposeful self who had come to this room.

"I haven't finished what I came for. I'd like to stay a little longer."

"I think it's better if you don't. Because of Theo."

"Why because of Theo?"

"She's going to fight this."

How foolish and blind could he be? I wondered. Theo would never fight my leaving her son. She had never wanted Adam's daughter for him in the first place.

"There's nothing she can do," I said. "I'll take Peter and go away as soon as I can. Of course you'll be able to see him any time you want, Joel. I'll never stand between you."

But he was shaking his head, answering me with a deadly calm. "No, Christy. That's what Theo will fight for. You still aren't yourself, you know. Peter is safer with me, and he'll stay here."

I hadn't expected this sudden dark force in Joel. There was too much about him of which I'd been unaware. I seemed to have been blind for half my life.

"Of course he will go with me. I'm his mother." I sounded a little shrill to my own ears. "There isn't anything Theo and you can do to take him away from me."

"I think there is, Christy. Do you want to fight this in the courts? Do you want that humiliation and eventual defeat?"

"I'll fight it anywhere," I said. "Peter belongs with me."

"Are you rich enough, Christy, to stand against Theodora Moreland? And against me—her son?"

He was beginning to frighten me.

"I'll get the money," I told him. "I have friends who will help me. Fiona will help me."

"Fiona owns nothing but her husband's debts," Joel said, and there seemed a new callousness in his voice. "She's not going to stand against Mother, who calls the tunes for her to dance to anyway. And where Peter's concerned, you have me to contend with. I'll fight."

"We'll see," I said. "We'll see."

I had to get out of the room. I had to get away from this firm new Joel Moreland, who looked at me so straight and hard. My legs were unsteady as I walked to the door, and he did not move to open it for me. I went into the corridor and followed it to the stairs. When I reached my room I stood in the red center of the carpet, with the room glowing about me and I found I was shivering again, as I used to shiver in the hospital. Was it all going to come back? How could I bear it if it did?

Someone had been there in my room—the closet door stood open, and hanging on a rack inside was the costume I would wear to the ball tomorrow night. How was I to put that dress on now? How was I to go down there and dance to music when my world was crashing about me? If I couldn't have Peter, I could't leave Joel. If I couldn't leave Joel, I couldn't go to Bruce. And without Bruce? I didn't know. Now I was truly alone.

16

The rest of that day seemed endless. There was a dinner party for Theo's guests that night, but I avoided it. I walked outside in the rain and I walked again the next day, when the rain had cleared and we had another lovely touch of Indian summer. I didn't dare to visit with Peter, lest he be disturbed by my mood of desperation. I saw Joel only in passing, and I avoided Bruce. I was not yet ready to tell him what Joel had said.

There was, however, no escaping the ball that night. When the time came and I was dressed, I stood looking at myself in the mirror in my room. The gown was a rich midnight blue, with a V-neck and short cap sleeves—a style that had been particularly flattering in its day, with its princess cut that hugged waist and hips, and a front overdrape like a ruffled apron, caught up into a slight bustle at the back. The skirt below hung full and straight to the floor.

Slowly I turned from side to side, studying myself in the long mirror. I had dressed with care, as though dressing for Theo's ball was all important in my life. At least it was a distraction. I could not yet accept or absorb the things Joel had said to me, and I tried to put them away from me for the evening. Tonight I suddenly wanted to be beautiful again, a woman again. I wanted to forget. I even wanted to dance, with Bruce admiring me, and I was unable to think my way past that simple goal.

I had been letting my hair grow and while it was still short, I had been able to brush it upward in a vaguely pompadour style, catching it in place with a rhinestone comb that had belonged to a grandmother I had never known. My face and throat and bare arms looked white in contrast to the dark, brilliant blue—last summer was one in which I'd acquired no tan. Someone had sent a small pot of pink geraniums to my room, remembering Sargent's portrait of Zenia, and I broke off a thick green stem with a cluster of blossoms on the end, catching the pungent geranium odor as I did so. This was the same scent that must have haunted Zenia while she was posing for her portrait. An odd choice of flowers on Sargent's part, but perhaps he had taken what was at hand. I wondered what Zenia had been thinking about while she posed. Perhaps of some lover? As I would think of Bruce? I felt close to Zenia that night. She no longer seemed far away in the past, and I found myself wondering what she had been like when she was young.

When a tap sounded at my door I turned from the mirror. It was Peter, in pajamas and woolly robe, hobbling on crutches, his leg still in a cast. His eyes were dancing with excitement.

"I wanted to see you!" he cried. "Bruce told me you'd look like the painting—and you do. You look just like Zenia. Beautiful."

"I'm not sure of that," I said. "But thank you just the same."

I moved about the room, gesturing with the geranium, basking in my son's approval.

"I've seen Fiona," he informed me. "She really looks like Lady Macbeth in that picture she showed me. But she isn't happy about the ball. I think she's scared about something. Come with me, Mother, and let's go find Grandma Theo. I guess she'll make everybody's eyes pop."

"She'll be down in the ballroom by this time," I said. "Shall we go and look at everything from the balcony where you're going to watch?"

Tonight he was not holding me off, and he was pleased with the idea. We went along corridors that were no longer empty, Peter using his crutches with surprising skill. Overnight guests were coming out of their rooms, and the lady who walked ahead of us wore a white dress with blue coin dots, and a velvet bow tied about one bare arm. I remembered the Sargent portrait.

Peter and I took the back stairs and when we reached the balcony where musicians had once played, all the color and sound and scent of that crystal and crimson room rose to envelop us. The band Theo had hired was already playing romantic tunes on the floor below, though dancing had not yet begun, and Theo was reigning with Ferris beside her, as she stood beneath a reproduction of Sargent's famous portrait of "Madame X." Her sleek black satin gown with brilliants for shoulder straps, her piled-up red hair, with the scarlet flower over one ear, and Diana's diamond crescent shining above her forehead, were true to the portrait, and she carried off the costume as though she had been a great beauty, even a young beauty, so that one almost believed these things were so. Only her green eyes were not the eyes of the painting, but belonged exclusively to Theodora Moreland.

I could not look down upon this room, however, without remembering. The last time it had been bright with lights and music was the night my father had died. The pang of loss stabbed through me once more, familiar, yet never wholly expected. Before he had gone upstairs to his death, Adam had danced with me once that night. It almost seemed that my searching gaze ought to be able to find him among the throng below. There would always be a sense of unreality about what had happened.

The ballroom was not crowded as yet, but more and more people were coming through the double doors at the far end and the great chandeliers above their heads shone down on color and warmth, and lent a certain vibrancy to the gay scene. Theo had done well, I thought, to use no decorations in the beautiful room. The gilded ceiling and painted wall panels, the crimson window draperies, the quilted satin benches around the walls, were enough in themselves to give the great room beauty and dignity. Below the balcony the musicians played old tunes that had worn well, and though they belonged to a later day than the room itself, added to the romanticism of the scene. Theo was hardly a romantic person, but she liked the dramatic, and it was mainly Fiona who had influenced her.

Dresses of the late nineties were more flattering than present day and the women who stood about the floor talking, or gathered around Theo, were beautiful and glamorous. No restrictions had been placed upon the men and they wore everything from white tie to the more decorative dinner jackets of the present, with frilled shirt fronts and cuffs.

Beside me, Peter's eyes glowed with excitement at the brilliant scene. "I'll watch when you dance, Mother," he whispered. "I think you'll be the most beautiful of all."

I hugged him to me. "I won't be that, but thank you anyway. Don't stay up too late, darling. If you like, I'll come up here after a while and see you to bed."

Bed did not interest him, but he nodded vaguely. "Crawford wanted to come and stay here with me, but I coaxed Theo to tell her not to. She'd spoil everything."

There was a faint murmur in the crowd below us as it parted near the far doors to let an impressive figure come into the room. Jon Pemberton had arrived dramatically in top hat and tails, with a gleaming diamond-studded shirt front—the only man in the room who had dressed for the Sargent era and the great days of Newport. A scarlet-lined cape swung gracefully from his shoulders and he had chosen not to surrender cape, hat or cane to the cloakroom attendants. He was a bit of a peacock himself, apparently, but good-humoredly so, and he seemed to thrive on being the center of feminine admirers as he moved about the room. I saw Theo eye him skeptically, and she gave him a slightly mocking greeting when he came her way, but I suspected that he was not one to be disparaged even by Theodora Moreland. Like Bruce, he would always be his own man.

More than once I saw him glance up at Zenia's portrait, and more than once his eyes searched the room, so that I wondered if he were looking for me, to match me with the picture. I would go down in a little while and dance with him, if he wished. In a way, I would feel safer tonight with Jon Pemberton, who was an outsider, than with either Joel or Bruce who would tear at my emotions.

So far, neither of these two had appeared, and I was surprised at Joel's being late. Nor had Lady Macbeth joined the throng, and I wondered if Fiona might choose not to come at all. Perhaps I should have looked in on her before coming down here.

There was a break in the music, and then a new start. Theo and Ferris had moved out onto the floor and others joined them so that the great room was soon filled with decorously waltzing couples following Theo's lead. As I watched, Peter nudged me.

"There's Dad. He's just come in." Peter moved away from me down the rail, the better to see his father.

Joel looked handsome in black tie, contrasting with his usual slightly careless attire. I felt a stab of the old tenderness. I remembered helping him with that tie in the past, and noted that it was badly done. But that was no longer my affair, I reminded myself. I was still watching for Bruce. When I saw him I would go down the balcony stairs.

"Do you remember the last party?" a low voice said behind me.

I swung around to find Fiona there. She looked dramatically in character in the role of Ellen Terry's Lady Macbeth, the metallic blue of her gown glittering in the light from the chandeliers, the long green sleeves shining. On her hair she wore a gilded coronet and there was a golden girdle about her waist. She held her head proudly, like a queen, but her face was unnaturally white and strained, and she had touched her lips with no color, so that she looked like a pale ghost of herself. Perhaps that was the way the Lady herself had looked on a certain fateful night.

"I remember," I told her. "Last New Year's Eve I danced with Adam down there."

"I didn't." Her tone was expressionless. "We were angry with each other and I wouldn't dance with him. He didn't stay down there long anyway. He said he had something important to do and he went upstairs."

"I feel as though I ought to be able to find him down there if I look enough," I said. "There are still so many times when I can't believe he's gone."

As she stood beside me she spoke in a low voice which Peter, at the far end of the balcony, could not hear.

"Christy, you remember the time when Theo made you believe you'd had a lapse of memory? It wasn't true. I helped her with that—and with other things. I came to your room that first night you were here and touched you, and I put those things out on the carpet of your room. Because I wanted you to go away, Christy. For your own good. That was all I wanted."

"I've been sure of this," I said. "But did you wear my father's jacket and lead me downstairs that night?"

"No—no. I never did that. I don't know who it was."

"Why did you hide Ferris's gun?"

She hesitated. "I—I didn't want to see it used. I've been afraid, Christy. Ever since Adam died, I've been afraid."

"Do you know that gun is gone from where you put it?"

"Yes, I checked. But there's nothing more I can do."

"Why are you telling me all this now?"

"Because I'm not going to help her any longer, Christy, no matter what she does to me." She stepped to the balcony rail and gripped it tightly with both hands, as if to steady herself. "I can't bear it," she said. "I hate all this—the music, the lights, the laughter. It's all completely phony. How can Theo do this? When Adam—"

I didn't think she was acting now, as she'd done that time with Ferris in the library. All she was telling me had the ring of truth.

"Then tell me the rest, Fiona. Tell me about Adam."

She gave me a long look in which I sensed doubt and uncertainty. "It's too late. Theo has seen us. Ferris is coming over. There's no escaping now."

Peter thumped back to my side on his crutches as Ferris mounted the balcony stairs. "You have to go down and dance with Dad," Peter whispered. "Tell him I'm up here watching."

His words brought the renewal of pain over what I must do to him.

"I'll tell him," I said. But I didn't want to dance with Joel. I would remember too well the last time I had danced with him on this floor in another lifetime, when I had been another, gentler woman.

"Theo wants you, Christy," Ferris said as he reached the balcony. "She wants to show you off under Zenia's portrait."

I nodded. "I'll go down. Have fun, Peter. Don't get too tired. There are a couple of chairs over there if you want to sit on one and rest your cast on the other."

Ferris and Fiona went ahead of me down the stairs and when they reached the floor he drew her into his arms. They moved out among the dancers, and I saw in Ferris's eyes a look that startled me. Was it an affection for Fiona? Or something else? If he hated Theo, how did he feel about Fiona?

As I followed slowly down the stairs, still carrying my pink geranium blossoms, I saw Bruce come into the room from the opposite end. He saw me halfway down from the balcony, just as I saw him, and he stood still watching me, his eyes hardly wavering. It had been he who had said I must dress like Zenia. I wanted him to be pleased. In his evening dress he was the handsomest man in the room. Jon Pemberton was merely striking.

I made my way around the edge of the room to reach

Theo, who had stopped dancing and stood beside Joel, and though I lost sight of him when I reached the floor level, I suspected that Bruce would be making his way in the same direction.

Theo nodded her approval as I neared her. "Yes, the costume is a success. Bruce was right—you bear a resemblance to Zenia."

"As do you to Madame X," I said.

She accepted my tribute as her due, bowing her head slightly, so that Diana's crescent dipped, as though she had been a tall woman, condescending to my lesser height. It was marvelous the way she could carry off the illusion. The brilliants twinkled on her shoulders, but her green eyes were brighter—emeralds in their own right, though shining with a malice that I could never escape.

Joel said nothing and he hardly looked at me, nor did he ask me to dance, which gave me a sense of relief. But Bruce was there quickly, impressive in his black jacket, and without words being spoken I was out on the floor in his arms, dancing to a medley of Cole Porter tunes. My foolish geranium glowed pink against the black of his jacket as I held it in my left hand. I couldn't bring myself to tell him that I had talked to Joel. I didn't want to remember what Joel had said. Not tonight. Because of Adam and the last time this room had been lighted and filled with people, pain waited for me at the edge of every thought, and I only wanted to push it back for a little while and be happy in Bruce's arms. He must have sensed my mood for he held me gently and there was tenderness in his eyes.

When the music came to a halt, we stood applauding with the other couples on the floor. Bruce nodded repeatedly in recognition of guests whom I knew only from seeing their faces in newspapers or on television. Bruce belonged to that larger world in which Joel, for all that he was a Moreland, had never cared to move.

"You make a perfect Zenia," Bruce said in my ear. "I knew you would. There are even secrets in your eyes—

the way there are in hers. What do you know, Christy, that you aren't telling?"

I glanced up at the portrait over our heads and saw what he meant. Zenia Patton-Stuyvesant had not looked at the artist who was painting her. She gazed off into the distance enigmatically, so that one could not help but wonder what she was thinking. It seemed to me that the look was not a happy one. Was that the way I looked tonight? Unhappy because of all the doubts that beset me? I didn't want to be like that. I wanted to go to Bruce without pangs for what I must do, without question or hesitance. Yet life itself held me back.

I tried to rouse myself from disturbing thoughts. "Have you seen Fiona?" I asked. "She's marvelous as Ellen Terry's Lady Macbeth."

"I've noticed. I saw her dancing with Ferris, looking like death. What's wrong with her?"

I shook my head. The music had started up again, but before Bruce could draw me into his arms, there was an interruption. Moving straight across the floor, so that couples stepped out of his imperious path, came Jon Pemberton. He had finally parted with cape, top hat and cane, and his blond hair stood up in an impressive crest, his blue eyes were alight with a wry humor, and his wide smile was entirely for me.

"Mrs. Patton-Stuyvesant, I believe?" he said, with a bow right out of the Gay Nineties. "Or may I call you Zenia?"

I had to laugh at him. "You know Bruce Parry, of course?"

He took his eyes from me for a moment in order to greet Bruce. "Of course. Hello, Bruce. Will you permit me to steal this lady for a while?"

"Considering that she's my great-aunt, I can't imagine stopping you," Bruce said wryly. "We'll have another dance later, Christy."

Couples were moving about the floor again, but Jon Pemberton did not lead me among them.

"Don't expect me to dance, Zenia. I'm foul at that sort of thing and I'd step all over your feet. Besides, there are more important matters to be accomplished tonight. Joel said he was willing to have you introduce me to the house —its special places. First, Zenia's sitting room. Joel said I must see that—it would characterize her. Will you show it to me? While *you* are in character? Will you play her part for tonight?"

His highhanded exuberance could not be resisted, and in a way it was welcome. It furnished distraction and a suppression of pain from the past and from the present.

"Of course," I said. "That particular room fascinates me. Somehow I feel at home in it. But Bruce is the one who can tell you more than I."

"Not necessarily. He remembers her when she was old. You will remind me of her when she was young. I just want you to *be*—looking as you do now," he said.

As he led me from the room, the band broke into one of the cornier old tunes—the "Tennessee Waltz." That same tune I'd danced to with Joel a thousand years ago— last New Year's Eve. One of Theo's tunes. Again the surge of pain was sudden, unexpected. Strange how the senses remembered the old love, even when the new absorbed all one's being.

We escaped from the throng and made our way across the Marble Hall to the stairs. Caterers were in charge of the buffet supper that would be served at midnight in the big dining room, and we passed a man carrying a huge tray. With swift audacity Jon pilfered two anchovy rounds and we munched on them, laughing, as we climbed the stairs and walked along the second-floor corridor to Zenia's wing.

The sitting room seemed very familiar as I found the switch that lighted the Tiffany lamp. Jon Pemberton sighed with satisfaction, moving about the small, crowded room.

"It's wonderful that Theo had the good sense to preserve this," he said. "It will give me Zenia as little else could. I'll come back tomorrow and write it all down, but for now I just want to look and absorb. Do you mind if we don't talk?"

I wondered why he needed me, and I wanted to get back to Bruce. "Why don't I leave you here so that you can spend all the time you want finding out about her through her things?"

"No. Don't forget that tonight you *are* Zenia. Go over there and sit at her desk. Be Zenia. Do what she might do. You're part of the picture."

I didn't mind too much. Even when I was dancing with Bruce I had to remember the things I had yet to tell him, the things Joel had said. Tonight I didn't want to think. I wanted only to lie fallow and feel nothing. Not old pain or new. Helping Jon Pemberton was an escape at least. Tomorrow I would marshal my forces and try to seek a way out of my dreadful maze. Now I would be Zenia.

When I had seated myself at Zenia's elegant rosewood desk, I picked up a tarnished silver penholder and looked at the rusted nib. There was a blackening silver inkwell on the desk and I lifted its lid to find the dried brown crumbs of long-vanished ink in the glass well. Zenia's book of orders for the day lay on the blotter and I flipped it open to read the names of her servants, notes for the cook, for the head parlor maid, the head gardener. In my imagination I began to identify with her. A real woman, who had sat at this desk—more than a hazy shadow from the past. Flesh and blood as I was flesh and blood.

"That's it," Jon Pemberton said. "Absorb yourself in her things. Forget me."

He moved about the room, an oversized figure in its intimate smallness, touching Zenia's possessions with big, careful hands. I returned my attention to the desk. There were numerous pigeonholes, most of them empty. Any important letters or papers would have been taken away long before this. I pulled open drawer after drawer, to find nothing of consequence. In one place, however, there seemed to be a space for a drawer where no drawer existed. I spoke over my shoulder.

"I do believe I've found some sort of hidden compartment. A lovely Victorian secret drawer!"

Jon Pemberton was beside me at once, leaning past me to examine surfaces, plain and carved. But if there was some point of pressure that might give up the secret, he didn't find it, and in a little while he went back to his tour of exploration.

I didn't want to give up. Since there was nothing else to do, I too pressed and poked and pushed. I opened the top drawer beneath the dropleaf and felt about in its emptiness. Something against the top of the drawer—the bottom of the desk—felt like a lever and I pushed, experiencing a childlike excitement. What secrets might Zenia have hidden away?

Squeaking a little from long disuse, the wooden side of a compartment on the upper desk began to move. I released the lever and found that I could push open a panel upon a hidden recess. This time I said nothing to the man who was looking dreamily at Zenia's mixed bag of pictures on her walls. In the recess were two books and I drew out the top one. It was a gold-embossed leather diary, and I felt a stirring of excitement as I opened it to pages of faded script. That same deliberate script that I had seen in Zenia's morning book.

Zenia's name was on the flyleaf. The first date was a little after the turn of the century, but the notes were cryptic and hardly detailed. She had not bothered with dates.

F.G. here today. Happy.

F. pays attention to me. Arthur forgets I'm alive.

Arthur away on business. F. came. We were discreet because of the servants. But Rosie can be trusted.

Arthur still away. I'm in love.

Papa forced this marriage. I wanted to wait. He said love

was silly, sentimental. Who married for love? Arthur was rich and railroads important. And now there is love. What am I to do?

Rosie says Mr. Townsend next door has been snooping around. He and Arthur are very thick. I don't think he could have seen anything.

I feel sorry for Maddy Townsend, married to that awful man. Theron is vicious. He loves power. So does Arthur, but in a different way. All that room of armor and weapons. Frightening.

Theron watches. F. hasn't dared to come.

Today I met F. in town. I feel reckless and wicked. And happy. Nothing sordid. A small, plain room with a lovely view of the harbor. I watched a boat with a white sail on the green water. F. loves me and I him. If only I could run away with him. Imagine what Papa would say—and Arthur.

Arthur home. No more meetings. I think he suspects nothing. But what am I to do? How can I go on living with him?

That awful Theron Townsend is making trouble. He and Arthur have always been close friends. Maddy came to see me. She is on my side. Theron is going to talk to Arthur. So I will talk to him first.

Arthur says he will never let me go. He called me a silly fool and said I didn't know when I was well off. Townsend has been having me watched. They know about my trips to town. I've written F. to go away. Rosie took the letter.

There was a space in the jottings, and then they took up again at a later date.

No word from F. Arthur says he went off alone on a hunting trip. But I think he would have let me know. I am frightened.

F.'s mother came to Newport. Arthur and Theron Townsend talked to her. Convinced her of the hunting trip. But no word for too long. Perhaps some accident. That's what they say.

I don't believe any of this, but they have satisfied F.'s mother. She is sending friends up to the north woods to look for him. He will never be found. I know that now.

How can I live? How can I bear to see the sun come up over the ocean on a new day? Arthur says I must give a party. I must stop any gossip that might be starting.

Some of the time I am numb, without feeling. I wonder if I have become a ghost? I wonder if I will live in this house to a great old age and wander its halls, remembering. There is to be a ball, as Arthur wishes. The invitations have gone out. I am a stronger woman than I thought. Or a weaker one. Should I speak out. I am afraid. I have no proof.

The ball is tonight. Now I have need for strength. I must dance tonight with horror for my partner. I know what happened to F. I found the book in Arthur's study. The poems by H.W.L. Page 83. He had marked the poem. And I knew. I wondered which one of them killed him—Arthur or Theron? Arthur, I think. And who performed the ghastly deed of hiding the body? The two of them together, undoubtedly. I have brought the book here and I will put it away with this. Someone must know someday. Someday F. will be found and the answer must be given. Shall I go to Redstones? Do I dare?

I felt a little sick as I read. It was as if I had written these words with my own hand, my own blood. I had nearly forgotten Jon Pemberton, and he, fortunately, was paying no attention to me. I took the second book from the recessed hiding place, knowing very well what I would find. It fell open naturally to page 83, as though it had been opened to that old chestnut of Longfellow's a great many times. The words seemed to leap at me from the page with old melodrama that had suddenly become real.

> *Speak, speak thou fearful guest!*
> *Who, with thy hollow breast*
> *Still in rude armor drest*
> *Comest to haunt me.*

I turned back to the few pages left of the diary.

Last night I danced at the ball as though nothing had

happened. Am I a monster too? But how can I speak out and cause a scandal that would destroy us all? When I know F. is dead. What am I to do?

Mr. Sargent came to the ball. Arthur wants him to paint me, but what will he see in my face? I am to begin the sittings tomorrow.

Every day I sit for Mr. Sargent. I am beginning to find the scent of geranium sickening. Every day I try to hide my secret from him. He paints with elegance, brilliantly. He records the moment as he sees it—but I think he does not see very deeply. I am safe. Sitting for him is a respite. Arthur is pleased with the picture. Arthur does not guess what I know.

I cannot write any more. I will never keep a diary again. There is too much which cannot be recorded. But I have at least dedicated my life. I know what I shall do. I can punish Arthur through the weapon of torment. I will never love again and I will never place another man in jeopardy, but I will give Arthur a life as unhappy as I can make it. He will pay for what he has done.

The last lines Zenia had written were scrawled in a strong, reckless hand. They were not like the meticulous writing that had gone before. I would never know whether she had gone to Redstones or not. I closed the diary and put both books back in the recess. It was terrible to think of her later life, lived always in deception and for the purpose of revenge—until the final ending when all the other actors were gone, and only she walked these halls in madness. Or had that very madness meant respite for a mind which had faced horror for too long a time?

In any event, it was not for me to turn these things over to Jon Pemberton. Joel and Bruce would have to decide whether the true story should be told. Since everyone was gone, perhaps the story should be written in all honesty—as could now be done. But Jon Pemberton must wait until Joel and Bruce could think about this. And Theo.

His voice startled me from across the room.

"You look like a very lost lady, Zenia-Christy. I think Sargent never saw all that your face might have told him."

I stared at him in distress, because my own story and Zenia's were beginning to be intertwined. I lived in another day and my problems were hardly the same. Nor were the cures apt to be the same as they had been in the day of Arthur Patton-Stuyvesant and Theron Townsend. But I too was married, and had my "F." I was being blocked from going to him because Joel and his mother held my son. I was even blocked by my own feelings about Peter and the fact that I must take him from his father.

"I think I'm a little tired tonight," I said. "I don't feel like going back to the ball. I'll just go down to get Peter and see him to bed. Then I'll go to bed myself."

He came quickly to stand beside Zenia's desk. "Give me a little more of your time tonight, will you? There's something else I want to see—that later portrait of Arthur. Painted, I believe, shortly before he committed suicide. *If* that's what he did. Will you show it to me?"

I had no wish to go upstairs to the Tower Room, but his request was not unreasonable, and I sensed that he had absorbed himself into the mood and life of the house, as it had once been, and I could serve him best if he saw that portrait now. Besides, though I didn't want to see the room again, I wanted to look with new eyes at Arthur's picture. Tonight it would tell me a great deal.

"All right," I said. "I'll go and get Peter, see him to bed, and come back here."

Jon waved a cheerful hand at me as I went out of the room. I walked along the corridors and down the stairs, aware of my midnight blue gown that was made in the pattern of Zenia's gown in the portrait, and I felt as though I too were a ghost who walked with horror. Spindrift was a house of death and tragedy—Zenia's and Arthur's, and mine because of Adam. Because of Bruce. But

281

no one was going to kill Bruce. Joel was a civilized man. His weapons were different. Nevertheless, I was trapped in my age as Zenia had been trapped in hers.

I had taken the back stairs and when I went through the door to the musicians' balcony, the band down below was playing "Love Walked In." I tried to shut the tune away from me. I didn't want to hear those words echoing in my mind. There was no "sunniest day" for me.

Peter had given up watching and I felt a little guilty because I had not come to him sooner. He had stretched out on the floor beside the balcony rail in his woolly robe, and gone sound asleep, with all that kaleidoscope of sound and color moving brilliantly below him.

For a moment I stood at the rail, not watching the women in their Sargent gowns, but looking straight across to the place on the wall where Theo had hung Zenia's portrait. With all my senses, I *felt* that picture. A living, suffering woman had posed for it, had been alive to horror for every moment while she had endured its painting. Yet she had hidden all this from the painter. He had caught the faraway mystery in her eyes, but he had been more concerned with light and shadow than in portraying a woman. She was there as a lovely, surface thing, but there was no heartbeat in the picture. Zenia had, as she realized, not needed to be afraid of the artist.

I glanced about the floor and found Theo, Ferris, Joel and Bruce. But I could not find Lady Macbeth. Fiona, who hadn't wanted to come to the ball anyway, had probably made her escape. As I would do shortly. I had no desire to join any of the four who belonged to Spindrift. I would show Jon Pemberton Arthur's portrait, and then I would go to bed. I would take a sleeping pill to make me forget everything. Everything. I too needed respite. Tomorrow, like Zenia, I must find the strength to fight again. But my solution would never be like hers. I meant to solve my problem somehow. Only for tonight I would not think about it.

I couldn't carry Peter with that cast on his leg, and he

wakened drowsily, to stumble upstairs to his room with my help. He was half asleep as I got him into bed and covered him gently. Miss Crawford came in from her adjoining room and watched as I kissed him on the cheek and drew the blanket up over his shoulders. There was no animosity in her now.

When I moved to the door she came into the hallway with me. "Did Mrs. Keene find you?"

I shook my head. "I saw her earlier in the evening. Was she looking for me again?"

"Just a little while ago. She said it was important. She said she couldn't find you downstairs."

"No, I wasn't there all the time."

"I told her I'd let you know she was looking for you when you brought Peter back."

"Thank you. I'll look into her room and see what she wants."

It meant another journey to the floor below, but I hurried down and tapped at Fiona's door. Jon Pemberton wouldn't mind waiting. He was happy where he was.

There was no answer and I tapped again. Then I opened the door and looked into the room. The lamp beside the bed had been left burning, but Fiona was not here. On her pillow lay the gilded coronet she had worn with her costume tonight, but there was no other evidence of her presence. I would have to wait until she found me. But I would not stay up for her.

Jon Pemberton was ready for me when I returned to Zenia's room, and he was alight with excitement over plans for his book.

"I was bored with my last writing job," he said. "But I can't wait to get my teeth into this one. There's more here than meets the eye. I'll have to fictionalize, of course. That's my thing—storytelling—and there's too much here that no one seems to know the answers to. So I'll have to make things up."

"Perhaps you won't have to make up a great deal," I said. "I'm ready now to show you the room Arthur used as a retreat, and show you his picture. Not that the room has been kept the same, as Zenia's room has. But at least his portrait is there. It's called the Tower Room."

He nodded and gave me a sidelong look as we went back to the stairs, and I knew he must have been aware of Adam and that particular room. But he said nothing, and I was grateful for that. A heaviness of sorrow lay upon me. Sorrow for Zenia, sorrow for myself. And for Arthur, and Joel and Bruce.

"Here we are," I said, and Jon opened the door for me.

I went first into the room and old horror came up at me like a blow. Old horror and new. I had been here before. I had stood in this spot before. I had seen death before. As I saw it now.

Fiona lay sprawled where Adam had lain, and there were dark, wet stains on the blue of her gown. There was no carpet now, but patches of scarlet on the floor spread away from her body. I turned a little wildly back to Jon Pemberton, and I think I fainted in his arms.

17

When I opened my eyes I was sitting in a chair in the Tower Room, with Jon Pemberton shaking me, not too gently. "Pull yourself together, Christy," he was saying. "She's dead, and I've got to go for help. Can you stay here? Can you hold on?"

I managed to tell him that I would hold on, and he went away, leaving the door open. Waves of terror and nausea swept through me, but I breathed deeply, gulping in the air that would steady me, keep me from being sick or passing out again. When I put my hand to my face, I could smell the geranium scent on my fingers, but I didn't know where I had dropped Zenia's geranium.

When I had quieted a little, I sat back in my chair and stared at Arthur's portrait. I could not look at poor Fiona lying where Adam had lain. Zenia's tragedies were at least more remote and I must make myself think about them. That portrait of Arthur Patton-Stuyvesant had been painted by a lesser artist than Sargent a short time before he died. His grim expression must have been a guard against any revelation of his thoughts. He had been known as a hard and ruthless man. But there had been a weakness, a vulnerability that Zenia had been able to attack. In the end he had taken poison. Now he had watched this new death, impervious to anything that happened in this haunted room. I could well believe that he had died by his own hand—because of the torment to which Zenia had submitted him. And perhaps because of his own memories. Her prophecy in the diary had come true and she had lived to be a very old lady, walking the halls of Spindrift with her bitter memories, until she had peopled the house with those who were no longer there.

What would life be like for me, if I lived till I was very old? Fiona would never know old age. Fiona, who had been Adam's wife.

It was no use. I couldn't think of Zenia and Arthur now. I could only think of Fiona and who might have killed her—because she knew too much and was perhaps ready to talk. She had wanted to see me, Miss Crawford had said. Perhaps she would have confided in me then— finally. Since she had told me a few things earlier, she might have decided to finish her story. Now it was too late and she had been silenced for good. If only I had met her earlier! Perhaps then I could have helped to protect her from the hunter.

At last I made myself look at her there at my feet. She had fallen on her back, with one arm outflung, the pointed green sleeve in that creeping patch of wetness. The other hand was curled in toward her body and I saw for the first time the pistol which lay beneath it.

I was on my feet at once, bending over the gun, though I did not touch it. It looked like the one she had hidden in Zenia's desk—Ferris's automatic pistol. Had she killed herself? Had she done what they claimed Adam had done, repeating the pattern with ironic deliberation? Or had someone else repeated so useful a manner of hiding guilt?

An age seemed to pass, though it must have been only a little while before they were all there in the room with Fiona and me—Theo, Joel, Ferris, Bruce. Jon Pemberton stayed on and no one told him to go away. The police had been sent for, Theo said. She was angry, furiously angry. Adam's death had been bad enough, but she seemed to take Fiona's as a personal affront, and she was more concerned with its happening than she was with Fiona herself.

"If Cabot had only lived—" she said once, and Ferris tried to soothe and quiet her. I remembered Fiona's words—that Ferris detested Theo. Yet he played his role well and Theo leaned on him more than she did on Joel or Bruce. But she did not lose entirely her habit of authority. Once she looked at me with critical eyes. "Are you all right, Christina? Joel, see to her. She looks dreadful, and she'll have to talk to the police when they come."

Joel came obediently to my side, but he did not touch me. "Perhaps you could go and lie down for a little while, Christy. We can get you when you're needed."

I had borne enough and I answered them hotly. "Nearly a year ago someone killed Adam in this room. Now the same person has killed Fiona! When are you going to stop what's happening, Theo?"

Ferris cut quietly into my challenge, though there was tension in his voice. "Adam killed himself and now Fiona has done the same thing."

"No!" I cried. "No, I don't believe it!"

"Don't excite yourself, Christina," Theo said ominously. "If Adam didn't kill himself, perhaps Fiona was the one who shot him, and now she has taken her own life in remorse. God knows she's been upset about something."

We all stared at her, and she looked almost pleased, as though she had finally concocted a theory that would put a final period to everything, leaving no loose ends.

But I wouldn't accept such reasoning. "I don't believe that, and I don't think you do either. Fiona was frightened about something, but she wanted to live."

"In any case," Bruce said, "it's going to be up to the police again."

Joel said nothing at all.

I looked at Bruce desperately and found his gaze upon me unhappily. He still had no right to come to me, to take charge as I might have wanted him to. Nevertheless, when Joel moved away, Bruce came to stand beside my chair. He made no effort to offer empty comfort, but merely stood beside me and I regained a little courage, knowing he was there.

Jon, of us all, was the mere observer, and I suspected

that he was making mental notes that would creep into his writing later, but at least his eyes were kind when he glanced in my direction, and in a strange way he and I shared this event. We two had found her. We two had experienced the first horror and the shock. It had been worse for me because I knew Fiona, and because I had been through this same dreadful experience in this very room less than a year ago.

The questions were waiting at the back of my mind, but I held them off. I didn't think there were two murderers. Whoever had killed Adam had killed Fiona, regardless of that gun forced to her hand.

The rest of what happened that night seemed to fade into a blur. Lieutenant Jimson was there again, and others of the staff that appeared on such occasions to take care of their grisly tasks. I could tell Jimson very little. Fiona had been worried about something. I had a feeling that she knew who had killed my father—but that was only guessing.

This time Jimson was not so easily satisfied with the suicide theory, though it would have simplified matters for him. The situation was desperately difficult for the police, with all those people downstairs who must eventually be questioned. To say nothing of the large staff of servants and moonlighting townspeople who were under this roof. But the police had coped with all this before. Names would be recorded and the questioning would go on for days, weeks, even though these people would not be held here.

After what seemed a very long while I was permitted to go off to bed, and unexpectedly it was Jon Pemberton who saw me downstairs and called Miss Crawford from her room to stay with me until I fell asleep. By this time he looked a little incongruous in his tails and stiff shirt, but he had reverted to his easygoing self, undaunted by what had happened—the uninvolved, but interested watcher.

Only as he left my room did he drop back into character once more. He took my hand and bowed over it gallantly, bent to touch it with his lips.

"Good night, Zenia," he said. "There will be happier times."

But there had been no happier times for Zenia, and I wondered if there ever would be for me.

I tried to smile at him as he went away. Miss Crawford seemed perturbed as she helped me out of my costume and I think she wanted to talk. But I couldn't take any more, and I must have discouraged her. She saw me into bed and brought me water for my sleeping pill. She even asked if she should stay in my room.

"No," I said, "go back to Peter. And don't tell him when he wakes. I'll talk to him in the morning."

She went away, and I gave my weary body over to the luxury of a complete letting-go. I had no special fears for myself at the moment. Fiona had not told me what she might have if I had seen her earlier. I was safe enough for now. Even Theo's old tricks had been stopped and there was nothing to fear any more. So why did I lie here in cold terror instead of going right to sleep? Why must I remember Adam's dead face, and Fiona's, and the face of that grinning skull over at Redstones? Everything seemed to be mixing itself up in my mind as the sleeping pill took effect.

If only I could go to Bruce and stay with him. If only he could hold me and protect me. There had been no one to protect Fiona. Once Adam had taken care of her, had looked after her, even when she wandered, and when he died there had been no one. And now there was no one for me. There were only barriers.

Zenia had suffered her era's terror of public scandal. My terror turned in a different direction. The terror of being put back in the hospital if I allowed myself to be driven to explosive action. The terror of losing my son. Since my talk with Joel, I knew Bruce was already lost. My sore heart had to accept that. I had thought earlier of solving my problems—I had been brave and determined.

Or at least I had told myself that was what I would be to-morrow. Now it was already the early morning hours of that tomorrow, and I had no courage at all. I was as lost to love as Zenia, and there was nothing I could ever do to save myself.

The drug took effect eventually and I fell deeply asleep. My dreams were all confused and unhappy, but I could not remember them when I awakened late the next morning, except for the lingering pain they left behind. I opened my eyes to find Theo beside my bed. I remembered now that there had been a ball, and I wondered what she had done about all those people. But she was experienced in breaking off a party, sending everyone away when the police permitted. She had done it before. She looked rather ghastly this morning in a black wool suit, with no make-up on the mask of her white face, and her green eyes unnaturally bright. The crescent of Diana no longer crowned her red hair, but it had not been lately combed and she had forgotten to remove the wilted flower she still wore over one ear, like the lady in the portrait. I thought irrelevantly of the pink geranium blossoms I had carried and dropped somewhere without noticing.

"Are you awake, Christy?" Theo's voice was hoarse, as though from overuse. "Can you talk?"

I made an effort. "I'll try. Have you found out anything?"

There was a faint hesitation before she answered. "Nothing. Of course the police aren't committing themselves as yet. But Fiona must have talked to you. What did she tell you that might have led her to this?"

"I think she was about to tell me something, but she didn't have time. I think she knew who killed my father, and that the same person killed her."

Theo moved a chair over to my bed and sat down in it heavily. "If you really think she was murdered, Christy, who do you think did it?"

I could answer that easily enough. "I haven't any idea."

"That's just as well," she said, and I wondered if that

was a relaxing of her guard that I saw in her face? Almost imperceptibly, she seemed reassured, though her fingers twined together, betraying inner strain.

"Did you know that Fiona has been meeting Ferris Thornton over at Redstones?" she asked me.

I stared at her. "Why?"

"I thought you might know why."

"That time I saw candlelight in the windows—was that what was happening?"

It was hard for Theo to give up her habit of putting me down for my delusions. "I suppose so," she said grudgingly.

I puzzled over this in silence. It was Fiona who had assured me that Ferris no longer harbored any affection for Theodora. But he was years older than Fiona. As old as my father. My fuzzy mind suddenly remembered that Fiona had married my father.

"Was she in love with him?" I asked.

Theo said, "Don't be absurd," and I wondered if she still believed in Ferris's devotion to herself. Last night he had continued to play the game, but he had never been one to give away what he was thinking or feeling.

"How do you know they've been meeting over there?" I asked, realizing in surprise that though she had come to interrogate me, it was I who was asking the questions, and she wasn't even struggling against what she might once have regarded as impertinence.

"Joel has been keeping an eye on Redstones ever since you saw a light over there. He's seen them together, though he hasn't said a word to me until now."

Joel wouldn't have, of course. But anything might be pertinent now.

"Have you asked Ferris about this?"

Something strange and unfamiliar seemed to pass over Theo's face—could it possibly be that she was afraid? Was all that indomitable courage crumbling at last? And if it was, why was she afraid? How much did she know?

"Not yet," she said. "I don't know whether I will. Christy, would you ask him?"

"Why are you afraid to?" I challenged.

She rallied her forces at that and frowned me down. "Don't be stupid, Christina. It's just that there's this old legend of his being once in love with me and never getting over it. I even used to believe in it. But not lately. In the last year he's changed. I lean on him to assist me in business matters, but I don't altogether trust him any more. You used to be his favorite young person. He might talk to you. Will you try it today, Christy?"

"I'll talk to him, if you like," I said doubtfully. "But not now. I still feel a little shaky. I can't believe last night was real. I can't believe Fiona is gone."

"Nor can I," she said. "Stay in bed for a while. I'll send breakfast up to you." She seemed unexpectedly kind, but I was wary. "The police will be back. That Jimson person will be here again. He promised me that when he left this morning. Reporters have already been here, arriving from everywhere. I've arranged to see them later."

And I knew she would. Theodora Moreland had been bred on newspapers. Repugnant as her duty to the press might be on this occasion, she would talk to reporters.

"Have you had any sleep yourself?" I asked.

"I lay down for a while, but I couldn't sleep. No one came near me," she added, marveling—she who was accustomed to dancing attendants. "I had to send for Joel. He's upset too, of course. But Ferris and Bruce have stayed away, and there's no Fiona."

"I'll help if there are things you need me for," I found myself offering.

She gave me her old look which dismissed any hint that I might be useful or capable, and stood up.

"We'll see. I'll have to hire someone now. To take Fiona's place. But Fiona was like a daughter. She was my son's wife."

This was tardy sentiment. Theo had used Fiona, but she had not used her kindly.

"She was married to my father," I said.

Familiar antagonism bristled between us, and Theo went through the door without another word. I got out of bed and took a shower to wake myself up. I didn't intend to get up yet. My head still felt woolly and I couldn't face the world. I wanted to see Peter, but not in this confused state. I wondered if he had been told, and who had told him. My drugged sleep had made me derelict there and I could only blame myself. But I would go to him soon.

I looked in my closet for a warm robe I could wear in bed. Adam's plaid sports jacket hung among my dresses and I felt a pang of recognition. I put my hand on the sleeve as I had done so often when I had searched for him among his things. But now I knew they were empty of his presence. I could no longer find him there when I touched his jacket. The sense of loss was in me, but I no longer wanted to press my cheek against his sleeve, pretending that I touched him. Perhaps this was an indication of further healing. I had moved along the path that led away from intense grief. I had begun to accept at last the permanence of loss that I must live with. I would miss him in so many ways, but now I could begin to remember happier, more comforting times.

I slipped into the blue wool robe and tied the sash about my waist. Then I got back into bed. My head felt heavy, my wits dull. What had happened to Fiona still carried a sense of unreality. I had been through this before. Perhaps this was one of nature's buffers—a protection against the shock of death. For a while everything would move in a dream—unbelieved and unaccepted. Totally unreal. By the time this sense of unreality passed, as it must, the sharpness of pain would be deadened a little. Later I would feel everything deeply, but not with that first agony I might have suffered. I was beginning to realize how fond I had been of Fiona—fonder than I knew.

A knock on the door brought a drowsy maid with my breakfast tray, and in her wake came Joel.

When the lap tray had been set across my legs, and the girl had gone away, Joel stood silently beside my bed. We

293

had barely greeted each other. I could not forget what had been said between us yesterday and I felt no inclination to be friendly. When I had eaten some toast and taken several sips of coffee, ignoring him, he began to ply me with questions. There was a series of them, almost like Theo's. Exactly what had Fiona talked to me about the last few times I had seen her? Why did I believe that she knew someone had killed Adam? What conclusions had I come to from her words? There was a pressure here that I had seldom felt in Joel before.

I had nothing to tell him because Fiona had told me nothing, and Joel sat staring at me with frost in his eyes.

"Theo tells me you discovered that Fiona and Ferris were meeting over at Redstones," I said. "Have you any idea why?"

"Ferris is the only one who knows the answer to that," he said. "Perhaps you'd better ask him."

"But your mother says you've been watching Redstones."

He was silent, his look veiled, giving nothing away. I went on.

"Fiona did tell me that Ferris's pose of devotion to your mother has been faked for some time."

"We all knew that."

I set down my coffee cup and leaned back against the piled-up pillows, closing my eyes. I couldn't bear to watch that wintry expression. It was strange enough to try to face the fact that he no longer loved me, but I hated this new merciless quality in him, this new, unrelenting force. Or was it new? Had he been like this all the time—like his mother? Had I been blind in the past to something that was only now surfacing to my clearer vision?

"Perhaps everyone else knew," I said, "but I didn't. I always believed the legend."

"Ferris has wanted Fiona to marry him for some time," he said.

How ignorant I had been!

"Then why didn't she?"

"Perhaps she couldn't be silenced that way," Joel said.

My eyes flew open. "What do you mean by that?"

"Nothing. I was trying to startle you, and I see I did. You are alive, after all."

It was my turn to ignore a challenge. "Has anyone told Peter?"

"Theo wanted me to. So I did."

"How did he take it?"

"I think this is too big for him to understand. I don't think he has fully taken it in."

Like the rest of us, I thought.

"I should have been the one to tell him. I might have softened it," I said.

"Then why didn't you?"

I had already accepted blame for this in my own mind, and I spoke more humbly. "I'll go to him this morning. I've been rather knocked out myself."

Joel got up and walked out of the room without answering that.

I knew I couldn't stay in bed any longer. Bed was an escape from the menace that might now turn against me. Fiona's death did not leave me safe. Everything she had been afraid of still existed to threaten me—the truth about Adam's death. If Fiona had told me what she knew, would I be alive this morning? Which one of them was trying so desperately to save his own skin?

I put on a navy blue pants suit and tied a yellow scarf defiantly about my neck. Because I didn't want to go about looking as Theo had, because I wanted to *look* brave. I smoothed on my lipstick with a careful touch. Then I went upstairs to Peter's room.

Miss Crawford was nowhere in sight, but a small table had been drawn beside the window where sunlight poured in, and Peter and Bruce were seated on opposite sides of a chessboard. Peter looked up at me with a smile as I came through the door.

"Mother, I'm beating him! I'm beating him for the first time!"

So much for the tragedy of Fiona's death. The young could sometimes bounce back more easily than we thought.

Bruce's smile was weary, and I loved him for coming here to be with Peter. "I'm afraid my mind isn't thoroughly on the game. But you're a good player, Peter."

"That's because you taught me," Peter said.

I watched as he studied the board to make his next move.

"Where is Miss Crawford?" I asked.

Bruce nodded toward the next room and I went to find the governess lying on her bed with a cold compress on her head.

"Can I do anything for you?" I asked.

She reached up to push the cloth away. "Thank you. I feel better now. It's all been so awful. Especially after what Mrs. Keene said to me last night."

I pounced. "What was that?"

The woman on the bed winced and put a hand to her temple. "I blame myself now. I'm very upset, Mrs. Moreland. I should have behaved differently. I know that now."

I tried to speak more quietly. "What do you mean? What happened?"

"Mrs. Keene came here while Peter was downstairs. She wanted to leave a letter with me. It was to be delivered to you if anything happened to her. I asked what she meant by that, but she wouldn't explain and she was behaving so strangely that I didn't want to take the responsibility. She seemed a little—irrational—and I told her that she should give the letter directly to you herself. Did she bring it to you?"

"No. When I saw her she said nothing about a letter. And later, when she was looking for me, we didn't meet."

Miss Crawford moaned faintly. "I should have done what she asked. I know that now. But her manner frightened me. The way she looked in that costume—like death. Death to come, wasn't it?"

"Don't blame yourself," I said. "She shouldn't have troubled you with anything like that."

"I don't suppose it's likely," Miss Crawford said, "but perhaps she gave the letter to Mr. Parry when I wouldn't take it."

"To Mr. Parry?"

"I think she was looking for him, as well as for you."

"I'll ask him," I said.

The governess roused herself and slowly got up from the bed. "My head is better. Thank you, Mrs. Moreland. I can stay with Peter now. Mr. Parry rescued me when I was feeling dreadful. But I took some pills and they've begun to work."

From the next room I heard a shout of triumph. "Checkmate! Checkmate! Will you play me another game, Bruce?"

When I joined them, Bruce was rising from the table. "Not now, Peter. I'd like to talk to your mother for a while."

Peter looked disappointed, as though he had wanted us both to stay with him. When I held him close for a moment and dropped a kiss on his cheek, he clung to me, but he did not mention Fiona. For now, at least, he had thrust all that dark knowledge away to the back of his mind where it might surface later. When it did, we would have to talk. Then, having made my comfortable deductions, as I went out the door with Bruce, Peter said something that startled me.

"It's like television, isn't it?"

I stopped in the doorway, realizing his meaning. I knew Theo indulged him with anything on TV he wanted to see, and because of violence on programs he must have watched, he could accept violence in the real world as something commonplace. Horror lay in such a world and Peter already needed help. While my overreaction to Adam's death had upset him, it would be far better for Peter to feel grief than to dismiss what had happened as ordinary. But now was not the time to deal in depth with the concept of death. I needed to find wisdom of some sort in myself before I talked to him.

As we went down the corridor, Bruce touched my arm lightly. "It's a bright morning—let's go out to the pergola."

I asked nothing more than to be with him quietly until my energy returned. Then I must decide what to do. I had been drifting long enough. I left him to pick up a jacket and met him again at a side door.

It was a warm morning for November and I raised my head to the renewal of sunshine as we stepped out the door on the other side of the house from Redstones. I was glad not to look at that structure now.

The pergola stretched its long white trellis in the direction of the sea, and there was that lounging greyhound in weathered stone at its entrance, its ears cocked alertly, its tail curved around the base of the pedestal. Peter had always loved the greyhound. When we'd come here when he was small he used to like to ride on its back. I gave the sun-warmed stone head a light pat as I passed it. There were so few pleasant memories Spindrift had for me.

Italian tiles paved the floor beneath vine-covered trellises, and dappled sunshine lay upon their terra cotta squares. A white bench invited us and I sat down on it, with Bruce beside me. For a time we stayed there in silence, drinking in the deceptive peace, letting warmth seep through our chill. There was no real peace and the chill went bone deep, but for a little while I was at ease. There were things I must talk about with Bruce, but they could wait a little.

When the silence grew long, I began to speak of faraway matters. "I haven't had time to tell you, but I found a diary last night that belonged to Zenia Patton-Stuyvesant."

Bruce was thinking of the present and for a moment it was as if he didn't know who I was talking about. Then he said, "Zenia? A diary?"

I told him what I had read, even to the finding of the Longfellow poem. It was a distraction from the present, at least, and he heard me out. As I spoke I noted how worn he looked from lack of sleep. As with all of us, what had happened had taken its toll. But Zenia's story could interest him, since he was her great-nephew.

"So that's what happened. I'm afraid Spindrift has a grisly history." Abruptly, he returned to the present. "Have you seen Theo this morning?"

"Yes. She came to my room. She looks pretty awful. I expect we all do."

"She'll have to face what's happened now," he said.

"She pretends not to know anything."

"Of course. She's got to put up a wall of protection at all costs."

"Protection for whom? I can't believe Theo would protect a murderer, even if exposure should mean telling the truth about Hal and what the paper was doing."

He didn't answer that, and my mind went woolgathering over my own words. Theo would never hesitate to turn Ferris over to the police if she believed him guilty, any more than she would hesitate to do the same thing with Bruce. There was only one person she would protect at all costs—her son. And not for a moment could I believe that Joel was capable of the crimes which had been committed.

Bruce was speaking quietly, and I forced myself to listen. "Perhaps it's Theo who must be protected now. Whether she wants me to or not, I think I'll stand by. I don't want to leave her to Ferris any longer."

I glanced at him quickly. "For any particular reason?"

"No. Only a sense of uneasiness."

I could agree with that. Ferris was still a mystery to me. I had known him all my life, yet I had realized in this short time I'd been at Spindrift that I did not know him at all.

"Maybe we can persuade her to close Spindrift and let us all go back to town."

"The police aren't going to permit that for a while," he reminded me. "Christy, have you talked to Joel yet?"

I didn't want to tell him, but the time had come. "Yes. I talked to him yesterday. I let him know that I wanted to end our marriage. He said he wouldn't oppose me, but that he and Theo would see that Peter stayed with him." I could hear my voice, drained of emotion because I had gone numb again since Fiona's death. In a little while I must wake up and start feeling, but for now any emotion at all seemed dangerous. There was no answer ahead and I was afraid to feel.

Bruce put an arm about me and drew me close. "Don't think about it now, darling. We'll work it out in time. You've had too much to endure since last New Year's Eve."

"Miss Crawford told me something just now that might make all the difference," I said. "Fiona tried to leave a letter with her last night that she was to give me. Crawford wouldn't take it, and Fiona never delivered it. She didn't come to you with the letter, did she?"

Bruce shook his head. "I met her briefly in the hall last night, but she didn't say anything about a letter."

"Then unless she destroyed it, it must be around someplace."

"If you're right, we'd better find it. I'll get back to the house and have a look."

I was glad that he found the matter of the letter urgent, but somehow I had little hope that he would find it.

It was just as well that he moved away from me at that moment because a man appeared suddenly in the opening to our shelter, and while I stared in astonishment, he began to speak hurriedly.

"You're Mrs. Christina Moreland, aren't you? The younger Mrs. Moreland? And you found the body last night, didn't you? Will you tell me—"

But Bruce was on his feet, tall and formidable. "Mrs. Theodora Moreland has promised you an interview. That's enough."

The reporter stayed where he was and I knew that our moments of privacy were over.

"Let's go inside," I said to Bruce.

"How did you get past the guards?" Bruce asked the man, and was met with a cocky grin.

As we fled back to the house past the end of the long veranda that fronted the ocean, I saw Ferris standing at the rail, and I paused.

"I want to talk to him. Go along to Theo, Bruce."

The reporter had followed us, but Bruce turned to him again with a look in his eyes that must have decided him to choose the course of discretion, for he disappeared toward the front of the house. I gave Bruce a wry smile and went up the veranda steps.

If Ferris heard me coming down the long stretch, he gave no sign. His look was fixed upon some point far out on the sunny water, and as I walked toward him I had time to wonder if I was afraid of him. Yet how could I be? If he had been fond of Fiona, he could not have been the one to end her life. If he had been fond of her.

I went to stand beside him at the rail silently. He turned his head and gave me a brief glance and no greeting, then fixed his attention upon that distant spot again.

"Why did it happen?" I said softly. "Why Fiona?"

No muscle of his face moved, and he still did not speak.

"I cared more about her than I knew," I went on. "She hasn't been like herself for a long time."

"No," he said. The one word of agreement.

"Have the police any theory yet?"

He shook his head. "I'm not in their confidence. None of us is."

"You know what she believed, don't you?" I pressed. "She knew that Adam was murdered."

"I don't think she ever said that. Nor do I believe that he was."

"You're wrong, Ferris. She knew. She was going to tell me, but she didn't get to it. Miss Crawford says she even wrote me a letter that I haven't received. Perhaps if that letter is found—"

"If there is such a letter, it might be better if it's never found," he said evenly.

I stared at him. "Why do you say a thing like that?"

"Perhaps Fiona did know too much. She wouldn't tell me what she knew, but she died because of it. Don't look for that letter, Christy."

So Ferris too did not believe in Fiona's suicide. I remembered the question Theo had asked. Now was the time to put it to him.

"Theo says the light I saw at Redstones that night was because you were meeting Fiona over there."

For the first time he turned his head and looked at me, seemed to examine my face gravely and judiciously before he came to some conclusion.

"I can tell you about that now. Once, more than a year ago, Fiona and Adam went over there to explore. Adam remarked that it would be a wonderful place for the hiding of treasure. As you probably know, she and Adam had a furious disagreement before he died and during their argument he said he had written down a complete exposé about Hal and the Moreland papers in his log, and that he had hidden these pages in Newport for safekeeping. But he wouldn't tell her where.

"He said he was going to blow everything into the open, and Fiona was afraid of what would happen if he did. A few days before he'd told me the same thing and I had an argument with him about it."

"But in the end someone managed to stop him," I said.

Ferris went on as though I had not spoken. "Afterwards, both Fiona and I wanted to find those pages, and she remembered what Adam had said about Redstones being a good hiding place. So we searched there together. And once I went over alone at night—the time you saw my light. Of course we found nothing. But I didn't leave any candles behind over there. I didn't mind leading a search of the place with you and Theo because I supposed nothing would be found. I was surprised when that candle turned up."

"Joel left it there. He had more candles in that flight bag he'd put in a closet. He told me he wanted something to be found, so Theo couldn't say I was imagining things."

"I suspect he wanted more than that. Joel and Bruce were both curious about the light you'd seen and they started watching the place. So Fiona and I gave it up as a bad job. We didn't want word of those log pages to get out."

Never had Ferris Thornton talked to me so openly and I decided to push matters still further while he was in this expansive mood.

"Theo was using Fiona to play tricks on me when we first arrived, in order to frighten me. But she said she never put on Adam's jacket to coax me downstairs. Was it you?"

"No, of course not," Ferris said calmly.

"Was it you in Zenia's study with the scarf?"

He looked out across the ocean again. "Fiona told me about that. She said you'd found the pages of the log and they were taken from you. But not by her. Or me."

If he had done these things he wouldn't tell me anyway. He had lied before, and he was on guard again. When he turned suddenly and grasped me by the arm I was thoroughly startled.

"Stop your searching, Christy. Stop it. If you keep on you may not like what you find. Let the police handle this. It's not your job."

I flared out at him. "The police were wonderful in Adam's case, weren't they? Putting it down to suicide!"

He moved away from me at the rail and his attention seemed fixed again upon some distant spot. I couldn't bear his dry lawyer's manner any longer. If he had loved Fiona, I supposed that he was grieving for her in his own way, but it wasn't my way. Something had to be done— something, something!

And I was the one who had to do it. I was the only one left who cared, who wanted to do it.

I turned my back on the sunny day and went through a door into the gloom of Spindrift halls. The answer was here—here in this house—and perhaps I was closer than ever to finding it.

18

The days that followed seemed to move past in an undistinguishable haze. The outsiders who had come to Theo's ball had all gone home. But those who belonged in the house had to stay.

For all my determination and desire to take some useful action, there seemed nothing I could do. For all that I had felt myself close to the truth, there was no handle I could take hold of. No new evidence of any kind had turned up. No one was discovered by the police to have any enmity toward Fiona, and while there was some doubt this time, they were coming to the conclusion that she must have killed herself. Adam's death had left her grieving and unsettled, they said, and Theo did her best to further this conclusion. She wanted everything to quiet down, wanted the police to release us so we could all go back to New York—and she wanted to keep hidden whatever it was she knew or suspected.

The one positive thing I managed during this time was a talk with Peter about death, and about the reality of death as distinguished from death in the make-believe world of television. It was true that violent death happened in the real world, I told him, but it was never to be taken for granted casually as a proper pattern of life. Fiona was real, and Fiona had died, and we would grieve for her. She should not have died violently. This was never the answer to any problem and it was not a solution good people chose.

I don't know how much of what I said got through to him, but at least I tried.

During this period I became aware of one thing that

had not existed to the same degree before. Theodora Moreland was terrified. Someone was nearly always with her now—Bruce or Ferris or Joel—and sometimes she even tolerated my presence and company. But whomever she was with, the terror persisted.

Not until the day when the police finally withdrew and we were left free to go wherever we wished, did I discover who it was she feared.

Ferris had come to tell me that he was going to town and that Theodora wanted me in the library. The strain of the last weeks had left Ferris looking worn, and it seemed to me that he had aged greatly. But if, as Fiona had told me, he disliked Theo, he continued to serve her well—or was it that he was simply watching her? I didn't know which.

The morning was cold and a heavy fog had rolled in from the sea. I put on navy wool pants and my red turtleneck sweater before I went downstairs to see Theo.

The library was, for me, a room stamped with Fiona's presence. I remembered her pumpkin-yellow caftan, and I remembered her graceful movements wearing it. Once more a fire blazed in the grate and I could almost see Fiona sitting there on one of the oyster-white sofas. Would there have been anything I could have said or done that day which would have changed or prevented what happened later? I didn't know. But I did cast a hasty glance at the balcony, and as far as I could see there was no one there.

Theodora Moreland stood beside one of the long windows looking out at the fog. She no longer neglected her dress, as she had done for a time after Fiona died, and the long jade green gown she wore became her, with her high-piled red hair that added to her height. Dangling jade earrings danced as she turned her head to look at me and then gave her attention once more to the side view from the house.

"What's he doing out there?" she said.

I went to stand beside her and look out into the mist.

At the entrance to the pergola Joel stood with his back to us.

"He has always loved the fog," I said. "Once when we visited San Francisco he spent hours on the streets, just walking about in the fog. Peter loves fog too."

"How can he bear it?" Theo murmured. "It was foggy the day Iris and Cabot died, and he's always blamed himself for that."

"What is it?" I said. "What's the matter?"

She left the window and went to seat herself on a sofa near the fire and I saw that she was shivering.

"Come here, Christy," she said, and her voice commanded me.

I went to sit beside her, grateful for the warmth of the fire, cold without knowing why. Her fingers were nervously busy, playing with her rings.

"I'm afraid," she said. "I'm terribly afraid. Something awful is going to happen. I can't hold it all back any longer. I'm going to be run over, annihilated. I'm going to be punished. I didn't mean—I didn't mean—" she broke off.

I said nothing. I didn't want to stem this outpouring, wherever it might lead.

"He's going on with it," she continued. "There's no way I can stop him."

"Joel?" I breathed the word faintly, not believing.

She went on as though she hadn't heard me. "I didn't mean what happened. I didn't mean him to go so far. Now I can't stop the avalanche. It will be safer if I can get back to New York. There's danger here. Danger for you too, Christy. He's begun to be afraid of you, afraid of what you know."

"Adam was killed," I said. "And so was Fiona. Is that what you mean?"

"Yes—yes! And now it's too late to stop what's been started. I didn't mean this, Christy. I didn't mean what happened."

"And you've been protecting Joel?"

Before she could answer there was a knock on the door and Bruce came in.

"You wanted me, Theo?"

She recovered herself with an effort and reached into a pocket of her gown to draw out a ring of keys. "Ferris has gone to town for me. Will you go over and see that Redstones is locked up and all the windows are closed? I'm returning to New York this afternoon. The servants can close up this place. I never want to see it again."

Bruce took the keys from her. "I'll take care of it, of course." He glanced at me questioningly, but I had no answer for him. I supposed I would go back to New York with Theo and Joel. Bruce had his own car. When would I see him again?

As soon as he had gone Theo jumped up and went to stand close to the fire, as though warmth would never return to her body, and the flames lit reddish lights in the green of her gown.

"Tell me what happened," I said. "Tell me what really happened."

She turned upon me with a suddenness that startled, her eyes alive with malice. "So that you can turn me over to the police? That's what you'd like, isn't it? Then you'd have Peter—when you don't deserve him. You don't deserve him at all!"

There was a violence in her that I had never sensed before, and I didn't want to stay in the room with her a moment longer. I ran the length of the library and let myself out the door. If she was afraid of Joel, it was not because of anything he had done; but because of her own guilt.

I had to see Bruce again and I had to see him right away. Out on the veranda the fog rolled in billows, so that the rail was barely visible, I turned in the direction of Redstones, but as I followed the long veranda to the far steps, the mists thinned for a moment out on the lawn and I saw Joel walking there. My footsteps must have sounded on the bare planks because he turned and looked toward me and we could just make each other out through the veils of fog.

"Christy!" he called, and suddenly I was afraid. I didn't want to be alone with him out there.

I ran down the steps and let the fog swallow me. When I looked back I couldn't see him, and he didn't call me again. In moments Spindrift was invisible and I couldn't see Redstones either, but I knew its direction. The iron curlicues on its fence brought me up short, damp and cold beneath my hands. I followed the tall black spears and found the gate open.

The fog was so thick in pockets around the house that I dared not run, but I found my way along the weed-grown driveway until the house loomed suddenly before me, its peaked roofs wreathed in fog. I stumbled up the steps and through the unlocked front door to the clammy cold of the front hallway. Here mist penetrated in thin wisps, and that single suit of armor with its open visor seemed to leer at me, reminding me of other armor and another, desperate time.

From upstairs came the slamming of a window that told me Bruce was still there. I called to him up the stairwell, and he came at once to the banister, looking down at me.

"Christy! What are you doing here?"

"I had to see you again before you left. Bruce, I'm afraid of them both. Theo and Joel. I'm afraid to go home with them. Theo's changed and she's talking wildly. Will you take me with you when you leave?"

"Are you going to leave Peter behind?" Bruce started down the stairs.

"No. I'll go back for him, if you'll wait for me. Perhaps you can take us to that apartment you found in New York?"

"Of course, if that's what you wish. What's happened, Christy?"

"Theo is afraid of Joel for some reason, and she was almost threatening with me just now."

Bruce came down beside me and put his hands on my shoulders, quieting me.

"There's nothing to worry about. Let's sit here on the stairs and talk a little. Then I'll finish closing Redstones and we'll pick up our things, get Peter and be on our way to New York."

I couldn't feel altogether easy, even though Bruce was with me. "Joel's walking around out there in the fog. What if he comes here?"

Bruce laughed. "I don't think you're really afraid of Joel, and I'm not either."

He pulled me down on the steps beside him and his arm was around me, holding me close. Yet the old numbness was upon me and it frightened me that suddenly I could feel nothing.

"Listen to me, Christy," he said. "When I leave Spindrift today, I'm through with the Morelands. I'm going away. Will you come with me?"

"I'll come with you to New York," I said. "But I'll have Peter and I want to keep him. I can't come to you to stay until everything is worked out."

"Peter and I get along fine," Bruce said. "I've always wanted a son. We'll have him with us in the end."

I huddled close to his warmth, clinging to safety in a sort of desperation, wishing I wasn't numb to everything but fear.

"I'd like Peter to grow up like you," I said. "Like Adam. You are like Adam, you know." Once I'd promised myself to make no more comparisons—yet here I was doing it again. With, of course, the wrong result.

I had annoyed him, and he took his arm from around me. "No, Christy. There's been enough of that. I'm not in the least like Adam. If that's the image you're harboring, it won't do. You're wrong, and I don't want that sort of love. You've got to love me because I'm myself—Bruce Parry. Not because you think I resemble someone else."

"I know. I shouldn't have said that. But just the same,

there is a resemblance and I value it. You have Adam's courage and his integrity."

"Integrity? Are you so sure about Adam?"

I remembered the things Joel had said, but I didn't want to hear them again from Bruce. Nevertheless, he went on.

"Do you think Adam was wholly blind to what was happening on the paper? Any more than Ferris was blind? Or I? I let you think I was, but it wasn't true. And now I want everything out in the open and honest between us. That's the way love has to be. We all saw men being destroyed, and we were selfish enough, fearful enough for our own jobs, so that we closed our eyes. All but Joel. Hal had to keep the whole thing away from him because he knew Joel would never keep still. Theo knew that too. Knows it now. That's why she's afraid. Not even she could have kept Joel quiet, once he had an inkling of what was going on. She suspects that Joel will fight this through in his own mind and blow everything sky high. That's another reason I want to be away."

When I tried to protest, he quieted me with a hand on my arm and continued.

"Those faked letters obtained from supposedly unimpeachable sources, the photographs retouched, faked—all these were so Hal could wield the power he wanted to wield. Anyone who stood against Hal Moreland was wrong and had to be stopped, destroyed. And I helped him, Christy, I helped. I'm not proud of it, but I did."

I couldn't bear the things he was saying. In his effort to be honest with me he was running himself down without mercy.

"No!" I said. "If you helped it was because you were caught in some way I don't understand. And Adam—he would never have gone along with all that."

"But he did, Christy. He did until the day when he began to realize what Theo Moreland meant to do to you. Even then she was bent on breaking up your marriage and taking Peter away from you. She could never forgive you for being Adam's daughter. When he realized that, he threw his own safety to the winds. Maybe his integrity was a bit tarnished around the edges, but it was never as bad as the stories Theo cooked up after he died, about his dealing with the underworld and all that."

"I knew those things weren't true," I said.

"No, they weren't. But some of the things he did earlier were true enough. At least his love for you was never tarnished, Christy. You've got to understand all this. You've got to love people as they are, not because of some dim-witted ideal you like to hold onto."

His words hurt me. I wanted him to be my ideal, just as Adam had been. I couldn't accept what he was telling me.

"How much do you love me, Christy? How well could you love me if you knew all about me?"

There was a passionate plea in his voice and I had to respond to it. I had to fight down all doubt and escape this terrible numbness.

"We'll forget all about this," I said. "This wasn't what you wanted to do, I know, and—"

"Stop it, Christy!" he cried. "That's not the kind of love I want. I want a woman who would give up everything for me, no matter what I am. Love me at all costs. If necessary, give up her son for me. I thought you were a woman after my own heart—determined, courageous, a little ruthless. I'd always thought you were wasted on Joel."

I was silent, frightened. This was my future life that was being laid bare and threatened.

"Let me tell you something more," he went on, relentless now. "You'll remember that Adam and Fiona quarreled seriously the night he died? That was because he told her what he was going to do. She felt tied to Theo, tied to Adam's comfortable job. She couldn't bear it. When he left her she went straight to Theo and told her that he planned to expose what Hal had done. Theo sent for me. She told me to stop him."

"No," I whispered. "No!" It seemed to be the only word I knew.

"Yes, Christy. Oh, I didn't mean to kill him. I only went up to the Tower Room to talk to him, threaten him with a few unpleasant things that might happen if he went ahead. But he had a gun and he waved it at me. We struggled and you know what happened. The gun turned in on him—and that was that. It was an accident, but I had to get out of there, and I did. Not even Theo knew for sure what had happened. She didn't dare question me because she was really to blame. I never told anyone. But she knew I had gone there."

I could hardly breathe. It seemed as though my heart had constricted so that it would never beat again. I did not recognize my own strained voice when I spoke.

"What about Fiona? She was up in the Tower Room that night, wasn't she? I found her earring. She must have seen you go in when she left. Did you kill Fiona too?"

"Christy, Christy, be reasonable! I had to stop her. What else could I do? I knew Theo would never talk because I had only to say that she had ordered me to kill Adam. Fiona loved me once. But she was afraid of me. For those two reasons she kept silent. But I knew she was getting near the cracking point. She was ready to tell you everything. And I didn't want that. If it had to be done, I wanted to do it myself."

"Then it was you in Zenia's sitting room—with the scarf?"

"Darling, I'm sorry about that, but I had to have those pages. I'd searched, but all I found was Ferris's gun in a drawer. When you sat down to read I had to stop you because I knew my name would be there. That scarf hung over the arm of a chair, so I picked it up. I didn't mean to hurt you—just to take those pages and get away."

His monstrous, reasoning words seemed to run on and on in my ears. Like a cold and fearsome river, drowning everything. Yet the ultimate shock quieted me. Now I must know everything.

"Was it you who wore my father's jacket that night?"

His smile was rueful. "It was Theo's idea to frighten you after she'd drugged your drinks. But I saw other possibilities. I wanted to get you downstairs alone with me—where we could talk and I could make a beginning with you."

Strangely, I could reason too. "But your raincoat was wet, as though you'd just come in from outdoors."

"I planned that. I left it outside in the rain and while you were busy trying to hide from me, I took off the jacket and put on the coat. But none of this matters now. All that matters is whether I can be sure of you, Christy. Will you still come to me when you can?"

I shrank away from him on the stairs, sick with horror. It was all too terrible to be believed. Bruce was the man I had imagined myself in love with. But the shrinking of my body told me the truth—and told it to him as well.

There was nothing I could say. I rose from the stairs carefully and slowly. I went down the few steps to the hall and moved toward the front door. It was as if by moving gently, quietly, I could make my escape.

He let me reach the door before he stopped me, his hand like a band of steel on my arm. "No, Christy. You can't go out there. Not now."

I turned and looked up into his face. He seemed the same as always, and his eyes were not unkind, but I knew the truth about him now. It was for this that I had deceived myself so recklessly, so foolishly. I had only loathing for myself, and beneath the loathing the beginnings of pure terror. Now it was going to be my turn.

"Don't look at me like that, Christy." He drew me suddenly to him and kissed me roughly on the mouth. "Do you think I could touch a hair on your head? You won't be hurt if you do as I say. I want to give you a chance."

I didn't know what he meant by that, and I could only wait for him to go on. How black his eyes were—with depths beyond the surface kindness.

"Come," he said, and he began to propel me toward the rear of the house.

My thoughts tumbled wildly, seeking for a way of escape, but his hand was cruelly tight on my arm and I could only move in the direction he chose.

When we came to the basement stairs, I knew without any doubt what he meant to do. I knew what was going to happen to me, and for a moment my knees weakened and I clung to him.

"No, Bruce—please!" I whispered.

He peeled my clutching fingers away, not ungently. "I'm sorry, Christy. It's the one place I can leave you safely. The hatch door is heavy. Once I've closed it you'll not be able to open it from underneath. Not on that rickety ladder."

I thought of the damp stone walls of the vault, the chill, the darkness. I thought of that suit of armor which had kept its terrible secret for all those years. I could go mad down there. And when would they find me? They would think I'd run off with Bruce and would probably never look in that place for me at all.

Behind, Bruce gave me a little push. "Go down the stairs, Christy. I don't want to carry you."

I started down the basement stairs ahead of him, free for the moment because he no longer clasped my arm. Yet nevertheless trapped and helpless. There was only one goal toward which he would lead me—the armor room at the far end of the basement, and the vault that opened in its floor. I was to know a worse imprisonment than my son had known. Bruce too believed I was trapped. But he didn't know this basement as I knew it, and he didn't know that I might fight for my life. There was no numbness now. I had come painfully alive.

I left the fifth step with a flying leap and landed on the stone floor. Then I ducked behind the first large object in that shadowy place. I shoved over a ladder in Bruce's path, disappeared behind the furniture, ran toward the far wall where a window still stood open. The packing case that had helped me before was still below it, and while Bruce sought me among the shadows, I climbed up to the window and scrambled through to roll on the ground beyond.

Fog was thick around the house, and fog could save me. I ran in the direction of the fence where the mist was dense, and clambered up over the spears, dropping to the other side. I could already hear Bruce climbing out of the basement, but he would expect me to go to the gate. A small gift of time had been loaned to me.

Spindrift was visible where the mists had blown thin, but I dared not run for the house. I had no friends there. Toward the ocean billows puffed and rolled like smoke, hiding everything. In moments I was lost in damp, choking vapor and stumbling along the Cliff Walk. I had no sense of direction now and I couldn't even see the rocks above the ocean. Somewhere along here there had been erosion and the path was gone. Unable to see, I might be dropped into the ocean at any step. I didn't know where I was going—only that I must go, that I must put distance between me and this man who was my mortal enemy.

When a black figure loomed suddenly ahead of me in the mist, I clapped my hands to my mouth to stifle a scream. But it was Joel, and I stood staring at him, trying to find my voice.

"Bruce!" I gasped. "Out there! I know everything that happened, and he—he was going to—"

"Hush," Joel said, and I broke off.

There had been a sound. Someone else was following the Cliff Walk, stumbling over the broken places, coming this way. Bruce had heard us.

Joel caught my hand and pulled me along over uncertain ground until there were rocks beneath my feet and I was following him down a steep path. Fog thinned ahead of us momentarily and I saw the outline of the boatshed below. Joel drew me roughly down the path until he could enter the shed ahead of me, pull me in behind him.

"Get into the boat," he told me. "Hurry."

I didn't hesitate, but dropped down into the cockpit, while Joel went to slip the rope. I knew what he meant to do. He would take the boat out into the fog. On the water we would be out of Bruce's reach and there would be nothing Bruce could do. But I knew too what it would cost Joel to do this—to go out there in the fog, venturing our lives. Yet now I wasn't afraid. I had the feeling that he would bring us back safely.

Then it was already too late. While Joel worked at untying the rope, Bruce walked into the shed. He glanced at me in the boat and then stood watching Joel.

"Leave that alone," he said.

Joel looked around, and once more I measured the difference between the two men, measured it with my heart breaking. Joel was lithe but slight, lacking in weight beside Bruce's powerful hulk. When it came to brawn, Bruce could defeat him. Brute force would always win. Joel let the rope go and straightened, watching Bruce from the far end of the slip. The water that he feared lay immediately behind him.

I looked around the boat, around the shed for any sort of weapon—but there was nothing in view. Not so much as a wrench. I reached for the dock, to climb out where I could stand beside Joel, but he spoke to me sharply.

"Stay down," he said.

Bruce smiled at us gently as though he found our actions amusing. "This is really too bad, isn't it, Christy? You had your chance, you know. But now it's gone." He took a step toward Joel.

"Stay where you are," Joel said, and there was an unexpected ring of authority in his voice.

Bruce paused, mildly astonished. "You aren't exactly in a position to call the tune, are you?" he said.

I almost ceased to breathe. Bruce had only to rush Joel to put him into the water. Then it would be my turn.

"You'd better do some thinking this time," Joel went

on. "If you leave now, maybe you can get away. Maybe you can even get off the island. I saw your car in the driveway, ready to go."

"And leave you two to sound the alarm?" Bruce said. "I've had enough of this. You're both going to have an accident. An unfortunate boating accident in the fog."

He started toward Joel and I clung to the dock helplessly, the boat moving under my feet. Then I saw that Bruce had halted in his advance and was staring at Joel—staring at the small but deadly-looking gun Joel suddenly held in his hand.

"I know how to use this," Joel said. "And you needn't think I'll hesitate. My father taught me to shoot quite well, you know."

Bruce looked down at me in the boat, measuring distance, I was sure. I think if he could have used me against Joel, he would have. But I was out of reach.

"You'd better take my first offer," Joel said. "Leave now and get as far as you can."

The weapon in Joel's hand did not waver, and the black muzzle pointed directly at Bruce. Yet I could hardly believe it when Bruce gave up. He scowled at us both, and without making any more speeches he wheeled about and went out of the shed. We could hear him climbing up the path, and in a few moments he was gone and there was silence.

"He won't get far," Joel said. "Awhile ago I phoned Jimson and told him to come back with his men." He held out the gun for me to see. It had a carved wooden grip and the barrel was short and sturdy. "It's a derringer from Hal's Western collection back in New York. Theo brought it with her. There aren't any bullets."

I managed to crawl out on the deck, but my knees were weak and I couldn't seem to rise. Joel pulled me to my feet.

"Are you all right, Christy?" The distance was still between us.

I faced him. "I haven't been all right for a long time. I

know that now. I've been wrong about so much. So terribly much."

"You need to let Adam go," Joel said. "You need to come back into life."

"I know," I said. "There are so many things I'm ashamed of."

He was shaking his head at me. "You've been right a lot of the time too, and I've been anything but blameless. There's been too much listening to Theo. Too much stiffnecked Moreland pride. But I have fought for you, Christy, in my way."

"Joel, is there any road back—to where we were?"

He smiled at me—that bright, shining smile I hadn't seen for so long. "Not to where we were. Perhaps to something better. If you want to try, I think we can find the way."

I went into his arms and he held me gently for a moment, kissed me on the cheek and let me go. It was a beginning—nothing more. But I knew now that it was not Adam or Bruce who had been strong. It was this man who stood beside me. Quiet and unassuming, he had never yielded on principle.

We started up the path from the boatshed together, to find that the fog was thinning up above, drifting away.

"How did you discover the truth about Bruce?" I asked.

"Through that letter Fiona wrote to you and never delivered. She hid it in a manuscript I was reading and I came on it today. I took it to my mother and I made her tell me everything. But I had to decide what to do so that you wouldn't be too badly injured. I was afraid you were going off with Bruce today, Christy, and I was determined to stop that if I possibly could. I almost waited too long."

From the direction of Spindrift we could hear someone calling, hear voices, hear Theo's tones in a rising crescendo.

"There will be a bad time ahead," Joel said. "Theo's going to be in trouble. She deserves it, but she's still my mother and some of the circumstances will help her. We'll do what we can, Ferris and I."

"Yes," I said. "I know how bad it will be. But she has a lot of courage, Joel. At least she has that. When the police are through with us here, can we go home? Can we take Peter and go home?"

We had stopped side by side on Spindrift's sloping lawn, and we could see the men now and the cars near the house.

"If that's what you want, Christy," Joel said.

The flood of feeling that went through me brought tears to my eyes, and the pain of emotion was more welcome than anything that had happened to me in a long time. I was Joel's wife, and that was all I wanted to be.

"It's what I want," I said. "More than anything. Just to go home with you."

He took my hand tightly in his and we walked toward the house together. I knew his stature now, and I did not think my foolish eyes would ever be blinded again.